COVENANT

By Sabrina Benulis

THE BOOKS OF RAZIEL

ARCHON

COVENANT

THE BOOKS OF RAZIEL

SABRINA BENULIS

HARPER Voyager

An Imprint of HarperCollins*Publishers*

Harper Voyager and design is a trademark of HCP LLC.

HarperCollins books may be purchased for educational, business, or sales promotional use. For information please e-mail the Special Markets Department at SPsales@ harpercollins.com.

First Harper Voyager trade paperback edition published 2014.

Library of Congress Cataloging-in-Publication Data has been applied for.

ISBN 978-0-06-206941-2

14 15 16 17 18   OV/RRD   10 9 8 7 6 5 4 3 2 1

FOR MY LOVED ONES, WHO HAVE TAUGHT ME
HOPE AND FAITH ARE THE ONLY
WINGS NEEDED TO FLY

Acknowledgments

I am always so grateful for the wonderful family and friends who encourage me in my dreams and inspire my best efforts. My first round of thanks of course goes to my husband, Mike, who patiently listens to my ideas, helps me tackle writer's block, and despite his engineering background isn't afraid to lend an opinion on nitpicky grammar issues. Thanks from the bottom of my heart to my parents, Gary and Sharon, for lifting my spirits during tough times and always being my first and best test readers. A thank-you to my family and extended family for always telling me to hold my head high in each and every accomplishment, and another loving thank-you to my close friends for sharing my excitement as I reach the milestone of book number two.

A sincere thank-you to my agent, Ann Behar, for unswervingly believing in my talent, and to the team at Harper Voyager who made this book a reality, especially editor Diana Gill, assistant editor Kelly O'Connor, and copy editor Laurie McGee. My gratefulness also goes to Nekro for once again producing an outstanding first cover for this book.

My heartfelt thanks goes to the readers and fans, whose enthusiasm for Angela's story always lifts my imagination to new heights. The new glossary at the end of the book is for your benefit!

How could I forget to thank my cockatiel, Caesar, for being my special writing buddy?

And, finally, a thank-you to God for absolutely everything and so much more.

COVENANT

Genesis ~ The Story So Far

In the beginning of all things, there was a song, and starlight, and a Garden within eternity's shadows. There, God created three great angels, and they were destined to rule all of Heaven from three majestic thrones.

Israfel, the Creator Supernal, was considered to be the most beautiful of these angels. A vision of bronze feathers and grace, he found favor in the eyes of God and Heaven and soon outstripped his siblings in both popularity and power. His brother, Raziel, the Preserver Supernal, became known for the virtues of wisdom and gentleness. And then there was Lucifel, the Destroyer Supernal embodying creation's fathomless darkness and depths, who despite her taciturn personality still managed to snare the hearts of creatures.

The storms and upsets of the universe could not touch these three angels. Sickness and death were beneath them.

But they were not immune to the passions of the heart.

As Israfel's favor grew, so did Lucifel's frightful envy and discontent.

Seeing herself as an equal to her sibling and with a loyal band of angels to support her claim, Lucifel finally broke with the established order and challenged Israfel's position as Heaven's supreme ruler under God. When Raziel—who had always seemingly vacillated in his loyalty between his siblings—took Lucifel as his lover, a bloody revolution exploded. The children of their forbidden union disappeared and were presumably executed, but in retaliation Lucifel engulfed Heaven in a War that ended in Raziel's suicide, Israfel's abdication, and her own tragic destiny.

Though defeated by both fate and circumstance, Lucifel chose to begin a new regime in lower, darker places. Yet she was swiftly imprisoned in her new kingdom of Hell.

Those who had once worshipped her in her glory were now her fearful jailers. They called themselves demons.

In the darkness below all things, caged and alone, Lucifel's ideals twisted even as her shadow of influence grew. From Hell it then spread like a poison, touching even the mortal world.

Though her true motives remain unknown, she is now suspected of wishing to open Raziel's fabled Book, seeking to use its power to silence the universe and the light within it that mocks her. Lucifel moves quicker by the day to manipulate events in her favor. But Raziel's death was not completely in vain. He has returned as the guardian spirit of a human girl to see that his sister, Lucifel, fails in her goal. This human girl is called the Archon.

The Archon is the only soul believed to be capable of opening the Book for the power of good. But like all creatures She has a choice and will either stand against Lucifel and destroy her or kill her only to take her place on the Throne of Hell and begin a darker era of Ruin.

In either instance, Her decision must be made quickly.

With the ties that once held the universe together brutally severed, an order long teetering on the edge of collapse has started to slide toward complete annihilation. A silence more threatening than Lucifel's looms over all creatures—

one without hope of resurrection. The whereabouts of the Lock and Key of Raziel's Book are unknown, and the task of opening it to save what remains of the world verges on the impossible.

The Archon is a soul born in mortal misery, and she has only recently grasped the virtue of friendship. There are many who believe that her dark destiny is—like Lucifel's—unavoidable.

But if Ruin and Death born of three unhappy angels sparked the end, it is also true that covenants broken can be remade, and that the wheels of fate can be turned backward despite all odds. Hearts call to one another, undoing the knots that have strangled hope and imprisoned peace. For darkness to exist, there must be a brighter light. The world has always known pain, strife, and wars.

Yet it is the bonds between souls that have moved the stars.

Zero

Many doors begged to be opened in the city of Luz. Kim was certain he'd at last found the only one that mattered.

Like all ominous things, it had materialized in the darkest hour of his life. Now he stood in front of its immense black wood and gasped for breath, cold sweat trickling down the side of his nose. A thousand warnings sounded off in his brain, and his lungs ached as they sucked in the freezing air. His hands had gone numb. Ice shellacked the tips of Kim's hair, and the strands swept punishingly against his neck. The wind strangled him with every breath, searching relentlessly for other lives to snuff out, sighing like a cold song through the alley.

A hiss shivered through the bone-cold night, and the breeze died for a moment. The damp and stone-filled city had hushed, as if waiting. Flurries drifted serenely to the ground.

Kim glanced over his shoulder, shuddering. Fear throbbed through him in waves.

He would have to move fast. He didn't have much time to make a decision before *she* caught up to him.

The door beckoned, suspicious and dark. Should he? Shouldn't he?

Kim stared at the door, gasping for breath. He peered at

the odd carvings and symbols in the wood. Impulsively, he reached for the snake-shaped iron knob.

Reality twisted and warped like a flash of lightning. Without warning the iron serpent came alive and lunged.

Inch-long metal fangs sank into Kim's palm. Needles of agony wrenched through his arm.

Kim cursed under his breath, tears of pain bunching at the corners of his eyes. He snatched his hand out of the snake's reach, wrapping fingers around his injured palm. Blood seeped hotly between his fingers. The iron snake recoiled back to its original position, glaring at him. Its reptilian eyes glowed with an unnerving yet familiar shade of orange. *Try again*, they seemed to say.

Frantically, Kim searched every inch of the wood for a keyhole. But there was none, and he realized with a newer shot of panic that he had no key anyway.

Another icy hiss echoed through him, drifting through the alley along with the snow. A soft rattle, like the sound of tiny bones rubbing together, cut through the silence.

Kim peered around again, sweaty bangs screening his vision.

A pair of phosphorescent yellow eyes gleamed back at him from the end of the cobbled road. Sickle-shaped black wings flickered once within the night. The glow of a gas lamp brushed the tips of his cousin's nails, and then her devilish form melted back into the darkness.

In a few more breaths, those nails would rip him apart. His hunter was badly hurt, but that wouldn't buy Kim enough time to escape.

He glanced around pathetically and sucked in more horrendously cold air. Silvery ice shellacked the surrounding walls of brick and stone, the hard ground. Snow tumbled in the renewed gusts of winter wind. He didn't want to die in the cold depths of Luz alone. Too much life awaited him, and possibly love.

He clung to that last hope with fanatical loyalty.

Kim clutched the cross necklace at his chest, and his mind raced and filled with thoughts of Angela Mathers and how much she needed him without even realizing it. He pictured her brave face, deep red hair, and cool blue eyes. He felt her kiss on his mouth and ached for the part of his heart he'd unwillingly left with her in a moment of irrational anger. But instead of Angela's voice, he remembered her angel Israfel's prophetic words: Kim was about to get exactly what he deserved.

A terrible, crushing sensation threatened to stop his heart. The hair stood on the nape of Kim's neck. His veins throbbed with terror. Blood rushed and roared in his ears. He fought off the screams rising up into his throat. Unseen and silent, death's stealthy approach pierced him like a knife to the back.

Kim threw himself at the door, pounding on the wood with his fists.

Seeing Angela's face in his mind one last time, he knew he'd give anything to reach her again. The screams left his mouth at last, reverberating in the icy air. Someone, anyone—for the love of God, let him in. Footsteps were behind him and ragged breaths and pitiless teeth and the thought was unbearable. He banged harder and harder, ignoring the threat of another bite from the snake because his hands were dead with cold and pain.

He would do anything, if someone would save him.

The world paused. A voice like a snake's touched the edge of his thoughts.

Anything? It sounded amused.

Yes. Yes. ANYTHING.

A tremulous *click* broke the silence.

Kim jumped backward and stared, his heart pounding. The immense black door had opened, and a sliver of nothingness peeped at him from the gap between door and wall. Like a man in a trance, he opened the door wider, revealing a worn stone stairway that led down into a dimly lit darkness. A stale but warm breeze wafted upward from the depths. There was no telling what waited for him down there. Within his soul, Kim heard a faint plea not to go, never to enter. For a single moment longer, he hesitated.

Pain crashed into him like a thunderbolt.

The door slammed shut. Kim whipped sideways into the bricks, scraping his cheek on bitter ice.

His hunter rolled to the slippery ground next to him, her sparsely feathered wings beating the stone in a frenzy. Ice cracked and split beneath her weight. Cold air rushed over Kim in merciless waves.

Scabs covered Troy's black pinions, and her entire body had become even leaner with hunger. Growls of rage peppered her almost unintelligible words. Kim stole one more glimpse of his cousin's lethal angelic beauty, the sight of her sharp teeth, the terror of her hypnotic eyes, and he wrenched himself from the slick wall and once again flung open the door.

Troy grabbed his leg, cutting more blood out of him.

Frustrated shrieks sliced into him like her nails. Her broken ankle had cost her time and speed, but it was her other injuries that had brought her close to starvation. Kim screamed a prayer.

Shuddering, she let go.

In a second Troy was on her hands and feet, preparing to pounce again. Kim swung himself through the doorway.

Troy's bony hand grasped the bloody tatters of his coat and pulled. Kim slammed to the ground. Troy's wings buffeted him, punishing his legs and waist. She scrabbled for a foothold on the unfamiliar ice, and he fought against sliding into biting range. Troy's hot breath reached his skin. The chain of his necklace threatened to choke him.

Kim pulled with all his strength.

The coat fabric ripped from between Troy's fingers. The necklace chain snapped. With a cry of triumph Kim dashed for the stairway again and turned, slamming the door shut.

Troy crashed against the opposite side.

Kim staggered back, nearly pitching down the stairs. Grasping blindly, he clung to an iron bar on the door's inside, trying to keep his balance. In a fury of Jinn nails and thundering wings, Troy scratched against the door and rasped his name, screeched out her fury. Her voice was like a song of terror.

The door shivered beneath the onslaught. Kim was sure a mere two inches of wood separated them.

It didn't seem to matter. Something was protecting him and Troy knew it.

Her hisses of defeat continued, burning Kim's ears like a relentless fire. He let go of the iron bar and stood at the top of the stairway, keeping his hand on his other bleeding palm, whispering every exorcism prayer in his memory.

Hours passed. Every so often, chalk-white fingers and sharp nails slipped under the door, searching for Kim's skin. Above the howling wind, he heard Troy's hiss or the rattle of the bones in her hair, and sometimes the screech of the crow that haunted her side. So he waited with her, certain that one of them would eventually give up but that, God willing, it wouldn't be him.

Finally, unbelievably, she left.

Kim's sanity returned by degrees. With it came suffocating hunger and thirst. He'd been running from Troy for so long, food and drink had become hasty and disgusting occasions. Now the overwhelming need for both began to overcome his terror at what might be waiting outside the door. He touched it, weighing his fortunes. No, he couldn't bear it anymore—

Kim set his jaw, pushing on the door from the inside.

It wouldn't budge. There was no interior knob either, only the iron bar that had left his arm muscles aching. He was trapped.

A warm breeze rose out of the darkness and brushed against his skin. The ice coating his hair dripped onto the stone.

Kim patted his chest, sensing emptiness. His cross necklace was gone, probably lying on the icy ground where Troy had torn it from his neck. There was no sense in grieving. That memento his foster father had given him was now long past its usefulness. The memories it symbolized would best stay where Kim had left them, half buried in the snow. Besides, he couldn't return even if he wanted to.

With the most furtive glances, Kim examined the staircase.

He breathed hard, his chest aching. His throat was raw from screaming, and as he stood, every muscle shrieked back at him in protest. Carefully, he edged onto the first step of the stairs.

Troy's steady breathing sounded from the door's other side.

She'd never left at all.

With his next step, she breathed louder, as if growing desperate.

Kim knew better than to walk down a mysterious set of stairs, after entering a mysterious door, all because he'd made a desperate promise. Yet he had no other choice, and deep inside, he couldn't help feeling that this was somehow the right one. A whisper at the edge of his memories—the same voice that had questioned him at the door—called from far below. Perhaps this was the moment he'd been waiting for.

Here is your chance, the voice called to him again.

Despite Kim's better judgment he believed it. He needed to believe it. So he left death behind to meet salvation where it waited—darker and darker down.

One

*A long time ago, I dreamed of these moments.
I wished with all my soul they would never
come to pass. Then I met Her.* —SOPHIA

Angela Mathers tapped her pencil against her desk and swept a long strand of blood-red hair from her eyes.

A deathly but earnest quiet filled the classroom. Many of the Westwood Academy students hunched over their clipboards and papers, scribbling away answers for the winter exams. There was a scrabbling noise—a rat scurrying along the floorboards. The Vatican novice moderating the class glanced up from his own stack of papers, searching each student with a piercing glance and a sly twist to his mouth, hoping to find a cheater here or there. His gaze lingered on Angela a moment longer, and then with a disapproving shake of his head, he went back to his papers.

The rat continued on his busy way to the crack beneath the classroom's double doors and slipped out unnoticed.

Angela sighed and set down her pencil, staring at the white flakes drifting outside the windows. The Latin classroom's gabled panes were enormous, taking up a quarter of the building, and through them the island city of Luz gleamed with festive flickers of gold. For the first time in a century, the typically chilly but wet winters of Luz had been graced with a never-ending gala of snow.

For days, it had been gusting throughout the city.

A sudden flurry of black shapes weaved in and out of the gale, finally coming to rest on a peaked roof to the north. Crows—big ones. Angela squinted, certain she could see even more of them circling the far-off grove that was Memorial Cemetery, like specks above a sea of white-capped trees. Shadows on an eternal patrol, they were one of the few creatures that had chosen to remain in Luz throughout the increasingly and unprecedentedly harsh winter. Morning and evening, they swept in enormous flocks from the cemetery to the city and back again.

Why? Angela's heart skipped a beat as a crow larger than the rest flew to the windowsill and peered inside the classroom. *What are you trying to tell everyone?*

The crow's eyes met Angela's.

For the briefest second, its irises flashed as yellow and scintillating as candle flames.

It can't be—

Angela sprang to her feet, knocking her chair sideways. It clattered to the tile with deafening force.

She struggled to right the chair and hide her burning face. Irritated voices and eyes followed her. The wood made a horrible scraping noise as she pulled it back into position.

Sophia glanced up from her own exam, frowning. "What is it?" she whispered.

"Nothing—it's nothing," Angela said quickly. She slumped back in her chair, almost groaning aloud when the novice's shadow darkened her exam. Angela did her best to look nonchalant, even as his hand grabbed her test and yanked it out of her reach.

He flipped through a few pages and sighed heavily.

Novices were Vatican officials in training, and Angela had discovered much to her chagrin that most of them just loved diligent students. Something told her she wouldn't be scoring any points in her favor today. The test dropped back onto Angela's desk. "Miss Mathers, might I suggest that you spend more time writing your essays and less time staring at the city vermin outside the window. You only have one more hour to impress me with your writing skills. I doubt you'll do it, but at least show some effort, hmm?" He adjusted his glasses and pushed the frizzy hair from his eyes. "Back to work, everyone. Noses to the grindstones. Your parents aren't paying this Academy for bird-watching sessions."

The hurried sound of students returning to their exams echoed throughout the room.

Vermin? "I like crows," Angela muttered under her breath.

The novice stopped stalking away from her desk.

"Feathered rats," he said definitively. He strode away from her with heavier footsteps but took a detour to slam a hand against the window. Some startled crows spiraled off into the evening.

Angela sighed.

What is it that makes people define what vermin is and isn't, anyway? Those birds are just trying to survive like everyone else. They can't help that they were born crows.

"What was that all about?" Sophia whispered from the desk at Angela's left. She kept her head down, letting her chestnut curls hide her mouth as she wrote in her distinctive, elegant script. "Did you see something?"

Angela paused. It had probably been her imagination. Ever since that night almost one year ago, she'd been consistently disappointed by what she'd seen and heard. In a few short days, Luz had exploded with supernatural craziness, but besides the odd weather, one more year had settled the city into some kind of disturbing normality. Everyone was somehow forgetting about the tremendous storms, the Devil's black rain, and the Jinn who'd murdered students to stay alive. The vicious demoness Naamah, the tragic Fae named Tileaf, and the dazzlingly beautiful angel Israfel were being relegated to memory and myth. Stephanie Walsh—Luz's most feared witch—was alive, but in a mental institution. Angela's brother Brendan was dead. Her friend Nina Willis was dead. Kim was most likely dead—or worse. But the Vatican had made certain to hush up every other detail, and woe to anyone who dared discuss those strange days. Time healed all wounds, and it was fast healing Luz's scars as well.

"No, I didn't see anything," Angela whispered back. She wasn't sure whether or not that was a lie. Her eyes could have been playing tricks again.

She winced inwardly as sudden pain streaked through her palm.

Sophia paused, but didn't say anything. She looked up at Angela, and her gray eyes seemed veiled. "If you say so. I hope you're not hiding anything from me. Anything important."

"I'm not," Angela said.

Angela smiled at her best friend and turned back to her test. She tugged on her arm gloves, focusing more on her left hand, but eventually the odd pain became too much. Angela slipped off the fabric, careful to hide her hand inside the desk slat.

She didn't want Sophia—or anyone else—to see and worry.

From the dimness, an Eye glistened back at her from where it rested in her palm. Lucifel's Grail often resembled an emerald with a fathomless onyx pupil, but now it seemed horribly alive, staring at Angela as if it wanted to speak and warn her of something. A thick and sour sensation swelled inside of her.

Something was about to happen. She knew it.

Angela looked around the classroom again, seeing nothing out of the ordinary. But the sensation grew, and grew, and by the time the exam papers were collected, and she and Sophia began to gather their books, she wanted to throw up. She clutched the back of her chair, swaying as students trickled out of the classroom. Soon, only one remained— Janna Hearst, a gangly girl with red hair like Angela's and downturned gray eyes.

Sophia wrapped her cold hand around Angela's wrist. "There *is* something wrong. You look awful."

"No . . ." Angela whispered. She gripped the back of the chair harder. Her hand holding the Grail ached and burned. She bit her lip, speaking through gritted teeth. "I'm fine . . ."

"No, you're not—"

Janna sighed and gathered one more book, turning to leave the classroom.

In the second that she turned and faced Angela, there it was. The look.

Oh, God, no.

Janna dashed out of the room, obviously headed for the stairs that led higher into the building. Surprised shouting, and even some laughter, followed her escape from the halls.

This can't happen.

Angela ripped out of Sophia's grip and stared into the abyss of her friend's dark eyes. "Death," she whispered. And then she ran, whipping out of the room toward the immense stairwell.

An intimidating crowd of people blocked Angela's path through the corridor. The Westwood Academy Exhibit Hall had changed for the worst since the terrible storm last year, and what room there had been was somehow halved by masonry equipment and plywood. With Luz's shipyards cut off from further imports, the Vatican had hastily constructed makeshift walls over the most damaged sections of the hallway. Angela sidestepped piles of junk, weaving a path through a seething mass of humanity.

Some of the students realized who she was and began to whisper. More began to part in waves, staring as she dashed up the western stairwell.

Angela dropped the only schoolbook in her hand near a bewildered sophomore. No need for dead weight.

She raced up the stairs, taking two at a time with her long strides. Through the gabled windows, she could see that a thick wet snow continued to fall. Layers of ice shellacked the elegant angel statues placed on the turrets. The golden light of their upheld lanterns glistened on the stone steps.

"Angela!" Sophia's usually sweet voice thundered up the stairwell.

Angela continued running. Her heart raced, and her hand burned like an inferno. She had to make it to Janna before the worst happened.

She reached the top of the stairs, throwing open the heavy door to a vision of white-flecked night.

Snow tumbled into her face. A murderously cold wind blistered her cheeks.

Janna stood at the roof's edge, her back to Angela, staring out at the golden glory of Luz. Despite the storm, the island was aglow in Christmas beauty, every window kissed by a speck of flickering light. Turrets rose to the east like mountains set with stars. Janna stared at them and then glanced at what was directly below her: a cobblestoned street nestled near a sea channel. Her short hair whipped around her chin and neck.

"Janna!" Angela screamed over the wind.

Janna turned, and wide-eyed fear blossomed on her face. But Angela knew it was the fear of being stopped, the torment of failing even in death.

"Go away!" Janna screamed back. Tears rolled down her cheeks. She turned back to the city and lifted her foot, but then stepped back and hugged herself as she sobbed. "I mean it—go away. I want to be alone!"

"Janna, just wait!" Angela said, racing for her.

I might not know why you are doing this, but I understand the feeling. You can't be like me.

"Don't come any closer!" Janna said, strangely horrified. "What are you doing!" She took a step backward, teetering on the building's edge.

Angela's hand cramped and burned fearfully. Crows erupted from the darkness and began to circle above, their bodies breaking icicles from the turrets. The birds swirled down around Janna in a sudden maelstrom, and she shrieked with terror. A madness of screeching crows resounded above the wind. Janna swatted one of the birds aside and wobbled on the ice.

"*You can't do it,*" Angela screamed. "*Janna, don't—*"

She slid forward and grabbed Janna by the arm.

Angela shuddered as the ice betrayed them, wheeling both

her and Janna in a desperate struggle, arm in arm—right over the roof. Angela's hand exploded with pain, smacking into the stone wall. Her breath was knocked out of her lungs, her last words fading by a whirlwind of ice and terror.

High above, Sophia's anguished voice followed their descent like an arrow.

It was too late.

The wind roared, biting with icy teeth. Angela screamed even louder, her voice cracking with agony. Janna wept. Luz bled out its color in streaks of yellow and white. Birds screeched and shrieked as if bemoaning each girl's fate.

It felt like seconds. It felt like eternity. But eventually, something hit Angela hard and she knew the same happened to Janna. And then they both forgot everything besides an unwanted, unexpected darkness.

Two

Angela knew she was dead.

She vaguely remembered falling, and perhaps the pain of actually dying, and now she was in this vaporous place of dreams that was nothing like what she'd hoped or expected. When Angela had helped empty the Netherworld of every last human soul, she'd never taken the time to think about what would happen when more humans died once that world had been sealed shut.

Now she knew.

Until someone or something ordered her otherwise, she was stuck in a universe of shadows. It wasn't exactly fair. Although—and Angela somehow sensed her grim smile—she could no longer remember why that was the case.

She stood in the vaporous half-light of death, dreaming. And then, eventually, a nagging worry tugged at her.

This wasn't right. She HAD to live for . . . someone.

Angela gasped as a dark doorway appeared in front of her, its immensity seeming to congeal from the shadows of her mind. The black wood disguised strange words and carvings of even stranger creatures, and instead of a knob, she found herself reaching for a metal snake. Shocked, she pulled her hand back and felt her entire being recede from the danger in front of her.

Angela couldn't explain why or how, but she was absolutely certain. It was madness to open the door.

She glanced around, suddenly aware of the snow falling around her. From a distance, voices could be heard.

"Janna?" Angela whispered.

Instead, two shadowy figures walked around either side of Angela and steadily toward the door. One was a male, tall but with a slender build and raven hair plastered down with snow. The red streak in his bangs had grown out almost to nothing. He was a wreck, his long coat torn, his pale skin streaked with bruises and cuts. But Angela would recognize those unearthly amber eyes anywhere. It was Kim. He was alive.

A cold hand seemed to clench her heart and squeeze. Angela reached out to at least grab the edge of Kim's sleeve, but she was a ghost grabbing for another ghost.

She stumbled forward through snow—and through his ghostly body—and watched helplessly as the door opened to a staggering blackness.

Kim glanced over his shoulder; he met Angela's gaze and silently mouthed her name.

With a heavy sigh like a man defeated, he started his descent.

Desperation cut like a hot blade through Angela. The other shadow belonged to Sophia.

Sophia wore the beautiful silver dress from the day she and Angela had first met, but her gray eyes were downcast, and her chestnut curls had also flattened beneath the snow.

She turned at the threshold of the great door and looked pointedly at Angela. There was decisiveness to the moment. Angela knew without a doubt that this was the last time they would ever be together.

Angela ran, aware that she was screaming again, and that it hurt.

She didn't want to go through the door, but she also didn't want to be alone in this terrible place. Being without Kim? Or even Israfel? Her heart had gotten used to that by now. But being without Sophia was out of the question—and Angela ran harder.

Sophia stood her ground before the door. The alien words of Raziel's Book appeared, moving and twisting across her skin. Her eyes blazed, and her hair whipped from an unseen wind. There was a deadly earnestness fixing her pretty face. She was saying something, but Angela could barely hear. A great roar had started to overtake her from behind.

A rushing storm and a light raced with her.

Angela was steps away from Sophia and the door.

Now, Sophia's words made themselves heard. "DON'T FOLLOW." Tears dripped down her delicate cheeks. She appeared inconsolable. But Sophia did the unthinkable anyway, and as the light overtook Angela, as Angela's soul tore away from her, Sophia entered the blackness and shut the door.

Three

And my first and last thought was: how could
she leave me alone? —ANGELA MATHERS

The pain forced Angela to finally open her eyes and come to terms with it.

Her bones ached. Her muscles felt like they'd been yanked out of her and then stuffed back beneath her skin. But the dim light of her room in the recently minted Emerald House had a soporific effect, and she lay there gazing out the window that first met her reopened eyes, watching in silent bewilderment while the snow fell and the reality that she was still alive sank in.

Slowly, she inspected the rest of her room, gradually turning her head to the left.

Her recent paintings of Israfel—all half-finished failures—peppered the area at the foot of her bed. Across the room on a small table, a pendulum clock marked the hour as half past five in the afternoon. Near the ceiling, her doll collection peered down from carefully placed shelves, row after row of them, perfect with their glass eyes, porcelain bodies, and fine lacy dresses. Sophia, looking like a life-size doll, sat by

Angela's bedside and regarded her with a grim expression, her breaths slow, even, and somehow admonishing.

She wasn't at all the terrible vision from Angela's nightmare. In fact, she seemed even more delicate and frail.

Sophia sighed and offered Angela a glass of water from a tray at her bedside.

"Thanks," Angela said, wincing at the pain in her voice box. She relished the water as it trickled down her raw throat. Then she gave the glass back to Sophia and stared at the girl's velvet slippers, still thinking of the terrible dream.

I was dead. That's the only explanation. After all, I can't dream anymore—I gave my dreams away in order to be with Israfel.

"Look where it's gotten you," Sophia said softly.

"What?"

She can't read my thoughts—

"Your recklessness," Sophia said shortly. "Whether it was you trying to kill yourself all those years ago, or whether it's you on a new, self-professed mission to stop someone else from doing the same, you never think things through, do you?" She rubbed her eyes in a gesture that was still elegant. "Do you remember what I said to you when you woke up after your first brush with death? After you used the Glaive to its utmost power to destroy Lucifel's shadow, despite Tileaf's warning? 'And now you know the consequences.' I could say the same here. Now you know the consequences for trying to be a savior."

The mention of Tileaf's name ricocheted through Angela like a bullet. She chose to ignore the guilt for now. "I would do it again."

"Really?" Sophia whispered.

"Yes. I would try to save Janna again, even if I didn't

have a chance. I don't regret a single thing about it." Angela shifted up and let out a little yelp of pain. "Okay, maybe some things. How old is this mattress? It feels like a board."

Sophia stared like a scolding mother at Angela for a while. But the usual soft smile cracked her porcelain features soon, and she helped Angela sit up in the bed, rearranging some pillows against her back. When Angela was comfortable again, Sophia clasped her hand gently. "You are the Archon, Angela. But overcompensating for that destiny won't help you. I know it bothers you that people say the Archon is evil, but—"

"I don't regret *trying* to save Janna, and I would do it again. End of discussion."

Sophia sat back, biting her lip. "You're misunderstanding me."

"I couldn't just let her die, Sophia."

"I know."

Sophia let the silence grow, staring out at the snow.

"Because I understand," Angela said, "what it feels like to chase after dreams. To forget this world for something else. And I know what it is to regret that decision." Angela glanced at her failed paintings of Israfel, suddenly aching to throw them into the fireplace like she had all the others that preceded them. She had been chasing after the angel of her dreams since childhood, had almost thrown away her life for him, had actually found him, and had been bitterly disappointed. Maybe that—as well as the cold fact that she could no longer dream about him—explained why every painting since the day he'd saved her from the edge of death had been a mess. "You're right—look at where it's gotten me. My arms and legs are a canvas of scars and burns. And he's out there in the glory of the universe, flying and singing without a care."

"I wouldn't quite say that," Sophia said grimly. Then she laughed. "But it's like you to make the Creator Supernal sound like nothing more than a spoiled songbird."

Angela allowed herself to smile. Despite what had happened, it was always difficult for her to be too pensive around Sophia.

But . . .

"Sophia, what happened to Janna? Is she alive?"

Sophia stood from her seat. "Yes. She is. Though unlike you she's in the sick ward across campus. Honestly, it's a miracle that you both survived. In fact, the entire event seems like it will be the talk of the Academy for weeks. Everyone has a theory about how and why you two didn't die. Some people are whispering about your face-off with Stephanie Walsh last year, despite the warnings from the priests otherwise. They think that you are—in fact—a witch. Or worse . . ."

Angela didn't know what to say to that. She kept quiet for a moment, taking another drink of water. "So why didn't we die, then?"

Sophia turned around, her face lost in shadow. Her words sounded guarded. "I have my own theory about who saved you both."

Who? What did she mean by "who"?

Angela sighed. "Well—come on. Out with it."

Sophia hesitated but finally walked across the room and grasped something dark sitting on Angela's dresser. "I was the first to find you and Janna, so I thought it wise to take any incriminating evidence the priests didn't need to see. I found these near both of you, where you'd been *set down* on the ground."

She returned to the bed and dropped two lengthy black feathers in Angela's lap.

They were more fitting for an eagle, not a crow, but Angela knew they didn't belong to any normal bird. She picked them up, holding them to the candlelight, her hands shaking. Surprisingly, the feathers took on a slightly bluish sheen in the glow of the room.

Like a blackbird's feathers . . .

Outside, the wind howled through the turrets.

The hair stood on the back of Angela's neck, and she realized she was holding her breath. In her mind, she pictured a black-winged devil that was also the perfect predator, watching her stealthily from the depths of the night.

"Troy?" she whispered, directing the question at Sophia. "Do you think these belong to Troy? But why would she come back now?"

Angela tried to suppress her shivers, but the horrid sensation stayed with her like it had in the classroom. Suddenly, it felt like foolishness to talk any louder.

Sophia said nothing, letting Angela inspect the feathers while she tidied the dorm. At last, she returned and said very gently, "It's impossible for two people to survive that kind of fall, Angela. Someone helped you. I doubt he or she was human. That's all that I truly know for sure."

Angela struggled to breathe normally and think sensibly. She didn't want to admit it, but the idea that Troy was still out there, bound to Angela and eager to find her again, struck her with real fear. If Troy searched for Angela, she would find her eventually without a doubt. And then—well, Angela often tried not to think about that.

Angela coughed in her other hand and then set the feathers back down. "How did you manage to keep me here at the Emerald House instead of in the sick ward? You know how strict the superintendents are about—"

"They don't need to see anything . . . important." Sophia averted her gaze. A distinct sadness weighed down her voice. "I know why you went after Janna, Angela. Next time—it would be better if you didn't keep things from me. Now, whenever you're ready, you should come downstairs and I'll call the Order and let them know. They've been clamoring to talk to you for days."

"For days . . . I've been asleep that long?" Angela buried her face in her hands, groaning at the thought of dealing with the Order again. They were going to use Janna's case to further their cause, and hopefully with Angela's support. She knew it.

"Yes," Sophia reiterated, "for days. You don't know what it's been like to deal with their scrutiny—not to mention the priests. When you come down, I'll have a sandwich ready for you. All your uniforms are in the closet. Where you *never* leave them."

Sophia stepped out of the room and shut the door. The sound reverberated through Angela like thunder.

She flashed back to her strange dream and nearly shouted Sophia's name.

Just as quickly, she slumped back in the bed with her arm over her eyes, letting out some shaky breaths. Sweat beaded her forehead. The wind sighed again, and Angela lifted her arm to peer out the window. The snow continued unceasingly, almost forebodingly, but the gargoyle statue near the gables glittered within the flurries, strange and beautiful in the Advent candlelight. Ice coated its arms and wings, hanging from their stone tips like glittering daggers.

The stone devil wasn't real or alive. But Angela knew for certain that Troy was, and that she was possibly out there somewhere, watching.

Yet Angela's guilt was almost equal to her fear. She wanted to scream at herself for not telling Sophia about how the Grail had burned and warned her of Janna's impending actions. But how had Sophia known that was the case? The question nagged at her.

Angela glanced at her left hand, at its arm glove.

She tugged at the fabric, dreading something inside. Then she very slowly and carefully slid it off.

Bandages had been wrapped around her palm. Angela undid them, swallowing back a sick feeling.

The Eye that was the Devil's treasure gazed at her, more alive than ever. Worse still, tremulous beads of blue had gathered at its emerald corners. The Eye blinked like a nightmare, and the blue liquid seeped down to Angela's fingers.

She brushed at a droplet, startled by the stickiness against her fingertip.

Angela gripped the edge of the bed with her other hand, trying to hold on to her recently regained consciousness. Her vision danced and swirled like the snow. A spreading chill worked its way to her heart, and the warnings of danger from her odd vision rolled back in a sudden wave, suffocating her. Yet there was no one to see the truth but Angela, and outside, the drifts fell cold and silent, not betraying the dreaded reality.

Lucifel's stone was weeping tears of blood.

Four

---

*Suddenly, I realized the universe would soon be
different, and the world I walked upon eagerly
awaited the change.* —ANGELA MATHERS

Luz. It was a city that Angela loved one day and hated the
next, always refusing to accommodate her indifference.
After eating her sandwich and gulping down another glass of
water, Angela had spent her time waiting for the Order's arrival by sitting in an armchair near the hearth room's blazing
fire, occasionally glancing out at the snow and the Christmas
glory of the city, waving away any of Sophia's attempts to
make her more comfortable.

Then, fighting her aching muscles, she'd tossed her blan-
ket aside and selected a particularly thick book from the library at the far end of the chamber. *A History of the Vatican
and Its Territories* had been printed in gold leaf on the spine.

Angela had hefted the book onto her lap as she sat again,
leafing absently through pages illustrated in fine ink. She
passed dates that seemed too old to be believed, then exited
into a period of glorious Renaissance, and at last skimmed

on to the technological explosion of the twentieth century. That last century had ended in a political upheaval that practically rearranged the world, giving the Vatican more power than it had possessed since the Middle Ages.

Now Angela flipped to the chapter devoted to Luz—the island city that was one of the twenty-first century's wonders of the world, and perhaps the Vatican's crowning achievement. The accompanying illustration perfectly captured Luz's sense of gothic claustrophobia. Completely at odds with the world around it, Luz's spires and shaky architecture seemed more like an act of defiance against the laws of physics. The city was a living cry against the sensibilities of the modern world and aroused as much fear as awe.

Its existence had become a stinging reminder of the mysterious and unfathomable. In Luz, anything was possible, and everyone accepted it, and no one bothered investigating anymore. Its location off the affluent and ultramodern American continent seemed like deliberate irony.

But it remained rudely isolated and frustratingly beyond science and progress.

Luz even stockpiled its own food. The recent troubling weather had cut off imports, but the city had sniffed at the world's concern. No, the newspapers had reported its authorities saying, we're just fine here, thank you. Many wondered, though, whether the city had merely shut its doors to ride out an apocalypse only Luz would survive.

The fact that the island only held so much food suggested a brutal swiftness to the storm.

Angela glanced at the snow outside the window and bit her lip.

She continued to read absently, aware of Sophia's fairy sweet voice humming in the background.

Luz is not the first city to be owned by the Vatican.
Regardless, there are many who continue to argue the
ethics of any one religion having the ability to establish
a sovereign government, most pointedly to establish
said government in a world where continental democ-
racy has become the rule as well as the norm . . .

Angela clenched her throbbing left hand, rubbing the
glove that covered it.

She knew the reasoning behind it very well. Luz was an
antiquated city of stone and candlelight where technology
hid and the supernatural thrived. It was the only city in the
world that welcomed humans with red hair like herself—
the persecuted embodiments of a dreadful prophecy of Ruin.
For that reason, Angela loved her new home. What she did
not love was the cold-blooded reason behind the welcome,
and perhaps the city's existence. In reality, Luz was a literal
capstone over Hell, and there were some who believed the
Archon who fulfilled the fearful prophecy would be Hell's
new ruler. So the Vatican encouraged "blood head" atten-
dance at the illustrious Westwood Academy, treated blood
heads with deference and constant pandering, and helped
grow latent supernatural abilities to perilous levels, all in the
hope of finding the fickle, dangerous Archon and stamping
him or her flat.

The ploy hadn't worked.

Angela allowed herself a smile. *I'm the Archon, and I'm*
alive after all. And the day I rule over Hell will be the day it
freezes over.

A sudden rush of cold air swept into the room, tickling at
the garland on the hearth.

Angela shut the book hastily, cursing to herself as Sophia

guided members of the Vermilion Order into the Emerald House foyer.

The Order was made up of red-haired students like Angela, but they pointedly refused mention of "blood heads" unless absolutely necessary. The nasty term had been adopted after the Archon's prophesied blood-red hair became common knowledge. Angela understood the Order's position on the matter entirely. But more than anyone, she also knew how hard it was to reconcile the past with the present.

She allowed herself a deep sigh.

Yes, Angela had been happy that the past year wound on uneventfully. Quiet, peaceful. Not a sign of the horror that took place in this city, or at the Academy, to be found. That was what she'd hoped for when she first came to Luz—a normal life despite being a blood head. And she'd found it, somehow able to leave the dreams that haunted her behind. Yet they never seemed to stop pursuing her.

The noise of boots shaking off snow, of coats taken and pleasantries exchanged, echoed into the empty house. Angela set her quilt aside and stood up to greet the Academy students noisily entering the room, doing her best to look genuinely happy to see them. She shared a glance with Sophia that screamed, *Get me out of this.*

Sophia shook her head and tried to hide her laughter.

A good-looking university student with peppery red hair shook Angela's left hand.

Angela winced, flexing her palm. She winced even more after spotting a female novice and two younger priests standing among the Order's numerous members. This wasn't going to be good. The priests' stoic expressions said it all. Angela was cornered this time.

After everyone exchanged a few more nods and greetings,

Sophia took the lead and guided everyone into the Emerald House's adjoining dining room. The table was large enough to seat at least twenty, but Angela and Sophia were the only two people in the Emerald House, the lone members of a now defunct sorority. They never ate in this room, always dining at the Academy's cafeteria instead.

Yet with her usual elegance, Sophia had done her best to make the room cozy and tasteful.

Red ribbons, candles, and imported pine garlands glittered throughout the room. A large platter of bread and cheese had been set at the center of the table, and a crystal water pitcher—still lovely despite a chip in its handle—cast back the light. The priests were the first to sit, followed by the members of the Order who dived into the cheese almost immediately.

Sophia gave Angela a knowing look and swept away into the hearth room again.

"Angela Mathers," an older priest directly to her left finally addressed her. "I hope you are feeling better. We're grateful you've taken the time to speak with us after your recent injuries." He scanned her up and down, his gaze lingering on the scars crisscrossing her legs. His voice had a creaky weariness to it, but sounded sincere. "The entire university has been asking about you, but we weren't about to say anything concerning your condition until we'd seen you for ourselves. You have a wonderful nurse in your friend."

"She is certainly an interesting girl," a young man with russet hair said. He searched Angela with his eyes. They were a dirty but strangely familiar shade of hazel. He smoothed out his overcoat, seeming to make a point of playing with the embroidery on the lapel. "Have you known each other long?"

"For about a year," Angela said, forcing herself to speak up. There were too many eyes on her. She hated the feeling.

"Really?" The young man settled back in his chair and smiled. "You'd think I would have seen her around more often. She's like a doll—not quite real. I would certainly have remembered her."

Angela cautiously met his gaze. "Sophia prefers to do much of her studies here in the house. Unlike me, she tends to get sick a lot in the cold."

The female novice to Angela's left chose this moment to pipe up. She folded her hands and regarded Angela keenly. "All the more reason for both of you to leave this shell of a sorority and merge with another society at the Academy. The two of you playing house in this rickety building is absolutely ridiculous. Everyone knows the Emerald House is nothing more than the remains of Stephanie Walsh's horrid Pentacle Sorority. Why cling to that kind of legacy?"

The old priest near Angela sighed. "Lizbeth, you would do well not to mention that name any more than necessary. The less talk here of the past, the better. Besides, I'm sure it only brings back unpleasant memories for Miss Mathers. For us all."

Lizbeth? Angela vaguely recognized her. Their schedules at the Academy were quite similar, though that was obviously more than coincidence now.

"With all due respect, Father Schrader, *blood heads* are more than witches," the young man with the russet hair said. "That's Lizbeth's point."

Angela looked up from her bread, searching every face. "And that's why you're all here, correct?"

There was a silence that felt oppressive.

"I know," Angela continued more softly, "that you want

me to join your Order. Because you think I have some kind of influence among students like us at the Academy. Why? Because of what happened last year with the blood head witch Stephanie Walsh? Need I remind everyone where she is now—locked in an asylum? I'm not your personal savior. You don't need someone like me as your leader and spokesperson."

Lizbeth took off her glasses and set them on the table. "Angela, do you know why Janna tried to commit suicide? Are you not aware of how we are being treated in this city since Stephanie Walsh's daylong reign of terror last year?"

How could I not be aware? If people don't admire me, they fear me.

"Janna was being bullied mercilessly in the past few weeks," Lizbeth said hotly. "And if it weren't for your help, she'd be dead. Tell me that doesn't give you a sense of pride."

Father Schrader raised an eyebrow. "It was a miracle they both survived, Lizbeth. Let us consider Miss Mather's good luck rather than her bravery. I beg you, Camdon, interrupt."

The russet-haired young man named Camdon took on a much more congenial tone. "What Lizbeth is getting at, Angela, is that we are being prejudiced against in the worst way possible. Janna is only one of countless others in her predicament. This Academy was made to be a haven for people like us, but if even that's been lost to us now, we should at the very least band together and look out for one another's interests. Stephanie's sorority was as corrupt as her, but with you at the head of this newly formed Order—"

"What makes you think that more segregation will help our cause?" Angela said a little hotly herself. "If anything, we should be working to dispel some of the myths about us and mingle with other people, not give them even more reason to be afraid!"

Camdon blinked at her. "You only say that because you're forgetting what it is to be ostracized, Angela. Because of Stephanie's accusations last year, the student body has given you a wide berth. You've had it too easy. Your life is too normal, and you're too respected now. But I guarantee—all that is going to change. It's only a matter of time."

Angela stood, pushing back her chair. "You're going to sit there and tell me that I don't know what it is to be *ostracized*? Is that it? So what are you saying? That Stephanie should have been right and I was the dreaded Archon after all? Is it better to live my life with the Academy's eagle eye on everything I do than for a few people to be afraid of me?"

And even though Angela was the Archon, she'd be damned that they know it. Better that everyone lived in their fantasy world where Stephanie was the beginning and end of all problems and Angela could be left alone.

Father Schrader was visibly nervous now at the mention of the Archon. He tasted his water, licking his lips. "Miss Mathers, let's not jump to conclusions and become overly emotional. The events of that horrid night are now lost to us, and we have the future of this Academy to consider. The proposition Camdon suggests is sensible at the very least. A student as admired and respected as yourself is doing no good rotting away in this empty sorority house. You would serve the world, and those like you, much more by becoming a mentor, a leader who could speak for those who are fast losing their voice. Don't forget, there are many now who are well aware of the circumstances behind the loss of your family, your brother . . ."

At the mention of Angela's brother, everyone went silent again.

Sophia chose this moment to reappear, staring at Angela from a shadowy corner. Her expression suggested only she knew the pain in Angela's heart and how deep it went.

Angela steadied herself, biting her lip. Tears welled in her eyes and she wished them away frantically.

Camdon stood, his shadow casting itself across the table. "Angela, I know what it is to lose the people you love. And that's why I am here on behalf of the Order, solemnly asking you for your help, to be our leader. Angela, do you know who I am? Do you recognize me at all, in any way?"

Angela regarded him. His face was soft but handsome. Yet all she could see were his muddy hazel eyes.

Recognition seared through her. She knew Camdon saw it behind her shocked expression.

"That's right. I'm Nina Willis's brother. Her half brother to be exact."

Angela slumped back into her seat, dazed. In her mind, she saw Nina dying all over again, plummeting into Hell so that Angela could live. It had only been a painful year since then, but even now the memories were more like half-remembered nightmares, their details blurring and fading with the passage of time.

Camdon took Lizbeth's place by Angela's side. Gently, he placed his large hand on top of Angela's. "Angela, you were a good friend to my sister. She was a troubled girl, unpopular and bullied. But you chose to be her friend—even until the end. If you won't do it for yourself, join the Order for people like her. For people like Janna. Give them something to belong to, and a renewed sense of pride."

Angela nodded, suddenly speechless.

Camdon Willis left her side. "At least think about it. You have some time," he said.

Yet Angela could feel him staring intensely at her.

As if that was the cue for everyone to leave, nineteen chairs slid away from the table and their occupants milled out of the room. Sophia followed them, hastily grabbed at coats and scarves set on the couches, and delivered them to their proper owners. Father Schrader was the last to leave.

He took his hat from Sophia and slapped it onto his thick white hair, already grumbling about the cold. He buttoned his long black coat from the waist up.

"The first snowfall in Luz in two centuries. The end is certainly nigh," he muttered to himself.

Angela stepped in front of him, blocking the front door. "Father Schrader . . . how is Stephanie doing? I . . . I've been curious . . ."

They stood next to a statue so lifelike it could have been a real angel listening to their secrets, his marble hand cupped around his marble ear.

Father Schrader glanced around furtively. "Not good, Miss Mathers. Not good. We can get nothing of sense out of her. No crucial information, not even a sentence worthy of note." His face darkened. "If it hadn't been for that demon, I would have said she was simply insane. Perhaps we should consider her fate to be a lesson: that pride indeed comes before the inevitable fall. Human beings were not meant to commune with angels, and vice versa. There are firm reasons why God has so definitively separated the two."

But what about the creatures who were in between?

Angela's mind flashed to Stephanie's missing ex-boyfriend Kim. He'd called himself a half-breed. The forbidden off-spring of a race of devils called Jinn and a human witch, he was an immortal vagabond who belonged nowhere. But Angela was sure Kim's hatred of the Jinn had more to do with being an outsider like Angela than he'd ever admit. Perhaps that explained why he'd been searching for the Archon in the first place, even his crazy need to see Angela seated on the Throne of Hell in Lucifel's place. Maybe what he'd really wanted all along was just to make a place for himself.

For both of them.

Angela shivered, almost feeling his touch in the drafts against her neck. It was impossible not to remember his golden eyes, his firm hands, or even the way he'd whispered in her ear. Everything about him had been suspicious, even his odd human name. Yet some kind of strange attraction had compelled Angela to listen and believe him, even to trust, as if their futures depended mysteriously on each other. She'd wanted to know so much more about him, but after the battle with Lucifel that had almost killed Angela, Kim had simply disappeared, leaving her with a thousand questions and no one able or willing to answer them.

Or maybe—and Angela shivered with an entirely different kind of feeling this time—maybe his past had just finally caught up with him.

She forced herself to finally ask one of those many questions. "Have you heard anything about Stephanie's old boyfriend, Father Schrader? His name was Kim . . ."

Father Schrader raised an eyebrow again. This time, he stared at Angela as if he could see right through her. "That one—I knew he was trouble from the start. No. None of us have heard a peep from that strange young man since Halloween night of last year. We've simply accepted the fact that he either escaped the island somehow or died in his attempts."

"I see. Well, thank you anyway. I was just curious. And by the way, Father—" Angela snagged him by the sleeve of his coat. "If I were to visit with Stephanie, what are the institution's hours during the week?"

Father Schrader gave Angela another long and wary look. "They allow visitors on Thursdays," he said quietly.

"Thank you," Angela said, letting go of his sleeve.

Father Schrader turned to leave but stopped abruptly, as if the oddest thought had just occurred to him. He regarded Angela again with a strange mixture of fear and awe, but then shook his head as if telling himself that whatever he thought he'd seen, he was surely mistaken.

Angela watched him leave the house and walk into the snowy night. The street was so silent, the universe could have been swallowed into nothingness. Overhead, wind whistled through gables on the roof, and to her left ocean water frothed weakly beneath a grate, half of its fury quenched by a blockade of ice in the sluice. The snow fell in a constant silvery stream.

Angela held out her hand. A flake kissed her skin and melted, leaving a tiny puddle behind.

Overhead, a crow screeched into the night.

Angela glanced up, scanning the darkness as a sudden fear clenched at her heart.

Without warning, two strong hands gripped her shoulders from behind and she screamed.

Five

We'd determined our fears were only yesterday's sorrows.
But even so, without telling Her, I began counting
the inevitable days to our good-bye. —SOPHIA

"Good Lord, you're a nervous wreck," Camdon cried, spinning Angela around to face him.

She almost collapsed against him, desperate for air and weak in the knees.

"I thought you'd left with the others," Angela said, gasping angrily. Her heart thundered in her chest. She pushed him away, steadying herself, still envisioning Troy swooping down from the blackness to wring her neck. "And why are you still here anyway?" Angela said, even less gently this time. "Didn't Sophia find your coat?"

How much did he hear when I was talking to Father Schrader?

Camdon smiled wryly. His expression revealed nothing. "I had to use the bathroom unfortunately, and your odd friend Sophia pointed me to the second floor. I'm the one who should be peeved, Angela. It's me—not you—who has to walk home in the cold alone."

"Next time, drink less water," Angela said.

She stepped around him, trying to get back into the house. Despite its draftiness and the horrible furniture, it was much more cheerful than Luz's new bone-chilling winter.

Camdon didn't budge. "Angela, are you going to the Christmas Ball this Saturday night?" he said, his voice softer than the snow.

Angela paused at the threshold of the door. "Why?"

"Because I don't have a date."

"And that means?"

"You're really going to make me ask you point-blank? You know how tough that is for a man, don't you?"

Angela stepped inside the house and shut the door.

She stood, thinking, and then opened the door again to Camdon's bewildered face and said briskly, "I'll let you know."

Angela didn't allow him time for a reply. She shut the door one last time and escaped back to the hearth room where Sophia waited with a paper in her hands.

"What was that all about?" Sophia said, amused.

"Camdon asked me to the Christmas Ball this Saturday evening. I told him I'd think about it."

Sophia's face blanched with shock.

"Oh, stop it," Angela hissed. "He's Nina's half brother and . . . I feel like I owe him."

"You mean you feel like you owe it to Nina," Sophia said, sighing. She spread her skirt and sat on the couch next to Angela. Silently, Sophia gazed into the fire, letting the light play on her preternaturally smooth skin and flicker in her fathomless gray eyes. At times like these, Angela remembered with a distant kind of terror that Sophia wasn't quite human at all but a Book in the form of a person. "And maybe you should go," Sophia said, her very human voice breaking the spell. "No need to stay here in this creaky house while everyone else dances the night away."

"But you'd be by yourself," Angela said.

Sophia smiled. "I was alone long before I met you, Angela. I am sure I will be alone long after we part."

Angela shook her head. "We won't part. I'm not going anywhere. That's such a pessimistic way to think."

"I know," Sophia whispered. She clenched the paper tighter.

"We'll find you a nice dress and you can come with me. I'd rather have you as a date than Camdon," Angela said, winking.

Sophia didn't laugh.

"What is this?" Angela snatched the paper from her friend's hands, sensing it was responsible for Sophia's sudden change in mood. She perused the odd script, her eyes narrowing. "What is this? A joke? Sophia?"

Sophia stared into the fire.

Angela inspected the paper. It was obviously very old and felt like parchment. The scripting was in English, but written with an unsteady hand that suggested the writer had never tried the language before. The words were terse and all the more terrible for it.

Angela Mathers, you will enter the door. Or Sophia will die.

That was all.

Angela blinked. All at once, she saw the door from her vision, and the dark stairs that led down, and down, and down. She saw Sophia standing in front of them in her terrible beauty as the Book of Raziel, telling Angela not to enter, her face saying to run away whatever the cost as she slammed the door shut.

That door? But who could have known about the vision I had?

"This is ridiculous," Angela said heatedly. "You're the Book of Raziel. You can't die . . . Can you?"

Sophia turned away. "Flip over the paper," she whispered.

On the reverse side, a very familiar poem had been written in pale ink.

> *Blackbird escapes hungry*
> *The Fly of doom*
> *Her hellfire smoke eager*
> *To scorch, consume*
> *All but the One seeing*
> *Who will assume*
> *The mantle and title of Covenant,*
> *Ruin.*

"Kim left me this poem before he disappeared," Angela said, her mouth suddenly bone dry. She forced Sophia to look at her again. "Where did you find this paper?"

"It was on the table where you and the others had been eating. It was on your plate, deliberately placed there. Along with something else."

Sophia left the couch and returned with a large but very dead black snake. She held the snake like a rope, allowing Angela to grasp it by the tail.

The moment it touched Angela's hands, it disintegrated to black ash and slipped between her fingers.

As Angela watched the ash fall, her heart seemed to drop out of her, plummeting with it.

What other warnings did she need? The crow at the windowsill, the bleeding Grail, the vision of the door, and now this. Fate was moving, and Angela didn't want to move with it.

"No," Angela said. "I'm so happy." She looked at Sophia. "*We* are happy."

"But did you really think the dream would last forever?" Sophia said softly. "Angela, I am the Book of Raziel, and I must be opened in time. The universe continues to crumble. Don't be mistaken by the beauty of the snow—the world is freezing slowly but surely, but as always, Luz will suffer first. It is all coming to an end. The only question that remains is, 'How fast?' Israfel is alive, and all of Heaven and Hell and the Realms in between wait for you, the Archon, to open me and make your ultimate choice. Just because we haven't found how to do so, either Lock or Key—that doesn't mean it isn't important anymore. There is no hiding, Angela. If Heaven doesn't find you time and again, Hell will. There is no escape from any of it—ever."

Angela held Sophia's dainty hands. "I've already made my decision. No matter what Lucifel does to me, no matter what Kim said, I refuse to be the Ruin and rule over a new Hell. So now, all we have to figure out is how to open you, the Book of Raziel, and prevent Lucifel from destroying everything. I won't let you die."

Sophia's eyes were downcast. "I have no fear for myself," she said, sounding oddly distant. "Besides, I did tell you I would always be by your side. I suppose we both have promises to keep."

"Exactly." Angela tried to ignore Sophia's uncertain tone. "So it's settled then."

"Not at all." Sophia shook her head. "I think you should talk to Stephanie, Angela. She was possessed by Lucifel, remember. Perhaps she can help you to stay one step ahead. I think it's crucial that you stay alert considering what has happened. Not everyone is on the Archon's side. Think about it—who left that note for you? An enemy, of course. And obviously that enemy could have been anyone in this room tonight. The Devil's reach goes far . . ."

"Either way, I don't care." Angela's hand burned, and the Grail throbbed beneath her glove. "I'll go through any door if that means you won't die. The only difficulty now is finding it."

Sophia wouldn't look her in the eye. "Sometimes, it's not that easy."

"What do you mean? It seems pretty straightforward to me."

"Sometimes, it takes more than decisiveness to turn back the wheel of fate. You say you will go through this door, but—perhaps I don't want you to. Perhaps you shouldn't."

"You won't die," Angela hissed. "*I'm not letting that happen.*"

Sophia opened her mouth and then seemed to decide on something else to say. "Angela, I am quite capable of taking care of myself. I did exist in Hell for a few millennia, after all, even if that was against my will. Whether a dark talisman or not, that snake was alive when I found it. So—as usual—I took matters into my own hands. If that's what it takes for me to be by your side and keep my own promise, then that's what I'll do. I'll try to get rid of the snakes in our path. The only problem is that they won't ever stop coming. Until you—the Archon—end this madness, it will only get worse."

Angela didn't have to ask exactly what had happened. Sophia was capable of all kinds of things she couldn't quite understand. That snake—magical or not—hadn't stood a chance.

This is it, Angela said to herself ominously, staring down at the ash. *This is the beginning. But of what? If only I could change everything, keep this moment, and never let it go.*

They were on the verge of something terrible, and Angela didn't quite know what it was. Is that what the door symbolized? Or was it something worse? And if it was a real door, and it led to somewhere awful, how long had Angela and Sophia been approaching it? Hopefully, Stephanie would know.

Enter the door or Sophia will die? That wasn't fair for anyone. And why couldn't they just tell Angela where to find the door in the first place? Maybe Sophia was right. Maybe—it was some kind of trap. But . . . Angela couldn't just sit back and do nothing.

Sophia took the paper back and perused it, a storm brewing behind her narrowed eyes.

"Anyway, I want to know who left that paper here," Angela said, suddenly angry all over again. Her suspicion cast itself on every last person who'd been at the table.

Sophia looked back at Angela, her gaze piercing and her voice firm. Her words seemed to echo from a faraway place—the same one where she'd warned Angela not to enter the terrible door. "I doubt you'll find out just yet. But if you do, keep this in mind. No matter how harmless they might appear—never trust a snake."

Thursday arrived with disturbing quickness.

Angela went through the motions of two days pretending that all was well, but her burning left hand consistently began to say otherwise. Besides the concerned glances of Sophia,

Angela oddly had nothing to contend with. The Order had given her breathing space—probably until the holidays were over—and there were no crows following her, or phosphorescent yellow eyes gleaming back at her from the darkness.

Yet something wasn't right.

Angela felt even more claustrophobic than usual, walking down the ice-slicked streets, and the faces that turned to regard her expressed constant fear and distaste, just like Camdon had pointed out. Even worse, the entire city of Luz hummed like a live wire with anxiety. The snow refused to let up, the cold increased ever so imperceptibly by the day, and the announcement had officially been made that citizens had to survive on whatever remained on the island until the spring thaw.

Angela wanted more than ever for it to be Christmas Day. She longed for cheeriness and a mug of steamed cocoa by the fire. Every normal, typical Christmas thing she'd never had as a child. But that was impossible when she had to find a mysterious door, enter it, and keep her best friend from dying.

So instead, she found herself standing in front of the Luz Institution where Stephanie Walsh had been sequestered.

The forbidding structure nestled directly on one of the tallest sea cliffs of Luz. All poorly mortared stone, its many towers jutted out from one another like tree branches. Even with the lights of so many candles in its windows, they resembled cheerless yellow eyes peeking from a black, many-armed monster.

Angela wasn't surprised to find the interior just as bleak, with seawater leaking constantly through various chinks in the floor. There were enough fireplaces to warm every patient and volunteer, but the glow the fires gave off seemed false.

The volunteer nun who'd been assigned to Angela had guided her through a dark brick lobby, where she'd quickly signed in as a visitor. Then they'd traveled up a long set of stairs to a floor where the stone had been whitewashed. Every corridor looked the same and smelled of antiseptic and musty blankets. At last, they'd arrived at a wing where a few volunteer novices chatted outside of a metal door marking a patient's room. A crucifix had been hung over the entryway.

Here I am.

Angela glanced at the sign nailed to the right of the door.

STEPHANIE LAURENTON WALSH

She licked her dry lips. Nervous butterflies tumbled in her stomach.

A nurse strolled by, staring for a moment at Angela's scars and blood-red hair. Panic shot through Angela. Any moment they would grab her and lock her up in Stephanie's place, imprisoning Angela for a past that wasn't quite her fault—just like they'd imprisoned her a few years ago. She could practically hear the lock clicking, sealing her doom. She could taste the terrible food all over again and hear the voices of the psychiatrists plying her endlessly.

Until she realized that it was Stephanie's door being opened, and it was a priest talking to Angela, encouraging her to make this opportunity count for them both. And then she was inside, alone with Luz's most notorious blood head witch.

Stephanie rested on a plain corner bench near her gable window, staring out at the snow. She looked simultaneously like the Stephanie that Angela remembered and someone completely different. Her dark red hair had been cut to her chin, and her green eyes had a vacant soulless glaze to them that reminded Angela of Sophia's most fathomless expressions.

She wore plain white sweatpants and a white T-shirt. At the edge of her bed, someone had left a bible.

A ceiling lamp flickered overhead.

Writing and odd symbols that Angela vaguely recognized covered the walls. She could make out a motif repeated over and over, the figure of a person on some kind of strange horse. Stephanie held the marker between her fingers, resting its tip near the edge of her lap. Angela tried to read one of the paragraphs to her right, but the scribbles made little sense. So she sat down and waited for Stephanie to talk. When nothing happened, she ventured in a small voice. "Stephanie? It's Angela."

Stephanie didn't move.

"It's Angela Mathers. Do you remember me?"

Nothing.

This, then, was the result of Stephanie's ambitions. Lucifel, the Devil, had possessed her and used her in an experiment to open Sophia, Raziel's Book. But the attempt had backfired, and Stephanie succumbed to the insanity meted out to any soul who wasn't either one of the greatest angels in the universe or protected by them. Initially, the priest had said she'd raved and called out strange names, at last settling into a chant that spoke over and over of eyes and darkness and unnameable terrors within a mysterious book. Now, she was mostly catatonic, expressing herself through her writing.

There was almost nothing left of the witch who'd helped murder Angela's brother and won a demon's affections.

Even now, Angela could hear Stephanie accusing her, saying how unfair it was that Angela was the Archon, and Stephanie herself had been left with nothing.

It had been Stephanie's most obvious regret.

This was awful. She didn't even seem to recognize Angela. Yet . . . Angela couldn't give up yet.

"It's Angela Mathers," Angela whispered, trying one more time. "The Archon."

Stephanie's green eyes widened. She snapped her head around and stared at Angela. She looked so odd without her heavy makeup, without her overly adult aura of sexuality. The more she examined Angela's sorority coat and scars, the more Stephanie's eyes welled up and her lip trembled angrily, making her seem even more childish.

She curled up, choosing the window again. "Angela," Stephanie said weakly. "You've come to laugh at me."

"No, I haven't," Angela said. "I came because I need your help."

Stephanie turned her head aside, but there was no denying that she seemed curious, almost astonished by Angela's admission. After a while, she peered back, as if making certain Angela was still there.

Angela came closer. "Do you have anything you want to say to me? This is your chance. You can talk, and I'll listen."

"You're the Archon," Stephanie murmured.

Angela nodded. "Yes."

"And I—" She clenched her fingers and pitched the marker onto the floor. "I'm the Ruin."

No, Stephanie. But you let the real Ruin of the universe, the Devil, possess you. And now look at what's happened. You're a shell of who you used to be.

Thank God, there were no mirrors here.

"I want Angela Mathers to know," Stephanie whispered, "that her secret is safe with me. She's the only one who can stop her, after all."

"Stop who?" Angela said a little too quickly.

"Lucif—" Stephanie's mouth snapped shut. She wrapped her arms around herself like the name was literally painful.

"Stephanie," Angela said, kneeling down in front of her. "Someone told me that if I don't enter a door, Sophia is going to die." Angela glanced at the tiny window in the room's door, hoping they weren't being observed too closely. She took out the paper from her pocket and showed it to Stephanie. "Do you know what this paper is referencing? Does it have something to do with Luc—" Angela caught herself, closed her eyes, and tried to stay calm. "With the Devil? Please, I need to know."

Stephanie took the paper and examined it, front and back. When she read the poem on the back, a strange wash of recognition came over her face. "Kim wrote this," she said simply.

"What?" Angela leaned forward, her heart racing. "Are you sure? But that's not his handwriting—"

"Don't trust him," Stephanie whispered, and she grabbed Angela by the arm. Her grip was like iron, but her hands shook. She peered at Angela intensely. "Don't trust anyone, Angela."

"Why?"

Stephanie laughed. "Look at me—that's why."

"That's not a real explanation," Angela said, aware she was losing her patience.

"All right, fine," Stephanie said, becoming icily serious again. "Kim said he loved me and he lied. Is that enough of a reason for you?"

Angela tried to speak more gently. "Do you know where Kim is?"

"In Hell," Stephanie snapped. "Where he belongs. Stay

away from Kim, Angela. Kim's father was a blackbird. He can't change who he is. And if he's not mine, you can't have him either." Stephanie wrung her hands together, whispering meanly, "Not you, or me, or anyone else."

Angela stood up, taking the paper back from Stephanie. This conversation was going nowhere after all. She should have known better than to think that Stephanie would have the answers so desperately needed. But Stephanie had a terrible though real connection with Lucifel, and if anyone wanted Angela in trouble, it was the Devil. Perhaps Stephanie's mind was just too far gone to be of any real use, just like Father Schrader had said.

"Good-bye, Stephanie," Angela said. She wanted to say something more, but came up empty.

She had just turned around again when Stephanie clamped down on her arm even tighter than last time.

"*Wait*," Stephanie said. She sounded truly afraid this time. "Don't go. Don't leave me alone. I'll tell you where the door is."

"You know?" Angela said, astonished but still worried that Stephanie was hedging again.

Stephanie glanced around the room, her eyes wild. "You don't understand. Luci—I mean, *she* makes me see things. Hear things. She said you would come and talk to me and that I would have to help you."

Angela stared at Stephanie, fear throbbing inside of her.

"They won't let me send you letters, Angela. So I wrote the words on the wall. Otherwise—I'd forget. There are so many of them."

Words on the wall? But all Angela had seen was nonsense, gibberish—

She gasped.

It couldn't be . . .

Angela snatched the paper from her coat pocket and held it up to the light on the ceiling, its scribbled side facing the lamp. There they were. The same symbols and words that had been written on the paper, Stephanie had written backward in her whitewashed cell. All over the walls of the room, Angela could read the poem's verses in heavy block scripting.

Her eyes darted wildly, taking in words here and there.

Blackbird escapes hungry . . . hellfire smoke . . . the One seeing . . .

And in thick letters: *Covenant. Ruin.*

Stephanie forced Angela to look at her again. "It's only a matter of time. It's only a matter of time until the blackbird escapes her cage."

"You mean Lucifel?" Angela said. Her voice was almost nonexistent. "Someone's going to let her out of her prison?"

Again? But that was right—Angela only fought Lucifel's shadow, and that had been terrible enough.

Stephanie breathed heavily, her face white and fearful. "It's only a matter of time. Get ready, Angela. I know where the door is, but when you go through it, you will have to go down very, very deep. Very, very far."

"To where?" Angela said, her breath nearly leaving her.

Stephanie couldn't even look at her anymore. "To Hell."

Lucifel is definitely the one behind this. Sophia was absolutely right.

"The door?" Angela almost shouted. "Where is it, Stephanie?"

Stephanie looked completely bewildered. "It's right in front of you."

"I don't have the time for riddles!"

"It's true, it's right in front of you," Stephanie shouted back. "Right here!"

Angela whirled around, seeing nothing but four walls with writing on them. "*Where?*"

"Anywhere," Stephanie said, but she regressed into a whimper as if realizing how ridiculous that sounded.

Angela shook her head and pushed back her hair. She wanted to scream, but instead she leaned against the wall and tried to gather her thoughts. This was the best she would get out of Stephanie—confirmation that it was Lucifel ultimately behind the dreadful note. There was an entrance to Hell in Memorial Park now, but there had been no activity from it since last year, and every time Angela checked, it remained the same—buried in rocks and dirt, the ground sealed tightly from invaders. Sophia had helped her put some wards in the earth and those had apparently done the trick, making the former cemetery just another barren spot in Luz.

Perhaps it wouldn't hurt to check one last time.

But when to get there? Running through her mental schedule, Angela realized she would have to wait two days for the park to reopen to visitors for Christmas. The Vatican guarded it so closely otherwise, she'd never get past the gate.

So that was it then. But it was also better than nothing. Better than a dead end.

As if sensing their conversation had finally ceased, Stephanie clung to Angela with mad fright behind her green eyes. "Angela, please don't go. You can't stop Lucifel—you can't save Sophia."

Angela fought with Stephanie, but the girl clung harder.

"Please, don't go through the door, Angela. You'll never come back and it will be the end for everything. *Lucifel will kill you and open Sophia, and then it will all be over. Don't you see the snow falling? Can't you see the universe dying? Angela, listen to me. Ride away. Don't let them get you. Ride, ride, ride—"*

Stephanie's words became frightening shrieks of despair. In an instant, the door to the room slammed open. Angela found herself torn from Stephanie's terrified grip as a group of nuns and two nurses in white attempted to pin the girl to the bed. Stephanie kicked and swore, but they subdued her after a short time with an injection from a small needle, and it was all over.

It seemed like only a few minutes more until Angela was thrust back out in the snow and ice, her heart pounding, her left hand burning, and the Eye certainly weeping blood, unable to find a door that apparently was right in front of her.

Six

That night, I dreamed I rode a horse to a revolving city
of stars. Then I plucked one of those stars from the sky
and gave it like a jewel to her. —ANGELA MATHERS

Friday arrived with more snow than usual, and a terrible sense of tension in the air.

Two more days until Angela could enter Memorial Park.

She couldn't stand it, and she often found herself pacing throughout the Emerald House after her classes, waiting for more mysterious notes that never arrived, keeping an eye out for more snakes that never appeared. Now, everything was too quiet without a single sign of Troy, of her crow familiar, Fury, or even of members of the Order. Angela slipped off her arm glove and examined the Eye, which had also stopped bleeding and aching for a good while. She would have thought the past two days had been nothing more than a bad dream, except that over and over in her mind, she could hear Stephanie's panicked screams, and her ominous prediction that if Angela entered Hell, she would also never return. That Lucifel would ultimately win.

I can't take this anymore. Why can't I make time go by faster?

She slid out a chair in the kitchen and slumped over the table, sucking in the warm scent of spice pie. In the hearth room, Sophia sang carols as she wrapped presents.

"Merry Christmas. Merry Christmas, and good cheer to all . . ."

Angela cradled her head in her hands, her mouth suddenly pasty and dry. Her ears continued to ring with Stephanie's words as they blended with Sophia's song, becoming a hundred times louder.

Angela's first real Christmas and she had to spend it like this. It wasn't fair.

She listened for a while longer to Sophia's song, then got up and grabbed the spice pie from the counter, heading into the hearth room with the pie, some plates, and two forks. Sophia was busy putting the finishing touches on a package, her small fingers in the middle of deftly tying a red satin bow as Angela entered. She paused while Angela set the spice pie in front of her, and then without a single comment Sophia returned to her work.

Sophia was waiting for Angela to speak first, but what else could be said at a time like this?

At any moment, Angela felt like the earth's jaws would open and Sophia would fall into a black pit of nothingness, screaming while white bony arms yanked her down harder the more she tried to escape.

Outside a crow screeched.

Angela flinched, almost dropping her pie on the floor.

Sophia looked up from her gift-wrapping, visibly concerned. "Angela, worrying won't change anything."

Angela grunted and shoveled a forkful of pie into her mouth. "I'm not worried," she said between chews.

Sophia shook her head. "You're a terrible liar." She stood, searching through the presents for something. "And I think you need to get your mind off all this for the next two days. Go to the Christmas Ball with Camdon, and then we'll go to Memorial Park the next morning and check the Netherworld Gate again. It's all we can do, and fretting about it won't change anything. Besides, Lucifel isn't stupid. She knows you will need a reasonable amount of time to find the door. Her main concern will be that you actually enter it."

"You mean that's where you come back into the picture," Angela said, setting down her empty plate. "Fine. I guess you're right . . ."

But she couldn't escape the terrible feeling that Lucifel would prod them through that door somehow.

"I know I'm right," Sophia said certainly. She leaned down, picking up one of the gifts. "Besides, going to the Ball will shut the Order up for a while. Just showing your face at a public event will make them happy."

Angela sighed. "I hate it. We should have a society that welcomes everyone and anyone, not just blood heads. They have the whole thing backward, and it's just making everyone that much more suspicious of each other."

"Very true," Sophia said gently, her expression pensive. Then she turned and handed Angela a fist-sized but prettily wrapped package with green paper and a silver bow. "For you," she said, smiling beautifully. Her stormy gray eyes held a gentleness Angela had never seen before. Sophia's voice was musically sweet. "I always loved this human holiday the most. Merry Christmas."

"Oh," Angela said, grasping the gift like it was made of gossamer. "Thank you . . . Sophia, I—"

This was it. Angela's first exchange of gifts. Ever.

She laughed, and then she laughed again for laughing in the first place.

She could have stared at the crisp green paper all night, completely absorbed in its pattern of stars and its tinsel bow. She felt like she held a gigantic diamond. "Wait. Hold on," Angela said hurriedly, setting the gift on the floor and rushing upstairs to the cedar wardrobe in her room. She rustled through a pile of clothes on the floor, emerging with a package sadly wrapped in old newspaper. By the time she returned and handed the gift to Sophia, her cheeks were on fire and she was gasping for breath. "I'm sorry," she said, already feeling unbelievably inadequate. "I didn't know you could find fancy paper on the island—"

"Thank you, madam," Sophia laughed, plucking the gift from Angela's hands. She smiled so brightly now, the whole world could have fallen in love with her. "Shall we open them together then?"

They settled onto the floor to sit opposite the fireplace and each other, and what began as a delicate tug of ribbons and strings devolved into a frantic competition to see who would open her gift first.

Paper crackled loudly as it was tossed aside.

Sophia won, lifting first a silver chain and then the necklace's pendant into the air. "Oh," she said softly, her pretty mouth formed into the exact letter. "Oh . . ."

"I was hoping you'd like it . . ." Angela had spotted the necklace in one of the Academy's fine jewelry shops and had bartered most of her own jewelry to purchase it. The delicate silver chain had a white sapphire star swinging from its end, with an engraved silver feather wrapped around its points so daintily, the entire construction looked like it might blow away if you breathed wrong. "I—I thought it would look perfect on you—"

"It's beautiful," Sophia said, so softly she could barely be heard. "The most beautiful thing anyone has ever given me." She stared at Angela, her face deeply serious. "Ever."

"Really?" Angela said, blushing.

"Yes." Sophia swung the chain around her neck and fastened the clasp. She walked over to her reflection in the window, examining her treasure with a vacant sorrow in her eyes. The pendant glittered above the scoop neckline of her silver dress, like a tiny star had dropped from heaven onto her skin. "Thank you," she said. Her eyes shone glassy. "Thank you. I promise I'll wear it all the time."

Is she crying?

"Sophia?"

"Yes?"

"What's wrong? If you're not sure about the necklace, I can return it. It won't hurt my feelings, I promise."

Sophia's beaming happiness continued to fade fast, like she'd just remembered a crucial thing that needed to be said but never could, and the more she stared at the necklace, the more that painful struggle became obvious. Angela could see the unsaid something hurt her—hell, it was hurting both of them. For a brief second, Angela considered running over to grab her, hug her, promise a million times over that they would never be apart.

That's what it is. She puts on a brave face, but that note, the door . . . it's bothering us both.

"It's nothing, really," Sophia said, staring off beyond her

reflection. "I just . . ." She touched the pendant again, her eyes newly clear and dry. "It's very beautiful."

The silence grew between them and Sophia shrugged, seeming to completely return to her usual self. She spun around smiling, but that smile seemed so much more forced this time. She was holding everything in again, and from the look on Sophia's face, Angela knew no matter what she said or did, her friend would continue to hold back.

Maybe it was all Sophia knew.

"Now," she said, gesturing at Angela's gift. "Open it."

"All right." Angela glanced down at the gift in her lap, realizing all she had left to unwrap were the folded ends of the paper. Neatly, she untucked both ends and slid out a box exactly like the one she'd given Sophia. Her eyes widened. "You're kidding," she whispered.

Angela opened the box. Gleaming back at her, the same necklace she had given Sophia rested on its little cushion.

"It seems we think alike," Sophia said softly.

She watched Angela walk over to the same window and use the reflection to clasp the chain around her neck.

Angela touched the sapphire, wordless.

Sophia appeared behind her with an even sweeter smile than before. "We'll always be together, Angela. I promise. You are the Archon, and I am the Book of Raziel. But we are also much more than that. Friends. Always."

Friends . . .

Still unable to say anything, staggered inside by the strength of the bond that had formed between them, Angela hugged Sophia and held her tight.

It was the sudden knock on the door that made her jump, forcing her to let go.

Seven

---

*The angel Raziel wore a coat of stars, and his winged
ears shone with jewels. His beauty was something
the human mind cannot comprehend. But he never
attended the formal dances of Heaven. Always wise,
he knew stars are dimmed by vanity.* —SOPHIA

The loud knocking continued.

Together, Angela and Sophia stared at the door like it was
what they both feared, a portal that would spew out demons
eager to rip them apart too soon. With the noise ringing in
her ears, Angela found the strength to slowly walk to the
door and peer out the peephole.

A man in a long black coat, with a sizable box tucked
under his arms, whistled to himself as he waited on the porch
stairs.

Slowly, Angela opened the door. Her chest tightened, and
her hand burned. "Yes? Can I help you?"

He glanced at her, startled. "Are you Angela Mathers?"
he said brusquely.

"Yes . . ."

"This is for you then." He thrust the box into her arms.

Angela staggered back a little from the weight. "Um, all right, but—"

"Good day to you, miss," he said just as brusquely. "Have a Merry Christmas and Happy New Year."

He sped off the stairs and down the street, his silhouette disappearing in the haze of snow.

Angela lugged the box into the house and shut the door, keeping more snow from entering the foyer. Sophia was already by her side, inspecting the tall package with tense wariness. There was no return address, and the box looked battered at the edges. They stared at it like they had stared at the door, neither speaking.

"Well?" Angela finally ventured.

Sophia pushed her aside. "I will open it," she said in a tone with no room for argument.

With lightning-fast efficiency, Sophia wrestled open the wrapped lid and ruffled messily through layers of packing paper. Plunging her hands deep into the box, she pulled and lifted out a dress by its midnight blue straps. The dress itself had a short train, but the fabric had been studded with crystals that looked like miniature stars.

Sophia's face was pale as death.

Angela's was probably paler. Her memories raced, and once again she saw ancient images of the angel Raziel in his beautiful blue coat studded with white jewels. This dress's fabric could have been exactly the same, fiber for fiber, though of course the cut and style were miles apart. Someone knew that Angela was the Archon, a human being whose soul shared a special bond with the dead angel Raziel, and the idea that they weren't being subtle about the knowledge punched her in the gut.

She could barely breathe as Sophia set the dress aside.

Plunging in again, Sophia took out a silver masquerade mask studded with more white jewels. Finally, she discovered a note.

Angela grabbed it impulsively.

You seem a bit shy, so I thought this might change your mind. I think it would look beautiful on you at the Ball. I'm sure my sister would have agreed. Perhaps I will see you there.

Camdon Willis

Angela let out a shaky breath, sudden relief flowing through her. She'd felt like her nerves had been cut, but now life could return. So—the design of the dress was a coincidence after all.

Yet Sophia's brow remained furrowed. A worried expression had tugged her smile away. "You have to go to the Ball now, I suppose," she whispered.

"Well, you're coming with me," Angela said. "And I don't care what Camdon thinks about that. Until we inspect Memorial Park together, I'm not going to leave you alone." Angela pushed back her long blood-red hair, taking a deep breath. "How can I not go? Did he really have to mention Nina like that again? I don't know what I think of this guy, but I do know that he's smart. I guess it couldn't hurt . . ."

"Of course not," Sophia said. But she clasped her pendant tightly and never stopped looking at the dress.

Saturday evening arrived, leaving only hours until Angela and Sophia could go to Memorial Park and hopefully put an end to their fears. But for the time being, there was the Christmas Ball to think about, and it was admittedly wonderful to forget everything besides music, food, and the joy of being together on one of the most magical nights of the year.

Angela steadied herself against Sophia, trying to climb the stairs of the Grand Mansion in her ungainly high heels. Despite the opulence of the night, the atmosphere weighed upon her, like flakes of iron fell instead of snow. Trying to look experienced and at ease, Angela nodded at other students entering the building. More than a few wore masks in red or gold that matched her own, and their eyes peered at her in curiosity from behind jewels and dyed crow feathers.

Everyone passed across a low courtyard flanked by enormous angel statues.

Angela refused to look up at the statues. The angels' stone eyes could have been following her alone, though that had to be her nerves flaring up.

Yet every second fled by painfully. Foreboding hovered and waited. Maybe they shouldn't have come, after all—

"You look worried," Sophia said. She climbed the steps beyond the unnerving statues gracefully, deftly swishing aside her silver dress's lace when it got in her way. Her chestnut hair had been braided and sectioned into two elaborate pigtails that would have looked silly on anyone else.

But Sophia had the magical ability to look good doing and wearing almost anything.

"Or," Sophia continued, "is it just that you're not used to wearing an evening gown?"

"Point taken." Angela sighed, wishing there was a mirror somewhere. She felt odd, like every other strand of hair was out of place. She took off the mask, finding it suddenly silly. "Actually, I don't think I look too bad considering I've never been to a formal dance in my life. Though I think I have you to thank for a decent appearance."

It was true. Sophia had splashed lipstick onto Angela's mouth, rolled up Angela's long blood-red hair into a high bun with two glittering combs to keep it in place, and forced her to borrow shoes with heels resembling pointy spikes. Angela had kept the arm gloves, but instead of wearing her favorite leather gloves with holes for each finger, she'd donned elbow-length gloves of opaque black lace.

The result was that Angela looked much older, and she stood half a head taller than everyone around her. But no one could help her balance.

"That's it," she said shortly. "I'm taking these shoes off. God, they hurt like hell."

"What? You can't do that," Sophia said, laughing incredulously. "Your feet will freeze—"

"Watch me." Angela said, taking off the heels and strolling over to a blonde with black slippers, another straggler entering the Ball late. "Fifty florins to trade shoes," she said.

In minutes the transaction was done and Angela was a little poorer but a lot more comfortable.

Sophia shot her a rude look. "You know—I happened to like those shoes. I've had them for at least fifty years. A year for every florin, I guess."

"Sorry," Angela muttered sheepishly, aware of Sophia's glare as they entered the Grand Mansion's large marble and stone foyer. Angela shivered and rubbed her arms, trying to look more interested in her surroundings.

The Grand Mansion was the special building reserved by the Vatican for Academy dinners, dances, and special holiday festivals. Most students lucky enough to even consider attending the fancier parties had a wealthy background, parents with connections to priests or novices in Luz, and at least a good measure of popularity. Angela was wealthy, having inherited much of her late parents' fortune at her brother's death. She had a connection to one or two priests, and the distinguishing fact that she had managed to survive Stephanie Walsh's insanity counted for something. But she was still a blood head, and Camdon was right—attitudes had started to change.

She and Sophia were an hour late, and the entry hall seemed oddly empty once they stepped into it, yet there were still enough people passing by to make travel slow. A few individuals smiled at Angela, but others steered noticeably clear. Sophia stayed by her side, refusing to shrink under the scrutiny.

"Can I help you?" a man standing at the entrance to the grand ballroom said, glancing at Angela with open curiosity that evolved almost instantly into hostility. He wore a crisp tuxedo, his darting eyes almost the same shade of black. He held a paper in his hand, seeming to scan it already for whatever he thought her name might be. "Which party?"

There was a nasty clip to his voice.

Music poured from behind the enormous curtain, elegant melodies overloaded with the song of violins and the occasional tinkling of piano keys.

"Which party?" Angela repeated.

She had no clue. In a second, she was a naïve new student all over again.

"The one for university sophomores?" she said, already angry at herself for sounding so dumb, and worst of all, for arriving without a plan to meet anyone at the entrance. "I was invited by another student. Camdon Willis."

Sophia made a slightly irritated sound under her breath.

A brief sense of urgency shot through Angela, and she gritted her teeth. "Listen, I have to get in there. I look the part, don't I? Isn't that enough—"

"You most certainly do not *look the part*," he echoed her snappishly. He leveled his pen at her. "And if I didn't know any better, I'd say this was a prank. Who do you think you're kidding, walking in here with those hideous marks on your arms? What do you think this is—some hellish little blood head Halloween party?"

"What?" Angela knew her eyes were narrowing. "You think these are fake scars—"

"Yes," he whispered. "I do think they're fake. I think *you're* fake. And I'm rather sick of you blood heads marching into everywhere like you own the place, like you've always deserved special treatment for your . . . handicap."

He was almost hissing at her. The faint scent of alcohol clung to him. The room darkened around them, though Angela couldn't tell if it was the slightly drunken anger in his words, the anger growing in her, or the sad flicker of the wall sconces that caused it. Through the marble and stone, an unhealthy cold continued to seep inside and pick at her.

"If I had my way," the man whispered hotly, "you'd all be taken off this island and eradicated. Why does the Vatican still humor you?" He laughed. "Though it's not surprising. I thought it would be the end of you all after what happened in St. Mary's, with that witch—"

Angela's heart raced. She braced herself against the stone. "You knew about that?"

"My sister died in there," he said between clenched teeth.

Angela sensed him stifling a deep urge to throttle her.

"Some demon killed her. A demon summoned by a person"—he pointed his pen directly at her—"like you."

"It wasn't me who killed her," Angela whispered. Her mouth felt deathly dry. Her left palm burned where the Grail throbbed and throbbed.

Sophia was noticeably angry, her gray eyes almost flashing. But the man was either too tipsy or too upset to care.

"It might as well have been you who killed her," he continued hotly. "You're all the same. One of you is the Archon
and will be the Ruin of us all, yet we can't stop you or get
rid of you before you get rid of us. Do you know what it's
like to live in constant fear? This island is cut off from the
mainland, from the whole world. We're isolated, covered in
more ice and snow by the hour, waiting for more angels and
hell-spawn to arrive and turn everything upside down and
backward again, and yet you and all the others continue to
live like it's all a game, or a Christmas miracle. Well, I don't
think there are any miracles," he said, his tone so loaded
with pain that Angela couldn't even defend herself anymore.
"So—what now? Still want to enter the party and have a
grand old time?"

"Yes, actually." Camdon stepped through the velvet curtain, slightly stooping as he entered the room. "Don't you?"
he said to Angela.

Angela bit her lip and turned aside for a moment.

Was she really the kind of person who needed a knight in
shining armor to save her?

Not at all. You know where that's gotten you before.

"You know her?" The man gestured at Angela, clearly
disappointed Camdon was a blood head and that he might
say yes.

"It doesn't matter," Angela said. "Because I'm going
inside no matter what you say. Come on, Sophia. Let's not
waste any more of our time."

"Yes, she's with me," Camdon said wryly and eyed Sophia
as well. "They're both with me. Now if you'd excuse us . . ."

Camdon grasped Angela by the arm and yanked her into

the grand ballroom without another word to the fuming guard. Sophia followed only a step behind. Heat rose to Angela's cheeks, mostly because she hadn't gotten the chance to storm through the curtain on her own.

She shook Camdon off and cornered him against the wall. "What the hell do you think you're doing? I had everything under control."

"Sorry, sorry," Camdon said, raising his hands. "It didn't quite look that way to me. What was I supposed to do, just stand back and watch?"

Angela let him have some breathing space. "Why do you want me here?" she murmured, trying to smile at the immense crowds of people. The gray marble ballroom was thick with shade and flickering candlelight. Garland and glass ornaments in the shape of globes and stars hung everywhere from the cathedral-style windows. This was the largest room in the Grand Mansion, but hundreds of men in fancy coats, tuxedos, suits, and even the frocks of the novices had overloaded it to capacity, and women in velvet and heavy furs suffocated whatever space remained.

Angela's midnight blue gown received both admiring and envious stares.

"Isn't it obvious?" Camdon said. "You're pretty, and I wanted a partner to dance with." He looked her over politely. "You do look lovely, by the way. I'm flattered you wore that dress. Someone told me it would suit you perfectly, and I have to admit that person was absolutely correct."

"Someone?" Angela said. A dull fear echoed inside of her. "Who?"

Camdon shook his head and smiled. "It doesn't make a difference. Besides, I'm sure Nina would have agreed as well.

And my sister's opinion always counted for more than people understood."

"Stop it," Angela whispered. "You can't keep mentioning her like that, Camdon. I know you're sad. So am I. But—tonight, I—"

Please don't make me keep feeling guilty, she wanted to shout at him.

Camdon sighed. "It's okay. I understand. I guess I just feel guilty sometimes. Nina was the opposite of other people. She actually wanted to be a blood head like us—she thought that would make her fit in at this Academy. Looking back, it all sounds so ridiculous considering how attitudes have changed. I suppose I just feel like I owe her something, every day. Because I couldn't be there for her when . . ." He sighed. "Well, anyway, after tonight that will all change."

Angela peered at him, an even more strange sensation ripping through her.

What did he mean by that?

"Sophia," Camdon said, nodding at her. "I hope you won't mind if I ask your friend to dance. I've been looking forward to it for quite a while."

"Not at all," Sophia said softly. But her eyes betrayed her wariness, and she stared at Camdon as if she could see right through him.

"May I?" Camdon said, holding out his hand to Angela.

Angela hesitated and then accepted his offer. Camdon took her by the hand and led her farther out into the crowds of people. Then he grasped her waist, imitating the couples next to them perfectly, swinging her onto the dance floor.

Here, the music was louder and the chatter more constant. But Angela couldn't stop a strange feeling of being watched, and not in a good way, like a million hateful eyes bored into her back, vanishing into the shadows whenever she spun around. For a moment, she thought she could see Troy's crow familiar, Fury, hopping from one window to the next, peeking with a flash of phosphorescent eyes through the panes.

She prayed it was only her imagination.

Angela glanced up at the vast and heavily shadowed ceiling. In far corners, angel statues hunched over the crowds. Remembering how the statues lining the Grand Mansion's courtyard had made her feel, Angela relaxed a little.

"So have you taken my words into consideration, Angela?" Camdon smiled. "I think it would be good for every blood head at this school if you joined the Order. It would help our cause immensely."

His hazel eyes peered into Angela's with the same strange intensity as the day they'd met.

Unwillingly, Angela's mind flashed to the night when she and her angel Israfel had danced together, when she had flown with him, and he had sung to her, turning his own falling feathers into a rain of crystals. How would he have felt to see her like this now? Not in a dirty school uniform, but elegant and feminine, and altogether . . . not herself.

Maybe it didn't matter anymore. Israfel was gone. Kim was gone. This was reality—for now. Yet it didn't feel right.

Angela glanced at Sophia.

Sophia continued to watch them with eagle eyes from across the room. Slowly, she raised her eyes to the ceiling. Did she sense something up there?

A cold and familiar chill worked its way up Angela's spine.

"Camdon," Angela said, "don't take this the wrong way, but I refuse to be convinced that segregating ourselves from the rest of the Academy will help matters. Why not create an Order open to any and all students, so that other students can mingle with people like us and see that deep down, we're really no different than them?"

"But we *are* different," Camdon said in her ear. "We can do things they can't."

"That's only because we're more confident. Because the Vatican turns a blind eye and encourages us to tamper with powers that we shouldn't."

"All blood heads aren't witches or warlocks, Angela. True, Stephanie and her Pentacle Sorority were a good example of what can happen when the wrong people tamper with powers they don't understand. But we can do good with those abilities too. In fact, that's partly why I wanted you here tonight. I needed to show you, Angela." Camdon's face became stony, and his eyes narrowed, examining her.

"Show me what?" Angela whispered.

Suddenly, the world turned in slow motion. A sick feeling worked its way into her stomach, and she knew what Camdon would say before the words even passed his lips. They tolled like a bell of doom, drowning out the elegance of the night.

Camdon pulled away from Angela but remained by her side. His smile seemed odd and out of place as he looked over her shoulder at someone approaching from behind. "I brought my sister back."

Eight

Long ago, I fixed the dreadful price of
a soul's return. —LUCIFEL

Dead silence descended on the room. The music stopped. Hushed words and whispers whirled around Angela like a tornado.

Softly, footsteps approached her.

She couldn't turn around. A sense of dread and elation, the strangest feeling she had ever known, had stopped the world.

Camdon beamed brighter than ever, and Angela now realized that the intensity she had found in his eyes was a type of madness. She stared back at him, unable to express in words the sudden horror she felt at his touch and the way he'd spoken in her ear. But she didn't need to speak, because another voice called her name from a shadowy realm beyond the grave.

"Angela," Nina Willis said from some nearby spot behind her.

The silence in the room pressed like a vise. Most people who had known Nina when she was alive seemed rooted to the spot, either confused or vaguely terrified. In the background, someone muttered a hasty "Hail Mary." Others cried softly, but whether from relief or fear it was impossible to tell.

But no one moved.

"Angela," Nina's voice said again. "Aren't you going to say hello?"

It can't be.

Nina was dead. She went to Hell in Angela's place, so Angela could live and help everyone else. *She was gone forever.*

Slowly, Angela turned around, her knees feeling shaky and weak.

Nina Willis stood in front of her, looking almost exactly as she had when she was alive. *Almost.* Her hair, which had always been frizzy and unkempt, had been pulled back into a smooth and careful braid. Nina's eyes, which had always been so bloodshot, were clearer than Angela had ever seen them. She wore a dirty white dress that Angela recognized instantly as the dress Nina's body had been buried in. Oddly, there wasn't a single scar on her neck marking the spot where her throat had been cut.

It was like looking at Nina's twin—someone very similar but not quite her.

"You—you're dead, Nina," Angela whispered lamely. Tears rolled down her face. What else could she possibly say? It was a miracle she hadn't fainted on the spot.

Nina took a very deep and alive-sounding breath, and she gazed at Angela with the most open and sincere expression possible. "Not anymore. Someone brought me back." She lifted her dirty hands, showing off the mud caked beneath her fingernails. "Do you know what it's like to crawl out of the ground, Angela? Not—very—pleasant. But I'd much rather be here than in Hell where I don't belong. Just imagine it; I fell into Hell and lost all sense of place and time, wandering aimlessly. Then I was grabbed and thrust into a new body just like my old one. Remade. Oh, that couldn't be the end of it though. I had to escape and crawl out from under that huge tree in Memorial Park—out of Hell. On my hands and knees, tunneling and crawling, rolling around on the snow once I reached the surface, learning how to breathe again. It was awful." Nina hugged herself, shivering. "And then I heard someone familiar calling me here—to this building. And I saw you dancing. Was it you, Angela, who brought me back?"

Nina has a new body just like the old one. She's a Revenant, a person resurrected from death through Lucifel's power. Sophia's body is exactly the same—just a machine that can be destroyed over and over again, only to come back for the next round. This means . . .

Angela glanced over her shoulder at Camdon, who stared at Nina with undisguised elation.

This means . . . I found the real snake Sophia was talking about. Camdon is helping Lucifel. Why?

What could she do now?

Angela's mind raced. She turned to Nina, and back to Camdon again, trying to think and think fast.

He'd already started stalking in Sophia's direction. A hot fear raced through Angela.

That's it—Lucifel blackmailed him into making an exchange. Camdon gets Nina, and as part of the bargain Lucifel gets Sophia. Damn it!

It was too late. Sophia simply couldn't move fast enough. She took two fearful steps backward and dashed for the room's exit, but Camdon grabbed her by the waist. The terrified screams of the crowd began. Noise and movement thundered throughout the Mansion.

Angela's left hand burned all over. Beneath her glove, the Grail throbbed, slowly and dreadfully blinking open its great Eye. A deep shudder ran through her and up into her body.

How dare you, her mind hissed inwardly. *You're not taking her from ME.*

She tore off the glove and raised her hand at Camdon.

He shouted in terror and raised his own.

A searing red light flashed throughout the room, illuminating the farthest corners. A great portal opened up behind him, some kind of vicious cut in the fabric of reality. Camdon screamed fearfully as Angela strode toward him. Her entire being was now focused on grabbing Sophia and crushing Camdon like a fly if the need arose.

"*Te libero,*" he screamed even louder. "*Te libero.*"

I release you.

Angela was almost on top of him as three enormous snakes burst from the portal.

She never had a chance.

The largest of them wrapped itself tightly around Angela's body, pinning back her arms, and squeezed.

Nine

Sophia had been right about everything. Yet somehow, I still couldn't accept the truth: that the wheels of fate would forever turn, whether or not I agreed. —ANGELA MATHERS

Angela gasped for breath. Her ribs would snap like twigs at any second. She screamed hoarsely, already suffocating under the weight of muscle and scales. Her ears buzzed, her vision swam, and every time she struggled even an inch, the snake squeezed tighter.

The cold screech of a crow sounded outside, crying in warning.

Angela recognized that sound.

Sudden hope rushed into her.

It can't be—

A crushing weight knocked Angela and the snake to the ground, rolling with them.

Angela shut her eyes, groaning with pain. Her muscles and bones still hurt from her fall with Janna, and now they sang in agony again.

Suddenly—she could breathe.

Angela threw off the snake's now limp and bleeding body. She rocked to her feet.

Troy, the beautiful but nightmarish Jinn, stood in front of her.

The snake regained some life, and Troy pounced on it again, biting it viciously at the head with her pretty mouth filled with sharp teeth. Her great sickle-shaped black wings thundered blasts of air that mixed with the portal's screeching wind. The phosphorescent yellow eyes of Angela's darkest nightmares blinked at her with acknowledgment. Pointed ears pressed back against Troy's choppy black hair, expressing her irritation as her chain earring swung side to side in the gale. The hellish snake whipped beneath her, attempting one last grasp at life.

With the little bones tied in her hair rattling viciously, Troy split the snake down the middle with her nails and tossed its body aside.

More thunder echoed from above.

Angela glanced up toward the ceiling, astonished to see a male Jinn with the blue-sheened feathers of a blackbird streaking down to meet with another snake. On a perch next to the angel statues, a much smaller Jinn waited and watched with owlish eyes.

Sophia was right. She knew. Troy had been watching Angela all along.

A hideous hiss assaulted Angela's ears. She turned around to find another snake rearing above her.

I don't think so.

Angela dug her fingers into the Grail, flinching as warm blue blood leaked from the cut. How long would it take for the blue blood to crystallize and for the infamous Glaive to settle long and lethal in her hands? Seconds.

As the snake arced down to bite off Angela's head, she swung the Glaive's curved blade to the right.

The demonic reptile thudded in two twitching pieces to the floor.

Terrible growls followed its demise. The light and wind from the portal intensified. Angela searched for Sophia and Camdon within the red brilliance. Hopefully they weren't gone. Without any more thought, she raced again in the portal's direction. The closer she came, the better she could see. But the Glaive drained her energy more with every step.

Sophia—HE CAN'T TAKE YOU.

The most terrible growl yet erupted from deep within the portal.

Angela halted, shivering despite herself. A moment of tense silence descended.

"*Stay back,*" Troy screamed with uncharacteristic fear.

Angela had no time to go backward. She could only duck as something huge and leonine exploded from the portal, soared over her, and landed heavily in the middle of the ball-room floor. The ground shook. The chandeliers rattled.

She held her breath, riveted and terrified.

What was that thing?

Slowly, a face ringed by a copious mane of black hair turned and glared back at her. The portal's light glistened along the curves of the creature's eyeballs, the straight fence of its teeth. The hunter took another noisy breath, flapping four enormous wings and then it rounded on Angela again, its limbs splayed and stiff, its hackles rising along the slope of its enormous back. It pawed at the ground with disturbingly human-shaped hands.

Worse yet, Angela sensed intelligence behind its preda-tory eyes. Briefly, she matched the creature's movements to those of the twin angels who used to guard Israfel, sensing a similarity, though not understanding why.

The creature's green eyes narrowed as it examined her.

That was it—its eyes were exactly the same.

"*Here,* Hound," Troy hissed from her corner with frightening anger. She unfurled her wings, answering her enemy with an open mouth filled with teeth.

Unimpressed, the wolfish beast paced nearer to Angela.

Troy switched to a ferocious growl, rage bubbling up from her throat and escalating into a chill screech.

Troy's distracting it. Risking her life . . . for me.

It was working.

The Hound snarled at Troy, and then it prowled nearer with heavy footfalls. A sulfurous odor emanated from the beast's body like a cloud. Its four wings snapped inward, restricted by the suddenly inadequate width of the room.

The male Jinn streaked out of nowhere again and hit the horror head-on, throwing them both to the ground.

Troy lost little time, pouncing with him. All three terrors rolled together, biting and snapping in a ball of feathers and teeth. Blood spattered across the tiles. The battle continued for an eternal minute.

Without warning, the male Jinn lost his footing.

That was all it took. The Hound grabbed him by the wings, bit fatally through his neck, and hurled him into the wall.

Troy froze for a mere second but bravely resumed her battle. For the first time, Angela saw terror behind the Jinn's eyes.

Heedless of all else, Angela rushed for them both.

She had barely taken a few steps when the Hound tossed Troy aside and galloped for Angela, leaping with its angelic face and baring rows of horrific teeth. Its jaws were wide enough to tear off Angela's head.

This is it.

She lifted the Glaive to meet the nightmare. Troy shrieked in pain, and the Hound released a bloodcurdling cry of agony.

Then it fell on Angela, and the world around her blinked out like a light left on too long.

Ten

Time passed within a world of shadows and dreams.
Every pain seemed small compared to the new
ache in my heart. When I awakened, I felt like a
different soul. Then I knew—she had gone, taking
my spirit with her. —ANGELA MATHERS

"Angela? Angela? Hold on—give her some space . . ."

Nina's voice. Nina's touch, shifting Angela's body to the side and holding her head steady.

Angela awakened little by little, realizing only by degrees that she was alive and had cheated death yet again.

Her memories were vague and disjointed. There had been screaming and light and suddenly a crushing blackness. Now her eyelids fluttered open and she lay in the chilly snow, gazing up at more flurries as they drifted from the dark sky. Coughs shuddered up her throat, but she barely had the energy to cover her mouth. Her entire body felt like it had been drained. Angela had used the Glaive, and, like every time before, the consequence was utter physical weakness. If she had used the weapon to its full potential, she would have died.

"How do you feel?" Nina said. Her face appeared above Angela's. Thick flakes of snow salted Nina's hair. "You were so damn lucky. The Hound fell on the Glaive and died. Troy had to rip the corpse off you to keep you from being crushed to death."

"Troy is still alive?" Angela reiterated.

A low growl to her right said yes.

Angela tried to sit up but slumped back into the snow. She stared at the spiraling whiteness all around her. The snow was so clean and pure, and yet so ominous. A sour tang saturated the air. She'd know it anywhere by now.

Blood.

"How did we get outside?" Angela murmured.

"Troy carried you," Nina said, lifting Angela's arm and wrapping something around it. "After what happened, we couldn't stay there. She said the priests would come and know you're the Archon. In fact, the whole city is going crazy. It's amazing we managed to get out of there at all . . ."

It was hard not to picture Luz taking every blood head and locking them in the darkest prison cells near the sea after tonight. Camdon's sad desire to see his half sister again had cost those like him everything. No wonder he'd wanted to segregate blood heads more. He knew exactly what he was doing and what the ramifications would be.

Sophia! He took Sophia!

"Nina," Angela said, grasping her by the arm, "where are Sophia and Camdon?"

"Camdon?" Nina said. She seemed confused. "Was he there? How do you even know him? He'd been studying abroad for almost two semesters."

Nina hadn't seen him? Well, that was possible. Nina had been focused on Angela and nothing else.

"Never mind," Angela said. "What about Sophia?"

There was a rush of air and a throaty croaking noise. Angela flinched as Troy's familiar named Fury landed beside her in a blur of black wings and yellow eyes. The Vapor in the form of a crow ruffled her feathers and inspected Angela with a penetrating look. Satisfied by what she saw, Fury proceeded to preen at the blood in her own feathers. She deftly tore out a crusty lump of down.

"Sophia is gone," Troy said. She crouched beside Angela on her haunches, breathing deeply. There was a strangely vacant look in her glowing eyes. "The human you call Camdon took the Book of Raziel to Hell, obviously in a pathetic exchange for the resurrection of his half sister. The Hound and the snakes were sent by a demon. It matters not which one—only that it is extremely powerful."

Blood rimmed Troy's lips and stained her nails.

Like Nina, she was different than Angela remembered and oddly subdued, perhaps because Troy had somewhat resigned herself to the Bond Angela had forced upon her. She also looked terrible. Many of Troy's feathers were missing or broken, and she flexed her left foot uncomfortably as if she'd sprained it.

"What was the monster that attacked us?" Angela demanded of Troy. "Was that the thing you just called a Hound?" Angela finally sat up and clutched at the sapphire pendant where it rested on her chest.

It was her only link to Sophia. Suddenly those moments they'd shared dissolved into painfully ancient memories.

"They are former angels," Troy said, "of a rank that does not resemble the others. When some fell, they became creatures of Hell."

Former angels . . . Angela noted the Hound had resembled

Israfel's guardians. Were his bodyguards derivatives of that dreadful creature? She didn't even want to think about it too much. The Hound was dead and had hopefully dissolved like the black snake Sophia had killed a day ago.

"The male Jinn?" Angela said softly. "Is he really dead?"

"Yes," Troy said with a low hiss. "But the heir is alive, and that is all that matters."

Timed exactly to her words, the small Jinn Angela had seen in the ballroom scampered into view and regarded Angela curiously. It was a female and very much like Troy with a pert, attractive face and glossy ebony feathers. She cocked her head at Angela and dropped a stone she'd been carrying, flicking her ears nervously.

Nina pointedly ignored the Jinn chick, sat back down on the ground, and settled her head against her knees, lost in thought.

"Her name is Juno," Troy said, but without any suggestion of motherly fondness. "She is my niece and my sister Hecate's, the former Jinn Queen's, only surviving heir from the Warrens. The male was Eris, another exile like myself who wished to protect the Sixth Clan's bloodline. There has been revolt in the Jinn Underworld because of the disintegrating dimensions. My sister Hecate believed in you, the Archon, but there are many who no longer cling to the covenant Raziel originally made with us. Out of desperation and fear, they murdered my sister who wished to protect you from death, and any and all who defended her ideals. I managed to smuggle Juno out of Hell to Earth before they could murder her as well. But that now makes me a traitor to the newly ruling Clan. Just like Sariel . . ."

Angela searched her memory, at last remembering that Sariel was the Jinn name given to Kim by his father. Troy,

Kim's cousin, had been hunting him for centuries as revenge for murdering the very father who had tormented him with fear. Now, she was stuck in the same ironic predicament.

Was that why Troy looked so terrible? The great hunter, the High Assassin of the Jinn, was now the one being hunted by her own race.

"You cannot imagine," Troy continued, growling dangerously under her breath. "You cannot conceive what torment he has put me through. Killing him is now the only way to keep myself from being killed. It is my only welcome back into the Clan after saving Juno."

"Why would you even bother going back to them?" Angela said. She immediately regretted it.

Troy's ears flipped back in anger. "An ignorant question from a typically ignorant human. But you are forgiven. After all, what can you really know of the cycle of life and death?" She fluffed her wings in the whistle of the wind, gathering the black pinions to her body. Her yellow eyes narrowed as she stared out into the darkness. "You think my only goal in life is to protect you? No, there are far more reasons for the things I do and you should be grateful. Hunting Sariel was what brought me back to this wretched Earth. Protecting you despite the threat of losing my life merely kept me here."

Kim is alive. But he's escaped Troy somehow. Was it—

Angela remembered her vision and the shock of seeing Kim appear in front of her, ravaged and worn, entering the same door she now had to find.

Angela tried not to show on her face the hope she felt in her heart.

Troy watched her keenly. "From the very beginning, I never arrived in this human waste of a city or spared Sariel's life for the fun of it. It was all for you, Angela Mathers. Or for the Archon, I should say. I should have been certain about your identity when you Bound me to yourself and took the Grail, yet you didn't smell like Raziel—and I was forced to act. But if you are not actually the reincarnation of Raziel, and his spirit is merely protecting you, what is the difference to me?"

Troy snorted, as if irritated at herself for that crucial mistake.

"You're apologizing for trying to kill me last year?" Angela muttered.

"If that's what you want to call it," Troy said slowly.

The Jinn clearly didn't like admitting to any kind of mistake, especially one so tremendous.

"I was sure you hated me." Angela pressed. "That you would kill me if you ever saw me again."

"Foolish, foolish girl," Troy laughed. She grinned evilly. "Though now that we are Bound, you must understand. I am the only one who will kill you. I will never let anyone else have that privilege. But as it is, you are the Archon and you must open the Book. What you humans so idly call Hell is the home of my people, whether we wish it or not. But none of us seek its end, and slowly but surely, it is falling apart."

"The dimensions, the Realms," Angela said for her.

"Are crumbling, yes," Troy said, licking her teeth grimly. "The destruction has begun here on Earth and is spreading outward from this human city. It is the reason behind this coldness, and this strange endless substance you call snow. The universe is freezing, in the early stages of dying. Only you can stop it. But first, the Book must be opened. And right now, we must take the Book back."

Troy gazed at her, and it hit Angela hard and painfully.

This was the moment she had dreaded for over a year. Upon her in all its oppressive torment, now she faced the daunting terror of entering Hell itself. What would she find there? The idea of temptation somehow scared her more.

Yet—Angela still couldn't see herself actively taking Lucifel's place. She couldn't.

I WON'T.

First, though, she had to find the door that Stephanie said was right in front of her. Angela couldn't help feeling slightly happy that Troy was available for answers.

"Troy," Angela said, ready to rummage through her skirt pockets for the piece of paper with Kim's familiar poem on the backside—until she remembered she had an evening dress on. "Before Kim disappeared—"

"*He is in Hell,*" Troy said. Her sudden growl made Angela jump. "And I will hear no more about him."

So he was there, after all. Then what did that mean for the rest of Angela's vision? Why didn't Sophia want Angela to save her?

The rage in Troy's voice had been so intense it could have taken on a life of its own. As if Kim had been right in her grasp, yet slipped out of it. The Jinn's hair bristled frighteningly, and she glanced savagely at Juno who had dared to come too close with another prized rock.

"How did Kim get there?" Angela said, daring the worst.

"If you must know," Troy spat furiously, "he is on the side of the demons. Working with those who wish to see you on the Throne of Lucifel. The night of Nina Willis's death, he used one of their little magic tricks to escape. But his demonic friends rejected him and he got no farther than the Netherworld. Empty as it was, he was forced to turn back.

My only consolation for failing to kill him that night will be setting my teeth in his neck in the comfort of my own warren."

"But how did he—"

"*Enough,*" Troy said furiously, her wings thundering powerfully in the snow.

This was the old Troy that Angela remembered. God, the Jinn was completely different when it came to Kim—whether the thought of him, or his presence—she hated him absolutely. Probably more than before, now that he'd escaped her.

So the spectacle of Troy's wrath settled the matter. Angela couldn't mention Kim's poem, she didn't dare. It would have to wait.

As if sensing the tension needed to be broken, the little Jinn named Juno sidled closer to Angela and tugged on the hem of her dress. "Yes," she said shyly, a pronounced hiss at the end of the last syllable. "We'll help you." She offered Angela the rock she had found. It would have been nondescript, but there was a tiny crystal in its center. "Here. For you. A promise from me."

Troy watched Juno with an annoyed yet ironically reverent silence.

"Thank you," Angela said, taking the rock with her throbbing left hand. With the other, she patted the chick's head, letting herself smile as Juno nuzzled back.

I can't believe it. They're actually cute when they're small.

Had Troy been like that once upon a time? Innocent and happy despite so much hunger?

"Do not be fooled," Troy said, swatting Juno away. The Jinn chick playfully returned, treating her gesture like a game. "They learn to defend themselves young."

The chick snarled, biting into Troy's hand in a teasing

manner. Yet blood blossomed on Troy's palm and dripped to the icy ground. The little Jinn lapped it up with blazing thirst behind its eyes.

"We will have to leave quickly," Troy said. "I am not eager to kill for this little one's appetite."

Angela didn't need any more explanation than that. She stood shakily, rubbing her aching head. "But there's one problem. I don't know where the door to Hell is. I was thinking that it might be in Memorial Park—"

Troy shook her head. "That entrance has been sealed off."

"Not completely," Nina said softly, staring at the dirt caked beneath her nails. She stood up with Angela and looked at her pointedly. "But it doesn't matter anyway."

"What are you saying?" Angela said. A shot of adrenaline coursed through her.

Nina took a deep breath. "I know where the door is. Follow me."

Eleven

So many souls had gone this route. And so few
realized what it meant to turn back. —SOPHIA

Camdon Willis pressed against the cool stone wall of Hell, trying to catch his breath.

He couldn't believe he was alive, and that the plan had succeeded. So—Angela Mathers was the dreaded Archon, the human being whose existence signaled the possible end of the world. But what was so special about her friend? He calmed himself and stared at Sophia, the doll-like girl who remained tightly in his grip.

Since they'd entered the portal and it had closed, she refused to look him in the eye. The expression on her pretty face was unnervingly icy.

"Hello?" Camdon whispered, glancing into the semidarkness. Embers glowed softly in the walls at regular intervals. He squinted and was sure he could make out strange hieroglyphics etched into the rock.

As his eyes adjusted more, he noticed a chair in the center of the circular chamber. A man sat within it, his legs hanging carelessly over one of the chair's arms. He was playing with a centipede like it was a marionette, lifting his fingers to tug on red strings of light connected to the creature's spindly legs.

He turned and his reflective orange eyes bored intensely into Camdon. A careless mop of black hair with violet streaks framed his very pale, very perfect face.

Camdon froze, relaxing his hold on Sophia.

"Well, well," the man said softly. He opened his hand and the red strings disappeared. The insect scurried off his leg into the blackness. "You've brought her, after all. It seems you humans can do some things right."

"Yes," Camdon said. He pushed Sophia by the small of her back toward the chair.

She stopped just shy of it, glaring royally at her new jailer.

Camdon stopped with her, unable to rip his gaze away from the man's reptilian pupils, the fine scales above his eyelids. "You're the demon who resurrected my sister?" Camdon said hoarsely.

Now he understood why they'd always communicated in shadows.

The man nodded. A very out-of-place smile settled on his lips. "What's wrong?" he said. "Were you expecting someone different?" He licked his lips with a forked snake's tongue. "I'm a little peculiar, I know, but I also thought I was still somewhat attractive. Then again, it doesn't surprise me that humans are afraid of snakes. You are rats, at any rate."

"You have what you wanted," Camdon whispered. "Please let me go back. My sister needs me."

The demon stood from the chair, his tall and lithe frame oddly intimidating. Slowly, he tipped back his head and laughed. "Needs you? Oh no, Camdon. You have it all wrong. Your sister doesn't need you at all. In fact, she's coming right back to me."

Dizziness swept through Camdon. His entire being chilled to the core.

That couldn't be true.

The demon leaned over him, his face suddenly hard and cold. "Do you really think I'd let a pawn like her out of my grip for one second? Lucifel wouldn't stand for that, boy. She and the Archon are coming to me. Sorry to burst your little bubble of sibling bliss. And once someone enters my labyrinth, they don't leave unless I say so."

Was it all a trap from the start? Camdon couldn't bear to think of that. He'd been so alone without Nina those semesters abroad. He'd been responsible for her happiness, and he hadn't been there to save her from death. Now, finally able to make amends, he was losing everything all at once.

"Please let me go," he whispered, backing away from both the demon and Sophia.

Sophia still refused to look at him, but this time she seemed stifled by pity, and her eyes shone glassy.

"Please," Camdon whispered faster. "Let me go home with my sister. I'll do anything. Anything—"

The demon slumped back in his chair and yawned. "So sorry, but I already told you the rules. Besides, how am I supposed to entertain myself until the Archon arrives? It can get so boring here in the dark, no one and nothing to talk to for so very long. One almost prays for excitement. Now that I have my little mouse, why should I let him go?" The demon pointed behind Camdon. "There are two tunnels behind you. Make your choice, boy. To keep things interesting I'll give you a head start—you see, I don't want to come off as unfair."

The fear scorching into Camdon felt like an inferno. He glanced at Sophia, but she squeezed her eyes shut and turned her head aside, as if she saw something terrible coming. She gripped the pendant at her chest and whispered, praying.

He spun on his heel and ran, the terrible sound of hissing and the demon's laughter echoing behind him.

Camdon ran and ran, but the snakes were faster than him.

Right when he thought he could catch his breath again, one of them reared out of the darkness.

Of all names, he shouted Angela Mathers's as it lunged.

Twelve

*Even so, I thought I could save
him.* —ANGELA MATHERS

"Ouch," Angela said. Strange electric shivers ran through
her whole body. Her arm ached.

She winced at the pain in her left hand and paused in
lacing up her boots. The aching had become pulsing waves
of fire.

Gingerly, Angela unraveled the bandages from her left
hand and stared at the newly bleeding Grail of Lucifel. The
Eye blinked within Angela's flesh, and more blue blood oozed
outward to the center of her palm. Blue blood—according to
Sophia, this was the color that ran in the veins of the Supernal angels. Sometimes Angela wondered who this Eye truly
belonged to, but she would shake away the question just as
quickly. Right now, it felt best not to know.

Odd. This pain was exactly like what she'd experienced
before Janna tried to commit suicide, though much fainter.
Like Angela was too late to stop whatever had occurred.

Something bad just happened. Sophia!

"Angela, are you ready?" Nina said impatiently from outside the bedroom door.

"Yeah, in a second," Angela shouted back. It took her a minute to rewrap the Grail and slip on both arm gloves. She finished lacing her boots and stood, smoothing out her red-and-black plaid Academy skirt, yanking up her tights. Angela had been against the tights, but with only her school uniforms available and no pants, she needed to stay warm. Opting out of her uniform blouse, she'd pulled on a musty-smelling cardigan and her sorority overcoat with the emerald eye stitched into the lapel. One of Sophia's gray scarves completed the odd ensemble. "Okay, I'm good to go."

There was no time to waste anyway.

Angela burst out of the bedroom and grabbed Nina by the wrist, dragging her down the stairs. She didn't bother glancing at any of Sophia's few possessions as they raced out the front door of the Emerald House. The necklace that linked Angela and Sophia together remained and that was enough. Everything else just hurt her inside.

"You shouldn't move too fast," Nina said. "You're still injured."

"We have to move fast. I can't explain, but something bad has just happened and it might have been Sophia who was hurt this time. I don't think Lucifel would kill her before I enter the door but—we can't be too sure of anything."

Every second that passed was a treasure lost.

Traveling from the area of Luz near the Grand Mansion back to the Emerald House had been too slow and difficult. Troy, Juno, and Fury could stick to the shadows and rooftops, but Angela and Nina were human beings with human feet. With Nina's expert guidance she and Angela had taken a lot of back alleyways and tunnels, but they had been in constant danger. Blood heads were being stopped everywhere on the streets for questioning, maybe worse.

They'd been lucky to reach the House.

Troy had agreed to Angela's wish to return so that Angela could change into an outfit much more suited to Hell than a blue evening gown. She couldn't even look at the dress Camdon had sent her and had thrown it onto the floor and left it behind without a second glance. Her intuition about it being tailored specifically to resemble Raziel's angelic outfits had been correct. Whatever demon had helped Camdon was also toying with her deliberately.

"I don't understand why Lucifel would kill her," Nina said as Angela shut the door. "Lucifel needs the Book of Raziel, right? At least, that's what I learned before I died. Let me know if the game has changed, why don't you?"

Angela stared into Nina's hazel eyes, searching her out. "You do have a point. But—I can't help feeling that Lucifel knows something I don't. Or maybe she's just completely insane by now."

"Maybe," Nina whispered. She looked uncertain.

"Whatever she's planning, though, it's not like I have a choice. I have to reach Sophia."

Nina nodded, snowflakes kissing her hair. She smiled. "Same old Angela, though you seem a lot more confident than you used to be. I like that."

"Glad to cheer you up," Angela said. She still found it difficult to talk to Nina so frankly when she'd been dead for so long. She rubbed her left hand and took a deep breath.

It was like she was hallucinating or talking to a ghost.

"Now what?" Angela said, sighing. "You mentioned that you know where the door is?"

Nina's expression was even more anxious. "I do. I already told Troy and Juno, and they'll be meeting us there. But, Angela, there's something that's bothering me. I know you don't have time for explanations, even though I have a million questions. What have you been doing? What happened with Kim, with Stephanie? I don't even know, and I want to know more than anything in the world. But tell me this—how do I know where this door is? I'm afraid it has something to do with the demon that brought me back. I'm afraid I'll hurt you more than help you. That you shouldn't go through the door no matter what I say."

Angela held her breath, considering.

Nina was right. But—

"You know I can't leave Sophia with Lucifel," Angela said, trying not to sound too harsh.

"Of course not," Nina said, pulling her back again. "It's just that it all seems too perfect. I'm afraid they want you and Sophia in Hell for a terrible reason, Angela. I'm afraid that you won't come back once you get down there."

Just like Stephanie had said. And what if she and Nina were right? Maybe it didn't matter if Angela was the Archon— maybe she was going to lose this round of the game no matter what she did. But she had to try.

Angela held Nina's hand and steadied her as best she could. "*You* came back, Nina."

Nina's eyes widened. "You're right. I was in Hell and I came back."

"So what do you remember from your time in that place?"

"Nothing." Nina shook her head. "Nothing worth remembering anyway. My time there is already becoming a blur. Once I died and my contact with the angel Mikel was severed, I was no better than any other ghost in the Neth-

erworld. That's what bothers me, though. I should have de-
parted to that high place where the other souls that promised
to help the Archon had gone, but something or someone held
me back. And here I am."

"We'll get through this," Angela said. "And then I'll
answer all your questions. But I've made up my mind, Nina.
Take me to the door."

Nina opened her mouth but shut it again, visibly forcing
her lips into a tight line.

"And, Nina?"

"Yes?" she said, brightening again, seeming hopeful
Angela had changed her mind.

Angela surprised her with a sudden and tight hug that
almost sent both reeling. Angela clasped her close, letting warm tears fall on Nina's shoulder. "I'm glad you're
back," Angela whispered, shuddering and trying to hold
back more tears. "When you died, I couldn't—I didn't . . ."

"I know," Nina whispered back, also letting tears slip
down her face.

"I won't let it happen again," Angela said, wiping at her
eyes. She let go of Nina and smiled.

Nina smiled brighter. She rubbed at her tears. "I know."

Without another word, Nina began to guide Angela as far
from the Emerald House as possible. At first, the streets were
unfamiliar ribbons of ice and cobblestones, and then they
began to sink down into the lower abandoned levels of the
Western District of Luz. Very few people walked the alleys,
and even fewer inhabited some of the ramshackle homes and
apartment buildings. Those they happened to meet regarded
Angela with open fear, sometimes running in the opposite
direction.

At last the candles disappeared from the windows. The wreaths stopped gracing moldy wooden doors.

They descended into a maze of streets that became more familiar with every step, and then Angela and Nina stopped at the grandiose decay of St. Matthias Church. This was where Angela had finally found the beautiful angel who'd haunted her dreams since childhood.

Israfel.

The church was exactly as she remembered it.

Angela crunched through the snow up to the chain-link fence surrounding St. Matthias, curling her fingers through some of the metal openings. The wet and the cold seeped through her gloves, and she let go after a short time, just listening to the heavy silence. Snow drifted in front of her, joining the pristine whiteness already covering the ground. More whiteness draped the building, reflecting the light from distant candles in a faint golden aura. Otherwise, the rich darkness of Luz's new and never-ending night hid the weathered statues, the forbidding doors, the sad cracks and gaping holes in the stained-glass windows.

St. Matthias was now boarded up, ready for repairs, but except for a few workmen's tools half buried in snow, it was hard to believe anyone had visited for weeks.

There were a few footprints around the tools. Bird tracks, maybe from Fury. Troy and Juno were sure to be inside already if this had been their destination. But Angela wasn't a Jinn, and she didn't have wings.

Angela jiggled the lock on the gate. It refused to budge.

I suppose there's only one way in. Just like last time.

"All right," she muttered to herself, "here goes nothing."

"Need help?" Nina said, offering a hand to push Angela up.

Angela waved her away. "Thanks. I might as well do it myself though."

"Whatever you want," Nina said. She shrugged and began scaling the fence.

Angela hitched her boots in the links at the fence's bottom and started to climb, up and up, until she reached the barbed wire and had to swing her leg wide, hoping her skirt didn't hitch on the razors like last time. Angela swung her second leg over, and then lost part of her footing. She fell sideways, trying to catch herself with her hands on the way, slamming into the fence bottom on the other side. The metal jangled. Her hands chafed even through the gloves. A sharp pain raced up the side of her thigh.

Damn it all. She'd cut herself anyway.

A thin stream of blood oozed from where the barb bit her skin. She pulled off one of her gloves, dabbing at the cut until it stopped bleeding, peering into the darkness while the snow and silence seemed to increase.

Nina dropped down beside her on both feet.

"Since when do you have the reflexes of a cat?" Angela almost felt like glaring at her.

"I was always a good climber," Nina said, kneeling beside her. "I used to run errands for a curiosity shop when I was in high school. Climbed one too many fences in my day. Always thought I was going to die doing that, honestly."

"Curiosity shop?" Angela ventured.

Nina shrugged. "It was owned by a fortune-teller named Mother Cassel. She happened to be a blood head too, though she had to work in secret, because the Vatican hates blood head fortune-tellers. They're pretty much illegal in Luz. Sometimes I got the impression she was trying to turn me into an apprentice of some sort, or even pass on the shop to me. She always thought I had unusual psychic talents for an everyday person. Couldn't quite figure it out. She used to help me try and interpret my dreams about dead people, because we'd given up on stopping them. It was a lost cause."

"Well," Angela said softly, "not quite." She stood and brushed off the snow from her legs. "So why do you think the door is here at St. Matthias?"

"I don't know. I just do. Is this place important to you? It seems like you recognize the church."

"Yeah, I do."

Nina waited for an explanation, but Angela motioned her toward the door. "Come on. The sooner we get in there, the better."

They ascended the stairs, and Angela listened to the gentle shift of the snow beneath her shoes.

She'd opened the doors easily last time, as if by magic. Hopefully, she'd have the same luck tonight.

She gripped the brass handle, pushing on it. God, it was like holding ice.

Locked.

"Great," Angela whispered, stepping backward. She kicked at the doors, but they held firm, snapping back against the weight of her boots. "That's just great."

A shudder ran through the doors. The wood groaned and splintered, buckling outward.

Angela jumped aside, trying not to scream as Troy's bony arm emerged from the hole and continued to make a space wide enough for Angela to step through. She waited for Troy to pull away and stepped into the church, ducking beneath jagged sections of door with Nina behind her.

Troy waited in a corner mired by darkness, Juno near her legs.

"You could have just used the knob," Angela muttered.

"Practice for later," Troy said, hissing under her breath. She disappeared for a moment, and then she and Juno reappeared farther away, watching both girls delve deeper into the abandoned church. Fury croaked somewhere high in the rafters, her bird chatter echoing eerily.

The church's interior seemed to waver in the half-light, and it remained cloaked in white where snow had fallen through holes in the roof. Angela stepped down the aisle, cringing when her boot cracked through a frozen puddle.

Unwillingly, she remembered Israfel's voice, his breathtaking beauty, their dance together, and the falling feathers he'd turned into a sparkling rain of crystals.

She remembered their kiss.

Where are you now, Israfel? Whose side were you on in the first place? Maybe Raziel's, but I don't know about mine.

Her angel had even called Angela by Raziel's name.

She closed her eyes as the memories came rushing back, faster and faster. Angela proceeded cautiously, trying to make as little noise as possible, failing miserably whenever she hit another puddle she couldn't quite see. Then she was in front of a familiar and oddly pristine stained-glass window with a young woman, an angel, and the lily that was the gift between them. Angela turned around, certain that Israfel would be standing behind her like a dazzling star in the darkness, just like he had that incredible night.

Instead, Nina stood behind her, appearing bewildered that this shell of a church held some kind of importance.

But there was one problem.

Perhaps it no longer did. "Nina," Angela said with real fear. "I don't see a door."

Thirteen

*My mother named me out of guilt. She'd dreamt before
I was born that a red-winged angel stood over my
cradle. He told her to name me Hope, but she looked
at my hair and refused.* —ANGELA MATHERS

"That's impossible," Nina said gently. "The door is right here."

Angela spun around, her gaze darting wildly here and there. "There's nothing here, Nina. I don't see any kind of special door anywhere."

At least, not like the one from her vision.

Oh God, this couldn't be happening. Angela couldn't have lost the game already.

Troy snorted impatiently from her perch. Obviously, she wasn't about to offer any further help. Perhaps she had none to give.

Nina paced and rubbed her forehead, trying to think. She paused. "Have you been given any other clues?"

Angela rubbed her arms, desperate to rein in her rising panic. "Just that the door was right in front of me, and that it could be anywhere."

"I KNOW it's here," Nina said firmly.

Angela huffed in exasperation. She slumped into a mildewed pew and cradled her head in her hands. "This is awful. I feel so close, but so far."

"Try to stay calm. We'll figure this out," Nina whispered. It was clear she was forcing herself to sound more confident than before. "Why don't we just take a minute or two to really think, okay? That couldn't hurt things. Just a minute or two."

"Okay." Angela nodded. "That's true. Maybe I do just need a few moments. There has to be a connection to the door and this church. But what?"

Angela closed her eyes and tried her hardest to block out the world—the relentless cold, the shivers running up her arms, the throbbing Grail, her desperation—and to think. Her mind wandered here and there, and she pictured the church and Israfel inside of it as he had been that long-ago day when they'd met. That was the one real tie she had with this place. She'd been trying so hard to paint his image, as if to hold on to something she'd lost, and had at last figured perhaps she should lose it after all. Now, she began to find it again.

She could see his eyes, so large and so piercingly blue, the shade of the deepest seas.

His hair shone a gorgeous color between starlight and silver.

His wings stretched like white banners between heaven and earth. Israfel's voice beckoned to her more achingly than the nightingales of so many poets, and for one cruel and impossible moment, Angela heard her heart respond.

A powerful wave of longing rushed over her—the nostalgia for what had been, for what could have been, and for what should possibly be. Angela had decided to hate Israfel rather than love him. He had abandoned her and taken her brother away forever.

So why, right now when she looked deep inside of herself, did that decision hurt just as much?

It was like she'd lost a very crucial piece of who Israfel really was.

And for some reason, it was her task to find that piece and put it back where it belonged.

It was painful to admit but Angela would do anything at this second to see Israfel again and complete that task. She had to. Unlike the recent necessity of protecting Sophia, this was a mission that had been with her from some mysterious beginning.

You would do anything? A familiar and gentle voice echoed from within her.

Yes, her heart said without hesitation, *I would do anything.*

With a sudden shock that sent Angela's heart hammering, she realized the voice in her head was Raziel's.

She opened her eyes again and saw the door.

It appeared exactly as in her vision, except solid and completely real and directly across from her, set against a wall of the church as if it had been there all along.

Nina gasped. Fury soared down from the rafters screeching in triumph. Troy dropped to the ground with Juno beside her, already inspecting every inch of the door's black wood with blazing eyes and suspicious growls. She slid a nail along one of the carvings set in the door but paused at the metal doorknob shaped like a snake—the same one Angela had drawn away from in fear while steeped in her vision of Kim and Sophia.

"This is it," Angela said, approaching the door quietly. She feared if she made too much noise it might disappear and leave only ashes behind. Nothing about it seemed real now. Angela carefully eyed the creatures carved into the wood, part of her worried they might be eyeing her. Her gaze lingered for a moment on a strange horse with a menacing horn.

Troy snapped her wings open, sheltering Juno behind them. "It is the same door that Sariel entered." Troy's voice was crisp with frustration. "But I could not get in myself."

"Sariel?" Nina said.

"That's Kim's given Jinn name," Angela said. "His father was a Jinn like Troy."

"Oh . . ." Nina looked like she wanted to ask more and her face paled, but she bit her lip.

Angela reached for the snake-shaped knob, her heart racing. "Here goes nothing—"

The metal snake came alive like a horrid nightmare, its long fangs snapping cruelly for her hands.

She drew back in shock.

"*Now, now, dear,*" a voice whispered from between the snake's reptilian lips. "*You should introduce yourself before gripping me in such a familiar way. Your name?*" The snake returned to its original position and glared at her with orange eyes. Unlike Troy's eyes, they bored through Angela in a different way that was also entirely unnerving. But this wasn't the instinctual stare of a hunter. Angela couldn't name what it was at all—and that made it ten times worse. "*Come now, even I can see you're in a hurry.*"

"My name is Angela Mathers," she said softly.

"*Oh?*" The snake pretended an amused tone. "*And to what do we owe the pleasure of your visit, Archon?*"

So they knew Angela's true identity. She set her jaw, speaking between gritted teeth. "I'm going through the door. I was told that if I don't go through the door, my friend Sophia will die. So here I am."

"*A dreadful situation*," the snake hissed. "*Regrettable*."

"Let me in," Angela said. "NOW."

The snake sighed. "*You're as much of a spitfire as I've heard. Unfortunately, I can't just let you in. There are rules, you see.*"

Troy inched forward, searching the door again for signs of weakness.

"What rules?" Angela prepared to take off her left arm glove and display the Grail. She was tired of this. There were too many obstacles already, and she couldn't imagine any more in front of her.

"*Rules of fairness. This is my labyrinth, and I know it top to bottom. So I think it's only polite to offer you a handicap, to make our interaction a bit more balanced. I have the advantage here, of course, and without a challenge, there's little reason to play. So here's my offer—if you are willing to sacrifice one of your companions, and believe me they won't last long in this maze—I will take you directly to the Book of Raziel and I promise her unharmed. Otherwise . . .*"

"Otherwise what?" Angela hissed herself.

"*Otherwise, I've already won.*"

Sacrifice her friends? Sacrifice Nina? Sacrifice little Juno who'd escaped death in the Underworld and believed in Angela? Sacrifice Troy who had risked her life to make sure Angela stayed alive?

Angela ripped off her arm glove and showed the Grail to the horrid snake.

In a noise like thunder, Troy sheltered herself and Juno from the terrible sight with her wings. Nina cried out and crumpled to the ground, hiding her face. But the snake showed nothing but amusement behind its disturbing eyes.

"Bastard," Angela muttered. She bit into the Eye with her fingernails, summoning the Glaive.

"*Impressive,*" the snake said coolly. "*But that's not quite an answer.*"

"Then here's your answer," Angela said. "*No deal.*"

She thrust the Glaive's blade through the snake. With a horrendous cracking noise, its iron body exploded into thousands of silvery shards.

Fourteen

*One more moment. One more, and then
it all began.* —NINA WILLIS

Angela leaned down, her hands on her knees as she took
deep breaths of chilly air.

She stared at the pieces of the door's iron knob littering
the ground. Not a single trace of the snake remained, but its
icy voice echoed in her head. Betrayal, it had said. *Certain*
betrayal. And a game over before it had barely begun. Her
ears rang with the sound of the metal snake exploding into
bits.

A scream of frustration threatened to swell out of Angela.
But it died in her lips, and she slumped even farther.

*God, Angela—what have you done? How the hell will
you get through that door now?*

Troy's derisive snort shot through Angela like a bullet of
fire. "Splendid," the Jinn said bitterly. "Perhaps we can pray
our way inside."

"*Shut up,*" Angela shouted.

Fury had been hopping across the ground, pecking with
her large black beak at the little pieces of metal. Angela spun

around to face Troy and the bird flapped out of the way, screeching in distress.

Troy tensed her wiry muscles but seemed more surprised than angry.

"What else was I supposed to do?" Angela said a little less heatedly. "Did you really think bargaining with a demon was going to get us anywhere? You heard what that snake said. How the hell was I supposed to agree to that kind of bullshit?"

Troy snorted again, and her ears flipped back in annoyance. She dug her nails into the icy ground but stayed silent.

Nina wobbled to her feet and walked over to Angela, helping her stay steady. "Just calm down, okay? Do you feel all right?"

"Yeah." Angela rubbed her eyes. "Yeah, I'll be fine. I'm sorry. It's just—"

Stupid. Stupid. What a stupid thing for her to do. Angela deserved for someone to yell at her. Sophia was right again. Angela was so stupidly impulsive sometimes.

"Forget it," Nina continued. "The last thing you need to do is explain. Even I wanted to smack that snake with something. Like you said, we'll figure this out. There has to be more than one way through that door, magic or not."

Angela shook her head and sat down in front of the door, resting her head on her knees. She shut her eyes and wished the weakness in her aching body away, but it was obvious that time would be needed for her to gain her strength back. An hour passed as the cold ate through to her bones, and memories rose before her like teasing ghosts. She thought of Israfel and that long-ago night, realizing with a sick sensation she might never keep that promise either.

Raziel had believed in Angela enough to show her the door, and she'd repaid him by ruining everything.

Juno's soft lisp floated out of the darkness. "Bad snake," she said. "Angela was right."

"Quiet," Troy snapped at her.

Juno rustled her little wings. Gradually, she crept closer to Angela despite her aunt's glares. Her small white hands tipped by sharp black nails poked at Angela's legs. Troy growled and almost grabbed Juno by one of her ragged little wings, but Angela gestured for peace.

"Stop it," she said to Troy. "It's okay. She's not bothering me."

Troy looked doubtful. "As you wish," she hissed, licking her bluish lips. She reclined on the ground and yawned, exposing some lethal teeth. Every so often, she glanced at Juno with undisguised irritation. "What do you want, chick?" she said at last. "What bothers you? There will be no food right now. Sacrifice as you did in the Warrens."

Juno cocked her head at Angela, one of her pointed ears flopping like a puppy's. "I wanted to ask her. What is Angela singing?"

"What?" Angela said, sitting up abruptly.

She was singing?

"It is a nice song," Juno said, her owlish eyes bright.

Troy shrugged her wings. "She speaks the truth. You've been murmuring like an imbecile for half an hour."

Nina hummed to herself as well, seeming to use it as an example for Angela. When she paused, she said softly, "It sounds beautiful. Where did you learn it?"

Angela brought up another sigh from deep, deep down. "Israfel sang it. That was the song he used to bring me to this church that one night. But, honestly, it seems even more familiar. Like I heard the song somewhere else a long, long time ago."

It really did have the sound of a lullaby. That probably explained why whenever Angela remembered or heard the song, she floated in some indefinable place, rocked into bliss as a musical voice crooned the words over and over.

"Sing it, please," Juno said.

Troy rocked up and snarled at the chick with a cascade of frightening anger. Her wings tensed, and her fingers clenched. "You will not listen to angel songs. You are the heir to the Throne of the Underworld. Angels are the carrion crows that left your ancestors to starve in Hell. *They are the monsters that destroyed our ancient city and dispersed our people, driving us to the brink of extinction. You will not—*"

"I," Juno said, straightening, "wish to hear the songs. They are part of our history, yes? As the Jinn Queen, I demand it."

Troy shook with wrath. She advanced on Juno with savagery in her beautiful face.

Angela stepped in front of Juno, shaking like a leaf as Troy came closer. Fury danced and screamed in the background, and Angela wanted to scream with her.

"Get out of the way," Troy muttered evilly, her hypnotic eyes focused on Angela. "The discipline of our chicks is none of your concern, Archon."

With the greatest hunter of the Jinn staring Angela down, terror rose up in her. Sudden fear choked out Angela's voice. Yet she didn't move.

Troy flapped her wings with thunderous force. Shards of metal tumbled in the wind beneath her. "Spoiled little brat," she snapped viciously at Juno. "When one of those angels rips off your wings, see then if I will come to your rescue." She stomped painfully on her wounded ankle to a dark corner, curled her wings around herself, and, with one more cry of frustrated rage, shut out both Juno and the world behind a screen of tattered feathers.

Angela allowed her heart to continue beating. She exchanged a wide-eyed glance with Nina that spoke volumes between them.

Whoa, Nina mouthed. She stepped away from Angela and Juno, choosing to sit on a pew and gaze out into the shadows. *I can't believe I just did that . . .*

For a terrible moment, Angela had remembered her near-death experience with Troy over a year ago, and it had nearly left her a babbling idiot. Now she could get her sanity back and try to remember why she'd challenged death in the first place.

"The song," Juno said imperiously, tugging on Angela's tights. The little Jinn blinked up at Angela, starkly serious.

Angela knelt down in front of the Jinn chick. "If I sing it, do you promise not to mention it again? You shouldn't make your aunt angry, Juno. Remember, she risked her life and is now an exile because she saved you from death."

Juno's ears pressed down and she hunkered like a scolded dog. "I promise . . ."

She appeared genuinely sorry and so much like a sad human child that it was almost impossible not to hug her. Then again, those little teeth had drawn blood from Troy's hands. Keeping that in mind, Angela focused and sang. But words weren't enough to knock down doors, and if anything, Sophia felt farther and farther away.

Were you there in the Garden of Shadows?
Were you near when the Father took wing?
Did you sigh when the starlight outpoured us?
When the silver bright water could sing?

Have you drunk from a river of amber?
Or eaten the nectar of dreams,
Where thoughts linger determining aeons,
And time stretches apart at the seams—

A sudden cry broke apart Angela's haunting memories. She opened her eyes again.

Troy crouched in front of Juno, protecting her behind her large sickle-shaped wings. Her eyes had narrowed to slits, betraying pain.

Brilliant light outlined the door, flooding the interior of the church.

Juno's eyes were even larger than before, though she shivered in pain from the light. Nina stepped beside Angela and gripped her arm, her face washed out by brilliance.

The door to Hell had started to open.

Angela lost her breath. The door groaned open farther against its will and her heart fluttered. The hellish carvings set in the wood resembled creatures made of starlight and pearl. Troy shrieked in horror, and Angela had to shut her eyes one more time against a luminous glory.

And then it was all over. The light faded to a dull memory and the door remained open, revealing the same ominous stairwell that had claimed both Kim and Sophia in Angela's vision.

Troy shuddered but unfurled her wings from around Juno. The Jinn chick crept nearer to the door, but swiftly changed her mind and returned to the shadow of Troy's great wings. Warm air wafted out of the door's expansive mouth, toying with Angela's curtain of hair.

From a safe distance, Angela examined the stairs. They

wound down into a darkness dimly lit by embers and strange glowing hieroglyphs.

"What in the world just happened?" Nina said reverently.

It wasn't hard to put two and two together. "I think it was Israfel's song," Angela whispered. She didn't like talking too loudly, as if it would attract some unseen horror from the stairway's bottom. "It opened the door . . ."

Is that why Raziel wanted her to remember Israfel? Or was it just a coincidence? If anyone had a power like this, it was the Supernal angels. Perhaps they really did know a song that opened doors to other dimensions.

"But I can't imagine how or why," Angela added. She looked to Troy.

The Jinn stared into the open doorway like a challenge had been thrown at her. Her blazing eyes narrowed. "There are no coincidences," she said as if answering Angela's thoughts. But her tone was oddly hushed.

Now that the door had opened, no one seemed eager to enter it.

A chill ran along Angela's arms. So far, Stephanie and Nina had both said that if Angela entered and walked down those stairs, she would never return.

But Sophia was there—in that dark, awful place where Lucifel reigned.

Trembling, Angela adjusted her arm gloves and cinched the laces on her boots. She stood up straight and took a step forward, and then one back. Troy and Nina waited for her, no one seeming to be able to decide on what to do next after so many early displays of bravery.

Finally, after the longest moment of her life, Angela walked toward the entrance to Hell.

Behind her, she listened to the footsteps of her companions, each of them gaining strength the more she advanced, feeding somehow off her own courage.

Even Troy was afraid this time. And what did it really mean if even she was afraid?

Angela was about to find out.

Without any more hesitation, she took the first steps down the stone stairway and into blackness.

It was almost too easy at first. Step by step with Fury hopping behind them, Angela, Troy, Juno, and Nina descended down a path that eerily resembled the stairway Angela had summoned one faraway night to let souls escape the crumbling Netherworld.

There might not be an escape for me this time.

Despite a sinking feeling inside, Angela turned back to the door. Surely, it would be there like a promise that safety wasn't far away.

The Grail throbbed in her left hand as a quiet fear stole her courage.

Of course, the door was gone.

Fifteen

---

*I sensed the song's true meaning had been lost over
time, changed into something else. Just like our
history. Just like my soul. Even so, I sang the words
because they always brought me home.* —ISRAFEL

Help me . . . save me, please . . .

Israfel chose to ignore the voice calling to him. He was
in no condition to save anyone right now. Lying in the
snow, weak and sleepy with cold, he had started to dream
about a time before all this madness when he lived in angelic glory, without pain or fear. The dances, the endless
nectar, the beauty of jewels and robes passed before the eye
of his mind. Angels of every rank bowed to him, the ruling
Archangel of Heaven, as he strode before them radiant with
majesty. The familiar crown weighed again upon his head.
Once more, his bare feet touched the crystalline floors of
the angelic city.

Someone please . . . help me . . .

Suddenly, he was in darkness. He was a caged bird tormented, forced to eat and drink to stay alive even though he
no longer wished to—because it had all been taken from him.

The nightmare came alive again, and Raziel plummeted to his death amid a rain of blood and feathers.

Quickly. Help me. BEFORE IT'S TOO LATE.

Israfel opened his eyes, momentarily bewildered by the reappearance of the snow and the filthy alleyway where he had fallen. His fingers slid across the ice, but he pushed himself up anyway, gazing out at the endless flakes of white sprinkling Luz's cobblestones in layer after layer of cold. He had saved Angela Mathers, the Archon that held his brother Raziel's soul, from death and this was how the universe thanked him: by separating him from his injured guardians, by keeping him out of Heaven, and by leaving him stranded and weaker than a newborn chick. Israfel no longer had any sense of how much time had passed for him on Earth, only that it had been too long and that human food was horrifically inadequate for him.

He clutched his stomach, feeling familiar movement inside and sudden queasiness.

Even if he starved, the hope living inside of him could not.

"Well, would you look at that," a human voice said from the darkness of the alley. Two dark silhouettes strode toward Israfel casually, completely unafraid. "Such a pretty thing and all alone. Nowhere to celebrate Christmas tonight, honey?"

Two men in tattered jackets stopped underneath a flickering gas lamp, carefully observing Israfel with frightful smiles.

He instinctively tried to reveal his wings, but they never appeared.

A frightful seizurelike shudder ran up his arms. He'd forgotten he was only slightly better than any other helpless mortal right now. Israfel caught his breath as one of the men stooped down and grabbed him by the collar of his coat, pulling him to his feet.

"Shit, she's gorgeous," the taller of the two men said. "What do you do for a living, honey? Are you a model? You could come model for us tonight. Get out of this cold, away from all the damned rats. Not a bad deal if you ask me. Don't worry, we'll treat you fairly. A hot meal, a good drink, a warm bed . . ."

His companion laughed. "You're scaring her, Ronan." He scrunched up his face, his nose red with cold. "Just knock her unconscious and take her before she puts up a fight."

Israfel backed up against the brick wall, steadying himself. "You shouldn't touch me," he said softly. "It might not turn out well for you."

"I'd beg to differ," the taller man said, placing both hands on the wall on either side of Israfel's face. "But if you come with us without making a sound, I'll try my best not to bash your head in. What's your name, anyway? Something about you seems familiar . . ."

"I have many names," Israfel said.

That wasn't a lie, of course. Humans apparently had so many names for him, he'd lost track of most of them.

"So we're dealing with a nut job, are we?" The man made a gruff noise under his breath. "Fine by me. Women like you aren't usually missed."

Israfel laughed. "Who said I was a woman?"

The man's eyes went wide. He glanced to his companion who appeared equally thunderstruck. "You're a man?"

"I never said that either . . ."

An unhealthy silence followed by the whistle of icy wind filled the alley. The man who had trapped Israfel at the wall stared at him with growing anger. His small eyes narrowed that much more.

Without warning he grabbed Israfel by the neck and began to tighten his grip.

Israfel allowed a second or two of pain, but as the memories of abuse flooded back—memories where he had stared into darkness for aeons while other hands held him and forced anything and everything upon him—he set his teeth and spoke through tighter lips. "Unhand me. NOW."

A clatter of metal against stone echoed down the alleyway.

Everyone paused, searching the darkness for the source of the noise. From behind a pile of garbage, a small human face peeked out at the unfolding drama. It was a little human girl with a ratty braid of red hair, her face smudged with layers of dirt. She held a makeshift platter of old food in her hands. So—she was the one who had been leaving little meals for Israfel since he'd collapsed here.

Realizing what was taking place, she stepped back, her face blanching with fear.

Without a word, she dropped the food and ran.

"Son of a bitch," the taller man hissed. "What the hell are you waiting for?" he shot at his companion. "Get that little blood head brat and make sure she doesn't get out of here alive—"

Israfel found his last bit of strength immediately.

He grabbed the man by the face, crunched through some bone, and pitched him face-first into the ground. The man screamed and rolled in agony.

Israfel left him behind, racing in the direction of the human girl and her pursuer.

He didn't have to travel far. Israfel slipped on the ice once or twice, but after rounding a sharp corner, he found both humans at a dead end.

The little girl cowered against the ground, her arms over her head.

The man stood over her, ready to kick her hard in the stomach.

With a burst of speed that sent pain into every part of Israfel's weary body, he raced forward, grabbed the man by the back of his jacket, and flung him like a stone into the wall.

The human's body connected with a vicious *thud*. He groaned and sank to the ground, blood gushing from his nose. One of his teeth had broken, and he spit out more blood before rushing at Israfel, his hands ready to punch him directly in the face or head.

Israfel caught him by the hand, eliciting a scream from the human as bones broke.

They struggled for a moment, and then Israfel kicked him directly in the stomach, sending him flying to the ground. The human hit the ice even harder than the wall, his cheeks bleeding. He rolled onto his back and moaned with pain, blood dribbling from the side of his mouth. Israfel stood over him, cold anger working its way through every part of his soul. This was the kind of wickedness that would have no place in his new universe.

"What—what the hell are you?" the man spat, gasping for air.

"*Enough*. Worms like you deserve judgment," Israfel said, pressing his foot onto the man's throat.

The human clawed at his leg, desperate.

"Oh—now you want mercy? Of course, there would have been none for me or the girl. Why for you? Why have the rules suddenly changed?" Israfel leaned down, his white hair brushing the sides of his face. "Now I'll tell you what I am. I am the face and voice that will haunt the rest of your miserable days. You might as well call me God."

The girl uncurled from her little ball, staring at Israfel with owlish and awestruck eyes.

No—he would never kill anyone in front of a child if he could help it. No matter how much they deserved punishment. Israfel had been a warrior at one time too, but he was a far cry from his sister, Lucifel. Innocence deserved preservation at whatever cost.

He lifted his foot from the man's throat. "I'd suggest you start to pray."

The human gasped like a beached fish on the ice. His eyes were closed, and his teeth chattered with cold. But he was very much alive.

Refusing to look back, Israfel took the little girl by the hand and stepped over the body lying prone on the ground. Together, they left the alley and the snow behind. She remained quiet for a long time, but as Israfel's steps slowed with his returning weariness, she began to gather her courage.

"Are you hurt?" she finally said in a tiny voice.

"I will be all right," Israfel said, gazing out into the darkness. In the back of his mind, he heard the voice from his dreams calling to him.

"My name is Tress Cassel," she said a little more loudly. "What's your name?"

Israfel smiled. "That is not important."

"It is so. Mama told me that a name holds a person's soul. It says everything about you. And we're friends now, so I'd like to know your name."

She was much like Israfel's guardian Thrones when they had been chicks. He could see them still, peeking above their nest to greet him when they had first been brought to his chambers in Heaven. Now they were ruthless bodyguards, a far cry from the spoiled children of aeons ago. He tried not to show the sorrow on his face, adopting the cold mask he'd learned from millennia as ruler of Heaven.

"My name is Israfel."

"Israfel . . ." She brightened at this revelation. "That sounds like an angel's name."

He stopped, yanking her to a halt. "You know?" he said, searching her innocent face.

Tress nodded. "You still had your wings when I first found you. So I didn't tell anyone who you were or where they could find you. You looked really tired and hurt. But the next time I came back, your wings were gone. But your eyes were still so big and blue, and your hair shone like the snow."

"Where do you live?" Israfel said, resuming their journey. "I'll return you to your home."

"Me and Mama live near the sea. I'll take you there, and you can stay with us. Mama's always telling me about angels and other people with wonderful names. She can see visions and has so many dreams. She told me where to find you and what to give you to eat. She said it was very, very important to keep you alive."

Israfel touched his stomach. His head had already started to ache painfully.

Then he stopped walking again, realizing what Tress had just told him. Her human mother was in tune with the Realms. If that was so, then she could help him return to Heaven through another route, perhaps circumventing the crumbling gateways between Earth and Heaven. Anticipation flooded him and made his heart throb. He knelt down and held Tress by the hand.

"You're so pretty," she said to Israfel, touching his white hair. "So pretty."

"Tress, you are a compassionate girl. I will reward you

and your mother for that as soon as I can. But first, I must return to Heaven. Tell me—does your mother have a large mirror in her house?"

"Yes," Tress said, beaming.

"As I thought." Israfel smiled gently. "I would be glad to visit your home, little one."

"Follow me then," Tress said and tugged on Israfel's hand.

Israfel bit his lip and followed her, but his thoughts were far away, too lofty to explain to the human as she continued to question his every expression and gesture. He stepped delicately across the ice and snow, noting with increasing distaste that this was not what he imagined for Earth in the future. But first, he needed to return home and set things right. He'd thought that impossible with the dimensions blurring and melding together. Yet here was a chance, however slim.

But one detail was absolutely certain. Archangel Zion, Lucifel's chick, had every bit of knowledge that Israfel was trapped on Earth and had very pointedly refused to send aid.

Israfel narrowed his eyes and set his jaw. That upstart would get what was coming to him soon enough. Soon Israfel and the Archon would open Raziel's Book together. Soon—everything was going to change and they would be ruling over a newly remade universe. But this horrific disintegration . . . Israfel had more than his share in its cause. His mind flashed to the Father's mangled corpse, oozing blue blood from a fatal wound.

Indeed, Israfel's stained hands might never be washed clean.

Tress wrapped her fingers around Israfel's tighter, humming to herself.

Help me . . .

That voice echoing in his head was familiar yet indistinct enough to be anyone's. Yet one thing was undeniable. The person crying out to him—

They were not only in danger, they were in Hell.

Tress's home was little more than a hovel with cheerful candles flickering in the windows, situated on a street crowded with other run-down buildings almost exactly like it. But it had a commanding view of the upper levels of Luz. Between the other buildings, the city rose up gradually like an enormous mountain of brick and stone layered upon more brick and stone. Turrets sparkled with light, seeming to reach almost to the clouds. Underneath, the ocean thundered ominously against the supports that held the city out of the waves.

Tress let go of Israfel's hand at the mildewed door. Some of the wood remained shellacked in ice.

She knocked on it once or twice in a distinct rhythm.

The door creaked open, letting out a dim light. Then it opened completely, and Tress guided Israfel into the house.

The building was even darker than it appeared outside, only a few candles lighting the most random spots of the room. Human junk lay everywhere. Tables, benches, and shelves overloaded with everything from cracked glass bottles to embroidered boxes barred Israfel's path. Necklaces hung from a coatrack, their heavy jewels throwing back the candlelight. A cloying, heavy scent filled the air, and smoke screened books stacked in haphazard piles. Everything suggested the remains of some sort of human shop flung into one small room. Israfel stopped in front of a large cracked mirror.

How human and weak he appeared. But his eyes were still large enough to give away the difference if someone peered closely.

"You've decided to come." A woman's soft voice broke the silence.

She stepped out of the shadows, opening her arms for the little one. Tress ran into them, almost glowing with excitement. "Mama, an angel! An angel! There were bad men in the alley, but he saved me from them, and—"

"Hush," the woman said, putting her finger to Tress's lips. "I know. Now go upstairs and continue packing your trunk. And wash your face—you're filthy."

Tress gave Israfel one more longing glance but obeyed and clattered up a rickety staircase.

The woman examined Israfel with veiled eyes. She was tall for a human, and her hair glistened a coppery red shade near the candles. A shawl covered most of her chest and shoulders, and her long skirt had been patched and repatched with dozens of colorful fabric swatches. "We don't have much time," she said very slowly. Her hand gripped the back of a chair, trembling a little. "My daughter and I will be going to the lower levels of Luz before the Vatican can find us. It's no longer safe for people like us here, but we can't leave the island. I do not have much help I can offer you."

"You know why I am here, woman," Israfel said gently. He stepped deeper into the room. "I thank you for your generosity in keeping me alive with your food. Being trapped here for so long, I am not quite myself . . ."

She watched the movement of his feet as if entranced, but quickly regained her senses.

"Why?" she said and took a step backward, instinctively putting distance between them. "Why do you stay on this Earth? You say you are trapped as well, but how?"

Israfel sighed. "Indeed, I tried to leave Earth over a year ago. But the Realms, the dimensions of the universe, are slowly collapsing one by one. This means that portals in and out of Earth are closing or disappearing entirely. I attempted entering a portal right as it sealed, and suddenly I found myself flung violently back to Earth. I was weak already, having used most of my energy to keep a human from death."

"The Archon," the woman said with grim certainty. "She is alive and moving among us, isn't she?"

Israfel watched her carefully. "And if she is?"

"Go to her," the woman said. "I am sure she can help you better than I."

"I cannot go to her just yet," Israfel whispered.

Tress's mother questioned him with a stony expression. "Raziel was your brother, correct?"

Israfel struggled not to show the pain on his face. "It does not surprise me that you know of our history."

He wouldn't tell her that the Archon was not Raziel. That she was a total mystery, with an unidentifiable yet enormously powerful soul. One that Raziel had deemed important enough to spend a possible eternity protecting.

"I am learned enough," the woman said. "The Vatican tries to keep much arcane knowledge away from ordinary citizens of Luz. But secrets and legends always have a way of traveling from eye to eye and ear to ear. For a long time, I flaunted the existence of my shop, knowing I couldn't be touched without evidence of witchcraft, as they like to call it. But with my daughter . . ." She turned aside, deep anxiety stealing her confidence. "It is not fair of me to put her in danger. She has suffered through much. We have grown poor simply trying to stay alive. Now that blood heads are being gathered, sought after . . ."

She shuddered.

"I will reward you well for your generosity as soon as I

have returned to Heaven," Israfel said. "But first you must help me leave this Earth. Your daughter told me that you have a mirror."

"Yes," the woman said. She walked to the cracked mirror framed in bronze at the far end of the room. "I have used it for scrying in the past. It is the only mirror in this city with a connection to the other worlds. I went through great pains to obtain it years ago, but never let visitors to my shop know about its existence. If word got out, my imprisonment would be certain. My death, a possibility."

Israfel stood in front of the mirror, staring at his fractured image. There was still enough glass for him to work with. "Woman, I would have you watch with me. You must say—"

"The words. Yes." She took a deep breath, appearing fearful.

"However," Israfel said, "when the visions begin, you must close your eyes. I cannot guarantee your safety otherwise. There are many aspects of the Realms dangerous to human senses. Your daughter?"

She searched the stairs for her daughter, and certain that Tress was upstairs and out of harm's way, she then pulled out a chair and sat far enough away from Israfel to think herself safe. "I'm ready."

Israfel stared into the mirror, listening as the woman mumbled softly under her breath. Human or not, the words she spoke would have the intended effect. It was the power and desire that counted. He watched and watched, sure of his skills. Israfel had spent enormous lengths of time staring into the Mirror Pools of Ialdaboth. He had discovered the Archon's existence in the reflection of those pools, one long and lonely time ago.

Help me . . .

His mind turned and shifted focus. An image began to form within the dark shadows of the mirror. Gradually, it swirled and strengthened, taking shape from his power.

Angela Mathers, the Archon, appeared in front of an immense and ugly black door. Israfel could not identify the companions beside her, but that mattered so little. He recognized the door that she was opening and entering. It was a portal to Hell. At least one still remained, perhaps because the Netherworld had been emptied. Previously, all humans had to die and pass through the Underworld to enter into Lucifel's kingdom. Yet with the Realms blurring together, old portals would close, and new ones would spontaneously form before disintegrating entirely. This one was a holdover.

Lucifel knew she was running out of time. She fully understood the risk of bringing the Archon through such a dangerous route.

Israfel clenched his long fingers. His sister must have known something about the Book that he did not.

Help me . . . Save me . . .

It was Angela Mathers's voice Israfel had been hearing. A sharp heat rushed through him as he remembered their brief kiss.

No. It was far beneath him to feel anything for a mere human. And if she was not really Raziel reincarnated, he had every right to crush his feelings whenever they arose. So why when Israfel looked at her did this odd confusion spring up in him? Why did he feel this need to understand? Why did he constantly wonder who she really was, and why Raziel thought her special? Was it her physical similarity to Raziel? What could it possibly be?

"I thank you again," Israfel murmured, breaking his trance. "I now have my freedom back."

The situation was not ideal. He would have to enter Hell through the same door. From there, he could find another stable portal back to Heaven.

There wasn't any other choice.

Yet the idea of entering his sister's mockery of a kingdom filled him with disgust. And worry.

Israfel pressed a hand against his stomach. If anything were to happen to him . . .

Then again, perhaps he could kill Lucifel first. She would not be the only monster he'd eradicated.

"You said you would help us," the woman replied, rising from her seat.

Israfel smiled. "In good time. As I said, I must first enter the other Realms and regain my power. But rest assured, I will keep my promise to you and your daughter. Please give her my farewell and my thanks."

He turned and started to leave the house.

"You will die before you can help us," Tress's mother said after him.

Israfel paused. His head throbbed, and his vision swam for a moment.

"You are very ill," the woman continued. "But what kind of disease can kill an angel? I wonder—perhaps it would be better for you to stay on Earth, after all . . . how much longer can you possibly have?"

"I still have time," Israfel whispered. "Not much. But some." He reached for the knob of the door, refusing to face her again. In the background, he could hear little Tress's shallow breathing. She had clambered back down the stairs in the short time Israfel and her mother had been talking. Israfel didn't need to look at Tress to sense the confusion in her soul.

A series of swift and violent knocks hit the door.

Israfel pulled his hand away.

"Vatican police!" a harsh human voice shouted in muffled tones. "Open this door now!"

Tress's mother gasped. She pulled Tress close to her, hiding the little girl's face against her thick skirt.

"Gloriana Cassel," the voice shouted again. "You are under arrest for the dissemination of occult materials, the corruption of Luz civilians, and for involvement in the murder of Westwood Academy student Nina Annabelle Willis—"

"Nina?" Gloriana gasped again. "She's dead? That—that can't be true."

"Mama, what's happening?" Tress said, crying.

More harsh knocks met the door. "Open up or we will be forced to break down your door!"

Gloriana held Tress closer, wiping at the girl's tearstained face. "Don't cry, dear. They won't hurt us. I'm sure we'll be all right." She looked at Israfel with hope in her eyes. "Sometimes help arrives in the most unexpected ways."

There was a pause while something heavy thrust against the door.

Gloriana and Tress stared at Israfel, pleading wordlessly.

Without a word, he glided away from the door and stood in front of them, pushing them even farther back with his hand. Gathering every bit of energy floating in the ether, he revealed the six wings that had been lost to him for so long in a blazing glory of light. Tress cooed in wonder as they unfurled in their expanses of snowy whiteness, but Israfel stayed silent and refused to look at her. He would pay dearly for using this much energy right now. Already, tremors of pain ran up his arms.

"Thank you," Tress said in the softest voice.

Israfel smiled in spite of everything. "You're welcome," he replied.

With a horrendous *bang,* the door slammed open and smacked into the wall.

"Everybody freeze!" the harsh voice shouted into the room.

Five men in long black coats burst into Gloriana's house, but immediately halted at the sight of Israfel and his six wings shining with majesty. One of the men had paused with a gun pointed in Israfel's direction. His hands shook like leaves in the wind, his thumb fumbled with the trigger. He seemed unsure whether to shoot or scream. His eyes widened with shock and terror.

The gun fired. A bullet raced for Israfel's head.

Yes, Israfel would pay dearly for all this.

He lifted his hand and tugged on the ether, willing the bullet to slow down. It came to within a foot of his head and clattered harmlessly to the floor.

Feeling dizzy already, he took the route typical of his long-ago days as ruler of Heaven and made sure not an ounce of pain, discouragement, or emotion showed on his face. "You would be wise to leave," he said in his most commanding and persuasive voice. "The battle will only get worse for you from here."

In answer, three more gunshots echoed throughout the house.

Sixteen

Every world connects to another. Time is perspective.
Journeys and stories are exactly the same, and what
humans call myth we know as reality. —TROY

Once, on a cold night that now seemed ages ago, Angela had dared to ask Sophia about the time she'd spent as the Book of Raziel trapped in Hell. They had been talking for hours, mostly about trivial topics that Angela knew disguised a deeper longing to share with each other. But sharing was something they both had little real experience with at the time. Angela had mistrusted relationships of any kind for too long, hardly knowing how to approach painful subjects. The strange distance in Sophia's eyes often suggested the same.

Now, descending farther into Hell, Angela flashed back to the coldness in their room as the fire had gone out.

"Sophia," Angela had said, grasping the Book's small hand, "tell me what it was like when you were in Hell for all that time. I want to know."

Sophia stared at her, trembling, like she didn't know whether the question was a joke or not. At that exact moment, the rain had ceased. Only later would Angela look out the window and see Luz's first steady flakes of snow.

"It was dark," Sophia whispered. "Endlessly dark. And stifling. There is an acidic river coursing through the deepest parts of Hell, and I can still taste the vapors stinging and numbing my tongue." She took a deep breath, like the memories called for a gathering of her strength. "I don't remember much else. I try not to. But I do know I passed countless years wishing. That's part of my punishment, you see. Ever since I died . . . I've been wishing."

"For what?" Angela whispered with her, forgetting to question just how the Book of Raziel could die.

"For this." Sophia had squeezed her hand and smiled.

Angela could still feel those chilly fingers.

Sophia—I'm going to get you out of here. You don't belong in this place at all.

Besides—there's still so much I have to ask you.

Sophia had mentioned once that she had originally died giving birth to children. The subject had never been brought up since, yet it plagued Angela, resurfacing at tense times like these.

Sophia's the Book of Raziel. She doesn't have any children. She must have been lying to me when she said that . . .

Angela clutched at her necklace, aware that her mouth was tightening into a line. No, Sophia wouldn't lie to her. Just like with Israfel, there was a part of Sophia that Angela couldn't yet comprehend. Perhaps *that* was the key to everything.

Angela gasped, a rush of adrenaline firing through her.

She tripped and stumbled off the last stone step, nearly falling onto the ground.

Troy was beside her already, examining footprints in the dust. Her nose wrinkled in distaste, and an evil look crossed her face. "Sariel was here," she said with a low hiss.

Angela steadied herself with Nina at her side. Her heart beat violently, anticipation flooding out her fear.

Juno hopped down beside Troy. The crow Fury perched precariously on Juno's shoulder.

The Jinn chick rustled through the gloom and brought a scrap of black fabric to her aunt. Troy tore the scrap from Juno's hands and studied it, her eyes narrowing despite the sickly glow of an ember set in the wall.

"That belongs to Kim?" Angela said, stooping down beside them.

Troy growled under her breath. She shoved Angela aside, searching for more clues. But there were none, and they found themselves standing in the gloom of a circular chamber covered from floor to ceiling in the alien writing that Angela found so disturbing. She rubbed the sharp peaks and curves of the script, sensing a familiarity.

Briefly, Angela thought of Stephanie's demon now long dead and the writing that had been tattooed on the demon's neck.

"What does this say? Can anyone read it?" Angela whispered.

Nina touched the scripting, running her fingers across the cool stone. "We live in deference to the Prince," Nina said, reading aloud and slowly. "We serve her and no other. She is our god. Let all who now enter this place fear and adore her . . ."

"*Quiet*," Troy snapped, thrusting Nina away from the wall. "Those are prayers, fool."

"To who?" Nina said, bewildered. She rubbed her arm. Troy's nails had left some thin cuts.

"To Lucifel, I'm sure," Angela said very softly. "Troy's right. We probably shouldn't read them aloud." She turned around, gazing at Nina. "Nina, how did you even know what those words said? How could you read them in the first place?"

Everyone looked at Nina, equally curious.

Nina shrugged. "I was dead once. Maybe that has something to do with it."

"You would do well to stay as silent as the dead until you're told otherwise," Troy muttered. She edged nearer to a series of lines and markings and set her hand against the stone, following a different set of symbols.

Angela peered at the markings closely. Nothing made much sense, until she used her imagination and recognized a river, a city of jagged spires in a great cave, and a vast plain. Other markings resembled nothing she had ever seen before. She did notice the etched figure of a horse with a large horn—it resembled the horse carved on the door they'd entered and the horses Stephanie had drawn on her walls.

Ride, she could almost hear Stephanie's voice saying in her head. *Ride away while you still can . . .*

"What is this?" Angela said sharply.

Troy's ears flicked. "A crude map of Hell. There is the Styx River," she said, pointing to the thick line in the map's middle. "Here is the demon city of Babylon," she whispered, sliding her nail to the etched city. Troy frowned, and she dug her nail into what remained of the picture.

Angela sighed. "You're right. It isn't much help. It doesn't even tell us where we are."

Troy glared at her as if to say, *Who would bother to return and say so?*

Then Troy stood on both feet, suddenly fearsome and tall, and paced forward into the blackness. As everyone followed her, the darkness receded slightly. It wasn't long until they stopped before three passageways, one to the right, one to the left, and one directly in front of them. A banner displaying some kind of serpent with plumes on its head hung in tatters from the middle tunnel.

"Oh, perfect," Angela whispered. "So we have to choose?"

"We don't *have* to," Nina said. "There are three tunnels and five of us. Counting the bird anyway."

Fury croaked from Juno's shoulder, but clearly wasn't about to leave it.

"No," Angela said firmly. "We're absolutely not splitting up. If we choose a tunnel, we go down that tunnel together."

But if they picked the wrong one . . .

This was awful. There were no better choices in a game like this.

But at least there were clues. The tunnel with the snake banner caught Angela's eye again.

That tunnel looked like an entrance to something. And the snake marking could mean that it would take Angela right to the demon who had helped Camdon. Or straight to Lucifel. Either way, Angela couldn't get Sophia back without reaching one of them.

"Okay," Angela said. "This one."

She walked closer to the entrance of the tunnel, searching the shadows for monsters. The air wafting toward her smelled stale and the air tasted almost vinegary. That at least matched with what Sophia had described to Angela about her time in Hell.

Angela stepped forward. The Grail in her left hand throbbed, and beneath the bandage, moistness—probably blood—wept into her palm.

That should have meant trouble. But there was nothing except silence and darkness.

"Wait. Hold on a second," Angela said, stopping everyone behind her. She tore off her left arm glove.

Juno scampered closer, but when the Grail appeared, Troy dragged her back. "You do not look at it, chick," she hissed.

Angela stared at the Eye, or the stone that resembled one, nestled in her palm.

Its onyx pupil glistened wetly and all too lifelike. Angela couldn't explain it then, she couldn't explain it now, but when she was sucked away into the Eye's depths she always felt a panic that swiftly evolved into familiarity, like she'd been in such a fathomless place many times before, grasping an infinity that was hers alone.

Troy had once thought the Grail's omniscient gaze would drive Angela mad, yet Angela had surprised everyone that day by claiming the cursed rock fearlessly.

Lucifel had been the first of the Grail's owners, and also the first to use it to conjure the Glaive, a pole arm of crystalline blue blood that practically fed on the lives it stole. Now this dreaded weapon was the Archon's property, the symbol of Ruin so many believed She stood for. The lives it had taken were now Angela's responsibility. But she had no desire for her friends to join the ranks of the dead. *What are you trying to tell me?*

The Grail wept a little more blood, and then the Eye blinked closed. Angela slipped on her glove. Like a gunshot in the silence, Fury croaked in alarm. Everyone tensed, gazing down the tunnel.

A tall figure strode toward them from within a heavy fog. Gradually, the mist receded and a young man with thick black hair touched by purple streaks emerged from the darkness.

Troy inched forward, flexing her nails.

"No, don't," Angela whispered.

"It is a demon," Troy snapped. "And this is my chance to kill it."

"They would have killed us by now too," Angela retorted. "Don't do anything until I say so. *That's an order.*"

Troy stepped back, muttering viciously under her breath. She grabbed Juno by the back of her rags and dragged her to a safe corner.

As the demon approached, Angela discerned the phosphorescent violet paint on his eyelids. He was barefoot, though his feet and eyelids were both lightly scaled. Otherwise, he was much like a human being with handsome, arrogant features, a mischievous smile, and horridly pale skin. Angela drew back only at the sight of his orange eyes and their snakelike pupils. A tattoo with the same demonic writing as the walls peeked above the low neck of his clothing.

He stopped in front of them all, examining each with burning eyes, lingering with interest on Troy and Juno.

Finally, his thin lips spread into a smile. "It looks like I'm just in time. You aren't dead yet."

Seventeen

*I had never been particularly afraid of snakes. Soon, I
realized that was an ill-fated flaw.* —ANGELA MATHERS

"Who are you?" Angela said. She hid her shaking hands
behind her back.

This demon acted much like Stephanie's, with the same
arrogance and the same assured way of walking. Only, there
was a stronger aura of power and danger. Worse, his eyes
matched the eyes of the iron snake Angela had shattered with
the Glaive.

"Let me guess," Troy said nastily. "You're a snake."

"How perceptive," the demon replied. He smiled.
"Though only half the truth."

Troy growled softly. She seemed on the verge of remembering something.

"You were the one speaking through that metal snake on
the door?" Angela shouted, unable to hide her anger like she hid
her fear. "Then why not kill us and get everything over with?"

"Wrong on both counts." He arched an eyebrow at
Angela. "I'm on your side, Archon. That should be clear considering I haven't tried to murder any of you. Yet . . ."

"Liar," Troy hissed. "Then tell us your name, snake."

He regarded her with amusement. "You haven't told me yours."

Troy curled her lethal fingers into fists. "It isn't our truthfulness that is being questioned."

The demon looked at each of them in turn, thinking. At last, a smaller smile tugged at his mouth and he said, eyes burning, "My name is Python."

Troy's rage was frightful. She arched her wings high and beat them with thundering emphasis. Dirt and pebbles scattered away from her in all directions. "*You. I should have known. Murderer and snake. Half-bred spawn of snakes.*"

"All true," Python said to her menacingly. "The Third Great Demon of Hell apparently had a snake for a father and has a whore for a mother. So sorry."

"A snake for a father?" Nina whispered.

"Yes," Troy said, never taking her eyes off Python. "His father was the feathered serpent Leviathan. His mother is Lilith. The Jinn know him only too well. This is the demon responsible for the fall of the Jinn city that is my namesake. Murderer and liar," she said, a deadly hiss escaping her again. "I should kill you right now, where you stand."

Juno dared a little hiss from behind Troy.

"That would be fitting for the High Assassin of the Jinn," Python remarked coolly. "Unfortunately, without me none of you will ever escape this maze."

"This is really a labyrinth?" Angela echoed back in anger.

"Oh, yes," he said. "The demon who owns it would very much like to see you dead. Or worse, to suffer. He is so very bored lately. More dangerous than usual. So he has decided to work with Lucifel toward her insane dreams. Mind you"—Python's voice became softer—"I don't exactly share them. If anything, I would like to see her caged for an eternity longer. But only you, Archon, will make certain of that. Also, I wish to thank you."

Angela flexed her left hand. Cold shivers ran up her arms.

She couldn't just trust a demon. But did she even have a choice? If this really was a labyrinth . . . they might never get out otherwise. No wonder the iron snake said Angela wouldn't win this game if she didn't give in to his demands.

Python nodded at Troy. "Because of you and this ratty Jinn, my mother's little protégée Naamah is dead. She was such a bitch, that one. I was glad to see her go."

Naamah had been the name of Stephanie's demon. Just the memory of that name sent ripples of dread through Angela's soul. But the idea that even Naamah had enemies here almost bothered her more.

"Mother loved her more than you?" Troy said sarcastically.

Python's face was colder than ever. "Exactly," he said. "And there's nothing *I* love more than hearing my mother scream. Whether in grief or rage or fear. It doesn't matter to me as long as I hear that lovely sound."

"You talk like she deserves it." Troy snapped. "I would have to agree considering an abomination like you lives."

"*Enough chitchat,*" Python said with a tangible hiss at the end of his words. His eyes burned brighter and he stared keenly at Troy before walking closer to Angela. He folded his arms, feigning disinterest while the silence grew and swallowed them all. "Archon, unlike your Jinn pet, I don't have the time for theatrics. I would like an answer from you as to whether or not you will accept my help."

"If I don't?" Angela said. Unable to look at him, she stared at the ground, trying to think and make a decision.

She sensed Python's gaze linger on the Grail hidden beneath her glove.

"If you don't," he said softly, "as I said before—expect difficulties."

"Can I have at least a minute to think?" she snapped at him.

"By all means." He bowed at her and strolled to the other side of the chamber, crossing his arms and leaning against the stone while his attention focused on first one person, then the other.

Angela motioned for everyone to come closer to her. Nina, Fury, and Juno approached, but Troy remained stiff and on guard, never taking her glowing eyes off the demon, refusing to budge a single inch.

Angela turned to Nina first. "What should we do? He has a point. We know nothing about our surroundings. Without him, we could be good as dead soon enough."

Nina whispered so softly, her voice was like a breath. "I don't like this, Angela. It's all too coincidental, like he knew we entered through that door. And his eyes are way too much like that metal snake's. They're probably the same person."

"He's not asking for the same conditions," Angela said. "His entire reason for helping us goes against all of that."

Juno cocked her head, listening to Fury's bird chatter. "Fury says it's probably a trap."

Angela regarded the crow as it gazed back at her with intelligent eyes.

"I don't like this either," Angela said. "But maybe we just don't have a choice. Besides, we have Troy with us. That counts for something, right, Juno?"

"Auntie is a great warrior and hunter," Juno said, but her expression was unfocused, unsure.

"I vote no," Nina said.

Juno flapped her little wings. "Me too."

Angela stepped back, rubbing a hand through her hair. That should have helped, but she didn't feel any closer to a decision.

Nina was probably right when she said not to trust this demon. And it couldn't just be a coincidence that his eyes matched the snake's on the door or that Angela had to fight the snakes Camdon sent after her and Troy. But if this demon's help got them closer to Sophia, and if they stuck together and kept an eye on him, maybe things wouldn't be so bad. They had no clue where to go first anyway.

Angela looked to Python who was examining his nails. He sighed loudly and glanced in her direction. "Well?"

"All right," she said firmly. "I've decided that we—"

"There will be no decision," Troy growled. "At least, none besides mine. We will make no deal with you, snake. Do you find us that weak and stupid? Slither back to your mother and weep with her. We will have nothing to do with you—"

"Troy!" Angela shouted, anger boiling over within her. How dare she? Troy was going to defy her directly, even though they were Bound to each other? Even though Angela was the Archon?

"Is that how you really feel?" Python said, looking at Troy with distaste.

Troy flapped her wings and rushed for him with blinding speed.

Python dodged, but Troy raked across his face with her nails.

He staggered back and examined the blood on his hand, wide-eyed. He touched his bleeding cheek, turning to Troy with an expression of respect mixed with deadly hatred.

Angela's insides froze.

"All right," he said to Troy with the worst kind of hiss. "You've made your choice then." He looked back to Angela with a smirk, suggesting that this wasn't the first or the last time they would meet. "Have fun wandering around in this rat maze, Archon. Perhaps you'll rethink my offer as you watch your friends get gnawed by Hounds. Those horrors don't run across fresh meat often."

A thick purplish mist spread around Python's body, and his form became shadowy before vanishing completely.

Troy licked the blood off her nails, refusing to look at Angela.

Hot with anger, Angela strode over to her and grabbed her sinewy arm. "What the hell did you do that for? I didn't give him my answer yet. *My* answer. Not yours."

Troy snarled and ripped her arm away. "I saved you the trouble of getting us all killed, Archon. If anything—you should be on your knees thanking me."

"You defied me!" Angela shouted.

Troy stood again, tall and deadly. "It was a trap," she said, breathing hard. She was clearly holding back the worst of her anger. "Perhaps it wouldn't concern you, Archon, if I or my niece died, but we have much more to live for than to become a snake's dinner."

Troy started down the tunnel the demon had emerged from.

Angela ran ahead and stood in front of her, blocking her path. "Next time you *will* obey me. You don't have a choice anymore. We're Bound, remember? I subjugated *you*. Not the other way around."

Troy displayed her fearsome teeth, smiling. She leaned into Angela with lethal fire behind her eyes. "But I don't think you quite understand the rules. I'll also be the one to finally kill you; remember that? And just like with Sariel, we can do that the hard way if you'd like. Continue to piss me off, and I'll go much slower than necessary when the time comes."

Angela laughed. "You can't kill me. I'm the Archon. You need me."

"For now," Troy said archly. "Until the Book is opened. After that . . ."

She stepped around Angela and continued down the tunnel.

Angela slammed her fists against the stone, groaning at the pain that shot through her arms.

Troy wasn't right. That's not the only reason Angela was alive. Raziel kept her alive for much more than opening Sophia.

Didn't he?

Juno approached and glanced at Angela compassionately, but, with Fury perched securely on her shoulder, she swiftly rejoined her aunt.

Nina stopped beside Angela and rested her hand on Angela's shoulder. "Forget about it," she whispered. "What's done is done. Troy was probably right. Nothing good would have come from that demon, Angela."

"Nina," Angela said. "There's more to me than being the Archon, isn't there? I mean, people's destinies aren't just set in stone, never changing. I have other reasons to live besides opening Sophia and helping people. That's a big responsibility, I know. But—there's more for me than just that, right?"

Angela thought of Israfel and Kim. She thought of Raziel mentioning a broken heart that needed to be mended, even though he hadn't mentioned whose. That was her responsibility too.

"Of course," Nina said, patting her on the shoulder.

She walked ahead to join the others and Angela followed behind, unable to stop the sinking feeling inside of her.

Troy wasn't right this time. There had to be more.

They paused again after the tunnel spilled them out into an enormous cave with walls glowing faintly in luminescent blue and green. Misty rapids tumbled over enormous boulders cut through the rocks to their left. Acidic fog filled the air. Angela sniffed at its harshness and paced, itching already to move forward. These breaks drove her crazy.

"Calm down," Troy said to Juno, though Angela felt the words were directed at her. "We must rest before we continue. The journey will likely be long."

Troy glanced at the strange glowing cavern, without any sign of its light hurting her eyes.

"I want to keep moving," Angela whispered.

Troy shook her head and gestured at Juno. "The little one needs rest. She can only move so fast and so far in a day."

"Then I'll carry her," Angela said. "Would that help?"

"You will not put a finger on her," Troy muttered. She yawned and her teeth glinted in the cold light. She looked at Angela again, almost begging her for the challenge.

"Fine," Angela said.

She took off her overcoat, suddenly warm. She was hungry, too, but didn't dare say a word when Juno was obviously starving. Besides, Troy would find food for them when the need arose.

Thirst was another matter.

Nina settled down for a quick nap, but Angela inched

closer to the stream, watching the foam bubbling on top of the water. She reached down to scoop some of the clear liquid with her hands.

Troy wrapped her fingers around Angela's wrist. The Jinn yanked her from the water, tossing her back to the tunnel wall. Angela rolled to her feet, hissing at the pebbles piercing her knees.

"What's wrong with you?" Angela shouted angrily. "I'm just trying to take a drink."

"If you do," Troy said, "it will be your last." She plucked a feather from her wings and held it over the water, then dipped the tip into a calmer part of the rapids.

She pulled it out slowly. What once had been a feather was now a tarry lump.

Troy flung it back into the water. It left a puff of steam before vanishing. "The Styx River flows through Hell, all the way down through the demon city of Babylon and to the Abyss. It is an acidic river that gains strength the deeper one journeys through Hell. This is only one of its minor tributaries. Its acidic fog eats away at our wings over time. It is why the most ancient demons are flightless. If you were to drink from this river, your innards would turn to mush."

Troy reclined on the stone next to Angela, watching Juno tap at a rock.

"Oh," Angela said. She sighed. "Well, then thanks . . . for not letting me drink from the stream."

"The water in those pools." Troy pointed at a little outcropping of rough stone. A tiny puddle of water had settled in one of the crevices. "That will be safe."

Angela nodded and crept toward the crevice. Trying not to look pathetic, she sniffed at the water, drank, and sat leaning her head against the stone. Angela rubbed at the sapphire pendant she shared with Sophia.

"How much longer do you think we'll be traveling?" Angela finally ventured. "Do you know where we are?"

"We could be anywhere," Troy said. "The maze will be self-contained, and the demon that owns it will have control over space and direction to some degree. Hell has many levels, but do not think that these levels follow the same rules of existence as on Earth. It took centuries for me to explore the mere part of Hell my Clan calls home. But eventually, all levels lead to the city of Babylon, and finally to the Abyss."

"What is the Abyss?" Angela said, staring into the darkness.

"The beginning and end of everything," Troy said shortly. She turned to her left.

Fury strutted over to Troy with a scrap of fabric in her beak. Troy took it and examined it, sniffing. Then she tossed the scrap at Angela.

Angela caught it. She found the cloth stiff. Blood had dried on the fabric.

She shuddered and dropped it hastily. "Whose is this?"

Troy's expression became grim. "It belonged to Nina's half brother. It seems the demon who helped him was not so keen on protecting him here."

Then Camdon really is dead. He threw everything away to bring Nina back.

Angela stared at Nina who continued to sleep peacefully, one arm over her eyes.

"Can you determine how he died?" Angela said, trying to stay calm. But she choked down the desire to scream and her vision blurred over with tears. She had hoped, despite everything, that Camdon had survived, that they might have bumped into him, even though he'd tortured them all by stealing Sophia. He wasn't evil at heart. Lucifel or one of her servants had merely taken advantage of his grief. Angela could still see the emotion on his face when Nina had appeared before him. "Do you think he . . . suffered?"

Troy shook her head but didn't speak. Her eyes searched the darkness warily.

"Then again, I don't know what's better," Angela continued. She looked at Nina again, and her heart ached. Losing a sibling was one of the worst feelings in the world. "Who could survive in Hell? I can't imagine what an ordeal like that would do to a human like me after a while."

Troy studied Fury as the bird tussled playfully with Juno. Her stare was always like a lion's watching a mouse. In a mesmerizingly predatory way, Troy was beautiful. It was only when she smiled that her sharp teeth broke the spell. At quieter times like these, her proud bearing always surprised Angela, until she remembered that the Jinn descended from angels and surely some of their elegance and beauty forever remained.

"There are some who survive Hell's second death," Troy said softly. "But they are the strongest and most noble souls among your kind, and often my people find them, and they are given a second life as servants. Fury was and is such a rare soul."

Angela watched Fury more closely, trying to picture her as a human girl who had hoped and loved. Now her beautiful soul had been trapped in a crow's body. But at least it had survived. "So then why did you kill and eat humans in Luz last year if you respect some of us?" Angela said bitterly.

"Because Earth is our Hell," Troy snapped back at her.

"The mortal world sickens Jinn over time and we starve slowly. I wouldn't have touched a single one of you—but I had no desire to die. Fury had the same resiliency, and as a Jinn I respected it. She suffered in her human existence much like you suffered, but she had also died sacrificing herself for a friend. Her compassion ensured her immortality, and I was able to resurrect her as my servant. Believe me—many of the humans I killed in Luz were far from noble."

Angela stared at Troy, almost hypnotized by the Jinn's glowing eyes.

A sense of honor was something she'd never expected from Troy's kind—but looking at Troy's expression now it felt right.

Kim had painted Troy as a villain, and their strange violent relationship and the circumstances had done little to say otherwise. But now it bothered Angela. What if she saw Troy as a villain because that was what Troy acted like in human terms? There was the key: Troy *wasn't* human. Humans called her a devil, but she was really a creature who lived in another world: one increasingly revealed as harsh and merciless. She didn't live by human rules, nor could she ever.

I suppose everyone is innocent at some point in their lives. Even Troy was like Juno once upon a time. Kim, too.

Oh, God, where is he in here? Is he dead like Camdon? I don't see how Kim could survive in a labyrinth like this alone.

"Troy?" Angela whispered.

The Jinn glared at her, seeming to anticipate her next question. "*What?*"

"Do you really need to kill Kim—"

"*Yes,*" the Jinn hissed. Her wings rustled angrily. She stretched her wounded ankle, biting back pain.

"But Kim said that his father—your uncle—was abusive,

that he had no choice but to kill him. And if you find that wrong—wouldn't it be just as wrong to kill him out of revenge?"

Troy laughed, turning aside. "You would judge me? You know nothing."

"I guess not." Angela breathed hard, swallowing back her fear and smiling at Juno as the little Jinn interrupted to hand Angela some pebbles.

"You and Auntie are friends," she said to Angela. "I'm glad."

I don't know if I'd go that far.

Angela glanced at Troy, but Troy pretended not to hear a word Juno had said. Only her flicking ear gave her away.

"Auntie is the greatest Jinn hunter," Juno continued. "She has made more kills than any Jinn in the Underworld. Well, other than Mama . . ." Juno's ears flipped back, and she appeared sad. Soon, she perked up again and said excitedly, "Do you see these bones in my hair?"

Angela noted the two tiny bones tied into Juno's hair. They were nothing compared to Troy's collection, but Juno wasn't humble at all.

"I got these on a hunt with Auntie," Juno said. "This one was from an angel, and this one was from another Jinn Clan."

Juno prattled on, doing everything but practically worshipping the ground Troy sat upon.

Troy listened with the slightest smile.

"You shouldn't worry," Juno said, finally winding down. "With Auntie, we'll be safe no matter what."

"Hush," Troy said.

Juno took another breath, eager to continue. Troy clapped a hand over her toothy little mouth.

"*Quiet,*" Troy hissed. She froze, her ears flicking to catch the slightest sound. Fury stiffened beside her. Nina cracked an eye open but didn't move, questioning Angela with a fearful expression.

Angela froze with them, hardly daring to breathe.

She saw nothing.

She strained her ears, struggling to catch suspicious noise over the tumult of the water.

Faintly, beneath the rush of the rapids, low and earnest snuffling could be heard. It approached them steadily. A cold sweat broke on Angela's forehead. Troy's wings shivered and her face took on a fearful paleness.

Juno hid behind her aunt, her eyes the size of saucers.

Out of the mist, three immense leonine shapes slunk closer to their group. The creatures snuffled more and lifted their heads, searching the darkness with shining eyes.

Hounds.

Angela glanced at their nearest escape—a tunnel on the opposite shore. But that meant crossing the lethal water.

Horror tightened Angela's insides and twisted them into knots.

This is what Troy got for refusing that demon's help.

Angela moved her hand as subtly as possible, aiming to take off her left glove. In her mind, she saw Sophia somewhere ahead of them tormented or worse. For her sake, Angela had to try to stay alive.

She exchanged a meaningful nod with Troy. As Angela had hoped, there was no apology in the Jinn's eyes. Troy, at least, felt certain of their fighting chance.

All right, Angela was ready.

But before she could act, the three Hounds snarled coldly, emerged from the darkness, and pounced.

Eighteen

No one wants my help. But when it arrives, the last word a soul whispers is "No." —PYTHON

Troy must have known Angela was about to summon the Glaive—and that it would make her disastrously weak.

She gripped Angela tightly by the arm and wrenched hard.

Angela crashed into the wall. She howled in surprise as stars of pain speckled her vision. Nina was by her side immediately, lifting Angela up again by the shoulders. But Troy and Juno faced off against the triple threat of the Hounds. One of the horrid creatures was smaller than the others with ragged wings. It looked like a baby.

Troy growled at it in a terrifying display of wings and teeth.

The two other Hounds stepped in front of their offspring, baring their own fence of teeth.

Faint laughter seemed to come out of nowhere. An odd purple mist began to mix with the fog from the rapids. Angela struggled to see, finally standing despite the pounding agony in her head.

She tried to rip off her glove again, and Nina clamped down on her hand.

"Let me go!" Angela screamed at her. She spun and tried to toss Nina sideways.

Nina held on, fighting with her. "You can't, Angela! It's too soon—the Grail would kill you—"

Angela ignored her and fought back harder. Fury screeched in terror above them.

Troy rolled out of the fog, snapping in a maelstrom of wings and blood at the Hound that had lunged for her wings. A nasty cut on her shoulder dribbled blood down her chalk-white arm. She lunged at the baby Hound again, threatening the worst. Turning, she advanced on one of the defensive adults, successful at striking a blow to one of its immense wings.

A long and deadly howl of pain erupted from the monster.

Juno emerged from the fog, leaping for one of the adult's eyes.

Troy stiffened in horror. She turned and grabbed Juno in midair, flinging her aside as another Hound clamped down on the spot with its enormous teeth.

There was a sickening *crack*—the sound of bones breaking. A sharp smell of blood saturated the air.

The mist thickened and Angela lost sight of Troy and Juno.

Nina pushed Angela toward the stream, screaming, "Hop to the opposite shore!"

Angela fought against Nina more, digging her boots against the pebbles at the shoreline. Her arm glove tore near the elbow.

NO. I have to save them. Troy would do the same for me. She IS doing the same for me.

The eerie laughter around them had faded. Now incredibly loud hisses echoed against the rocks until they became ear shattering. Angela covered her ears without even wanting to. The pain was unbearable.

A gigantic snake with a triangular feather-plumed head reared out of the fog, snapping lethally at one of the Hounds running for Angela and Nina. More bones cracked and broke. Snarls of fear and howls of agony reverberated against the rocks.

Another Hound advanced, breaking from the fog with its flanks streaming blood. Troy and Juno were still in the mist, shrieking and growling.

Nina clutched Angela's arm and froze. The Hound galloped to within a few feet of them.

The giant snake shot out of the fog, grabbed the beast by its torso, and tossed it backward into the rocks. It hit the tunnel wall with a sickening *thump.*

"*Go,*" Nina said, pushing Angela hard toward the stream.

Angela staggered, one of her boots hitting the edge of the water. Steam erupted from the toe of her shoe. The leather cracked and melted.

The giant snake's tail smacked into the walls of the cavern, sending a spray of rocks to the ground. A large and sharp rock hit Angela's hand and she cried out in pain, but she held on to Nina tightly. The question was how they would reach the opposite shore together. Angela's legs were long enough to help her reach the other side without touching the water. But Nina would be a problem.

She might never make it.

More rocks tumbled from the ceiling. Enormous chunks fell, blocking off a much smaller and tighter escape route near Troy and the Hounds. The force as they hit the hard ground shivered through the entire cavern.

"Hold on!" Angela gripped Nina tightly by the hand. Blood slicked her palms.

Nina lost Angela's hand and grabbed it again. Angela pointed hurriedly at the water and Nina nodded, understanding she might not make it across, but that she had no other choice. Angela clasped Nina's hand even more fiercely as the rain of rocks continued.

Together, they jumped.

Together, they made it across. Their feet hit the opposite shore. Angela dared to smile at Nina, allowing a moment of triumph for them both.

A large rock smacked into the side of Nina's leg, wrenching her from Angela's grip, shoving her sideways. Nina stumbled out of reach, one of her legs slipping into the water.

Her scream was agonizing. Nina yanked her leg from the water and collapsed on the shore, but the damage had been done. The smell of acid burning skin soured the air.

"No!" Angela grabbed for Nina. She could barely see through her tears.

Nina rocked in horrendous pain, clutching at her leg. She grasped for Angela's hand again, her face red as she sobbed.

Another enormous rock fell directly between them both, blocking Nina off completely.

More rocks fell, building the great barrier between them in an earthquake of noise. The world disappeared as purplish mist returned, blinding Angela to the fate of her friends. She climbed the barrier, heedless of the falling rocks as they hit her like a rain of knives, cutting her skin all over. Maybe—

just maybe—she could reach everyone again. To hell with the pain. The violet mist surrounded her in a thick cloud.

She cried for Nina one more time, receiving only Fury's faint screech in reply.

Before Angela could make any more progress, a strong pair of hands reached from behind her and dragged her away screaming into the blackness.

Nineteen

*I wanted to tell her the entire time—even
if you feel as helpless as a mouse in a trap,
never stop fighting.* —SOPHIA

Angela smacked into the tunnel wall, struggling furiously with her captor. The opening into the cavern where Nina, Troy, and Juno had been left behind was now completely blocked by boulders. Angela screamed until her throat hurt anyway. Insane as it seemed, maybe that would make a difference.

But someone had a firm grip on her, and he pinned back her hands and held her tight until she gasped for breath, hot tears rolling down her cheeks.

"Let me go," Angela shouted hoarsely.

"Not until you promise to behave yourself," a suave and familiar voice said. "I can't have you trying to scale the rocks again like a rat."

Angela struggled more, crying and screaming, fighting in vain until she slumped to her knees, weak and gasping. Her captor breathed steadily behind her, at last letting go of her wrists. Angela tilted back her head and let her tears fall, screaming again and again until she almost lost her voice. But she was too weak to move.

Finally, she let silence descend.

"At last," the voice said behind her.

"Go ahead," Angela said. "If you're going to kill me, do me a favor and make it quick. But I won't make it an easy job for you." Angela rubbed at her left hand, clenching it tightly. She would show her captor the Grail and force him to let her go. That was her only option. Depending on the circumstance, maybe she'd let him live, though keeping her from Nina and the others hadn't helped his cause.

"I doubt I'll hurt you," he said. "Let's just keep our interaction sophisticated and civil so the temptation never arises. Now, Archon—or should I just call you Angela—"

"*Don't you dare,*" Angela said between her teeth. "It's Archon or nothing." She lifted her left hand.

"As you wish." The demon Python stepped into the soft glow of the embers set in the tunnel walls, examining her with pity. The cut he'd received from Troy looked raw and wicked in the half-light. He stood over Angela, gauging her more with his bright orange eyes. Up close, she could see all the tiny scales that covered his eyelids down to the finest detail. He glanced askance at her upraised hand. "Well, I'm surprised at your coldness. If it weren't for my compassion, you would be dead. Deceased. *Gone.* Need I elaborate further?"

Angela glared at him, lowering her hand again. Python was suspicious—but now there was no denying that she needed him around. Still, she was angry. "Thank you? You don't need my thanks. You'd already determined on helping me. *I didn't ask.*"

"But you wanted to ask," he said, narrowing his eyes at her with icy perceptiveness. "All that while, you were calling to me in your mind, hoping to find me again. Looking for salvation somewhere, anywhere. I know you didn't like when that Jinn made your decision for you. Neither would I . . ."

Angela stared at her boots. Gingerly, she prodded the open toe where the stream's acid had eaten away at the leather.

"Ow. *Damn it.*" She rubbed her finger dry on her skirt. More tears dripped down her face.

What could she do now? Nina, Troy, and Juno might still be alive. Maybe there was a way in this labyrinth that would lead Angela back to them—maybe this demon knew it. But there was no guarantee. And if anything happened to Sophia in the meantime . . .

Python watched Angela wordlessly. For someone determined on helping her, his face held a marked chilliness. "Do you feel sorry for them? You shouldn't, Archon. Believe me, the Jinn doesn't feel sorry for you. And why are you mourning a friend who was dead and should have stayed that way? They deserved this suffering for their arrogance. I warned you well enough of the dangers to be found in this maze."

"Troy was trying to keep me safe," Angela snapped. "When she refused your help, she was thinking of me, no matter how stupid her decision was. She wasn't just thinking about herself." Though Angela had no way to prove that.

Troy's loyalty to her didn't seem to go *that* far. Perhaps Juno's only went as far as her aunt's. Yet their actions in the cave said very much otherwise. Maybe Troy was hard on Angela like she was hard on Juno for a reason—to keep them strong.

Wait a second . . .

Angela looked at Python again. "How did you know Nina had died already?"

Python smirked. "I'm a demon, girl. My eyes see many things that yours do not." He crossed his arms and leaned against the wall. "For instance, I can see the signs in this maze, hidden ever so carefully by its owner, that point to the way out. And you will not find the Book unless you find the way out."

"You seem to know a lot about this place," Angela said. "Why?"

"I acquaint myself with every high-ranking demon in Hell. I take the time to learn their strengths and weaknesses, their dreams and desires, their fears and joys. Everything. I can slip in and out of the smallest cracks, hear the slightest noises, and perceive the best disguised of all lies. They know I cannot be kept out, or for that matter, contained. So they do not bother to stop me when I enter and leave this place. I am different from the others."

The unnerving light behind Python's eyes returned.

A chill shuddered along Angela's arms. She rocked to her feet, fighting with the bile in the back of her throat. Angela closed her eyes but could still see Nina screaming on the shore. She fought back her tears, but the scream reverberated in her memories as Nina's leg hit the water. Angela had to keep moving anyway. Sitting in this awful place and doing nothing would only lead to more death and pain.

Certainly at least an hour had passed. Too little time to just leave—but Sophia also might die at any moment.

One more time, Angela tested the barrier between her and the cavern where Nina, Troy, and Juno waited. She pressed her ear to the rocks. Maybe she'd at least catch Fury's cries. Nothing. Only the sound of rushing water met her hopes. Desperately, she tried clawing at the boulders, but even the smallest of them was too big to move. Angela slumped forward, exhausted, her fingertips raw. She gasped and slammed a fist painfully against the rocks.

Python watched her without lifting a single finger to help.

Angela glared at him. It took everything in her not to scream again. "What do you know about the demon who owns this maze," Angela said. "Is he just helping Lucifel? Or is there more to this?"

Python laughed softly. "There is always more. But as I told you before, he's bored. Boredom leads to all kinds of mischief . . ." His expression turned distantly cold again. "I would love to satisfy your curiosity further, Archon. But the hours of Hell grow late, and we would do well to travel quickly. Many more creatures wait here in the darkness. Not all are as predictable as Hounds."

This all seemed too convenient. If Python had been following them, it obviously wasn't hard for him to figure out a way to separate Angela from Troy and the others. But Angela couldn't wander around here aimlessly and alone. Besides, if Python proved to be dangerous . . .

Angela flexed her aching left hand.

She glanced at the boulders blocking her path to her friends. Of course, nothing changed.

Troy, she said in her mind. *Come to me. Please.*

They were Bound together, and the unspoken law was that Troy needed to obey to some degree. But not a sound came from the fence of rocks separating them. It was as though the entire attack had been a terrible dream.

Don't worry, Angela said to her. *I have to keep going. But I also won't give up on any of you. We'll get out of this together. I know it.*

"Ready?" Python interrupted coolly.

"Of course not," Angela whispered. She set her mouth

into a tight and grim line as she followed the demon and left
the barrier, step by shaky step, behind.

Python led Angela in silence past dangerous chasms, around
immeasurable abysses, and against what she swore were the
edges of cliffs. Finally they emerged into a more civilized
part of the labyrinth, where carvings and writing covered the
walls anew. The corridors and halls felt frightfully twisted
and endless. Perhaps she and Python were encroaching on
the demon city Troy had mentioned. But the crude map of
Hell had suggested the opposite, and it was clear Angela
would have been hopelessly lost on her own.

Angela crushed a dizzy fear battering at her heart and
brain. She tried not to think about Sophia and the others
too much, concentrating merely on putting one foot in front
of the other, but it was difficult. She was thirsty, hungry,
incredibly tired, and every echo seemed to carry a familiar
voice, and with it a painful memory.

At last, they entered a vast hall where enormous pillars
stretched on and on into endless darkness. The ceiling felt
more like the sky, and their footsteps echoed eerily.

Faintly, Angela heard the rush and roar of water again.

She glanced at Python, but he continued walking in silence until they reached a gigantic set of solid onyx doors.
Like the door to Hell, these doors had also been engraved
with all kinds of fantastical and monstrous creatures. Angela
recognized carvings of the Hounds, though in the light of
the embers and braziers their forms appeared shadowy and
indistinct. There were no horses this time.

Angela focused on the shape of an enormous serpent with
a plume of feathers crowning its triangular head. It looked
almost exactly like the snake that had attacked the Hounds.

"Do you admire him?" Python said softly.

Angela jumped slightly, startled by the sound of his voice. She tried to calm herself, taking slow breaths.

Python gazed at the carving intently. "That is my father, Leviathan. He was one of the feathered serpents who sided with Lucifel in the Celestial Revolution. What a shame he didn't survive the War. Even a boy like me needs a hero . . ."

Angela's skin crawled. Her heart thumped wildly. More fear raced through her like liquid fire. Suddenly, it was a deadly mistake to be on the verge of another door with Python by her side.

"What is this?" she whispered. "Where are we?"

Python observed her indifferently. His voice was smooth and cold as ever. "This is an unavoidable passage. To exit the labyrinth, you must first reach its center or heart. That heart is what we are about to enter."

Angela's own heart hammered painfully. "What's on the other side of these doors?"

"Possibilities," he said unhelpfully. "Opportunities. Will you take them? That is the Archon's decision alone, my dear. Although perhaps it would be good for you to know that I've been keeping a person of interest inside, waiting for you. I think that individual will be of enormous assistance in making your choices. But in the end, time, temptation, and terror hinges on your sovereign word." Python bowed for emphasis.

"I suppose you're not coming with me?" Angela said. That should have been a relief, but it strangely wasn't. Not knowing what would happen next was the most exhilarating and terrifying feeling. She'd rather share it with anyone than be alone.

"Well," he said roguishly, "I haven't been invited to the

party. But unexpected guests make for exciting company, so don't you worry—I will be near. I've been yearning to see the truth, after all."

"See the truth?" Angela echoed him. What in the world . . .

She stared at the doors, her vision swimming.

"Well then"—Python leaned toward her ear, his tongue flicking against it—"I'll see you on the other side."

Angela shuddered. She swatted Python away angrily—and met with nothing but air.

He was gone.

She glanced around the immense chamber, at the columns, the hieroglyphs, and deep into the silent darkness. A warm breeze ran along Angela's arms and teased at her skirt. The Grail beneath her glove felt uncomfortably moist. It was probably bleeding again.

Angela wrapped her arms around her shoulders, fighting her chills. She turned back to the double doors and stared at them. Unconsciously, she clutched the sapphire star pendant on her necklace, whispering a soft prayer to herself.

I'm not giving up now.

She pushed gently on one of the doors, and it cracked open without the slightest resistance. Music flooded out of the opening and into the hall. Light burned Angela's eyes. Laughter followed her over the threshold. Angela gasped at the vision in front of her because it was too stupendous and incredible to be believed.

She had barely taken another step, and the laughter ceased, the music paused.

The door slammed shut behind her and locked.

Twenty

*Lucifel did her best to destroy our memories of
Heaven, but behind closed doors we never stopped
dreaming of the opulence we'd left behind. Some
even tried to bring it back.* —PYTHON

Angela froze. Her brain could have turned to jelly and nothing felt real.

She stood at the edge of an enormous ballroom constructed with onyx and glittering crystals. The black stone of
the columns supporting the room gleamed beneath braziers
studding their sides. The floor shone as smoothly as black
glass. Tables covered with every kind of goblet imaginable
lined the far walls, and a large fountain dominated the center
of the room. Beneath the red lights, the liquid spurting from
its center eerily resembled blood.

She stared openmouthed at the couples who swarmed the
room.

Mysterious figures of men and women with grotesque but
oddly fascinating masks dotted every square foot of space.
Some costumes resembled the same creatures carved into the
double doors. Angela recognized the scales of snakes, the

sharp teeth of the Hounds, and perhaps more menacingly, horse masks dominated by ribbed horns with tips glistening sharply in the half-light. Every dancer wore phosphorescent paint around the bare circles of their eyes. Most of the couples had paused to stare at Angela, inquiring about her presence with piercing expressions rather than words.

The silence continued. Angela had heard the doors lock behind her. Ringing the room, at least ten other sets of doors beckoned.

An inscription in demonic writing decorated an arch above the nearest doors. The more Angela focused on the writing, the more it transformed into letters she could easily read.

Within this room temptation lies. Beware
the drinks, beware the eyes.

She glanced in panic at the inscription above the other door to her left.

Trapped in dreams, one easily sins.
Now the unwanted trial begins.

Angela's trembling hand crept toward her left arm glove. The Grail burned so badly a scream also burned in her throat. But she didn't dare make a sound. Angela bit her lip hard. It bled and soured the inside of her mouth. She gazed out into the crowd of people—more likely demons—and waited for someone else to speak or move.

Without warning, one of the spectators broke away from his partner and strolled toward Angela. He was dressed exquisitely in black silk with purple lace at the sleeves. He peered at Angela through a mask that resembled the head of a stag complete with lethal-looking antlers. "And who are you?" he asked with surprising politeness.

One of the women regarded Angela with venomous eyes while intermittently sipping at a glass.

What's the use of lying? If this is part of the labyrinth, they already know who I am.

"Angela Mathers," she said firmly, bracing herself for an attack.

His eyes widened in surprise. Speedily, he knelt before Angela and clasped her hand before she could snatch it away. "The Archon," he whispered reverently. "Our ruler."

"Your ruler?" Angela said. Fire shot through her body. Hairs prickled on the back of her neck.

The woman sipping at the glass approached with studied elegance. Up close she was disturbingly tall with unbelievably green eyes. "Our sovereign who will overthrow Lucifel."

She knelt down in something resembling a curtsy.

Angela's world spun. The other women hastily copied the first, their wave of curtsies rippling outward. Some of the demons unfurled wings that were little more than bloodied bones and stringy muscle. Others obviously had none left to unfurl, and some were luckier, with ratty wings in shades of black or blond. Angela sniffed and frowned at the acidic taint in the air. It must have been the same acidic fog that Troy had said destroyed the demons' sensitive wings over time.

The demon in the stag mask held Angela's hand high. "This is the one who will sit on the Throne of Lucifel. This is the new Prince of Hell."

Angela looked around awkwardly, unsure of what to do next. The entire scenario was so odd and incredible. It all felt like a terrible dream.

Too many demons filled the room for Angela to fight them one-on-one. There had to be another way out of this. Python had mentioned opportunities of some kind.

Though he'd more likely been referring to Angela's role as Lucifel's rival.

Why did he really lead me here? There had to be a way around this place, despite what he said . . .

Certainly his crazy talk about "seeing the truth" had something to do with it. But what did that even mean?

Angela thought of the inscriptions above the door concerning temptation, and shivered. Her mouth had dried to the consistency of cotton, and her stomach bubbled painfully whenever she glanced at the drinks on either side of the room.

"Who will dance with our new sovereign?" the male demon said, presenting Angela once more to the crowd.

There were many murmurs, and then a tumult of shouting. Many of the demons glanced at one another. Finally, another male with an emerald mask stepped toward Angela. "I will dance," he said, stretching his hand toward her demandingly.

"*I OBJECT,*" a feminine voice echoed powerfully across the room.

Frigid sweat blossomed on Angela's forehead. Her heart raced and galloped like mad.

Now the dancers of all descriptions parted in waves, revealing a woman who sat on an obsidian throne at the other side of the room. She was taller than the other female demons and wore a simple mask glittering with purple and green gems. Feathers with red tips crowned her cascading waves of black hair. She slid from the throne, revealing an alien-looking yet beautiful dress with a high collar that sloped dangerously low from her shoulders. Her skin was strikingly dark.

"I object," she continued, "on the grounds that I myself have already chosen her partner in this gracious dance."

She spread her arms out to Angela.

"Welcome, Archon, to this festival, which is but one of my many celebrations day and night. But who has delivered you to my secret corner of Hell? Or have you come to us by your own power?" She smiled at Angela, though her honey-colored eyes held a familiar coldness. "No answer? Then I suppose a black bird dropped you here by chance on the way back to his nest in Babylon." She laughed softly and nodded at a tall but shadowed figure standing behind her throne. He stiffened but said nothing.

"Who—who are you?" Angela finally said. Unbelieve-ably, her words were carried from demon to demon, all the way to the woman speaking to her.

The woman smiled ingratiatingly. "I am Lilith, my dear. Though I have many other names . . ."

Lilith! Python's mother? Why would Python bring Angela to her of all people? He said they weren't working together—that he hated her. Did Lilith know what was going on?

No wonder Python hadn't been able to openly enter this room with Angela.

Angela tried to swallow the nervous ball in her throat. She clenched her hands.

"In any case," Lilith continued, "I'd been looking forward to your arrival. It is sooner than I'd expected, but perhaps things are not going well for you on Earth. No small wonder, considering the great danger that threatens the Realms. But as it is, you've arrived at an opportune and rather appropriate time." She looked to the demons arrayed near Angela. "This place is hidden from demons who are not my servants and friends. It is a privileged place of revelry and idle delights. A place where reality reflects dreams." She stared intently at Angela. "And dreams reflect desires. Archon, let this be a taste for you of the pleasures to come if you choose to rule over us in Lucifel's stead. You don't need to worry. Rely on my support." Lilith lips spread into a beautiful and terrifying smile. "One hundred percent."

Lilith waved a hand, and the female demons to either side of her drew away into the shadows.

The tall man who'd been standing behind her stepped into the flickering light beneath a brazier. His skin was pale, an even more striking contrast to Lilith's dark beauty.

He wore a mask resembling a crow's face with a pointed beak, and his beautiful black coat had been decorated with ebony feathers at the shoulders.

"Here is your partner, Archon," Lilith said. "Enjoy your time among us. Forget the terrors of the world for a while. Here—time passes differently."

Lilith laughed, and the dancers closed around her again, making her vanish as if she'd never existed. Meanwhile, the man with the crow mask advanced on Angela until he was steps away from her. Slowly, he knelt down before her and then he stood with his hand outstretched. His amber eyes peered at her with a burning and wordless plea.

Angela considered her options, which weren't very good.

Sophia—I'm coming for you.

With a deep breath, she slid her hand into his.

They danced interminably. Angela knew better than to touch any of the drinks to either side of her, but she often glanced at them with longing.

Her partner was very skilled and very graceful. He was also completely silent. Angela tried to peer beyond the confines of his mask and came away with the vague impression of a handsome face with sculpted cheekbones and a slim nose. The costume and the bad lighting kept her from taking in better details.

It couldn't be just a coincidence that Angela was once again at a masquerade ball. Her mouth set into a tight line. Camdon must have been inspired by whatever demon controlled this labyrinth to send her that midnight blue dress. Lilith spoke of Angela's desires being reflected here, and now that she had a moment to think, it struck her hard: Why *had* Angela really gone to the ball in Luz? It wasn't like her to give in so easily to peer pressure, even if she felt guilty about something.

Maybe I'm just trying to be normal. It's what I've always wanted, after all.

The elegant music paused.

Angela watched as most of the other demons clapped and laughed. On the surface they appeared to be legitimately happy, but their faces and eyes remained cold. The fountain of red water also disturbed her, and Angela tried not to look at it too much. She was about to let go of her partner, fascinated by a row of crystal flasks filled with liquid as red as the fountain's water.

He held her hand tightly, pulling her back. "Angela," he said softly, "don't you recognize me?"

She recognized his voice. Angela stared at him, frozen yet again.

He smiled and lowered his crow mask. It was Kim, as strikingly handsome as in the days when she'd first met him in Luz. That sculpted face, and those thin lips—Angela gasped as every detail came flooding back. His black hair was longer now, and the red streak dyed into his bangs had started to grow out. But he was a far cry from the vision Angela had of him entering the door to Hell. There he'd been a complete wreck. Right now, he was clean and certain of himself, as elegant as a prince.

Angela understood his choice of costume as a grim irony. The crow was the symbol of his cousin Troy's Jinn Clan.

"I'd been hoping you would recognize me before I needed to take off the mask," Kim said quietly. He stared at her with the intense and searing eyes of her memories.

"You're not dead," Angela whispered. Despite her relief, she didn't have it in herself to smile.

"Not yet," Kim said grimly. "But if Troy has her way, it's only a matter of time." He regarded Angela darkly. "Have you seen her at all?"

Angela nodded slowly, unable to stop staring at him.

Kim's breathing quickened, and his face paled more, but he kept calm otherwise. "Is she in Hell?"

Somehow, it didn't feel right to answer that question just yet. "Where have you been all this time?" Angela said instead, aware of a pathetic pain creeping into her voice.

He motioned to her to continue dancing. As she slid into his arms again, his warm whispers touched her ear. "After the battle with Lucifel in Memorial Park, you fainted. Israfel rescued you and left shortly after. That left me alone with Troy. I was sure she was dead. I was also wrong. She attacked me, and I was forced to use a blood crystal to try and escape. But"—his tone lowered—"the unstable portals kept me from traveling far enough. I was forced back to Earth. As soon as Troy realized this, she started hunting me with double the ferocity. I gave her trouble, but she almost caught up to me when I managed to escape into Hell. I was desperate, Angela. I had no choice. I needed to see you again, even if there was only the smallest chance of that happening."

His story matched Troy's version of events. But Troy had also said Kim was firmly on the side of the demons.

Angela closed her eyes, unwillingly remembering kisses in the dark as Kim whispered in her ear. Her heart ached. It was tired. She was tired. Angela fought the urge to collapse against him.

"The authorities in Luz are suspicious of you anyway, Kim. You can't go back. The Vatican police will arrest you now. Maybe worse."

Kim laughed. "They were suspicious of me from the start. Despite what I told you, I'm not really a novice, Angela. I had the knowledge of one. But I'm no priest. Only a pretender. But I forged the proper document and fit in with them well enough to learn what I needed over the years. Indeed, by now I know much more."

"But you are Troy's cousin," Angela reiterated.

Kim made a sound of disgust. "That is unfortunately true. Everything else is the truth, Angela."

"Even your name?"

Kim sighed. He held her closer. "Yes, I do owe you that at least . . . My mother didn't exactly love me as a mother should. I had an older sister who died shortly before I was born. My mother gave me her name, bitterly wishing I was someone else even from the first day of my existence. There—now you know . . . and I'm sure you of all people can understand."

Angela thought of her own name, how the mother who hated her had given it out of misplaced guilt, all because an angel in her dreams had leaned over Angela's cradle.

Angela relaxed a little. "And how about what you felt for me?" she said softly. "Was that the truth . . ."

"I hated you at first," he whispered. "Because you rejected me. Then, I realized we are alike. I can't leave you alone with feathered wolves. I want to be by your side. Angela, you said you would never sit on Lucifel's Throne. But remember, it might be your destiny. There might be no way to fight it anymore, and I want to be by your side when—"

"That's not why I'm here," Angela snapped. She pulled away from Kim.

He stared at her, smiling bitterly. "No, of course not."

"Sophia was abducted, Kim. And I'm here to find her and take her back."

Kim shook his head. "It's exactly like you to think there isn't more to all of this. Have you thought about *why* she was abducted?"

"Because Lucifel is insane," Angela hissed, suddenly irritated.

Kim gripped her arms so hard it hurt. "Or to get the both of you exactly where she wants you—helpless. Babylon is a web of intrigue, Angela. Remember, not every demon shares Lucifel's ideals. But some of them do. Take one wrong step, and you'll plummet off the cliff."

"I've done that plenty of times and survived," Angela said petulantly. She ripped her arm away from Kim. "But now I know how to keep myself from falling in the first place. What are you doing here, Kim? The same demon that guided me through the labyrinth so far said that he was keeping you here, just for me. But I walk into this craziness to find that Lilith thinks you're *her* prize to give. I want to know what this is all about, and what you have to do with it. Whose side are you on?"

"Yours," Kim said, his face utterly serious. "Lilith is protecting me right now, Angela. She offered to spare my life in exchange for getting you into Hell. I'm the black bird she believes dropped you at her doorstep. What she doesn't know is that Python, the son that hates her, is the one who slipped me into her nest. She thinks I'm a devoted human worshipper, nothing more. She's a powerful ally, Angela, but a dangerous enemy with no desire to see Hell's regime turn upside down. She doesn't want you on Lucifel's Throne any more than Lucifel does. This celebration is a trap."

Angela's blood ran cold. "Then why would Python bring me here if he knew that?"

Kim's gaze hardened. "Hatred is a powerful instigator of chaos. Think of it as a slap to his mother's face."

That sounds right, and yet . . .

Angela remembered Python's words about seeing the truth. Something told her Kim knew nothing about that little detail.

"I'm flattered by his confidence in me," she said sarcastically, trying to hide her growing anxiety. She glanced at the smiling faces around her. "Are they going to try to kill me? Right now?"

Now those smiles seemed so fake. Her pulse raced like mad.

"Soon enough," Kim whispered. His hand on hers shook. "The idea is to tempt you with the glamour of being their new ruler. To get you drunk with time and a sense of power. To make you forget why you are here in the first place. My job was to make sure of that, while in exchange Lilith would protect me from Troy. But I won't do it, even if Troy rips me to shreds." Kim touched her blood-red hair. "I'm going against so many things for you. The least you could do is thank me."

"What other kinds of things?" Angela said softly. There was a gentleness to Kim's gaze that frightened her as much as the demons in the room.

"My adoptive father's, for one," Kim said. "Do you remember that night you asked me about my cross necklace, and I told you my father gave it to me. I didn't mean the Jinn father that I killed. I was talking about the other one."

Angela blinked at him. Heat and pain scorched through her all at once. "You're like Stephanie . . ."

Kim shook his head. "I felt sorry for Stephanie when we first met. She and I shared a similar history. So my adoptive father encouraged our association. If Stephanie had been the Archon, I was given the order to kill her and eradicate the threat to Lucifel's position. Maybe—considering the kind of person she was—I would have. But I couldn't do the same to you. You'd done nothing to deserve the burden on your shoulders."

He said that, yet demons didn't seem like the type to adopt out of pure charity.

Hadn't Python said there was always something more behind everything?

So why had Kim's demon foster father adopted him—of all people—as a son? What could Kim do that no one else could?

"It haunts me," Kim said. His warm lips kissed the edge of Angela's ear. "Who are you, Angela Mathers?" Kim's face, usually so distant and cold, softened with real longing. "I need to know. You are not Raziel reincarnated. You're someone else. I think that is the real key you need to search for. It's the secret that Sophia has shut away within herself. It is the cause of Raziel's mysterious death. It might be the salvation of everything."

Angela closed her eyes, drinking in the strange but heady perfume clinging to Kim's clothes, the strength in his body.

She thought of Israfel with a sudden bitterness.

The music swirled around her, and for a moment she did find a refuge in forgetting everything else. How much more pain could she take?

Then she returned to her senses, and reality struck her like an arrow to the heart.

I have to get out of here.

Angela's mind flashed to Sophia, and to the lilting music Sophia often played on their recorder back in Luz. It was eerily like the music Angela heard now. Classical and unearthly, filled with sensual beauty with notes that gave you wings to soar to new worlds. She saw Sophia laughing, twirling around to the music. Sophia grabbed Angela's hand and forced her to dance with her, still laughing.

But how can I escape? There are demons everywhere. They'll know if I try to leave . . . Think, Angela. THINK.

A suave voice interrupted Angela's dream. A long shadow darkened her world. "May I have this dance?"

Angela opened her eyes as a tall figure slipped between her and Kim. Kim's face blanched and the crowd swallowed him, but strong hands gripped Angela and whirled her helplessly away. She looked up at her new partner and found herself face-to-face with a glittering snake's mask. Exquisite silver thread had been embroidered into her new partner's collar and coat. "Hey—" She struggled against him. "What are you doing!"

Fear tightened her throat. Her face flushed.

"Welcome to the ball, my beauty." The demon lowered the mask and smiled at Angela. Python's familiar orange eyes blazed right through her. "It seems you're not too bad at playing Cinderella. But it's too early in our little tale for you to rest in your prince's arms. And it's unfair of you to deny other suitors a chance to impress you."

Python tried to kiss her hand, but Angela twisted it sideways.

"What do you think you're doing?" she said again, incredulous. Blistering panic shot through her. The room chilled, and she swore her breath frosted the air. Her heart pounded in her ears like a drum. "Your mother will know you're here."

Python winked. "On the contrary, she'll never know I'm here unless she sees me. Considering that she has yet to scream and cry, she hasn't seen me."

"Thank you, then, for showing up to make things difficult," Angela stammered angrily, trying again to pull away from him. "But I'm not going to be your pawn. You're right. I've made a decision after all. That I'm leaving."

Python yanked her violently close so that their faces were an inch apart. He scanned her up and down approvingly. *How dare he.* Angela was about to spit in his eyes but never got the chance.

"Tell *them*," he whispered, "not me."

He nodded his head to the left. A throng of demons approached, carrying a throne more impressive than Lilith's on their shoulders. It was glaringly obvious they meant for Angela to sit on it.

She searched the crowd, but Kim had vanished in a sea of faces. Oh, God, what if they'd found out Kim was helping her?

"Forgive the awkward pun, but I suppose the ball is now rolling," the demon whispered. "So much for sweet dreams, princess. Temptation has arrived. Since I already know your decision, I can pity you in advance. But forgive me if all I can do is watch the drama unfold. Besides—I wouldn't want to miss the long-awaited revelations. Ah—so there she is . . ."

His eyes looked up, searching a balcony. Python must have found his mother at last.

He let go of Angela abruptly and vanished like smoke into the crowd. Angela staggered before the advancing group of demons. They dropped the obsidian chair in front of her with a menacing *thump.*

"May I help you, Sovereign?" A female demon with platinum blond hair gestured for Angela to sit. "We've brought you a throne."

"I don't want it," Angela muttered in a panic.

"Surely, you wish to be our ruler," the blond demon continued, though her eyes glittered dangerously.

"No," Angela said. "I don't. I don't want your Throne. All I want is to leave."

The female demon reached for Angela's wrist, and Angela screamed.

"NO."

The dancers stopped. The music faded to an eerie silence. Everyone stared at Angela from behind their masks with open surprise.

She was the cornered mouse, and they were the cats. Her entire body shivered.

Angela backpedaled more and knocked into one of the tables covered in goblets. One of the glasses fell and smashed at her feet, scattering shards everywhere.

Red liquid pooled on the floor near her boots. Slowly, the other dancers closed in on her from every direction. High above them, Lilith stepped toward the edge of an onyx balcony carved with pentagrams. She watched Angela with terrifying superiority behind her eyes. Her voice carried down from the dark heights, rising above the lonely noise of the great fountain in the room. "What an unwelcome turn of events," Lilith said condescendingly. "You would refuse your Throne, Archon? You would abandon your loyal subjects? Abandon me? How much smarter it would be of you to stay here. To . . . rethink your decision."

Angela pressed against the table.

That was the temptation and it had failed. So now—

"Well, Archon? Will you be our new ruler? Because if you will not—I'm afraid to say there's no real place for you here."

Lilith already knew there wasn't a place for Angela. If Angela wasn't killed now, it would be later.

She grasped at one of the glasses behind her and threw it at the nearest demon, splashing his wolf mask with the red liquid. He barely flinched and continued to walk toward her. Angela gripped her left arm glove and started to slide it off, lifting her hand high.

Some of the demons backed away cautiously.

Lilith's laughter rang through the room. "Now this makes for an interesting night." She looked to the female demons on either side of her. "I suppose the Archon has given us her final answer. But she'd do well not to act too rashly. Behold your prince," she said, snapping her dark fingers.

Two of the male demons emerged from the midst of the crowd, Kim held between them. He struggled, and one of them cracked him powerfully across the face.

Angela hesitated. She glanced wildly at the demons as they neared her.

Kim breathed hard, glaring at Lilith. A nasty handprint swelled on his cheek. "We had a deal," he shouted at her.

"And you broke it," she snapped back. "So much for your promises of success." She whirled back around to face Angela, pointing at the fountain. "Make her drink!"

Kim's face lost the little color it had left. He struggled harder. "Wait! Wait! I can still help you—"

"Enough!" Lilith shouted back. She pointed again at the fountain. "Take her!"

Some of the dancers rushed Angela, grabbing her. She screamed, struggling as hard as she could. A menagerie of masks with teeth and scales surrounded her. Cruel hands grasped her own and yanked them behind her back, tying her wrists together with a cord. The same female demon who'd initiated the curtsy in her honor now laughed in her face. The male demon who'd introduced her to the crowd grabbed Angela by her hair and dragged her toward the fountain.

The closer she came to its shining black stone, the more life and warmth fled her body. A familiar smell washed over her. Nausea followed it in heavy waves.

Drinking that red fluid would be the worst thing Angela could possibly do. What was Python's motivation in letting this happen? What could this have to do with the truth?

Finally, she reached the fountain.

Angela turned her head aside.

Two demons gripped her by the face and forced her to gaze down at her reddish reflection.

"It looks like Lucifel has won after all, Archon," Lilith said, her voice echoing with chilling effortlessness throughout the chamber.

Rough hands shoved Angela's face into the liquid. She sputtered, shooting up and out of it for breath. The hands shoved her down again and splashed the liquid into her mouth as she surfaced. Uproarious laughter filled the air.

Her vision swam. The world darkened. A resounding buzzing noise, like the beating wings of a giant fly, overwhelmed her. Angela swallowed as she gasped for breath, and the liquid poured down her throat. It was salty and oddly sour. She coughed and slammed against the smooth floor, distantly aware of her fingers clawing at the stone.

Sophia . . .

Angela had no more ability to think or to pray. There was only that one word, encompassing everything.

Then the nightmares took her.

Twenty-one

Out of the deep and fathomless darkness, a light appeared. With it, Angela's mind returned little by little. She could barely breathe and her head ached so badly she couldn't think straight.

Was this reality? Was it a dream?

Angela was no longer certain, but oddly her body felt unfamiliar.

Something was wrong. Angela began to walk and her legs felt longer, her body stronger. Gradually, she passed angels of all kinds, their beautiful faces often looking at her in quiet admiration.

She walked down a hallway with a glass floor and pearlescent walls. The entire world glittered iridescent as a prism, and the angels matched the radiance surrounding them, glistening with their jewels, their flawless dress, their intricate hair.

She should have been afraid.

Who was she? Why was she seeing this? What had changed?

A strange and overwhelming sense of calm filled her, like her soul had been drugged and dragged to observe this show it might not understand.

Finally, it dawned on her. Angela was in someone else's

body, and he *was in absolute control of it, steering her through dark but glittering corridors, past a row of paintings in colors more vivid than any she'd experienced on Earth, and finally into a private chamber with a great window that took up an entire wall. Shimmering curtains were all that separated her from a city glowing like a galaxy. Outside, a sea of crystal spires and incredible light stretched before her, their immensity revolving in the midst of space, stars, and nebulas. They glared down from the sky so intensely, Angela felt like she could reach out and touch them.*

The chamber itself was sparsely decorated. A round bed suspended from chains hung near the window, its insides spilling over with cushions and satiny sheets.

There was a dresser, and a vanity with a mirror. But there were few chairs, and only one or two other cushions for sitting. The entire room rested in shadows, while outside, the unnamed, glorious city spun like a gigantic wheel of fire. Angela—or rather, the angel she was trapped inside—walked slowly to the window and stared out of it. She shared his sense of awe, and a feeling that could only be described as longing.

Like she could spread these wings of hers and test their worth.

"Raziel," a gentle voice whispered musically behind her.

So—she was Raziel. No, she was in his memories. A silent, helpless witness.

Raziel turned his body and Angela turned with him. Israfel stood in the middle of the room, more casual and genuine than she'd ever seen him before, his hair loose and tousled, back to that gorgeous bronze color Angela remembered so well from her childhood dreams. But his eyes were brighter, and he carried his fully unfurled wings high, like they emphasized his happiness. He was breathtaking even without the heavy makeup and jewels, his languid eyes rich with emotion.

How young he seemed.

"Raziel," he said again, smiling. "You always come at the worst times. I was about to settle for the evening." Israfel looked at the floor with shyness in his expression. "You probably shouldn't stay long. I will have many matters to attend to in the morning."

Raziel strode for him, and Angela felt her hand reach out and touch Israfel's face.

He gasped, looking at her with a real fear.

Inside, her own heart seemed to race, and her entire self yearned for something inexpressible. Israfel pulled in close, so close, and Angela flashed back even within the dream to his mouth on hers that faraway night, the tenderness of his lips like the whisper of silk against her own. But Raziel turned aside at the last moment, and Angela was certain she could hear the tiniest sigh of pain leave Israfel.

He loved Raziel.

It was almost painfully obvious, even in the way Israfel breathed.

"Israfel," she heard herself say, but in a masculine voice that sent a whole other range of emotions shooting through her: mostly bitterness at the curse Raziel had placed on her life. "I have something very important I must discuss with you. You might want to sit down. This could take awhile."

Israfel pursed his lips together. But he obeyed and sat on a round cushion. "You have been gone for so long, returning nearly on the eve of my coronation anniversary," Israfel whispered. "Tell me that this surprise will be a pleasant one."

It sounded almost like a command.

"Israfel." Raziel knelt down across from him, taking his slender hands into his own. "My Archangel."

Crimson stripes blushed to life on Israfel's cheekbones.

Raziel sighed. "I have learned something of grave importance to you, and me, and Lucifel."

Israfel's expression changed, transforming into something Angela recognized immediately. These were the first traces of the chilly superiority he'd exhibited when she'd met him on Earth. "Yes," the angel said slowly. "What is it?"

Raziel hesitated, but only for a moment. "Listen to me carefully. I have learned from an undeniable source that . . ."

There was a silence.

Raziel was having trouble finding the right words.

"I—" He took a deep breath. "We are siblings, Israfel. You, and me, and Lucifel. The Father—he has known all along, choosing to tell us that this was not the case. But we have all been split from the same—"

Israfel shot up from his seat.

He stared at Raziel, his already large eyes enormous with anger and fear. His entire frame shivered, and he opened his mouth, and at first no sound came out. He was absolutely imperious, the same Israfel who'd let Angela's brother die, the same Israfel who'd made Stephanie's demon quiver with fright. She felt her soul quaver with terror. "What is this nonsense?" Israfel said dangerously.

"Israfel, listen to me—"

"Siblings." Israfel shook his head, biting his lip. "No," he whispered, "you lie. Lucifel has put you up to this."

"She has done nothing of the sort," Angela heard herself say too quickly.

Israfel took the retort as defensiveness. His eyebrows

arched angrily. "You always take her side," he hissed, his voice dripping with anguish. "Is that why you have come tonight? To gloat with her over my divided kingdom?"

"The Father's kingdom," Raziel said.

"But under my heel," Israfel snapped, "and everyone would do well to remember it." His expression changed, and he breathed hard and fast. "You love her, don't you? Why not just tell me and be done with it."

Angela reached out again.

Israfel flung her backward, a real electric shock jumping from him to her.

"Get back," he moaned. "Leave me alone. I wish to be alone."

Israfel sank to his knees, no longer questioning the truth of her statement. Was it because he had always sensed it to be the truth? Angela felt sick with him, horrified at seeing the proud angel sliding into visible despair, shocked as he was shocked, because if Raziel told the truth, then Israfel was guilty of a crime he'd never intended to commit. He was in love—but with his own brother? It was sinful, unforgivable—and it was clear he couldn't help himself. Heaven's Archangel was a mess, a wreck, and in this single moment, on his way to becoming a living ghost.

"Leave me," he whispered. He rounded on Raziel. "NOW."

Angela caught him by the shoulders, kissing him on the forehead as he gritted his teeth, nearly resembling Troy in her worst moments. Angela was sure he'd zap her again, but Israfel slumped, allowing Raziel's kisses.

The last one met his lips.

He moaned softly, and Angela felt herself standing. Raziel was going to leave him here, in a puddle of misery. Angela *wanted to shriek for Raziel to stop, to let her soul stay and comfort Israfel, because she could see it all too clearly. He had been on the precipice, hiding his suffering behind a carefully practiced smile. Now he was plummeting inside, falling off the invisible edge.*

Raziel aimed for the door.

No. No. This was too painful.

But she and Raziel were gone, back into the same corridor, the deep silence washing over them with a peace that suggested nothing had taken place.

How could Raziel do this? How could he leave Israfel there, when Israfel's pain was so obvious and crushing?

There was a soft sound of rustling and breath.

Raziel turned and Lucifel stood beside him, like an ashen shadow among more shadows, her thin body leaning casually against the wall, her face lacking any kind of smile. Her crimson eyes bored into Angela so keenly, Angela feared Lucifel could see another soul behind her brother Raziel's shell. Lucifel lifted her hand, showing Raziel two fingers.

"Two days," she said, her voice as ashen as her looks.

Lucifel resembled the embodiment of sickness, like she could die at any minute despite the hatred compelling her to live. Her skin was like Troy's, yet had an unhealthier cast to it, as if she'd been buried in a deeper darkness for years.

"And after that," Lucifel continued, "things are going to change."

She smiled in her terrible way.

"What are you talking about?" Raziel said worriedly.

Lucifel marched past him with her fearful stride, on into the darkness.

After that, Angela's mind shifted; she felt like a part of her heart had crumbled to pieces, and she screamed in hideous pain, watching from a dreadful place as Lucifel shrieked and moaned in agony, as an infant was torn from her by one set of hands while she lay on a white table in a beautiful room, blood streaming from her in torrents. Her rage was like a storm, and yet she could do nothing, so few were the sympathetic faces surrounding her.

Angela's mind shifted again, thrusting her into a montage of horror.

Israfel knelt down to stab Lucifel through the heart, crying out in victory.

Lucifel slaughtered people one by one with the crystalline blue Glaive.

Finally, Angela found herself on a stairway resembling the one she'd summoned to Luz, the very same Ladder the human souls in the Netherworld had used to climb high and far to safety. Its actual steps appeared to be made of both light and crystal, their size mind-boggling, their beauty almost indescribable.

The Ladder ended at a mass of glowing cloud, its outer rims swirling around an immense hole of nothingness. The spot resembled a dark blemish on the face of the universe.

A deep sickness wormed into the depths of her soul.

No. She had seen this before. She didn't want to again. Yet the more Angela screamed, the more Raziel's slender legs climbed the beautiful Ladder to the fringes of the heavens, taking her with him.

He sprinted toward the gaping mouth of nothingness.

He was tired, bloody. Panting and heaving for breath.

Feathers and crimson rained down from the sky, drifting in macabre clouds throughout the twilight. An immense war raged on around them. Angels fought, bled, plummeted, and died. Vicious-looking serpents with feathered plumes *on their heads snapped at their broken bodies. Raziel continued to run faster and ascend farther. Now he was at the threshold of the void at the bridge's pinnacle. He stepped beyond it.*

Angela screamed again, bombarded by flashes of light and the sensation of time and space warping around her. Still inside of Raziel, she knew they had entered whatever Realm hovered like a portal above the carnage below, and it appeared to her in these flashes of Raziel's memory as a grim and empty nightmare. There were dark walls, hieroglyphic writing emanating cold blue light, and a gaping sense of life-lessness. Still he continued, and at last he stopped.

There was another flash of light.

Raziel argued with someone, then begged and pleaded.

"Tell them the truth," he demanded, his great wings snapping in emphasis. "End this horror that you started."

Angela looked up with Raziel's eyes.

The face staring into hers froze her spirit with terror.

This was Angela's face, Angela's eyes. Oh, but also so much different.

This person was neither male nor female, yet somehow the creature still combined all the beauty of both—just like Israfel's unspeakable perfection. It had Raziel's sharp features—also Angela's. And it had the dark aura of Lu-cifel herself. Numerous wings extended from its back, every feather a shade of red, bronze, and gray. Bluish veins striped its skin with tigerlike beauty, creating a dreadful but lovely pattern against chalk-pale skin. Black hair fell from the creature's head in a curtain of pin-straight ebony, but those eyes—those eyes—

Its eyes were as green as the Grail, so piercing that they seemed to reach down into Angela's very soul and shred it apart with a glance. Raziel continued to speak, and this creature that resembled all the Supernal angels combined merely stared at him like the embodiment of terror.

She felt Raziel's mouth stop moving.

The godlike creature in front of Angela lifted its hand.

Light and fire tore through her, through Raziel. They twisted in mad horror. Raziel began to run, forcing her to run with him.

Still the blasts of pain assaulted them again and again.

Warmth—blood—poured out of Raziel. Angela thought she might pass out with pain as his wings were shredded to fleshy ribbons.

Another flash of light. Another shift in her consciousness.

Now she and Raziel tumbled off the same bridge they had used to enter the highest part of Heaven, and worst of all, Raziel could no longer fly. He plummeted. Angela felt all his inner agonies. There was an image of Lucifel and Israfel flashing before her—certainly Raziel's final thoughts, his greatest regrets.

The ether was so deep it felt like forever until some kind of ground rose up to meet them.

But Angela knew it had come when Raziel's pain ceased, and that last image of Israfel faded away along with the endless terror. Unwillingly, she called out to Israfel one last time.

She doubted he could hear.

Twenty-two

I remembered the day my heart broke, and from that hour,
I kept the echo of his dying voice within me. —ISRAFEL

Help me . . . save me . . .

Israfel opened his eyes, straightening his body from where it slumped against the wall of Tress Cassel's house. He tipped his head back, taking shallow breaths. Wind whistled through the broken windows of the building, teasing the feathers of his hair. Beneath the sigh of the icy air, Angela Mathers's voice echoed.

Help me . . .

The words were fainter than before. She was probably deep within Hell by now.

Israfel sighed and stared off into the darkness of Luz's seemingly eternal night. He flexed his wings. One of them had been shot with the humans' bullets and twitched painfully whenever he moved it. Another bullet had torn through his shoulder. Over the hours, both bullets had been pushed out by his body, and they now lay in little pools of blood on the floor.

Israfel picked up one of the bullets and passed it between his fingers, examining the smooth metal.

They were such insignificant things, and yet so painful.

Finally, he let the bullet drop and roll near one of the dead humans in the room. Every last Vatican officer had been killed, but there would be more. Israfel had been protected by enough guards in his many millennia of existence to understand what would happen to him next.

Soon, more soldiers would come, and he would either die or be imprisoned.

Israfel's astral energy had been woefully depleted by the battle to save Tress and her mother. Now he needed to wait to build up his strength. Meanwhile, Angela Mathers's voice grew fainter in his mind. At this point, it had almost gone silent. Israfel clutched at his stomach and took another shuddering breath. A door behind him opened and shut, and he flinched.

Feet padded in his direction. Gloriana stooped before him reverently, offering him a bowl of broth with vegetables.

Israfel smiled at her but waved away her kindness.

"It's the least I can do," she whispered. "Please."

He took the bowl and held it to his lips, sipping politely. But Israfel couldn't stomach much more human food. Nearly retching at the meaty taste of the broth, he dropped the bowl. Soup splashed onto his legs and the floor. Gloriana cried out softly, already mopping the broth from his legs with her dress's hem.

"Enough, woman," he said to her. "Take your daughter and go. You have kept your part of the bargain, and I have kept mine. There is no reason for you to linger here any longer. You know that reinforcements will arrive."

"They will kill you," Gloriana hissed with anxiety.

Israfel stared out into the snowy night. "I won't make it

easy for them. But if you are referring to their weapons, it will take many, many of those bullets to kill me."

Her eyes widened. "But if they shot you in the head—"

"Even so."

She looked him over with a pale face. "My daughter and I will always be grateful to you. If you ever need me for anything more—"

Israfel sighed with the irony. "It is you who need me. Indeed, everyone needs me. They simply don't know it yet." He covered his stomach with a hand and closed his eyes, trying to forget the pain in his head and wings. "But that is no one's fault but mine. Perhaps I deserve this humiliation for my sins. Greatness begins with fallen pride. It is something my brother, Raziel, often quoted. Proud fool that I was, I didn't believe him. Yet I loved when he said such things to me . . ."

There was a long silence.

"Aren't creatures like you above sin?" Gloriana said softly.

Israfel opened his eyes again to find Tress creeping into the room. She took one glance at Israfel and tears rolled down her round cheeks. He held out a slender hand to her, and she crept forward, taking courage from his kindness. "No. We are not above sin. We merely have different sins. Yet there are some common to all creatures with spirit and soul. I am guilty of some of the greatest sins that there are or shall ever be. Whether I wished it or not."

Tress held Israfel's hand tightly. "Are you staying here?" she whispered.

Her little head turned in the direction of the dead men, and Israfel grabbed her chin, forcing Tress to look at him. "Yes, I will be staying here. But you and your mother shall leave. That is an order, Tress. You will obey your angel, correct?"

She nodded and cried a little more.

Israfel stroked her cheek. "I had little ones like you once upon a time. They were twins, a male and a female, and they often cried out when I had to leave them alone, sometimes for days on end. It broke my heart to know their pain. Will you promise me that you will do what they could not, and refuse to cry?"

"What were their names?" Tress said. She rubbed her eyes.

"Rakir and Nunkir," Israfel said. "But they are no longer little like you, dear. You must be the same and become stronger for your mother."

Tress took a deep breath and let go of Israfel's hand. "Okay. I won't cry."

"Good." He let go of her chin. "Now go to your mother and do not enter this room again. I will see you again someday, little one."

She refused to say good-bye but brushed Israfel's wings with a finger. Tress picked up a fallen feather and held it to her chest. Then she raced out of the room to resume gathering together the last possessions that hadn't been broken.

"Thank you again," Gloriana said. "I hope that you survive, and that you find the Archon as soon as possible. For us all. But, please, answer this one question for me. If an angel dies, where does his soul go?"

Israfel remembered Raziel plummeting to his death. He remembered the millions of angels who had died that long-ago day when Lucifel nearly destroyed the hope Israfel was carrying inside of him. Yet the more he remembered, the more he knew that this human woman could not understand what he was about to say. "His soul goes back to its original home," he whispered.

Gloriana accepted Israfel's answer with a pensive expression.

Israfel closed his eyes and rested, listening to Tress and her mother mill around the room and gather a few more belongings. Eventually, the door shut, and they were gone to escape to safety, and he was alone with the smell of human death.

Without wishing to, Israfel stepped into the past that danced before his tired eyes. Sorrow haunted him. Sin stained his hands with blue blood. In the loneliness of Ialdaboth he existed, wept without tears, and dreamed without any real dreams. Time slipped past him like a swift current to nowhere.

Israfel, Raziel, and Lucifel were not like the other angels. It had taken the Father's death for Israfel to realize the terrible truth.

It had all been a carefully crafted lie. They'd never had a home at all.

Sleep overtook Israfel fitfully. His body was so weak that he could no longer sit up or keep his eyes open for long. After a while the howl of the icy wind poured into the broken home again. Hands grabbed him and tied back his wrists and wings. A soft cloth was wrapped around his mouth and cinched tightly at the back of his head. Finally, he was lifted and slid into something with a cold metal floor.

He awakened by degrees to a dark room of gleaming candlelight.

Israfel stroked the metal floor with his fingertips, and then found the strength to tilt his head and look up.

He was in a gilded cage with thick bars. A velvet cushion had been kindly set in a corner for him, along with one or two goblets of water. Prayer wards written in the Tongue of Souls had been fastened to the outside of the bars where he couldn't reach them.

Israfel peered between the bars, catching sight of a bevy of men with long black robes and coats cinched at the waist. They were human priests, discussing something in earnest, arguing every now and then with whiny upraised voices. Eventually a younger priest caught sight of Israfel awake and motioned in a panic for the others to be quiet. They all turned around and stared at him, fear shining in their eyes. Everyone knew Israfel shouldn't have been caged, yet no one had the courage to free him.

His physical strength was back to a considerable degree. Israfel bit cleanly through the cloth set in his mouth.

The satin fabric slid from his lips to the floor of his golden cage.

"Why am I in here?" he said softly.

The priests stared at Israfel, their eyes widening in awe at the melody of his voice. But no one moved.

"Do you know who I am?" he demanded. "If so, you shall release me now."

Silence.

Israfel pursed his lips, looking over each human in turn. He would be sure to remember their faces and souls.

At last, an old priest with thick white hair broke out of the shadows and approached Israfel's cage slowly. He knelt down and looked at Israfel with respect. "Forgive us, but we had no choice."

Israfel stood up, leaning over him. "Your name. I do not speak to a creature without the knowledge of its proper name."

"Schrader," the old man said with an awed but tired voice. "Please call me Father Schrader."

"My name is Israfel," Israfel said. He moved to extend his hand with the palm down as he had done so many times in the past as Archangel. But his hands were tied, and golden bars separated him from the humans anyway. He tried not to show his indignation as he felt crimson stripes blush along his cheeks. "Now you will explain to me why you have dared to imprison one of the Supernals. Was it not wiser to kill me?"

Father Schrader lifted his hands in supplication. "You don't understand. We know better than to kill you."

"But not," Israfel said dangerously, "to treat me with due respect?" He didn't give anyone time to answer. "Yet I can see you are all nervous fools. Perhaps you are right and this is your way of feeling safer. If so, remain in your happy illusion."

Israfel manipulated the ether and undid the ropes tying back his slender wrists.

The priests murmured in distress. A few stepped forward, but Father Schrader gestured for them to stand back. He turned again to Israfel. "Prince of Heaven, we are in dire need of your help. We have been aware of your presence in this city since your appearance a year ago in St. Mary's—"

"That pitiful church," Israfel said with real disgust. "It is now stained with the blood of your people. But make no mistake. I did not come for your sake, to save you from the demon. I had come for the Archon. Only one of those young women that night had proven herself to be the soul I was searching for. She is now gone from you. I too shall be leaving."

Father Schrader's face paled, and he appeared to realize something with shock. Silent for a while, he finally said, "Why haven't you left already?"

Israfel regarded him with disdain. The arrogant attitude of these men was so much different from the respectful innocence of Tress and her mother. "I cannot until I reach the proper door. But now that I am aware of its existence, I will find it soon, and then I will leave. Caging me will only prolong matters to your detriment."

Father Schrader turned back to his companions, and they discussed more, many of the humans gazing at Israfel intermittently with fear, some of them with wonder, a few with pathetic superiority. At last, they all seemed to reach an agreement on something. Father Schrader approached the cage and knelt down again. "Once again, we beg your forgiveness for caging you. You are right in your judgment of us as fools, Prince Israfel. We fear what we do not understand. To us, you are a figure of mythology and legend come to life and a few of us remember vividly the nightmarish evening in St. Mary's Cathedral last year. This is human fear at work, not disrespect." Father Schrader lowered his head with a shamed expression. "Right now, we are on our knees ready to give you all you desire in exchange for your generous help. The city of Luz is cut off from the rest of the world. The snow and ice continue and worsen by the day. Worse, there is a portal to Hell itself that has opened in our city. In the name of God, we beg you to seal it."

"One catastrophe among many more to come," Israfel said shortly. "You are right in thinking I alone can save you from the approaching silence. You are wrong in thinking that your worship in exchange is an acceptable offer. I need absolutely nothing from you."

"The Archon must be stopped," a young woman shouted confidently. She was one of the few females mixed in among the men, though she wore the same long black coat. Her face was scornful.

Father Schrader rounded on her instantly. "Lizbeth!"

Israfel gestured for silence. He turned to her. "The Archon will not be stopped. Her existence was to some degree inevitable. You are merely questioning Her potential. How like you to lack any faith in your own kind. Judging by what I have experienced of humanity, you are nothing but savages dancing on a planet as ephemeral as a snowflake. But this world is the linchpin connecting the Realms, and so I have no choice but to consider you and deal with you all. You have the eye of God on you, then. But closing one portal to Hell will not save you. Another may open elsewhere, and I will already be gone. This process will continue until I change things."

Israfel refrained from saying that he was satisfied with the circumstances. The humans were ready to take him to the threshold of the portal he needed to enter. As for sealing it, he was sorely tempted not to save them from their fate. From what he had seen so far, human pride and cruelty had few boundaries.

He stared at the priests, aware that he appeared weak and somewhat human but had thankfully managed to maintain a majestic demeanor.

Silence descended again.

"You saved Gloriana Cassel from being captured by the city's police force," Father Schrader finally said. "Why?"

Israfel narrowed his eyes. "I do not see why that is your concern."

Father Schrader cleared his throat. A distant look came to his eyes, like he was thinking of someone specifically as he spoke. "She and her daughter were blood heads. But they will not be able to run forever from the higher authorities in the city. If you help us seal the portal to Hell, we will work to suspend the arrest on her and grant blood heads throughout the city amnesty unless they are caught explicitly in the act of witchcraft."

Israfel kept silent, staring at each human again with icy coolness. He wouldn't show the emotion outwardly, but he couldn't allow Tress to die. She was his responsibility now. It would be a blow to his pride as an angel, as someone who had watched his own adopted chicks suffer in the past and the present.

Besides, as Israfel had said, closing one portal would not be the end of it all.

"Will you help us, Prince?" Father Schrader said. There was real hope behind his eyes.

Israfel knelt down so that he stared directly into the old priest's face. "If I do, remember this. When the new era comes, and I am lord over everything that exists, I can bring you back. You and your fellow men. You will then have new bodies, but they will belong to me, and unlike me, you will not be immortal. You will instead die and be reborn over and over again according to my wishes, but never leaving me, always clinging to my memory and my service. *That* is what I will receive as true payment if you do not keep your word."

Father Schrader folded his hands together and bowed in reverence. "Of course," he said. He trembled violently. "As you wish."

Israfel straightened. "Then I will follow you to this door."

His brief search was over. Israfel was about to enter his sister's kingdom, but Heaven would also not be far away.

He sang, manipulating the ether around him as he had learned to do so long ago. Israfel lifted his voice, changing the pitch and tone when required, allowing his own energy to throb throughout the small room. He sang the words he had awakened to that ancient day near the Nexus of souls, when he'd first opened his eyes to the starlight above him.

The atoms of the gold bars began to hum, rearranging themselves.

Israfel was the Creator Supernal. It was a trifle for him to open a cage. Before the priests' eyes, the gold froze. Israfel touched the metal, it shattered with a dull *crack*, and chunks of gold dropped to the floor like glass shards. As the pieces reached the ground, they melted again to blazing golden droplets.

Everyone flinched as the hot metal hissed against cold stone.

Carefully, Israfel stepped over the shining mess on the ground. He brushed by the prayer wards stuck to the cage, and they curled up, burning to ashes. Israfel tried not to display the horrendous pain in his head as the priests led him along dark corridors lined with devotional images. Many of his escorts proceeded cautiously, keeping a careful distance from him.

Eventually, their group stepped into an enormous room of dark stone. Green velvet curtains hung listlessly over the windows.

"The portal materializes in the shape of a door and changes positions all throughout the city," Father Schrader whispered. "It appears to respond to the desperate desires of souls."

"Because a demon has taken command of it," Israfel said. He paused in front of a blank wall that he knew hid the door. The energy of its presence throbbed throughout the room and into his bones. "All your study and theology, yet you've become no wiser about how my sister Lucifel operates. She is only taking advantage of your unfortunate situation. How did you find the portal here?"

The old priest sighed. "We used a deranged mental patient who claimed she could see it. She finally told us that she'd been seeing it for a while but hadn't summoned the courage to enter. She disappeared last night—after a long search for her, we believe she finally entered the door, and it hasn't moved since."

The human named Lizbeth drew in closer again, listening with her gaze riveted on Israfel.

"Because the demon inside has what he wants," Israfel said. "There is no further need to play games. What was the name of the girl?"

"Stephanie Walsh."

That was the girl who'd thought she'd been the Archon, but most certainly wasn't. Stephanie Walsh had been the adopted daughter of a demon. It seemed the particular demon toying with this portal knew exactly how to make the Archon miserable. Angela Mathers must certainly need Israfel's help. But the odds were not good that he'd reach her in time.

Israfel stepped forward and sang. The wall buckled, twisted, and then as if it had been hidden behind a veil, the door solidified in all its grotesque immensity. The priests gasped and ringed the room as reality warped before settling again, sending a dull pulse of energy through Israfel like a shockwave. He glided for the door gracefully and examined the carvings on its surface, tracing his finger over the black wood.

He smiled to himself at the audacity of the iron snake as a doorknob.

Apparently, this demon had a sense of humor.

"This is a childishly simple lock to open," Israfel said with a sigh.

There was a sudden flurry of raised voices, the scuffling of shoes on stone.

Israfel turned around.

The priests stood behind him rows deep. More of them had entered the room and taken their positions along the walls, in the center of the chamber. They all stared at Israfel with stony faces. Every single one of them regarded him with cautious arrogance. Many held long knives. Father Schrader was in their midst, but as a captive. He struggled with a wild fear in his eyes, but a blow to the back of the head stopped him quickly. He sank to his knees, gasping, anguish on his face.

"What is the meaning of this sudden idiocy?" Israfel muttered.

Lizbeth broke from her companions and approached Israfel without hesitation. "Prince Israfel, you are a great angel," she said softly. "You are one of the most powerful beings in existence. But unlike what Father Schrader so idealistically thinks, paying deference to beings superior to ourselves will no longer help humanity survive." Lizbeth stopped a safe distance away from him. Her expression grew more intense. "In the course of my more occult studies at Westwood's university, I recently became aware of something spectacular: the powers of angel blood. Angel blood can be used to heal wounds. When someone drinks it, it can reveal secrets of the past and future. And," she said in a much harsher tone of voice, "it can be used to seal portals to and from the other Realms."

Israfel's heart beat faster. Dizziness threatened him. But he remained stoic and majestic. "Come quickly to the point," he said icily.

Lizbeth took a deep breath. For a moment, she seemed

cowed by Israfel's imperious attitude, but she recovered. Her voice trembled anyway. "The Archon has abandoned Earth to its fate. Angela Mathers has left us to begin her reign over Hell. It is the end, and all we can do is try to prolong our lives as much as possible. But your words have also proven that God and his servants are not what we have been taught since our youth. We must now take matters into our own hands. With your blood, we will seal any more portals that arise."

Anger crackled inside of Israfel like a thunderhead. This kind of outrage was almost ludicrous.

"You would dare . . ." Israfel could no longer speak. His body trembled.

Lizbeth shivered but kept her voice firm. "Angela Mathers refused to protect the blood heads who shared her own suffering. That might have been her salvation. Instead, she chose a different path." She looked at Israfel, and her irises swiftly shaded over to a familiar bright crimson. "Much like how you chose a different path, right, Israfel?"

Israfel stiffened. His heart raced. Those were Lucifel's eyes. But it was not Lucifel speaking.

There was only one other possibility.

Lucifel and Raziel had two offspring born of their forbidden union: Zion and Mikel. According to official angelic records, they had been executed. But more than anyone else, Israfel knew those records to be cleverly constructed lies. With Zion's true origins thoroughly hushed, he currently ruled Heaven as Archangel in Israfel's stead. Mikel, the female of the twins, had been born without a body as a pure spirit. But Israfel had made sure to imprison her in a body as soon as possible.

Mikel was a disease almost as dangerous as her mother. Israfel had a strong suspicion she'd been responsible for much

of the Archon's suffering one year ago. If not directly, Mikel
had at least set the wheels of fate in motion.

Her ability to possess and manipulate had made her a li-
ability since the morning of her birth.

Now, she was in the body of this human girl. Somehow,
she'd escaped her cage.

Israfel stared through the human's eyes and into Mikel's,
aware of the venom within him burning through his usually
elegant expression. "So the real truth is that *you* have led
them to this utter foolishness, Mikel?" Israfel whispered. "I
suppose my pangs of guilt were misplaced. I was absolutely
right in caging you like your mother."

The surrounding priests murmured among themselves,
obviously confused by the new direction of the conversation.

Lizbeth—or more correctly Mikel—strolled closer to Israfel completely unafraid. The angel behind the girl's eyes
never took her own off Israfel's, just like when they'd entered
the room. Now he recognized this confidence for what it was.

"This is the result of your murders and your selfish cruelty, Israfel," Mikel murmured in Lizbeth's voice. "Blindness
on your part. You thought you could imprison me and that
would be the end of your troubles. You thought that tortur-
ing me would give peace to your own wounded soul. But
you are wrong in every way imaginable. My torture will not
give you peace. And besides, I found a way out of my prison
that you never expected. On the night that Angela Mathers
mistakenly summoned Lucifel's shadow to Earth, she also
summoned *me*. I entered the body of her friend Nina Willis,
but that poor girl was murdered shortly after, forcing me to
search again for another body to inhabit. This one suited
me well enough, and so I observed Angela day-by-day without her ever knowing. And I also watched you. I watched as

you suffered and grew hungry, weaker and weaker by the hour. Now, here you are as pathetic as I once was. Pangs of guilt, indeed. What did you think of being in a cage, Israfel? What will you think of the pain these humans will now inflict on you to keep themselves alive? Perhaps if you show me you've learned compassion again, I'll let you enter the door unharmed."

"You say I've tortured you, yet it was I who kept your rebellious spirit in check for aeons." Israfel laughed softly at the irony before him. Mikel dared to lecture him on the very faults she shared? He spoke again between gritted teeth. "Mikel, you think like the chick that you are. You know *NOTHING* of the pain I have been through in my many, many, many years of life. What can an infant like you possibly teach *me*?"

Mikel's anger burned through Lizbeth's face. Her whispers grew raw and petulant. "Just as I said, you think only of yourself. How many times must you be told, Israfel? Your actions, not mine, have brought this universe single-handedly to the brink of destruction. And in that black moment, you didn't think of anything or anyone. Not even my father, Raziel—"

"And as I said, you know *nothing*," Israfel reiterated. He tried to keep his voice as low as possible. He breathed hard, needles of pain running through his soul at the mention of Raziel's name. "Yet fool that you are, you would stand against me? If I survive, I can make you more miserable than you would ever think possible. There is no doubt you deserve it for this insolence." Israfel ached to smack her in the face. "You are your mother's daughter, chick. Certainly you've worked in her favor, manipulating the Archon into Hell."

Mikel's confidence faltered. Shock burned behind her eyes.

Israfel straightened proudly.

"There is much more to this moment than your twisted sense of justice. I know why you remain on this Earth. Who did you bribe to get Angela Mathers through the door? What other lives have you brought into your tragic mess?"

Mikel swallowed back her anger. Human tears bunched near Lizbeth's eyes as the angel's spirit affected her heart. "What does it matter? I merely led people to what they wanted most. I never forced them to do anything."

Israfel studied her carefully. Surely Mikel was the one who'd somehow involved the demon controlling the door. But she was too smart to reveal anything further. She had at the very least told some vulnerable human how to contact the demon and enlist his help—likely for some kind of personal gain connected to Angela. Then, the demon had taken the opportunity for what it was.

"Why?" Israfel said. "*Tell me, chick.*"

Mikel's voice cracked with pain. Her red eyes burned. "Because I want to die," she finally said in an anguished tone.

Israfel narrowed his eyes at her. "And only my sister can kill you."

Mikel and Lucifel shared certain special characteristics, and Mikel was an immortal spirit unable to be killed by ordinary means. It made sense.

"The Archon will refuse to open the Book," Mikel said. "But that action will set my mother free. Then, Lucifel will come to me, and the horror of my life will be over. The endless pain. The misery of living. I cannot bear being your instrument of torture any longer. I cannot bear this horrible nature I was born with . . ."

Israfel looked at her and real pity tugged at his heart. So many times he'd been tempted to feel the same way. But he couldn't help saying what he truly thought. "I will only say this one more time, you understand nothing and think like the chick that you are. You are not the only creature in the universe to suffer, Mikel. How dare you speak of selfishness when you have put countless lives in danger to end a life you see as pointless."

Mikel stared at him wide-eyed. She screamed and ran forward, striking Israfel across the face.

She fell back and wept, clutching at the hand she'd dared to raise against him.

Israfel gazed at her without any more emotion.

"All this time," she shouted at him, "and you've learned absolutely nothing new. Why should I save someone like you, Israfel? Now, you will reap what you've sown for so long."

The red light behind Lizbeth's eyes flickered and was gone.

Lizbeth stood in front of Israfel now, every trace of Mikel's soul and consciousness gone from her face. She blinked at Israfel as if she'd just awakened from some long and odd dream. She lifted her hand and examined it, seeming to remember that it might have struck an angel.

The surrounding priests had gone absolutely silent.

But the tension in the room had changed. They had witnessed Lizbeth's hand strike Israfel across the face.

The magical blood they sought trickled down the side of Israfel's cheek. He could be injured, maybe even killed. Israfel was a great angel, a legend, but he was still noticeably weak. They could follow through with their desperate act of sacrilege without any real repercussions. They might have casualties, but they could surely overpower Israfel with sheer numbers. Slowly, they closed in on him without saying a word.

Israfel knew better than to waste his strength just yet. It would take many cuts to kill him.

He looked at Father Schrader, who once again struggled with his captors.

The old priest's eyes were wide with horror.

Israfel unfurled his wings, silver light blazing around his body. He huddled on the ground and wrapped his pinions protectively around himself, knowing he had to at least keep the treasure inside of him from harm.

It didn't take much longer for the other priests to overcome their remaining fears.

With cries of triumph, they fell on him.

Twenty-three

I wanted to say with pride, that no matter how much time passed, or how much danger assaulted me, or how many temptations I met on my way, that my soul never changed. —TROY

The labyrinth's great tunnel was even darker than before. The water of the Styx River trickled and coursed beneath boulders fallen from the cavern ceiling. Piles of jagged rock littered the ground in every direction, and every so often another chunk clunked powerfully to the earth.

Troy lay silent and still, just breathing for a while.

Eventually, she pushed up shakily onto her hands and feet, rolling rubble off her back. She unfurled her wings and tried to stretch them but found herself blocked by the piles of rock to her right and left. She leaned forward but jumped back hastily, hissing with pain. Troy had broken a finger on her left hand.

Well, she had traveled for days on end hunting with worse injuries many times in the past. Her ankle that had been slowly healing over the course of days had at least gotten through the ordeal unharmed. Blood dripped into her eyes from a gash stinging her forehead.

The smell of more blood and burning flesh met her nose.

Troy flicked her ears, straining to catch any sounds of life in the darkness. A low moan and the sound of flapping wings could be heard beneath the trickle of the water.

She began to pick her way under, over, and around the rocks toward the noise. Troy climbed over one of the adult Hounds' corpses, her nails snagging in its mats of black feathers and hair. Her stomach growled with incredible hunger, and the smell of meat tormented her, but she never stopped until she'd left the corpse behind, turned a corner around a large rock, and found Nina Willis lying on her side, clutching at her leg and groaning softly.

Nina didn't even notice Troy approach. Her eyes were shut tightly, and her face was red from weeping. Fury perched by her side, one yellow eye cocked at the girl in concern. The Vapor looked at Troy.

Fury's thoughts touched Troy's mind like gentle whispers. *She is in great pain . . .*

Troy nudged Fury aside and sniffed at the steaming wound in Nina's flesh. The injury was bad. Surely the girl would eventually lose the leg.

Troy's wings tensed. Her stomach fluttered nervously. Nina's injury could be helped, but where was Juno? Troy straightened as much as the surrounding rocks would allow and sniffed the air, letting her ears do their work. Her keen eyes searched the darkness. Finally, she spied a tiny form huddled beneath a rock, its ragged black wings wrapped tightly around a body layered with little cuts.

Watch Nina, Troy said inwardly to Fury.

Juno's gaze locked with Troy's, her infantile eyes wide and moist. But she didn't move.

Troy neared her cautiously, and then settled down by Juno's side with her own wings folded tightly against her back.

Juno was bleeding, but otherwise she just seemed to be in shock. Troy tried to remember how her sister Hecate behaved when the other chicks were hurt. She tried to think back to the care her own mother desperately gave her. Leaning over, she clasped one of Juno's arms and slowly began to lick away the blood.

Juno whimpered and curled into Troy's side, trembling. Her little fingers clutched one of the Hounds' teeth, fallen from one of the corpses.

"You did well," Troy said. "Hecate would have been proud of you."

Juno took a little courage from the words and tried to show a braver face. They both knew that it was a miracle she had survived. Juno may have been the heir to the Underworld throne, but she was weak and a poor hunter. "Look, Auntie," she said with a hiss, holding out the tooth.

Troy broke away from her cleaning regimen and took the tooth from Juno, using one of her nails to dig out a hole. Troy then tied the tooth into Juno's hair, settling it next to the chick's much smaller trophies. Juno shook her head, and her eyes brightened at the sound of the bones and teeth rattling together.

"Clean yourself," Troy snapped at her, shoving Juno aside as the chick clambered back toward her.

Juno took on a wounded expression but settled into licking at the blood on her arms and wings.

"Now stay here," Troy said, and she wandered back to where Nina rested.

This time Nina noticed Troy creeping closer. The girl scrabbled backward despite her pain, rocks flying everywhere, momentarily horrified by Troy coming so near to her when she was so vulnerable. Fury screeched in distress. Then Nina seemed to remember where she was and why, and she slumped against the stone, completely exhausted by the pain. "Where's Angela?" she croaked pathetically.

Troy growled. "The demon must have taken her. We are now on our own."

Nina's face showed her fear, but she overcame her agony and tried to sit up to talk better, maybe even stand. Fury hopped nearer to Nina and clucked in displeasure.

Troy clamped a hand on Nina's shoulder and shoved her back down. "Not yet. It is too soon for you to move."

Nina slumped down again and rubbed at her tears. "How long will we have to stay here?"

"Until you can actually walk again," Troy said. "Perhaps a day. It is all we can afford. The only other solution would be to cut off your leg and carry you. Either way, you will lose the limb eventually."

"Cut it off with what?" Nina shouted.

Troy showed her teeth.

Nina shook her head violently. "I'll wait a day then."

"Of course," Troy said, not unsympathetic.

She sat on her haunches by Nina's side and tore some of the hem of Nina's dress. Slowly, Troy bandaged the wound. Nina gritted her teeth and sometimes screamed, but overall she sucked back the pain with admirable bravery. At the end of the process she was left sweaty and gasping, but the worst was now over. Her adrenaline would give her the painkillers she needed to keep going. That, and perhaps her concern for the Archon.

"I think that giant snake interfering was too convenient. And the rocks falling . . . Do you think it was a trap, to separate us from one another?" Nina said after a short silence.

Troy grunted. "You would be a fool to think otherwise."

"Will that snake demon kill Angela?" Nina said even more desperately.

"*No*," Troy said. "It is clear enough that he needs her alive. It is us he doesn't want here. Me especially."

Rocks tumbled nearby. Nina flinched, but Troy already recognized the familiar scrabble of little nails on stone. Juno's head popped up over a boulder, and then the Jinn chick climbed down the stone and over to Nina to curiously examine her injury. Troy held Juno back when she came too close. The chick was hungry too and couldn't be trusted around a weak human's wounds without supervision.

"But," Troy continued, "he will know eventually that this attempt to destroy us has failed."

"What next?" Nina said, coughing with pain. "We have to get out of here then—"

"Not yet," Troy snapped. "You are too weak."

"Then leave me," Nina shouted. "Angela needs you . . . not me."

Troy stared at her. "Never question why you exist and why you are where you happen to be. There is *always* a reason."

Nina looked at her wound and sighed.

Troy examined the shadows, her ears flicking nervously. "It is far from ideal. But we have no choice but to remain here for at least a few more hours. You must gather your strength. Juno and I must sleep. Even hunters like me cannot work miracles . . ."

Despite another glare from Troy, Juno curled next to Nina searching for warmth.

Nina stiffened, but when it became clear Juno wouldn't hurt her, she visibly relaxed. She stroked Juno's wings, tears of pain still rolling down her cheeks.

"Are you going to join us, Auntie?" Juno whispered with a little hiss.

"Yes," Troy growled at her. "Now be quiet and sleep. I will make sure to feed you when you awaken."

Juno watched her suspiciously, but eventually her golden eyes sealed shut. Fury returned with a strip of meat and swallowed it hastily before Juno could notice, then fluffed into a black ball on top of the little Jinn's warm back.

Troy settled beside them both in silence, but even when Fury and Nina also finally fell asleep, Troy did not stay completely true to her word and remained awake as long as she could, gazing out into the misty blackness, listening to the interrupted cascade of the Styx, searching for danger that could arrive at any moment.

For the first time in a long while, Troy broke down and let her wings shiver violently. Troy was afraid of few things but failure. Right now, she could not fail.

More than life depended on it.

Troy awakened to the noise of movement against rock.

She cursed herself inwardly for falling asleep, then cracked open an eyelid, searching the fog for signs of danger.

Their surroundings hadn't changed. Nina, Fury, and Juno slept curled together, their breathing timed to one another, the rise and fall of their chests slow and even. Troy watched them, swiveling her ears to catch the slightest sound. Nothing. It wasn't until her eyes had started to close again that she heard it.

A low and deep hiss. The sound of scales rubbing smoothly against stone.

Troy pushed up onto her hands and feet and peered into the shadows. There was the flicker of orange eyes, and then they blinked out. Faintly purplish glowing mist filled the air. A chilly breeze swept from nowhere and played with Troy's hair and feathers. She tensed her muscles, completely on the alert.

Abruptly, Python stepped out of the darkness and nearer to her field of vision. He was far enough away to stay out of immediate danger, but still close enough to keep Troy ready for the worst.

"What do you want?" she hissed lethally.

"A ludicrous question," Python said softly. "You knew I would return."

Troy flexed her fingers, rubbing her nails together. "Where is the Archon?"

"Safe," Python whispered. "And that's all you need to know."

"*Liar.*"

"Not at all," Python said. "You *also* know it is in my best interests to keep her alive."

Troy snarled angrily. "Alive doesn't mean safe."

Python smiled.

The hair began to rise along Troy's neck. Rage bubbled up within her. "Why not come closer so that I can rip into your face again? If you want to play, play with me. Leave the human and the chick out of it."

"You see"—Python shook his head—"that is where you're wrong. I didn't come to fight. I came to talk."

Troy snorted in amusement. "You do enough of that already."

Python's eyes flashed with irritation, but he regained his smooth composure quickly. "Troy, I have a pronounced aversion to your kind. You know that well. After all, am I not a legend to your ragged little race? And I'll admit, one of the crowning achievements of my life was to watch your namesake city fall, to see you all dispersed like vermin to every corner of the Underworld."

Troy clenched her nails into the ground so hard one of them snapped.

Python's snake eyes bored into her. "But you are a different one, Troy. I have taken interest in you since I first heard the tales of a Jinn hunter that was so feared, some of the rival Jinn Clans begged the demons to exterminate you. Seeing you in person like this is almost an honor. Despite what I had to suffer for it." Python rubbed the wound on his cheek. "But I am not like my mother. I can let the past go, even if you cannot."

Troy stretched her wings. "You are testing my patience with your incessant flattery."

"Not flattery," Python retorted. "The truth. You are different from most of your kind. Smarter, better senses, and dare I say somewhat more attractive on your own pitiful level. Perhaps I am not going too far in saying you are the epitome of what the Jinn can be, but most are not. Such a pity about your sister . . ."

Troy stiffened. "You know of her death?"

"Not just me. All of Hell. And from what I've heard, you are now an exile, abandoned by your own Clan because you chose to protect the Archon and Hecate's runt. Correct?"

Troy said nothing.

Python sat down on a rock and leaned back, crossing his legs. "But that isn't the only reason you're here, is it? You don't just want to protect the Archon. You want to return home. You want not only the safety of your world, but to enter it again as a hero. I suppose you think the death of your half-bred cousin will give you that."

He knew about Sariel? Troy shivered, her ears pressing back against her skull.

"I know where he is," Python whispered. "I can lead you right to him."

Troy froze.

Python's thin lips took on another smile. "Come with me, Troy. You and I can do each other much good."

"Why would you help me?" Troy snarled.

"It does seem quite the mystery, doesn't it?" Python laughed. "But if you need to know, I believe in you, Troy. Your sister was a pain to deal with and was frankly a weak and ineffective ruler for your people. You—on the other hand—I see as much more powerful and wise. You, I know, would put aside the old prejudices to keep your people alive. Yes, the runt is in the way. But what would it cost you to leave her and the human behind? Even better, kill the chick and you will automatically be Queen of the Jinn, correct? And I would make certain that your people would acknowledge the fact."

Troy stared at Juno, sleeping peacefully with one ear twitching. Juno was much like Hecate—impulsive, clumsy at hunting, and regrettably weak at the worst times.

Troy had suffered much to keep her alive. But would Juno be enough to keep the Jinn as a whole from going extinct?

Her heart began to race. Troy licked her lips.

"How easy it would be to just snap the chick's little neck," Python whispered. "She'd never even know. The same with the human. And, after all, what is she worth? No more than a walking pile of meat. Meat that could keep you alive, healthy, satisfied. It would only take seconds to make life easier for yourself . . ."

Troy breathed harder. Her vision swam.

"It must be so hard," Python continued, "to always live at the service of others. Keeping them happy and alive at your own expense. How much better to be Queen and turn the tables for a change."

Troy leaned over Juno. She saw Hecate dying. She saw her own mother starving to keep her alive. She didn't want the cycle of death to continue on and on, pitifully unchecked. And worse still, Sariel continued to escape her. Troy reached out and touched Juno's neck.

"All it takes," Python said, "is one twist of the wrist. Just one."

Juno rustled in her sleep. Her legs shuffled. "Auntie," she hissed softly.

The word scorched like lightning through Troy. She snatched her hand away from Juno and rounded on Python.

"*No deal, snake,*" she growled and flapped her wings violently.

Troy leaped for Python's neck. He dodged out of the way, leaving the nails of her hands and feet to scratch powerfully into the rock. Troy unhitched her nails from the stone.

She dropped back to the ground and raced for Python.

"You'll be sorry for your arrogance, you ragged crow," Python spat at her. "An idiot's refusal demands an idiot's reward."

Before Troy could slice into his face like last time, the purple mist surrounded Python's body and he disappeared. His orange eyes were the last thing to vanish.

Troy skidded to a stop among the jagged pebbles.

Fury had awakened and flew to Troy's shoulder, screeching in anger. Behind her, Troy could hear Juno and Nina awakening. They began to shout and begged to know what

was happening. Juno galloped to Troy's side and growled
out into the darkness, her miniature hackles raised, and her
wings stiff.

"The snake returned, just as I warned," Troy said, turning to face Nina.

Nina stared at Troy with wide eyes. "And?"

Troy breathed hard. "And I told him he wasn't wanted
here." Troy growled furiously at her. "Enough questions!"

"But—"

"*Silence*," Troy hissed dangerously. She slumped to the
ground, folding in her wings. She gasped for breath as if
she'd fought for hours, gritting her teeth and staring into the
darkness. Her wings shivered, then her entire body. No one
dared to come near her for a while. At last, Juno crept closer.

"Auntie," she whispered.

Troy ached to swat her away. Sariel had been so close yet
again. Now that chance was gone. Troy's people were at the
brink of disaster, and here she was stuck in a cavern with an
injured Revenant human and a Jinn chick who couldn't catch
a spider properly. She clenched her teeth and tried to keep
herself from doing something rash.

"Auntie," Juno hissed, "whatever happened, it is over
now. You are safe."

Troy relaxed a little, still shivering with anger.

"Thank you," Juno said. "For whatever you did." She
clasped Troy's leg.

Troy grabbed Juno's arm and made to fling her violently
aside. She relaxed and let go at the last second. "Come," Troy
said to no one in particular. "We will leave now and go forward. It is no longer wise to stay here."

No one spoke. But they obeyed and either hobbled behind
or followed Troy to the only opening available to them in

the cavern. The path was extremely dark, lit only by a few embers every one hundred feet. Nina would have immense difficulty in seeing, but she never complained. Troy led them in silence and refused to answer tentative questions put to her about what had happened. Yet the more she walked with Juno by her side, the stronger she felt, and the more a pride she'd never experienced before worked its way down to her soul.

It would be difficult. But there was no doubt inside her anymore.

Troy had made the right decision.

Nina read signs when they appeared, Troy did her best to catch and follow her cousin's scent, and after a while the journey settled into some kind of odd routine as they wound down, deeper into the labyrinth, probably closer to Lucifel with every step. Juno and Fury knew enough to stay in the background and communicate with each other through silence rather than words.

That left Troy and Nina to walk side by side through the long darkness.

Troy couldn't express the fear she felt inside. There was no proof, but she knew that Angela was in trouble and that they had to hurry. But the pace couldn't grow any faster with Nina injured and weak.

Nina often fell silent, her face taking on a grim expression that could have foreshadowed tragedy.

The lack of any other living presence in the labyrinth was troubling.

The demon who had lured them inside enjoyed the cruel game of seeing his victims struggle in his maze. Any period of relative quiet now seemed like the prelude to a grand trap.

Troy's wings quivered nervously as they exited a low and excruciatingly narrow passage. It dumped them into a cave that was more like a room with smoothly carved walls. The ceiling was so high that the torches set in its reaches resembled the stars. Troy knew that the labyrinth had to be connected at some point to the demon city of Babylon, and now she and the others appeared to be coming closer. Hieroglyphs covered the walls.

Nina ran her hand along the carvings, her face pale in the flicker of unearthly light. She muttered the passages, reading them to herself until she stopped, visibly afraid.

"We're trapped," she whispered.

Troy stared at her, her ears trying to catch any suspicious noise. "This entire maze is a trap. Do not speak unless you have something more useful to say."

Nina shook her head violently. "The writing says there's no way out. *We've reached a dead end.*"

"Impossible." Troy stomped over and shoved Nina out of the way, attempting to read the demonic script herself. Juno hovered by Troy's side, glancing from Troy to the wall and back again.

The words were hardly legible. Surely Nina had made a mistake.

"Stay here," Troy ordered everyone. She escaped into the blackness surrounding the flickering light and tried to inspect the fringes of the chamber. It was long and rectangular, the walls covered in writing that appeared ancient. Yet besides the narrow passage they'd used to enter, there seemed to be no real door out. Fury soared overhead, examining the areas Troy hadn't bothered flying to reach.

After a few minutes, Troy returned and Nina heaved a sigh of relief.

"You were right," Troy said. "We will have to turn around."

Nina shut her eyes, probably unable to imagine retracing that many steps only to get lost again.

Wait! Master! Fury's thoughts interrupted Troy's with sudden force. The Vapor landed with a thud at Troy's feet, dancing and flapping her large wings. *There is an opening in the ceiling, high above. But it can only be reached by flying. The human . . .*

Troy glanced at Nina. The girl would have to be carried.

"Tell me you're not afraid of heights," Troy said to her.

Nina's face lost the rest of its color. Perhaps she was remembering that night she'd fallen from one of Luz's high towers, and Troy had dived to rescue her from plunging into Earth's frigid sea. "We have to climb?" Nina managed to squeak out.

Troy grunted. "You would never make it all the way. Especially in such a pitiful state. I will fly and carry you."

"But—"

"Do you suggest that I leave you here?" Troy snapped. "Either way, make your decision. We don't have much time."

Nina seemed to search the darkness for an invisible clock counting down their seconds. Then she nodded and approached Troy awkwardly. "Won't I be kind of heavy?"

"I've carried trophies twice your size back to the Warrens," Troy said. "You are little more than air."

"Oh. Okay then . . ."

Troy wrapped her arms around Nina's chest and waist. With a commanding nod at Juno, she spread her wings and flapped them powerfully, bouncing thunderous echoes off the walls. In seconds they had lifted from the ground and begun to soar upward. It had been awhile since Troy felt the warm breeze whipping back her hair, the miraculous effect of the air buoying her aloft.

Nina's weight barely affected Troy. She ascended faster and faster, aware of Juno and Fury soaring close behind.

They aimed for a pinhole in the ceiling that became larger and larger the closer they approached. Large script circled their exit to freedom. Snakes carved into the stone stared back at them with cruel glittering eyes.

Nina spoke in Troy's ears, her voice shaky with fear. She was reading the words that surrounded the porthole. "*What you thought was Up is actually Down. In this room, a hundred Hells are found.*"

A scorching sense of danger shot through Troy. She spread her wings stiffly, trying to brake.

She was too late. Eerie laughter echoed behind the noise of Troy's wing beats. The stone snakes' eyes glowed brightly.

Troy's own momentum pushed her through. The others followed a moment later.

With a terrifying sound of metal on stone, the porthole closed like an eye blinking shut.

Twenty-four

The more I longed for home, the farther
away it became. —Troy

The world tilted and whirled.

Troy smacked into what should have been a ceiling but was actually a floor.

Nina dropped from her arms with a loud cry, and Troy accidentally bit the inside of her own cheek, smarting at the blood filling her mouth. The laughter had faded.

Troy cursed herself anyway. She should have recognized the illusion at some point on her own. Recently, perhaps in the monotonous course of their journey, the landscape had actually twisted upside-down. The effect had been so subtle, even Troy hadn't noticed as she should have.

She pushed up from the floor, spitting out blood. Her injured ankle throbbed painfully.

Juno huddled against her, even more wide-eyed than usual. Fury also seemed entranced as she stared out into the dimly lit room in utter silence. Nina groaned and rubbed at her head as she sat up.

"What just happened?" she muttered, wincing as her leg

brushed the floor. Most of the blood on her bandage had dried to an ugly black color, but the wound would continue to ooze for quite a while before decay set in.

Troy slammed her fist against the floor and gasped for breath.

She rounded on Fury. The bird broke from her spell just in time.

Troy swiped at the crow angrily, and Fury skittered aside, screeching. *Forgive me*, Fury begged in her whispery little voice. *You know I cannot read! I didn't know—*

Forget it, Troy snapped. She stood and rubbed at her hand, stroking her nails. *I will deal with you later.*

Fury shivered but wisely dropped the subject.

Troy stretched her wings and folded them inward again as she glanced at their surroundings. There were embers and the soft blue-green luminescence covering some of the ceiling that Troy recognized from her own home in the Underworld. But everywhere, obsidian as smooth and reflective as glass jutted from the floor in a new maze of mirrors. Juno had fixated on one of her hundreds of reflections and began to approach it cautiously. She tapped at it and retreated back to Troy's side, whimpering.

"What is this?" Nina said, wincing again as she tried to stand. Beads of sweat dotted her dirty forehead.

Troy looked to her right and left but found nothing besides more mirrors.

Somehow, there was probably a way out. But finding it in this mess of illusions would be dangerously time consuming.

She sniffed. Sariel's scent was now completely gone, though they were actually deeper in Hell, which would be better for finding Angela.

Troy examined herself in the mirror. The bluish tinge to

her lips looked faded and dull in the equally bluish light. Far from looking intimidating, Troy appeared as ravaged as she felt. Her hair was more knotted than usual, and her wings had only started to grow back the missing fourth of her feathers. Old scars somehow looked more prominent and monstrous. There seemed to be little left of the High Assassin who brought so much terror to the Underworld.

"There will be an exit," Troy said, turning away from her pathetic reflection. "The demon would be bored otherwise. So we must find the way out. Now."

Their little group was alone and terribly vulnerable. Troy dropped onto her hands and feet and prowled cautiously around their perimeter.

The room was smaller than the mirrors made it look.

Troy found the first corner to turn easily enough. There were even more mirrors here. The others followed and cautiously fanned out, their footsteps slower and more tentative the more they walked away from one another. Troy licked away at the blood inside of her mouth, her stomach growling pathetically. Nina wobbled and leaned against one of the obsidian mirrors.

"Are you all right?" Troy said, examining her keenly.

Nina straightened, but the tired look in her face didn't change. "Would you mind if I just stayed here until you found the exit? I don't think I'll be much help as I am anyway . . ."

That was reasonable enough.

Troy nodded. "Juno, come."

"But, Auntie, I think—"

"NOW," Troy said.

Juno scampered to Troy with Fury hopping behind at a safe distance.

"She will be fine," Troy muttered to Juno as they rounded

another reflective corner. "The more you haunt her with your presence, the less she will heal. She needs to become stronger, and without relying on the fickle compassion of a Jinn chick."

Juno's ears flattened, but she said nothing. Silently, she watched as Troy untied bones from her hair and dropped them at key areas to use as a path back to their starting point. The silence continued as they wandered in relative circles. Yet the more they wandered, the more Troy's impatience grew, and an evil sense of being watched oppressed her.

She stopped abruptly next to a bone on the floor that she didn't recognize. Juno smacked into her legs and plopped onto the ground, shaking her wings.

"Auntie?" Juno whispered.

Troy ignored her, trying to think, staring at the bone. Her mind had been working on a faint memory. Now it came back to her with crushing force. A rumor had been passed down among the Jinn that the demons had chambers like this one sprinkled throughout Hell, especially their city of Babylon, and that they used them not only as a way to punish transgressors and enemies, but as a battleground for two equally matched opponents.

Amid these mirrors, they would drop two Jinn and starve them before forcing them to battle each other to the death.

There was no reason to think this demon would ignore tradition. But he hadn't even bothered to have an opponent attack Troy or Juno.

That left Nina.

Troy broke away from the bone of her ancestor in revulsion. "Hurry. We must return!"

Without any further explanation, she galloped as swiftly as she could. Her feet slid across the stone floor, its chill leeching upward through her palms and spreading throughout her body.

The demon couldn't kill the girl. Angela would never forgive Troy for letting Nina die so easily, and besides, it was now a matter of pride for Troy to keep her alive.

At least that was what Troy told herself. Why else would she be acting so foolishly?

This time, the laughter that followed her sounded loud and clear.

Twenty-five

Only the strongest souls escape becoming
my marionettes. —PYTHON

Nina wasn't sure if it was her tiredness or her hunger causing her to hallucinate. She felt like a zombie staring at her reflection, trying to wish away her weakness and pain. Angela needed her, and Nina was stuck so far away. It actually hurt her inside, and the questions within her echoed that pain. Why had she been brought back from death? Who brought her back? Worse still, how could she prove she still had a reason to live?

Perhaps it was those thoughts that summoned Stephanie Walsh's image in one of the obsidian mirrors.

Stephanie was uncomfortably different from the person Nina feared so much before she'd died. Her red hair was much shorter and more ragged. Stephanie also looked older, as if she'd aged ten years in the span of one, with a weariness look pulling down all her features. She wore a white jumpsuit instead of the Pentacle Sorority uniform, and her characteristic smug smile had vanished. But her green eyes burned with a fiercer fire than ever.

"Hello, Nina," Stephanie's reflection whispered. "I must admit, you're the last person who deserves Hell. Was it me who put you here?"

Nina stared. That was one thing she couldn't remember. This was all so dreamlike and surreal.

A warm breeze brushed at her hair.

"I am sorry about that," Stephanie said. "If it was my fault." Stephanie managed to smile. "I know. I look different, right? My bloodshot eyes. My ridiculous hair. I guess I do deserve that. I made fun of you for all those years. You said you saw dead people in your dreams and no one cared or believed you. The people who did believe you tortured you for it. Now, I see people in my dreams. And I hear voices in my head."

Stephanie shivered.

"And *her* voice is the worst one of all . . ."

Nina shivered with her.

"One of those voices called me here, Nina. I didn't want to go through the door. I cried and begged not to. But this demon told me that if I did, I had a second chance. Angela is down here, isn't she?" Stephanie's voice hardened. "There's still a lot I need to say to her. Where is she, Nina? Do you know?"

Nina shook her head. Her heart raced and her limbs chilled. For some indefinable reason, she felt rooted to the spot.

Stephanie appeared to step closer. Instantly, her reflection multiplied with her shift in position, gleaming from countless other obsidian mirrors. She smiled again and flexed her hands.

"Nina, I know we haven't gotten along in the past. But I want you to think hard about something. What has Angela really done for you? What kind of positive influence has she been in your life?"

"She's my friend," Nina whispered.

Stephanie shook her head. "That's not an answer." She sighed. "Nina, I could help you. You deserve that, I think. I came here through a door too. I can lead you back to that same door. I can get you out of this place and back to Luz where you can live a normal, humdrum, happy life . . ."

"I can't go right now," Nina said. Her mind flashed to Troy, Juno, and Fury.

"Are you talking about that bloodthirsty Jinn? You can't leave a monster like *her* behind? Don't you think she'd do the same in a heartbeat if she had the chance?"

Nina thought of Troy harder and suddenly found herself unable to answer. She thought of how and why Troy might be staying by her side, and the more she questioned it, the more the kindness behind the reasons grew doubtful.

She swallowed nervously.

"Come on," Stephanie whispered. She walked closer, her reflections shuddering across the mirrors, twisting their positions. "I can see you want to get out of this Hell. Once we find Angela, we can leave together, you and me. Think of it as an apology for my part in getting you into this mess . . ."

Nina's mouth dried like a desert. Her heart hammered beneath her chest. "Can't I have a moment to think—"

"I don't have time," Stephanie snapped, some of her old nastiness returning. "It's not that difficult a choice, Nina. Angela doesn't care about you, or you wouldn't be here. That ratty Jinn who wants Kim dead doesn't care either. Do you really think an angel, demon, or anything like them can feel real compassion for a human being? I know better than anyone that they think differently than us."

A flash of anguish crossed Stephanie's face. She came closer, her many reflections looming larger.

Now Nina saw she held something shiny in her hands.

Nina's mind turned in every direction. She didn't want to believe what Stephanie was saying. But the more Nina considered, the more it seemed impossible for Troy to really care if she lived or died. To Troy, Juno, and Fury, Nina was a burden, an inconvenience. Nothing more. And Angela—what *had* her presence in Nina's life done? Nina had died once and she was about to die again. Angela was nowhere to be found right now.

Stephanie stretched out her hand, smiling.

Nina reached out for it, her mind still in a fog.

Then with a sudden flash sparked from the depths of her soul, she relived, in mere moments, countless happy, peaceful, and sad but meaningful memories. They ended with Angela's stricken face and her sorrowful voice, asking Nina a question that must have been tormenting. *There's more to me than being the Archon, isn't there?*

Once again, Nina felt Angela's warm hands holding hers; she heard Angela promising in her firm way to answer all Nina's questions if they exited Hell alive. Then Angela's hug held them together, and her hot tears hit Nina's shoulder. Those tears in Nina's memories felt almost as warm as in reality. It was true that Angela had been awkward with expressing her emotions in the past, almost cold. But Nina had learned that was just Angela's way of keeping her feelings safe. She distanced herself from others to protect her heart.

Now, Angela's soul was changing, and Nina's had changed with it.

She withdrew her hand from Stephanie's. "I can't go with you."

Stephanie blinked at her.

"Stephanie," Nina said, "what you said is somewhat true.

Maybe Troy doesn't care about me at all. Maybe Angela wasn't really my friend at the beginning. But she is now. And Troy could have left me for dead at any time while she and I were here. She chose not to. Besides, if I return to Earth, what kind of life can I live when most people remember me dead? I'd be nothing but a freak, just like I used to be. So my answer is no. I can't go back. I won't leave. I made a promise too—even if I didn't say it aloud."

Stephanie's sorrowful look returned. "You're a step ahead of me, Nina. No matter how many friends surround me, they're typically friends in name only. I guess you're making the right choice." She shook her head. "But that doesn't mean it's the smart one. Oh, well . . . I tried."

A lethal light appeared behind Stephanie's green eyes again, but this time Nina caught the briefest flash of reptilian pupils.

Nina should have known something about this was too perfect. Stephanie wasn't completely herself. Someone else was manipulating her thoughts, maybe even controlling her.

Nina shuffled backward.

Stephanie took another step closer, and her reflections disappeared. Now she stood in the flesh directly to Nina's right, staring at her while she clasped a long, sharp piece of obsidian in her hands. Stephanie's face blanked over oddly, and a pathetic fear replaced the hardness in her eyes. "That demon said if I killed you, he'd lead me right to Angela," she whispered fearfully. "I told him no, Nina. But then the demon told me—I didn't really have a choice. *Run while you can. Run—*"

Stephanie's voice cut off. Her face reverted back to a cold mask, and now the words that came out of her mouth were clearly someone else's.

"What a timely interruption," the voice hissed through Stephanie's lips. "Isn't it just my luck that the insane tend to be strong-willed. Well, why fight it? If you want to watch yourself kill Nina Willis, Stephanie my dear, be my guest."

Stephanie's face sapped to the whiteness of pure fear. "*No. No,*" she begged, but an invisible force jerked her arms up so that she raised the knife high.

Nina dodged just in time.

The obsidian whistled through the air.

Nina pitched hard against the ground, shrieking in pain as her injured leg touched the stone. She rolled, dodging again. Obsidian clanged against the stone floor. There was a harsh cracking sound, and it broke into four smaller fragments. Stephanie jerkily knelt down to pick one of them up. She was desperately trying to fight whatever control her captor still had over her, but it wasn't working.

Another fragment skittered close to Nina. She grabbed it, hot with fear.

Nina wobbled to her feet as soon as possible, took her chance, and ran.

Her running was more like hobbling. Every step felt maddeningly slow. She escaped into part of the mirror maze, turning corners like mad, trying to hide. But though Stephanie was slower to follow her, the laughter resounding in the air was not. Nina turned another corner, her heart pounding frightfully, her breath catching in her throat.

She met with her reflection on three sides and a large pool of acidic water steaming beneath the dim light. A dead end.

She turned and found Stephanie marching toward her resolutely. The jerkiness in Stephanie's movements was gone again. Whatever control the demon had on her mind, he'd gotten it back completely for now.

Nina threw herself against the nearest obsidian mirror, hoping it would smash. It didn't even shudder.

She pressed her back against the mirror again, clutching the makeshift dagger Stephanie had unwittingly given her. Nina didn't want to use it—but what choice did she have? She held it out, her hand shaking. She feared moving too much because of the acidic water. Nina doubted she could go through that kind of pain again and stay sane.

Stephanie must have sensed her hesitation. "You always were weak," she sniffed at Nina, advancing without a shade of fear, sidestepping the pool. "*That* was why I couldn't let you into my sorority, Nina. Well, this should at least be easy for both of us. I wonder what Angela will say when she knows you're dead again?"

Stephanie raced for Nina with deadly aim. More terrible laughter filled the air, echoing from everywhere.

A black blur streaked from nowhere and pounced on Stephanie hard. It knocked directly into her, flinging her to the floor.

There was a harsh *thud*. Stephanie groaned. Her body rolled to a stop perilously close to the acid pool. Half the clothes on her back had been ripped away, revealing bleeding gashes. Yet she sprang up onto her hands and knees with frightening quickness, in an echo of her best days as Westwood Academy's most feared witch.

"It's *you*," she hissed. "*You nasty bitch.*"

Troy licked the blood from her nails and advanced snarling in such a terrifying display, Nina could barely look at her.

Abruptly, the Jinn paused and stared at Stephanie with surprise.

Juno scampered around her aunt and stopped at Nina's

side, growling. Fury landed on Nina's shoulder, opened her wings, and screeched bravely.

"I'm ready for you this time," Stephanie said, though her face showed real fear again. Face-to-face with Troy, whatever good was left in Stephanie now resurfaced, fighting frantically for control. But it was obvious the evil overshadowing her mind was too powerful and already winning out.

Stephanie lifted her hand and pointed at Troy, shouting ominously.

"Exorcizo te, omnis spiritus immunde—"

An immense but invisible weight fell on Troy, crushing her. The Jinn's wings trembled. Staggering, she pushed herself up from the ground, shrieking from the pain. Juno screeched in pain near her spot at Nina's side.

Stephanie dared to come closer. "*—in nomine Dei—*"

On and on, Stephanie continued. Nina barely listened to the words themselves, because she also screamed over and over. "*Stop it! You're killing them!*" Her voice grew hoarse. She rocked to her feet one more time.

Troy groaned, forcing herself back to her feet but she could have been fighting against gravity itself. It looked like her stomach had been yanked out with a hook. She struggled anyway, staring at Nina with wide and truly agonized eyes. Juno moaned in her own pitiful corner, her little wings flapping in spasms.

Nina had to do something. Troy and Juno were risking their lives for her, and no one had forced them to do so.

Troy screamed. "*The demon is controlling her with strings. Cut the strings!*"

Strings?

Nina remembered how Stephanie's arms had jerked above

her head. She remembered the odd look on Troy's face when the Jinn confronted Stephanie. Whatever invisible strings happened to be there, Troy could see them.

Nina narrowed her eyes and concentrated.

Just barely, she could discern a patch of distorted air above Stephanie's head.

The agony was almost unbearable for her bad leg, but Nina steadied herself and ran for Stephanie anyway. She held out the dagger, and Fury flapped away in sudden alarm. Tears blurred Nina's vision, and the motion of the world slowed.

Stephanie turned, utter shock paling her face.

Nina swiped wildly above Stephanie's head and shoulders, and amid a flash of brilliant red light, they collided.

Twenty-six

Now, I sensed the real beginning of
my forever. —NINA WILLIS

The pain was instant and all-encompassing.

Nina couldn't remember what death had been like. Yet she knew it couldn't have been worse than this. More light flashed. A sound resembling the snap of steel cables filled the air. Nina tumbled with Stephanie to the ground, and something sharp slid between her ribs as her own dagger dropped from her hand. A searingly cold sensation went through her.

Nina screamed and flung Stephanie off her body as the floor rose up, hitting her mercilessly. Warmth poured out of her.

Nina's cheek smacked the stone. The pain dissolved almost instantly, and a deep numbness spread through her limbs. Yards away, Stephanie stumbled and collapsed so close to the acidic water that one of her hands dangled over the edge, twitching.

Stephanie lay still, but her eyes remained open and she gasped in shock and pain. A deep red stain blossomed on her white clothing. Nina's knife had accidentally stabbed her—but at least the terrible battle was over.

A penetrating silence came over everything.

Nina wanted to move, at least to see if Troy and Juno were all right, but her body refused to obey her brain. She breathed and prayed for what felt like forever. Then a shadow fell across her, and Troy knelt down with a frightened Juno by her side. Both Jinn stared at Nina. Juno was oddly quiet, her bright eyes glazed over. Fury sat on her shoulder, croaking sadly.

"How bad is it?" Nina whispered hoarsely. "The wound . . . doesn't hurt anymore . . ."

Troy shook her head, as if to say that was the worst thing possible. The bones still tied in her hair rattled gently.

"What about Stephanie?" Nina said.

Troy's eyes widened in surprise. Nina's concern seemed to be beyond the Jinn's comprehension. "She was a puppet on strings," Troy said grimly. "It is a dirty demonic trick, but a common one. It's even easier if a demon's tool happens to have a weak mind."

Nina tried to take comfort in the idea that Stephanie had fought one last time for control. Nina never could believe that people were completely evil. Even Stephanie had a side that cried.

Tears filled Nina's eyes, but she could barely feel them. All she had left was a world slowly beginning to blur away. "I bet you think I'm so stupid . . . You probably hate me. You thought I was a burden all along. I know. And maybe you were right. Look at me now." She choked back a long sob. "I'm dying again . . . but where will I go this time? I couldn't even figure out why I came back in the first place. There has to be a reason . . . right?"

"There is a reason for all things," Troy said softly. Her large eyes glowed in the growing darkness.

"Maybe it's because Angela needed me," Nina whispered. "She needs friends. Without them, I don't know what's going to happen to her. Maybe . . . that's the only thing keeping her from choosing to be the Ruin and reign in Lucifel's place . . . you know. For us . . ."

Juno's long ears flattened. She gazed down at the trickles of blood touching her fingers and toes. But she made no move to lick them.

"Now I'm failing her," Nina said. She stared at Troy, trying to focus more on those hypnotic eyes that were fading from her fast. "Troy, promise me that you'll be her friend in my place. I know it sounds silly . . . someone like you being friends with a human . . . but Angela is different, she's the Archon and . . ."

More tears swallowed Nina's world.

Troy's face came down to the level of Nina's ear. Her breath felt faintly warm. "No. She is not different from you," the Jinn hissed gently.

Nina's eyes opened wider for a second. "What? But that's not—"

"Fate chose her," Troy said. "As it also chose you. You are equals in that sense. I am not ashamed to call you an ally, Nina Willis. You saved me, and you risked your life for the heir to the Throne of the Underworld. Once upon a time, there were many Jinn who would have died for the honor of protecting their Queen. Now honor is gone, and the old order is collapsing. You have put almost all my relatives to shame with your courage."

Gratefulness swelled in Nina's heart. She felt herself cry more, but the tears, much like everything else, began to feel far away, as if they happened in another place and time.

"I will protect the Archon with my life," Troy said faintly. "And I will never leave her side . . ."

"Neither will I," Nina said slowly. "I just won't allow it . . ." This wasn't the end for her. Nina had cheated death before, and she could cheat it now.

But how?

A strange voice touched the edge of her thoughts. It sounded a lot like the one that had come from Stephanie's mouth but more friendly and understanding.

Work for me, it whispered, *and you can live forever. I'll even let you enjoy a life of privilege and wealth by your brother's side . . .*

Somehow, Nina sensed every last bit of that was a lie. *No thank you,* she said in her mind definitively.

The irritated face of a snake flashed within her thoughts and then it mercifully disappeared forever.

A great weight lifted from her. Nina was now alone, peaceful, and she began to slip deeper into a surprising dream. Her tears must have finally stopped—she could see Troy and Juno clearly again.

They were so strangely beautiful despite how fierce and frightening they could look. Troy especially had an almost regal air, her translucent skin looking as white as chalk, but with networks of blue veins so fine and delicate they resembled lace. The angles of her face were perfect. Yet she had the strangest expression, something Nina had never found in her before.

Compassion? Pride? Sorrow? Nina wasn't sure.

Yet there was an enchantment to it. It was not a bad image to take into shadows that finally shut out the world.

Twenty-seven

*So many creatures I had encountered died with
less dignity than she did. At that moment, it
occurred to me why Raziel had chosen a human
to be the Archon. There was something in their
spirits that existed nowhere else.* —TROY

Nina's body went still.

Troy took the girl's tangled hair and covered her eyes with
some of it. The smell of her blood was horrifically tempting,
and Juno appeared to think so too. Her little limbs trembled,
and she bent down to drink.

"No," Troy said, pushing her backward. "We *do not*
drink the blood of great hunters and warriors, chick."

Juno whimpered, her large eyes averted in her shame.
"Yes. I know . . . I just . . ."

"Hush," Troy snapped. She left Nina's body and prowled
nearer to Stephanie.

The girl lay near the acid pool, gasping and very much alive.
Fury strutted around her, inspecting Stephanie's wounds.

There could not be more of a difference between the two
humans. While Nina had held on to the peace that heralds

a noble death, Stephanie's face blanked over with horror the second Troy leaned over her, gazing into her wild green eyes. It was clear from this human's expression that she was insane. Her good hand clutched in terror at the ground, as if she could push herself far away from Troy with a few fingers. Her mouth was almost slack, her breathing quickened. Judging by her behavior, most of her body was probably paralyzed.

"Who brought you here?" Troy said with a low growl.

Troy's insides felt like they'd been crushed; her bones ached, and her muscles screamed in torment from the exorcism.

Stephanie said nothing, gasping more with fear.

"*Who*?" Troy said again, spreading her aching wings.

Stephanie watched, her eyes even wider than before. "A demon," she whispered.

"The snake?" Troy snarled.

Stephanie nodded, entranced by Troy's eyes. "He said he would take me to Angela again . . ." Stephanie made an expression like she'd just realized something important. "That was a lie . . . wasn't it? It was all a lie . . ."

Juno peered around Troy's arm.

Troy thrust her back. She set her fingers on Stephanie's neck, feeling for her pulse. The human was bleeding, but it would take her a long time to die if they left her behind. When Juno's head popped around the other side of Troy's wing, Troy signaled to her to come closer this time. Juno crept nearer to Stephanie, her little wings held low.

"We can leave you here," Troy said to Stephanie. "Or . . ."

Stephanie stared at Juno. "It was all a lie. I should have never listened. I should have never entered the door. Angela shouldn't have entered the door either. There's no going back now . . ." Her green eyes cleared, and a soft smile touched her face. "At least it's over now. No more voices in my head.

No more harsh noises interrupting my thoughts." She looked out into the distance. "Naamah . . . Mother . . . I hope you are proud of me . . ."

Troy settled down by Juno's side. The chick sat next to Stephanie, examining her closely.

"Do you see the difference between the two humans?" Troy said to her after a short time.

Juno nodded.

"This is the way of things," Troy said to her. "All creatures die eventually. Even Jinn and angels. We are in a sacred place to determine whether this particular human lives or dies. What is the right thing to do, chick?"

"To . . . kill her?" Juno said distantly.

Troy sighed. "Yes. She will suffer enormously if we leave her here. She was insane and does not deserve such cruelty. You must always remember that. It is what separates our race from the demons. What else will you do?"

There was a short pause. "I'm so hungry," Juno finally said.

"But how hungry? Could you survive without touching the human?"

Juno stared, clearly at odds with herself. Finally, she nodded.

Troy looked down at Stephanie and regarded her grimly. "Remember always, chick. In this world, hunger will always exist. And hunger is like the demons—cruel and unpredictable. You must never waste food, or as Queen allow your people to starve if you can help it. But you must also learn how to be strong—and to sacrifice when it is necessary— because every good Queen thinks of others first. Your mother spoiled you and kept you from the harsh realities of the hunt too much. Now the time has come to show me that you will make a good Queen some day. Show me that you understand what it is to live as others cannot. I will leave the human's fate to you . . ." Juno bent over Stephanie. She hesitated for a second, scrunching up her nose. "She doesn't smell right."

Troy passed a hand over Stephanie's eyes, forcing them closed. "She was possessed," Troy whispered. "You are smelling her tainted blood and soul."

Juno gazed at Stephanie sadly. Then she bent over her lower, and the reverent expression on Juno's face made her look remarkably like Troy's dead sister. Stephanie's suffering would now come to a mercifully quick end.

Pain raced through Troy's heart.

In her mind, she saw Hecate again and heard her cries in the nest as she and Troy jostled for food and struggled through hunger and pain to live. If Juno could exist in a better world than that, she deserved it. She and all the Jinn needed a universe where fear and famine were not ever-present ghosts. Yet change wouldn't come easy. To their own Clan, Troy and Juno were outcasts, and now the chick had no one to rely on but an aunt with poor experience caring for infants. Juno's position as the Jinn's new Queen was precarious. But Troy would make sure that, no matter what mistakes she made along the way, her sister's legacy continued. It was the one that believed in the Archon, and in her.

Jinn always kept their promises.

Troy had made so many, to her sister, to the Archon, to Nina—and most hauntingly to Sariel. Willingly, she lay down in exhaustion, closed her eyes, and remembered.

Juno's sacred moments did not take long. With Stephanie now dead, it was time for all of them, including Fury, to leave the nightmarish room of mirrors.

With renewed strength and determination, Troy stood

and examined the room. If she strained her ears, she was certain she heard an odd muffled noise from the other side of one of the walls. There was probably an exit on that side, hopefully from the labyrinth itself. The maze would most likely have more than one way out. What worried Troy was that the exit would lead not to Sariel or Angela, but to the demon city of Babylon.

This chamber had been used in the past and was certainly connected to the city somehow.

Troy sighed, her ears flicking nervously. They had already lost so much precious time. Anything could have happened to Angela by now.

"Are you ready?" she said to Juno.

Juno was done cleaning her mouth and feathers. She sat up, Fury croaking by her side. "You're going to leave her?" Juno said quietly. She looked at Nina Willis.

Troy walked back to Nina's body. She stopped beside it. "You are right. We will take something of her with us. For the Archon." Troy wanted to curse herself for not thinking of that sooner, but impatience and anxiety struggled constantly for mastery of her thoughts. "I will allow you to choose and take the piece, and then give it to Angela Mathers. What? *Why do you look at me like that?*"

Juno stared behind Troy, her eyes enormously wide. Fury had gone utterly still.

The air shifted ever so slightly.

Troy jumped aside, her wings flapping powerfully.

A white foot thumped down on top of Nina's body, settling on her chest. Troy dashed in front of Juno, spreading her wings protectively, rounding on their visitor with cold snarls of anger. She disliked demons, but she hated being surprised even more.

Her nerves felt frayed. Troy hadn't even caught his scent this time.

"I suppose it's going to be hard to name a winner here," Python said smoothly. He wore a feathered snake's mask, and he tugged it off, throwing it casually aside. Then he nudged Nina's body, shrugging. "But it was an entertaining battle all the same. Just like in the days of my youth, when mother and I would watch the games together. Sometimes— just like today—I would get the chance to participate. Stack the odds a little in my chosen champion's favor. Ah, Mother, you were so much less of a bitch back then." He stared more at Nina, and then smiled at Juno. "No appetite, little crow? How disappointing."

"*You do not speak to her,*" Troy thundered at him.

Juno stood rooted to the spot.

Fury had flown to another perch, but Troy could sense her nearby, waiting for her master's signal when the moment came.

"And just why can't I speak to her? Because she's your runty Queen?" Python spat.

"Because your malice should be toward me alone," Troy said. She remembered their conversation in the cavern. Troy shivered, unable to believe there'd been a moment she'd considered killing her own niece.

"Fair enough," Python whispered. His orange eyes burned. "Well, Troy, aren't you going to ask me about Angela Mathers? Or about your cousin, that annoying half-breed my mother took a fancy to?"

A growl bubbled up from deep within her. "There is no need, because you will not take me to them. I will find them on my own."

Python tipped back his head and laughed. "Really? But

that's why I'm here, dear. To stop you from getting there. You've come quite far through my labyrinth. It's commendable. You've been entertaining enough to watch. But I think I've had enough of *this* little game. I have bigger crows to cage, bigger rats to trap." His eyes blazed fiercely. "You've reached the real end now, High Assassin. And it's a pity. Think about what you could have been—Queen. Consider what you will be without my mercy—dead."

"Don't flatter yourself. I always sensed this was your maze, snake," Troy whispered. "If it weren't for the Archon, I would have escaped it long ago."

"How loyal," Python said with a dark cleverness in his smile. "And it was exactly that sense of nobility I was counting on."

The rage within her intensified. He had been playing them all for fools—and worst of all, enjoying every minute of it.

Somehow, despite her better judgment, Troy had believed enough of Python's lies to think that maybe—just maybe—he was truly on the Archon's side. But Nina's death had ended that for good. If only Troy could be where Angela was now, to protect her from Python's treachery. Angela's desperation to rescue Sophia would only keep blinding her to the demon's real motives, and those couldn't be in her favor.

He would spring for Angela's throat eventually. The grim question was when?

Python regarded Troy with amusement. "I see your mind working. And it's absolutely right—there was never any way out of this for you, or for the Archon. I play every chess game well, High Assassin. I certainly have a lot of time to plan my moves ahead. But not every pawn realizes who their real master happens to be. Look at Nina Willis, for example," he said softly. "When her half brother approached me, begging me to resurrect her body—how could I push aside such an opportunity? With Nina's unwitting help, Angela Mathers finally found and entered the door to Hell like a blind fool. It was almost laughably easy to get her inside."

Troy could hardly breathe. There was more to that story. There had to be. It was too much of a coincidence that Nina's half brother had known how to summon Python and ask for his help.

"Her brother was smart enough to find you on his own?" Troy smirked. "Perhaps you aren't as well concealed and clever as you'd like to think . . ."

Python lost his laughter. "It shows what a naive winged rat you are. Your own Clan betrayed you. What makes you think the angels wouldn't do the same to their own kind? It was an angel who led that weak human to me. Not his own mortal cleverness."

"What angel?" Troy said, her tone scoffing at the news. But she already knew.

Instantly, she thought back to the angel Mikel who had possessed Nina Willis a year ago.

Regrettably, Python had caught on to the ruse. His deadly eyes narrowed to something even more sinister. "None of your business," he snapped. "Now if you wouldn't mind, before I torture you and the runt, I'm here to collect the soul that now belongs by rights to me." He stooped down over Nina and muttered under his breath. A cold light began to outline the human's body and reflect brilliantly off the acidic water.

Troy's eyes burned with pain.

"Look away!" she said to Juno and rushed in front of her again.

Juno cowered, whimpering. The light subsided, and they could only watch in helpless horror as Python lifted a softly glowing bluish sphere from Nina's body. It pulsed, and tremors of brilliant light flowed over its surface. With the Netherworld closed and Nina already in Hell, her soul had regressed to its most pure essence. Python kissed the light in his hands. "What will the Archon have to say to me now?" he said under his breath.

Troy sensed what she planned to do next would mean certain death for both her and Juno, but there were few options left. While a few moments ago escape had still been possible, this new outrage deserved swift justice. It was now achingly clear why the demon had murdered Nina, and Troy alone stood in the way of his plans. Python had enough pawns already. Nina's soul would be one too many.

With her eyes still burning from the light, Troy leaped at Python.

Her hands reached for Nina's soul, were a second from grasping it.

Hardly concerned, Python waved his hand.

Power rippled through the ether and smacked into Troy. Her body whipped into a mirror, knocking the wind out of her as it smashed, raining shards around her body. Troy dropped to the ground, her muscles in agony, gnashing her teeth from the pain. Blood oozed from new cuts on her skin.

Juno shrieked in horror and was about to run to Troy's rescue, but Troy shot her a cold, hard glare. *Don't move*, it said.

Python sauntered toward Troy, annoyance souring his perfect face.

NOW, Troy said in her thoughts.

Fury streaked down from above. With a cold cry of victory, she plucked Nina's soul from the demon's grasp, cradling it between her large talons.

Python screamed, his face twisting with rage. He thrust out his hand and said something ugly in the demonic language, but Fury was already too far away. She soared out into the darkness screeching, certainly heading for the exit from the labyrinth. Fury had found it after all. Her next job would be to take Nina's soul somewhere Python could never steal it again.

Keep going, Troy said to Fury in her thoughts. *Go and don't look back.*

"You frustrating *bitch*," Python said, rounding on Troy again with blazing eyes.

Troy knew what was coming next. "*Run*," she hissed at Juno. "*Follow Fury.*"

The chick stared at Troy in pure horror. Violet mist erupted around Python, and his body began to dissolve, his orange reptilian eyes the single feature that never changed. Every part of him stretched and transformed into inky black smoke and scales.

"*GO*," Troy screamed at Juno.

Juno hesitated, and then she turned around and dashed off into the blackness.

The moment she did, the walls of the room seemed to rush in on Troy.

She had no time to escape. Obsidian mirrors toppled and smashed. Bones nearby cracked into shards. Thick loops of scaled and feathered flesh thumped out of the shadows and wrapped around Troy's body, coiling swiftly one at a time. Higher and higher they surrounded her. Purplish mist choked out her breath.

Troy tried desperately to crawl up and out of her prison, but the coils of scales and muscle tightened. In seconds she would be crushed to death.

A triangular snake's head crowned by a tuft of feathers swayed above her.

She snagged her nails into black scales and climbed as hard as she could. Fear and pain sent shocking waves of strength through her body.

The gigantic snake's head darted down, aiming to bite her in half.

Troy ducked sideways. Breath hot as steam passed over her.

The snake snapped back into position with movements almost too quick to see, preparing for another strike.

Python was now in his truest form as a feathered serpent, and the glorious plumes on his head had blended into a combination of violet and black, defining him as a demon. His enormous orange eyes focused on Troy. With the sound of an iron trap slamming shut, he bit again at her torso. His fangs gleamed like knives. "*Stop moving,*" a soft voice echoed from his entire body, "*and this will be over much sooner.*"

Troy latched frantically onto Python's scaly folds and climbed with all her skill.

He arched his neck, opening his lethal jaws directly over Troy's head. She dodged again at the right second, jumping for another foothold.

Her body slammed against Python's again, but she rolled, suddenly free of her scaled prison. The cold ground seemed to rise and strike her in the face and chest. Troy shot upright, ready to dash out of reach. A shadow loomed above her.

Pain more agonizing than a boulder breaking her bones ricocheted through Troy's entire body. Blood gushed in a hot river down her back.

Troy hit the earth hard, screaming.

Python's fangs had sliced her left wing. And now his

shadow hovered over her again as he prepared to finish his work. A suffocating coil of muscle slammed against Troy, pinning her to the earth. Her jaw snapped shut from the force, and dots of lights speckled her vision. The ground felt hard and cold as iron. Troy thrashed against it, but Python pinned her tighter, bit into her wing again, and twisted his head.

He was breaking Troy's wing off right where it met her shoulder blade.

Such pain. Indescribable anguish.

Troy shrieked, and Python twisted harder, intensifying the pain, pouring more liquid fire into the marrow of what was left of her wing bones. The final bits of Troy's wing tore away. Her ears buzzed and the world seemed to tilt. A horrific numbness crept across the left side of her back.

She struggled to stay conscious. Nausea turned her stomach upside down.

"You Jinn are too proud with these wings of yours," Python said, his voice echoing distantly. *"Perhaps now you won't be quite so judgmental. Finally, High Assassin, at least one of your kind can understand what it is to be a demon like me. Finally you can know the pain I feel when I remember what it was to flap my wings amid the stars. Your sister, the previous Jinn Queen, didn't quite get the message. Let's hope you can do a better job."*

Troy's entire body throbbed with unbearable pain. Yet now it struck her—she wasn't dead yet. But why? Python picked up her body and flung it to the side. Troy's head smacked into the ground again. Her cheek scraped the earth and she landed facing him, her remaining wing twitching in spasms, blood trickling from her countless wounds. Slowly, Python's serpentine body dissolved into violet smoke again.

In seconds he stood before her as a demon, but now he revealed what was left of his own wings. They were a mess of bone, metal rods meant to support what patchy skin remained, and ragged flesh. Steam from the acid pool nearby brushed at his ankles.

"Now we're practically twins," he hissed at Troy spitefully. "Queen or not, you'll do well to remember who your new master is, you feathered rat."

Something dark and blindingly fast burst from behind a broken mirror.

Juno.

With a loud cry of rage, she slammed into Python hard and they both pitched straight for the acid pool.

Juno broke away seconds before the inevitable and thumped back to the floor.

Python's slender body continued to tumble backward into the steaming water. Shock and anger contorted his face. His lips parted and he appeared on the verge of screaming or cursing.

With a sickening *crack,* his body exploded in a rain of black ash. Pieces hazed the air, drifting onto Juno as she raced for Troy and stooped down beside her.

"Your wing," she said in abject horror.

Troy fought to stay conscious, struggling to her feet despite more pain than she'd ever known. She staggered in the ash. Blood still ran down her back, but both she and Juno knew there was no time for Troy to rest or recover her strength. Even if Python was gone, they had to get out of this death trap to wherever Fury awaited.

Her gaze met with Juno's and locked tightly. Troy grasped her niece's arm and leaned against her for a moment. Jinn weren't skilled at showing gratefulness, and Troy was worse than most. But Juno understood, and she nodded at Troy with such a mature expression. It faintly resembled Hecate's in her nobler moments. Perhaps this little one would make a great Queen after all . . .

"Auntie, what's happening?" Juno shouted suddenly.

Troy broke from her trance and rocked forward. Ash had slipped from beneath her. The room darkened. She glanced up, straining to focus.

A mysterious wind whipped out of nowhere, blinding Troy as more ashes lifted into the air and whirled like black snow. Her eyes stung but she forced herself to see. Slowly the ashes condensed near the acid pool into the tall and familiar shape of a man. Cold laughter echoed through the chamber, and Troy's insides instantly knotted with fear.

Python wasn't dead.

They had only been battling his shadow—nothing more than a clone of himself created and sustained by blood and astral energy. And as it returned for the second round, the real Python remained elsewhere, very much alive, watching their misery and laughing about it incessantly.

"Did you really think it would be that easy to kill me?" The demon's smooth voice shivered throughout the room. *"The Prince taught me more than one trick in my days as a chick. Besides, I'm not stupid enough to play with the High Assassin of the Jinn without a backup plan. If only you weren't so rude, Troy, my dear. Perhaps then I would have reconsidered killing your niece . . . Oh well. So much for mercy . . ."*

Troy's heart almost stopped. A pain worse than the loss of her wing hammered her hard, because worst of all, despite the unthinkable torment Python had put Troy through, she'd never been his real target.

Juno's eyes widened. She tugged at Troy's arm desperately. "This way!"

This wasn't right. Troy was always the one protecting her niece. Reversing the roles twisted her stomach into a ball. But Juno was already ahead—and Python's shadow loomed behind.

Troy shivered and shrieked, and in a whirlwind of pain she sprinted after Juno, following her to the exit as Python's laughter echoed in her brain, nearly making her insane.

Troy would make it. No, she wouldn't, she couldn't. They would survive. They would die. Her thoughts warred with one another madly. Then Juno disappeared into a misty haze, and though Troy ran after her, the fog only thickened.

Every breath felt more impossible than the last. Troy entered a tunnel with a dull light at its end and she forced herself onward.

The final walls of the labyrinth peeled outward, widening.

Abruptly, the ground was pulled out from beneath her.

The fog vanished, and Troy found herself leaping from a cliff high above the demon city of Babylon. It glimmered below her, glorious with obsidian and flickering lights in a cavern large enough to be the world. Juno was nowhere to be found. There was only the immense city, Python's laughter, and the warm air embracing Troy's body as it wafted beneath her remaining wing. Troy could no longer fly.

She could also no longer think. Her eyes closed.

Without a single sigh left to her, she fell.

Twenty-eight

My situation felt hopeless. How could anyone survive
this kind of pain? Then I considered Nina's pain, and
Troy's, and Sophia's and even when it felt unbearable,
I pushed on toward the precious place where we'd
certainly meet again. —ANGELA MATHERS

The Grail sent throbs of aching pain through Angela's entire
body.

She stood before an enormous emerald Eye in a sea of
utter blackness, her feet somehow positioned on solid
ground. Within the Eye's shining pupil, Israfel's reflection
gleamed. He cried out in anguish, his wings beating in agony.
His white hair hung before his large blue eyes. Something
about him seemed so small and human. Then he faded from
view, and the Eye blinked shut.

Angela awakened suddenly, one last throb shooting
through her body.

Darkness suffocated her, but gradually her eyes adjusted.
She struggled to free her arms, but they had been chained
to the wall and the manacles bit into her wrists. The chains
jangled as she jostled with them, their noise echoing throughout the now empty ballroom. Angela swallowed, her throat

feeling raw, a sour taste coating the inside of her mouth. Her head swam. Over and over, she continued to see Israfel, Lucifel, and Raziel, arguing, interacting. Raziel's pain sliced through her again as he plummeted to his death. The legend was wrong. He hadn't committed suicide.

Somebody had murdered him.

The frightening but beautiful being with a hundred wings had shredded Raziel's wings and thrown him to his death. That same being whose eyes had been so familiar . . .

The person the angels called "Father."

Angela glanced up at her left hand. The arm glove remained in place, deftly covering the Eye bleeding beneath the fabric. Her mind whirled.

Israfel, Raziel, and Lucifel were definitively siblings. Israfel had been unable to bear the guilt of accidentally falling in love with his own brother. Lucifel had been discontent as well, though Angela could only guess why. There seemed to be more behind her venom than envy over Israfel's position as Archangel. And Raziel had tried to put a stop to the bloodshed but died miserably despite his efforts.

Angela shivered, finding herself face-to-face in her memories with that awful creature looming over Raziel. The cold hatred on its face had been almost impossible to look at.

Lucifel took Sophia to Hell after the War. Was that to keep her safe from that awful . . . thing?

What did Raziel really learn that led to his death?

Maybe Lucifel already knew.

Angela sighed and turned her head, still groggy. Kim was to her left where Lilith had chained him, sound asleep. Bruises peppered his face, and a nasty cut had been scratched into his cheek. The demon must have slapped him more than once. Yet she hadn't bothered to kill Angela. That didn't sit well with her. Angela struggled again with the chains and finally gave up, leaning her head back against the smooth cold wall.

I wonder if Nina and Troy are still alive . . .

The odds said no, but Angela couldn't help hoping. The tears she'd always promised to stop but could never really hold back slid hotly down her cheeks. Why did she hate tears so much? Because her parents beat her when she cried? Maybe it was because tears made her feel so weak and vulnerable. They were an admission of the pain she used to always try to run away from.

"Feeling discouraged?" a gentle voice said.

Angela gasped, whipping her head around to face the sound.

Lilith sat in the shadows on a velvet cushion, her dark legs crossed, and her long fingers drumming against her thigh. She slid out of the chair and strolled nearer to Angela. Without warning, she stooped down and gripped Angela roughly by the chin.

Angela's cheekbones screamed with pain. Any harder and her face might shatter. She tried to twist her head away without success.

"It serves you right, Archon. You really are quite a thorn in the Prince's side. I wonder if she ever really expected you to get this far. Not that it matters, because I'm here to make sure your journey comes to a screeching halt."

"Over my dead body." Angela spit in her face.

Lilith wiped her cheek in disgust. Muttering a curse, she slapped Angela powerfully across the mouth.

More pain raced across Angela's skin like lightning. She gasped, unable to lift her head again.

"You have courage, at least," Lilith said smoothly. "Perhaps it's the one thing that makes you resemble Lucifel."

"If you want to kill me," Angela said, still gasping, "why are you taking your time?"

Lilith smiled. "Because you don't deserve a quick and painless death." She knelt down in front of Angela, petting the same spot on Angela's cheek she had so cruelly smacked only moments before. "Do you remember a demon named Naamah?"

Angela's chest tightened. How could she forget?

"You do," Lilith said brightly. "Well, she was my protégée, Archon. Naamah's true parents died when she was young and so I took her in as a mentor. But I grew to love her, perhaps even more than my own offspring. She was a dutiful daughter. Our ideals divided in the end, but I could never bring myself to follow the Prince's orders and destroy her. She was too valuable to me as a person. That is—until you killed her."

"I didn't kill her," Angela shouted.

Lilith shook her head. "Perhaps not directly. But indirectly is good enough for me. Someone has to pay. Why not you?"

"What are you going to do? Just let me and Kim starve here?" Angela glanced around, trying to find anything that might help her or Kim escape. There was nothing.

Lilith chuckled sweetly. "That would be far too boring, Archon. I think we should just go slowly, see what makes you scream most, and work from there. I'm sure a replay of the torment you just went through in your visions should suffice. I saw quite a bit. It was very interesting, just as the Prince told me it would be. That whole business about Raziel committing suicide was apparently a lie." Lilith leaned down, her dress sliding to an uncomfortably revealing spot below her shoulders. "It makes me wonder what else is in that head of yours. Better yet, if angel blood can bring on visions, what can the blood of the Archon do? It wouldn't be a bad idea to experiment."

She put a nail to Angela's neck and slid it up to her chin. "The only question now, is how painful should it be?"

Her nail dug into skin.

Angela cried out, unable to help herself.

"Lady," a voice said from the shadows.

Lilith cringed, but she stood up and regarded the visitor. It was the same female demon who had curtsied to Angela. "What is it?" Lilith snapped. "You can see that I'm busy here."

"Your son wishes to speak with you," the demon said.

Lilith laughed. "I have no son. If you're talking to a snake, though, tell him I'll be there in a moment. Let him know this had better be worth my time. I'm tired of his constant interruptions. Milk," Lilith muttered under her breath. "I should have fed him poison instead. Perhaps it would only have made him more of a serpent . . ."

Lilith glared at Angela but silently left the chamber, shoving the other demon out of the way as she exited through a set of double doors.

The female demon's eyes brightened dangerously the moment Lilith was gone.

The demon walked up to Angela. Slowly, a purple mist rose up around her body, and Angela watched with a pounding heart as the demon's figure stretched and reshaped itself. Python broke out of the fog and quickly set to work on Angela's chains. His mouth was set in a cold line. Once Angela's arms were free, he stepped back and watched as she rubbed her wrists. "A simple thank-you would be sufficient," he said.

"You're the one who got me into this mess," Angela hissed back. "You knew what would happen when I walked through those doors."

"Touché," the demon said. He folded his arms and leaned against the wall. "But I had to see the truth. That part of my mother's plan I agreed to. This, I did not." The malice in his voice sent shivers up Angela's spine. "My mother's cry of frustration will be quite soothing in the end." He reached down and picked up one of the masks thrown carelessly onto the ground. It happened to be another snake's mask. He held it up to his face. "She is such a careless hedonist, she didn't even notice her own son at the ball. Even though I danced with her three times."

Angela tried to ignore the odd light behind his eyes when he said that.

"What did I drink?" She rubbed at her throat. Her head still hurt.

"Angel blood," Python said shortly. "Drinking it reveals the truth of many things. Thus the unfortunate need to plunge you headfirst into a pool of it."

Angel blood?

Angela steadied herself, trying not to retch. The idea of how many angels had needed to die in order to fill that fountain made her even more hideously sick. For all their gloss of civilization, the demons were almost worse than Troy and the Jinn. At least the Jinn seemed to kill out of hunger and necessity. This was different. This was murder for the fun of it.

She rocked slowly to her feet. "Then free Kim and show me how to get out of here. I know I can't have much time left. Sophia can be anywhere by now. Troy and the others—"

"Troy and the others?" Python sighed. "You still turn your thoughts back to them?"

He seemed to be considering something.

"All right. I suppose I will tell you." Python looked Angela straight in the eye. "Nina Willis is dead. Troy and the Jinn chick betrayed you, Angela. They have returned to the Underworld and left you to fend for yourself."

Angela swallowed, a shot of pain working through her. Her heart hammered. Her hearing buzzed. "No. That's not true. Troy wouldn't—"

"Wrong," Python said. "But I don't blame you for needing proof. So here it is."

He threw something resembling a large garnet against the wall. It shattered, sending a spray of red across the stone that quickly coalesced into a circle of pulsing light. In this light, Angela saw Nina lying dead on the ground. The girl's injured leg was clearly visible. Then the scene switched out, and Juno knelt down by a body dressed in white, just like Nina's. She bit the corpse.

Angela screamed Nina's name.

Python waved his hand, and the red liquid fell to the floor in hundreds of droplets. "I have been keeping a very close eye on those two Jinn," Python said. "Who can trust them, after all? It's their nature to kill at any opportunity, especially when they happen to be starving. You would be wise to forget about them completely. Come with me, and I'll make sure you find the Book without anything more to trouble you. Seeing the truth hidden in your soul was an unfortunate necessity. How can I help you when I'm not entirely sure you are indeed the Archon? But now that I know, I feel no more hesitation risking my life to keep the Prince of Hell caged."

"Troy wouldn't do that to Nina. Neither would Juno," Angela whispered.

Nina . . . You've died yet again? How could that happen? Where would you go this time? This is all my fault. Nothing is going like I'd hoped. How can I bring you back now?

Angela wiped at her tears. She clawed at the ground, sobbing. Misery clenched at her heart.

"Betrayal hurts," Python whispered, staring at her.

"Thanks to my wretched mother, I know that all too well. But look at it this way. When you know the truth about people, you also know how to keep yourself from being hurt by them in the future. Live for yourself alone, and all of your problems solve themselves." He knelt down in front of her. "You should just accept that sometimes the world isn't worth saving. Just imagine how easy life would be if all the trouble-some people disappeared."

"Troy wouldn't do that," Angela whispered again.

She knew instinctively that what Python had shown her was the truth, but perhaps not in the way he wanted her to believe.

It couldn't be.

He stared at her more, perhaps trying to determine how firm she was in her beliefs. "As you wish," he said, standing up again. "But I'll warn you now, people are never quite what they appear to be on the surface. There is always more. Everyone has a dark secret or two. It's only a matter of bringing those secrets to light. Every friendship is based on how well those secrets are kept hidden, and how effectively someone gets what they want."

"Sometimes, friends are friends, and there really isn't any more to it than that," Angela said firmly.

She and Python locked eyes for another moment.

"We'll see just how well your little friendships serve you in the future," he said darkly. His gaze shifted sideways. "Oh, your knight awakens."

Kim opened his eyes and glanced around the room until he saw Angela.

"I'll give you a few touching moments together," Python said meaningfully to Kim. "Then it's onward and forward before Mama's return."

Python took a slow step sideways and disappeared, as if he'd entered an invisible door.

Angela suppressed her shivers. The misery inside of her was all encompassing. Tears ran down her face, and she could barely look at Kim.

"What happened?" he said weakly.

Angela shook her head.

Kim hung his own, hair swinging into his eyes. "I understand. You obviously don't need to tell me." He looked around the room grimly. "I'm sorry, Angela. Maybe Lilith was too much of a force for me to reckon with." He sighed. "I thought I could at least stop her from making you drink the angel blood. Somehow, I think she was on to me all along. Perhaps not entirely, but . . ."

"No," Angela said. She stood and wiped at her tears. "You did what you could for me. Thank you."

"Are you still intent on finding Sophia?" Kim said gently.

Angela rubbed her forehead. "I don't have a choice but to go where this demon is going to take me. Whatever part of the labyrinth comes next."

"What will you do when you find her?" Kim said.

Angela said nothing, folding her arms and shivering.

"Will you try to open her—"

"One thing at a time," Angela said shortly. He was asking far too many questions that wouldn't change a thing. She wanted to scream. This was her life. Instead of being a normal young woman, instead of kissing Kim in a corner and dreaming about the next kiss, she had to run through a rat maze to find her best friend and keep her from being killed. But she didn't regret risking her life for Sophia's in the least. Besides, the more she remembered those moments of passion in Kim's arms from the previous year, the more they seemed like a shameful dream.

Right now, with Nina dead and Troy and Juno possibly gone, Angela's sole focus needed to be Sophia. Whenever Angela thought of Kim, Sophia's face overlaid his. Israfel was another matter altogether. Angela's bitterness toward him only grew the more she didn't see him anymore. But so did her pity.

Why had she seen him in pain, crying out, looking so very weak?

Kim laughed softly. "I know. I should keep my questions to myself." He took a deep breath. "I only wanted to protect you, Angela. Whether or not you take Lucifel's place, I can see myself by your side and nowhere else. You can't give me anything else right now, but at least give me that."

His anguished voice sounded genuine.

Angela walked over to him. Impulsively, she touched his face, gently brushing the dark hair from his eyes.

Kim closed his eyes and sighed.

"I treated you so cruelly last year," she whispered. "I'm sorry."

She bent down and kissed him softly on the mouth.

The sound of clapping forced Angela to rip herself away abruptly. She gasped. Python stopped clapping from his spot right beside her and leaned down, putting his face parallel with her own. "Very nice, but as I said, my dear, onward and forward. Besides, I'm starting to feel left out."

He mockingly leaned in for a kiss.

What is he doing! Angela pulled back instinctively, surprise and anger warring inside of her. Heat blazed across her face, and she remembered being locked in Python's arms on the ballroom floor. She breathed hard, shaking.

Python smirked at her, his orange eyes narrow with amusement. Then he turned to a visibly ruffled Kim, setting to work on his chains. "Touchy, touchy."

Twenty-nine

Those moments Angela and I shared merely
confirmed what I'd always known—She was the
person I longed to be. She was a perfect reflection
of the soul I might lose. —KIM (SARIEL)

The escape back into the labyrinth went smoothly enough that Python hadn't felt it necessary to run.

Kim held Angela's hand tightly anyway, helping her to step over fallen obelisks and scattered boulders that sprouted up in their path. She accepted his help without comment, often staring ahead of herself as if looking into a world more alien than this one. He wondered with a pang of jealousy if she thought of Israfel.

Angela's fingers strayed to a pendant resting against her chest. Kim saw it was a silver feather wrapped around a white sapphire star.

He let go of her hand and she strolled ahead, focused on her steps through the darkness. The tunnels here had been decorated with mosaics now half crumbled with age. Angela glanced at them, but she hadn't bothered yet with questions about what they depicted.

Python dropped back by Kim's side, and they watched Angela's progress together. The demon's face was cool, his footsteps on the stone even and measured. "You didn't lie," he whispered to Kim. "I can tell by the look on your face that you have feelings for her. Not that I blame you—she's quite a catch. But let's not forget she is the Archon, after all. I doubt she will hold on to you much longer once your usefulness fades."

Kim laughed with irony. "She told me so herself once upon a time. Unfortunately, unlike you, Angela is a bad liar, and she hides her feelings poorly. She's also much more compassionate than she behaves at times. She's someone who hides most of what she feels."

"A sign of weakness," Python said.

"That's only one way to look at it." Kim stared ahead, still unnerved by the demon's intense eyes. "I can understand how she thinks because we're a lot alike. I also grew up in a world that didn't accept me. I was called a devil's child, tormented because my mother was a witch."

Python raised an eyebrow. "Well, it was true, correct?"

Kim shook his head. "True or not, the misery other people inflicted on me shaped who I am. Just like Angela, I had to make hard decisions about my life and the direction I wanted it to go in. Eventually, I chose to break free of my torment—"

"With Mastema's help," Python said quickly. "Which is hardly the compliment it should be. But since you've chosen to work against your arrogant foster father this time, I'm willing to overlook the annoying connection between you two. What a fool. Couldn't he consider you might feel like rebelling someday?"

"Yes . . . with his help, the darkest period of my life ended," Kim whispered. He tried not to feel even guiltier than he did already. Now he knew Mastema's ideals for the insanity that they were—but Mastema had trusted Kim and raised him.

He shivered thinking of what would happen once Mastema realized centuries' worth of planning would be ruined by Kim of all people and things.

Kim sighed. "My real father was a monster—literally. I would have never found the courage to escape him otherwise. No one in my situation would have been able to . . ."

"And your courageous hunter of a cousin," Python said, "continues your Jinn father's legacy of terror." The demon sighed and touched a cut on his cheek.

Kim couldn't stop staring at the cut. Cold fear shot through him. He stopped Python, gripping him by the arm. "*Was it her who cut you? Where is she? Where is Troy—*"

Python grabbed Kim's hand, wrenching it off him painfully. "Busy," he said, continuing forward. "And she'll stay busy enough until I'm done playing with her. She's irritating, but also amusing to me. I don't get rats like her in my maze very often."

Kim breathed hard. Already, he imagined Troy's intense yellow eyes peering back at him from the gloom. "You shouldn't underestimate her," he said heatedly. He stepped in front of Python, stopping him again. "You should kill her as soon as you get a chance. Otherwise . . ."

"Otherwise 'what'?" Python said dangerously. "If anything, half-breed, you would do well not to underestimate *me*. Remember, this is my little portion of Hell, and what I say goes. I say right now that the Jinn rat lives. Don't worry. I'll keep my part of our little bargain and kill her eventually. But you should think before you overstep your bounds."

Kim couldn't help pressing his luck. Anger flared hotly

inside of him, mixing with his growing and desperate fear. Even if Python sawed off Troy's wings and plucked out her teeth, she was now too close for comfort.

Kim struggled to keep his voice lower. "Even your mother sees Troy as a threat. If Troy kills me—then what will you do? So much for freeing the Prince from her cage."

"My mother," Python hissed between his teeth, "is currently out of the picture."

"Do you really want to see Lilith dead?" Kim snapped.

Now Python's eyes narrowed to deadly slits. He stepped forward, leaning over Kim. "Don't get personal with me. I've already done you more than a favor by turning a blind eye as you took my mother to bed for your own personal gain."

"*YOU TOLD ME TO DO THAT. You said she wouldn't trust me unless I—*"

"Quiet," Python said, grabbing Kim by the mouth. The demon's fingers pinched Kim's face with a searing pain. "Quiet."

Kim burned to rip Python's head off. Instead, he looked at Angela who continued to pace cautiously ahead. He trembled and did his best to calm down.

"Good boy," Python said. He let go. His snakelike eyes bored into Kim. "When it comes down to it, you've grown soft, haven't you? You've changed. That blazing fire behind your eyes, the anger and bitterness that propelled you forward, it's all fading fast. You're right. You need all the protection you can get. You've grown tired, half-breed. If the Jinn does in fact reach you, there's no doubt in my mind as to who will emerge victorious from your little battle."

Python broke away from Kim and walked ahead of Angela.

She stepped backward in alarm but allowed the demon

to pass without saying anything foolish. Python's lithe figure melded briefly into the darkness.

Kim caught up to her, rubbing at the blossoming bruise on his chin.

"What happened?" Angela said, real concern on her face. "Did Python hurt you?"

"We had a little argument," Kim muttered. "Nothing to get worked up about. He knows it wouldn't be smart to kill me."

They paused for a moment. Angela glanced at a mosaic to their left. It had been made with glittering black, purple, and silver stones and depicted a gigantic snake within a shining garden.

"The Garden of Eden," Kim said slowly, gazing at it with her. "Before it was tainted by lies . . ."

Angela stared at the mosaic snake's orange eyes.

She then looked down the shadows of the tunnel where Python had gone ahead of them. She resumed walking and her pace was quicker this time.

"How do you know him?" Angela demanded. Her beautiful face, all sharp angles and large blue eyes, seemed even more severe in the ominous half-light. "What bargain did you make with him, Kim? Was it all about Troy?"

Kim couldn't lie to her now. Not with so much already keeping them apart. "Just like his mother, Python promised to kill Troy for me. But in exchange I'm to free Lucifel from her prison."

Angela skidded to a halt. Her expression was incredulous. "You can't do that."

"You don't understand," Kim said grimly. "I have to. If I don't . . . so much for helping Sophia."

"I really don't see how the two are connected," Angela said angrily.

"It's very simple," Kim said. "If I don't free Lucifel, you can't kill her either. She will take what is in the Book, Angela, and then she will silence the universe with it. Somehow. All I know is that my adoptive father believes in that insane ideal of hers, and I suddenly disagree. Lucifel knows now you are truly the only one who can open Sophia. She wants you both down here beside her for a reason. This is all one big convoluted trap. But better to take the opportunity while we have it."

Angela's voice grew louder. "Did you write that poem about a Covenant and Ruin and leave it in my dorm house so that I would find it? Stephanie said that was your writing . . ."

She must have meant the poem Python had forced Kim to write. Kim had felt it was underhanded, but the demon had claimed they could use it to encourage Angela through the door that much faster. He'd also made enough threats that Kim never really had a choice. "Yes, I wrote the poem," Kim said softly.

He refrained from saying that he hadn't been the person who'd delivered it. That had been Python's responsibility. Kim could only imagine what poor soul the demon had bribed to do it. Probably a student who knew Angela personally.

But Angela didn't need to know that just yet. She was already worked up enough, and confronting Python was far from a good idea.

"I think you're insane," Angela spat back at him.

Kim touched her long red hair. "What will you do then?" he said sadly. "Kill me?"

Angela stared at him. Swiftly, she slapped him across the face. She breathed hard and fast, her eyes glazed with tears. In stormy silence, she sped off down the tunnel.

Kim closed his eyes, touching another painful spot on

his cheek. He trembled. Angela didn't understand. He didn't want this either. But for her own good, there was no turning back. It was his unfortunate destiny, after all. Sucking in a painful breath, he started after her.

They were both brought up short by Python. The demon stood in front of two giant double doors made of black glass. He crossed his arms, searching Kim and Angela with his eyes by turns. "Have the little lovebirds finished their quarrel?"

Before Kim could hold her back, Angela strode up to Python fearlessly.

"What kind of lies have you been feeding me? You told me you wanted to keep Lucifel in her cage—now Kim tells me you want just the opposite?" Angela shouted in his face.

Kim knew better than to interrupt. He could only pray.

Python's expression tightened coolly, but he never lost his composure. "Death is as good a cage as any other. It is probably the only one Lucifel will never really leave. But I'd suggest you keep your voice down and your suspicions better placed. The Prince has spies everywhere. Sometimes the walls literally have ears . . ."

Python slammed a fist near what Kim had thought was the carving of a spider.

The insect's green eyes flared to life. Then it hissed and scuttled like lightning across the walls and down the tunnel.

Angela watched it go, horror written all over her face.

"My, my . . . what would you do without me?" Python said, smirking at her.

Forced to give up on confronting him, Angela peered at the glass doors behind the demon. Kim feared she might try to bust right through them without a thought, but she glanced at him and checked herself for a moment.

"So what is this? An exit? I *hate* doors now," Angela said, still trying to sound angry. "There's never anything good behind them." She nearly shoved Python aside, examining the latest obstacle to her freedom. "I don't want any sneaky half-truths anymore. This had better be the way out of here."

"It is," Python said. "At least—if you can get past the guards. We've reached one of the many exits from the labyrinth. Yes, there is more than one way out. That's the fun of the process, of course. A few ways out, only one terrible way in. After this threshold, consider yourself one step closer to the lowest reaches of the demon city of Babylon, and unfortunately for Lucifel, the Abyss. She's a smart god, however. The Watchers guard this way into Babylon. Regrettably, there are no shortcuts around them . . ."

"The Watchers," Angela repeated. She shivered. "What are they?"

She glanced around, apparently realizing what Kim had known for a while—that the hieroglyphs on the walls and the mosaics tiled beneath them had been established in sequence, as if telling a story.

In them, Kim recognized angels. Humans.

A tall figure with many wings confused him, but Angela stared at it keenly. Even he could see that its face vaguely resembled her own.

She gazed at it, seeming to remember something as her face grew paler.

Kim swallowed nervously. He looked to her, trying to remain calm as he explained. "The Watchers are angels who defied God by coming to Earth and interbreeding with humans. But the resulting offspring were either stillborn or died shortly after birth. Initially, God punished the Watchers by forcing them to guard the gateway separating the Underworld from Heaven for all eternity. However, after Lucifel's revolt in Heaven, they sided with her, hoping she would be their salvation. She merely moved them into Hell, where they now help guard the demon city of Babylon."

"They are beyond reasoning with," Python said. "Trust me."

Angela gazed up at the words hastily scrawled in demonic Theban over the odd doors. "What does that say?"

Kim read the words aloud.

One exit of many has been found
That much nearer to the infernal crown.

Python repeated the words, and smiled. "It's such an ominous but clever rhyme."

Angela glared at him. "There really is no other way but to go past them?"

"Only if you don't mind turning back and retracing your steps," Python said, regarding her with curiosity. "But that's up to you. If it were me, I don't think I would be that optimistic . . . especially considering your circumstances. But that's the mystery, isn't it? What would happen if you were to turn back and choose another path? Perhaps we'll never know. I suppose it's just another part of what makes a maze so much fun." He said those last words licking his bottom teeth and staring at her. "Mazes and stories are a lot alike," Python said. "So many twists and turns. And you never quite know if they'll end happily."

"I'm not turning back," Angela said. But the look on her face showed how much her heart was sinking.

Kim knew how she felt. What if that wasn't the right choice? And yet . . .

"Oh, I know you're not turning back," Python said to

her. "That's what makes you so much fun. You're far from boring, Angela Mathers."

Kim turned aside this time. It was hard to look at Python because he found himself hating the demon more by the second. "Let's get on with this," he muttered.

Angela glanced at Kim, seeming to think. She turned back to Python. "Should we expect your help in there?"

"Must I do everything for you, my dear?" Python said. "Indeed, I've done too much already. Very few make it this far through the labyrinth at all. Considering the trouble I'll now have with my mother, I should go back and console her for tragically losing the troublesome Archon. At the very least, I'll slow down her progress as she sends the Hounds of Hell to sniff after you. In short—no."

Purple mist billowed around the demon's feet and torso.

"But if you want my advice, make sure the Watchers don't get into your head. Those former angels are always too curious for their own good . . ."

The fog drifted away, and Python was gone.

Kim looked at Angela, his eyes meeting hers. He still felt her gentle kiss on his mouth, and he warmed inside despite the chill running across his skin. Angela didn't say anything, merely set her hand on the gnarled handles of the doors.

Her face steeled with resolve.

She stood like that for a minute or longer, seeming unable to take the next step. Her fingers shivered. She closed her eyes.

Kim could only watch as she held the handles firmly and pushed.

Thirty

Angela couldn't know it—but because Luz was the linchpin connecting the Realms, everything in the city mirrored Heaven and Hell to some degree. From Luz's shape, to its festivals, to its watchful statues—everything the Archon would be forced to endure had already passed in some way before Her eyes. —SOPHIA

Angela had expected yet another tunnel, hall, or corridor. But when the doors opened, she found herself gazing into a cavern that was so immense, it seemed to have its own sky. A completely flat and silent world spread out before her. There was no breeze and the air smelled stale. Great globes of light glimmered high above, like dim suns behind a haze of clouds.

Directly ahead in the distance, enormous obsidian pillars soared upward into the fog. They crowned a large but low hill of ashy sand. Was this the plain she had seen on that crude map of Hell? But the word *plain* seemed too small for something so incredibly vast.

"Careful," Kim whispered as Angela stepped forward.

Angela walked slowly through the ashen sand. She pulled

off the arm glove on her left hand. Kim froze for a moment beside her, staring at it.

"Do you have a weapon?" she whispered to him.

"Of course I do," Kim said. He inclined his head at her. "You."

"If you say so," she said, sighing heavily.

"And these." Kim slipped one or two crumpled paper wards from his coat pocket. For the first time since Lilith's Ball, Angela realized he was still wearing part of his crow costume. "But they won't do much besides stop them for a moment or less. Lucifel wouldn't use the Watchers as guards if they were that ineffective."

"All right. Stay close to me then, and I'll do my best." Angela looked away, remembering her cold slap to his already bruised face. She still found it hard to look Kim in the eye. The feelings were there, but their ideals clearly diverged. The rift between them just grew by the minute. For so long, Kim's face and touch had tormented her memories. Now he was even more handsome than Angela remembered, despite his wounds. But the resolve behind his eyes shook her nerves badly. It was clear he had no intention of turning his back on what he saw as Angela's true destiny. "It's too quiet," she whispered, trying to fill in the awkward silence.

Kim nodded, staring ahead.

Angela continued, more and more shaken by the immense quiet. Now that they were closer to the pillars, it was easier to see the strange hieroglyphic writing carved along their sides, all the way up to their triangular peaks. These pillars were actually obelisks, and there were hundreds of them, in hundreds of parallel rows, with each row a width of forty feet at the least.

Their geometric precision was only interrupted by rectangular indentations carved into their middles. Angela halted, her breath sighing out of her. She probably looked goggle-eyed with wonder.

Kim bumped into her and cried softly in surprise. His hands gripped her shoulders. Their warmth was comforting enough in the eerie silence that she didn't brush him away.

Slowly, Angela glanced around, her heart yearning to burst from her chest. Fear raced like fire into every corner of her being.

These obelisks held the most realistic angel statues she had ever seen. In comparison, the statues that had disturbed her outside the Grand Mansion in Luz suddenly looked like primitive lumps of rock.

Worse yet, the effigies were almost too detailed and natural. Some were male and some were female, their double wings were weather-beaten and portions of their bodies had been swathed in bandages. They wore coats of dazzling green and blue with thread glittering like silver. At any moment they appeared ready to move, sigh, or speak. An unexpected breeze whipped through the corridor, blowing sand into the air. Yet their glassy eyes never even blinked.

It was like some ghastly wax museum.

A creeping sense of being watched picked at Angela. She followed her instincts and dug her nails into the Grail. The Eye began to bleed and blue warmth dribbled down to her fingers.

Kim stepped back hastily. He stared as the Glaive formed between Angela's fingers and the blade crystallized. The weapon's haft and pole stretched in the opposite direction, settling to rest in her other hand.

Angela closed her eyes and listened to her heartbeat. Blood pulsed and throbbed through her hand, mixing with the Eye's as the Glaive sucked gently away at her life force. She would have to be careful and not waste too much valuable time here.

Angela couldn't afford to be weak now.

Though she couldn't help hoping maybe—just maybe—the Watchers would let them pass.

Angela walked slowly until she was in the middle of the great row of watchful angels and obelisks. She stopped.

Nothing's happening.

Whispers erupted around her. They seemed to hang in the air and then disappear like dreams.

Angela looked at the statues. The world spun as she held up the Glaive, her arms shaking. Kim breathed beside her, a cold sweat trickling down the side of his sculpted cheek. The whispers grew louder. His amber eyes widened. "Now," he said grimly. *"Get down."*

A hefty gust of air beat down on Angela from overhead. A long shadow darkened the sand.

She slammed to the ground beneath a hurricane of beating wings, and Kim fell with her, covering her as best he could. Sand blew into Angela's eyes, nose, and mouth. Her head rang from the force of her jaw snapping shut. She clawed at the sand, unable to bear being pressed blindly to the earth.

Just as quickly the wind ceased. The storm of plumage disappeared with it. Trying not to flail or scream, Angela spat the grit from her mouth and rubbed the sand from her face. Beside her, Kim knelt in a protective gesture, his face even paler.

A circle of curved wings now blocked every escape route.

Two of the statues, obviously not statues at all, loomed on either side of Angela. The same coats that had appeared so dazzlingly affluent from a distance had actually been

faded by exposure and time. Long tattered bandages covered half of the nearest angel's plumage, and a thread of
light stretched from its head to the inner nook of an obelisk.
Like Python had warned, these angels were literally guard
dogs on chains.

The Watchers' voices erupted in incessant, maddening
whispers. But their lips never moved.

Intruders . . .

The word echoed and returned again as if from a million mouths, assaulting Angela's senses. She touched her
ears, hardly able to believe the strange echoing effect in her
head as the words reached down into her consciousness and
plucked at it painfully.

Are you the one I love . . .

Where were you, beloved? Have you come back to me . . .

Each voice competed with the next, some crying about
lost love, others about loneliness and punishment.

An intense pain shot through Angela's head. She screamed,
only slightly aware of Kim's cry as he clutched at her, shouting her name. Angela hit the powdery sand beneath her. The
Glaive threatened to collapse into a pool of liquid.

Images filtered as quickly as lightning though her mind.
One second she was a baby reaching for a toy. Now she
was a child, locked in a closet while her brother slipped her
food beneath the door. There were Christmas carols, but as
always, no presents for Angela. Her mother shrieked at her,
called her a filthy blood head, and hit her. Her father didn't
make a move to stop it. Time abruptly shifted. Angela was
once again painting Israfel's image, with hot tears rolling
down her face. Then it was time to sit silently in the institution, staring at white walls in her equally white uniform. Fire
erupted in a blazing inferno around her. Scars flared to life

on her arms and legs. Her parents died in the flames. Her brother, Brendan, died after crawling pathetically to Israfel's feet.

The sight of it all tore at every fiber of her heart and soul. She begged in her mind for it to stop, please stop.

Where are you, my love?

The voices continued mercilessly. Angela cried out as she found herself dancing with Israfel again, as she recognized the pain behind his eyes. He was calling for her. But suddenly she was in Kim's arms, trying to forget her own agonies. Angela's soul twisted and writhed and she tried again to break free of the nightmares being forced on her, but the Watchers pried into her mind with all the greater aggressivness.

You were taken from me . . . now I must take you back . . .

Now Sophia appeared before Angela's tortured mind. She was delicate, beautiful, and lonely as ever. Sophia stretched out her arms to Angela, begging her not to enter Hell. Slowly, the peaceful world they had built together crumbled apart.

Pain threatened to stop Angela's heart.

But I have to enter, Angela argued with her. *For your sake. I have to.*

But what was that horrible screaming voice in the background, interrupting them?

The fierce grip on Angela's mind weakened abruptly. Her eyes snapped open. She clutched at her throat. It ached like she'd tried to swallow a knife, and her voice was raspy and raw.

That screaming voice had been hers.

She rocked to her feet. A deep shiver in the ground quaked up through her body, nearly flinging Angela back to her knees. Kim grabbed her by the arm, trying to hold them both steady. For a moment, the universe groaned, and the air warped. Angela clutched her stomach with her free hand. A thick wave of nausea twisted through her.

"It's starting," he shouted. "The Realms are growing more unstable."

No, Angela shouted back to herself in her mind. *No. I didn't finish this yet. It's not over yet. I can reach Sophia!*

The earth stopped trembling with odd suddenness. The silence returned.

The Watchers stared at Angela without a single trace of emotion. If they had been surprised by what had just happened, they would never show it. Instead, their eyes pierced Angela like fine needles. Their voices returned. Now, they sounded angrier, as if they had judged her memories and past and found them lacking.

Creature of dreaded omens . . . you are unclean . . . a thing that should not be. A soul without a name.

Nothing unclean enters this place.

Nothing enters this place that is not of this place.

Angela glanced back and forth between the two nearest angels converging on her. She held the Glaive up high, screaming out in terror despite the raw pain in her throat.

You are ours now—and the Watchers will deal with you.

She swung the Glaive, staggering slightly.

Blood sprayed back on her. Two of the dreadful Watchers dropped back into the sand, now truly lifeless.

Instantly, more of them soared in, followed by yet more in a punishing hell of angels. The world became a blur. Angela swung, she cursed, she hacked off wings that spiraled down into the sand, and she cut off arms that flopped twitching to the ashen ground. Blood hit her in the eyes.

She shrieked, twisting the Glaive so that it caught a Watcher in the chest, flinging it backward at least fifty feet.

Still they came, relentless and terrible.

Angela knelt on the ground, gasping for breath. The world wheeled and spun around her even faster than before. She couldn't hold out much longer. Already, she felt the Glaive sucking away all of her energy and turning her muscles to jelly. Her heartbeat slowed to the rolling rhythm of a great drum in her ears.

She shouted in surprise and swung the Glaive hard to her right. A Watcher dropped in two pieces to the ground.

Unclean? Is that what she really was? But Angela wasn't just the Archon—*she was a person too.*

More Watchers swooped in. Angela cut them down like a reaper of birds, wing after wing, beautiful face after beautiful face. The exhaustion was almost too much. Blood dripped in her eyes.

I'll never win at this rate. Sophia—wait. I'm doing my best. For you, for Troy, for Nina.

The thought of Nina dead again tore into Angela like a pair of ragged claws. Tears blurred over the unfair world around her. She shrieked and stumbled, but caught another Watcher before its hands could wrap themselves around her throat. Dizziness brushed at Angela, pitching her sideways.

Not yet! Not yet!

"*Exorcizo te,*" Kim screamed. His voice resounded over the cries of the Watchers.

There was a flash of brilliant red light. The angels drew back with angry cries.

Angela whipped around, her matted hair half screening her vision. She wobbled, and suddenly the Glaive collapsed. Blue liquid gushed down her arms and dribbled to the ground. She slipped and tried to catch her balance. Kim grabbed her hard and tugged her forward.

Ashy sand sprayed around Angela's ankles.

She ran, trying to keep up with Kim as he shouted in Latin. She stumbled once, twice, again and again in the powdery sand. She wrapped her hand around the necklace pendant at her chest. The Grail throbbed and burned so fiercely, Angela's hand felt as if it might melt into a puddle of flesh.

They exited the corridor of obelisks. The voices and the cries of the Watchers ceased.

Still, Kim refused to stop running.

Time slipped away in a rush of fear and pain. They could have been running for an hour, perhaps more. Still they continued. Angela kept up with him, her pounding heart and scorching adrenaline pushing her forward despite her dizziness. But there would be no relief for them soon. The sand stretched away in a vast desert, and at its end a great city loomed on the horizon. This was the dreaded demon city of Babylon—it had to be. Onyx and obsidian glistened in the hazy light of the lamps working as the cavern's suns. Brilliant fires touched thousands of the city's windows, glittering in patterns of red and yellow. Pyramids rose high into the fog. Everything was jaggedness and sharp edges, as if the city had been constructed with great black teeth. The low growl of thunder touched her ears, and Angela imagined the city was as angry as it looked. Soon the thunder evolved into an ugly roar.

It was coming from behind them.

Angela stopped for breath, her hands on her knees as she gasped. Taking another step felt like courting death.

Kim glanced behind them, his face grimmer than ever. "You're kidding," he shouted over the noise. He cursed in angry frustration. *"Damn it!"*

Angela turned and looked up. Her eyes widened.

Now she understood why the Watchers had drawn back. They no longer needed any more casualties when there was an entire army to chase after Angela and Kim. The horizon behind them seethed with dust and bodies and hellish light. A dreadful mix of demons and possibly human ghosts sat astride creatures resembling horses with long, ribbed horns sharp as spears. If they were unicorns, they were unicorns from Hell, and mesmerizing blue patterns of light flickered and flashed along their bodies in the gloom. Angela thought instantly of the horselike creatures on Stephanie's wall, the door, and the map of Hell. But those carvings had done little justice to creatures so otherworldly and fearsome.

Fear and wonder rooted Angela to the ground. She couldn't bring herself to look away.

The ghostly riders—were they human souls captured by Lucifel? Angela remembered with a hot pain in her soul how her own dead parents had chosen Lucifel over their only daughter when given the choice.

Perhaps they were among the army even now, aching to cut off her head.

"They're riding Kirin," Kim shouted to Angela. "Lilith must have sent them. *So much for her son's promises—*"

"What now!" Angela yelled back. Her throat still hurt and she no longer cared. Soon she might not have the chance to care about anything ever again.

"The Glaive," he screamed at her desperately.

Angela weakly tried to summon it again, but only managed to form a blue dagger in her hand. Her head pounded, and her left hand holding the dagger trembled violently. She staggered.

Kim stared at her wildly. He turned, seeming to search

toward Babylon, and then back toward where they'd exited the labyrinth. "*Python!*" he screamed. "*Python!*"

The army pursued them and was closing in fast enough that some of the demons sat low and intent on their charges. Very few of the demons had wings. They'd probably disintegrated long ago, and now they relied on the Kirin for long-distance travel. Kim cursed again and then his face changed, brightness and excitement sweeping over it. Two Kirin crested a low hill and galloped toward Angela and Kim from across the plain. Upon reaching Angela, the great creatures reared up and their paws thumped down powerfully in the sand. Their horns were even more intimidating up close. Saddles with the symbol of a violet snake carved into the side lay on their backs.

"He pulled through," Kim shouted. "Thank God! Quick! Get on!"

Angela had never ridden a horse before, much less a creature as fearsome as this. She balked at the Kirin as it snorted hot breath in her face. Its eyes glowed yellow like Troy's and held a striking intelligence.

Ride, Stephanie's voice yelled in her memories. *Ride away before it's too late . . .*

Was this what she'd meant? Had she seen Angela on one of these creatures in some hellish vision?

"*Where do we go?*" Angela screamed at Kim.

Kim brought one of the Kirin closer to Angela. He tugged on its reins sharply, turning it toward the city again. The Kirin struggled and then obeyed, stomping at the earth. "Toward the city, and then down alongside the bank of the Styx," he shouted. "Toward Lucifel's Altar."

Angela hesitated.

Kim can't get that far. If he does, he'll free Lucifel.

"Come on!" He lifted Angela and practically tossed her onto the Kirin's saddle. "This one will follow its mate. Just let the reins loose and allow it to follow my charge."

Angela settled down in the saddle without saying another word. She gripped the reins, staring at Kim as he jumped into his own Kirin's saddle and kicked it sharply at the flanks.

The noise of the army behind them rang and echoed deafeningly. It was almost upon them.

Angela's Kirin launched forward behind Kim's, and she cried out, gripping the reins so tightly her hands burned. Shudders ran through her as its heavy paws struck the ground. Air blew back in her face, whipping her hair straight back. Babylon loomed ahead. Closer, larger. Soon, Angela gave up on the reins entirely and wrapped her arms around the Kirin's neck, careful to keep her dagger away from its black mane. Their rollicking pace sent her teeth chattering.

They thundered on, but it was no use. Whether because of skill or luck, the army was now only a few yards behind them. The noise of Kirin paws striking the earth was so loud Angela could barely think.

One of the ghost riders broke free of the army and galloped side by side with Angela.

She stared at him. Her heart could have dropped into the pit of her stomach.

It was Camdon Willis. He was focused on the city like a mindless drone, and his transparent body glowed a ghostly red. As if in a dream, his face turned slowly in her direction. Their gazes locked. With a cry of recognition, he veered in toward her. He grinned in triumph—and swiped at Angela viciously with a nasty-looking dagger.

"Camdon!" Angela screamed.

He showed no sign of changing his tactics. Instead, he veered in even closer.

Angela straightened a bit, tugging on the reins. Her Kirin dodged to the right but moved back to avoid a rock in the sand. Grasping his opportunity, Camdon sliced at her leg. Angela yanked on the reins and swerved aside again, nearly slipping off the saddle. She kicked at the Kirin's sides and it galloped faster.

Nina's half brother caught up with nightmarish quickness. Soon they were again side by side and uncomfortably close. "*Camdon!*" Angela screamed one more time.

He wasn't himself anymore. Angela's brother Brendan had changed once his soul was possessed. Why should Camdon be any different?

Camdon dipped in to slice at her legs yet again. This time, a stinging pain raced through her calf.

She screamed.

Angela struck back with her blue dagger, swiping at Camdon's hands. The blade seemed to pass through nothing but air, but Camdon stared at her in surprise, his eyes widening with shock. His Kirin slowed and he looked at his hands like he'd never seen them before. Camdon smiled at Angela again, but now that smile was filled with gratefulness. He closed his eyes, as if relieved at whatever came next.

With a blinding flash, he burst into a thousand sparks of red light that blew back through her hair.

"*NO,*" Angela screamed. "*STOP!*" She jerked on the reins, desperately hoping for the beast to halt, her hands shaking like leaves. But it didn't seem to make a difference. "*CAMDON! CAMDON!*"

The Kirin rode on.

Thirty-one

Sophia's eyes held the same pain as my own
mother's when I disappointed her time and again.
And so, I couldn't help hating her. —PYTHON

Sophia was the Book of Raziel, but she also considered herself to be a person like any other. Despite that, she'd been treated as a creature with feelings by only two people in her entire life: Raziel and Angela. Knowing this, Python had given into his sadism and forced her to sit in front of an obsidian mirror, and its surface had displayed and continued to display every moment of Angela's journey from the second she'd entered Hell to save Sophia.

At first, Sophia had feigned cool indifference.

But the more Angela suffered, the more Sophia knew anguish blossomed on her face. She refused to beg—as the Book of Raziel it was not only beneath her, it was exactly what Python wanted and would make no difference. But Sophia did allow herself to cry. Unable to leave, unable to help, she sat in Python's chair exactly as he'd tied her there, watching and weeping.

"What do you think?" Python said. He leaned down

beside Sophia, whispering in her ear. Together they watched as Angela clung to the Kirin's neck, screaming. Angela had gritted her teeth and her bloodstained face looked as anguished as Sophia felt. Python sighed. "She'll get here, doll. Don't worry. The Archon has more spunk than I'd hoped. Soon she'll arrive, she'll open you, and then"—he smiled grimly—"a new era begins. If anything, this was too easy. Is it so much to ask to have a challenge now and then?"

This time, Sophia allowed the scorn souring her thoughts to be heard. "A challenge?" she whispered. "You're a fool if you think Lucifel doesn't know what you're trying to do."

Python barely flinched. "Her awareness doesn't matter if I win. Lucifel is the bird in the cage. *Not me.*"

"Continue in your world of delusion," Sophia said softly.

Python stared at Sophia with his intense, fiery orange eyes. He seemed to be considering her carefully.

"What is it all for, Python?" Sophia said. More tears rolled hotly down her face. "To spite your mother? Then I suppose you're not so different from the angels themselves, are you? Each and every one that falls, to my shame has done so with disgrace, trying to hide their sins behind painted smiles. But it is fitting that the sight of you destroying yourself should be just one more punishment for me among many. What an ironic testament to the flawed destiny I have brought upon you all."

Python opened his mouth, about to retort.

A flash of greenish light brightened his room. Lilith appeared from within the light, her dark and beautiful face tight with anger. She strolled quickly toward Python, looking like she would strangle him. Instead, she grabbed him by the collar, shook him, and threw him violently against the wall.

Python laughed. His face, however, was chillingly cold.

"Mother, how unexpected at this hour. Whatever could be wrong?"

"I know what you did," Lilith shouted viciously at him. "You rotten little snake. *Why do I put up with you?*" She raised her hand to strike him but seemed to think better of it. With a struggle, she lowered her shaking hand and regained her dignity. "But it doesn't matter. Your little game, my bored and boring son, ends here. I've sent enough souls and slaves after Angela Mathers to catch her, rip her to pieces, and scatter the bits to every corner of Hell."

"I know that," Python said insolently. He pointed at the mirror in front of Sophia. "Yet you've forgotten that not every slave in this chasm is loyal to you alone. Like me, some have grown tired of Lucifel's reign. I have my own cavalry, my own loyal regiment like every other lieutenant in Hell. And they also think it's high time to let the blackbird out of her cage. Maybe I shouldn't be surprised you overlooked that detail in your single-minded revenge."

Lilith stared at the image of Angela riding the Kirin and pursed her lips dangerously. She rounded back on Python. "You're an *idiot*. Do you realize what Lucifel will do if she learns about your betrayal? Isn't it hypocritical enough when my Naamah died for the same twisted fantasy?"

"What?" he whispered, advancing on Lilith. "What will Lucifel do? Give orders? Try to have me killed? Words and threats, given from her spider's web of chains. And if we're arguing about idiocy and common sense, I doubt you'll emerge with the upper hand. I gave you the soul of Camdon Willis, but you didn't use him to your advantage, Mother. Instead, he lived long enough for the Archon to send every bit of his essence back to the elements. What fine work."

Lilith stared him down harder. "Spare me your preaching," she said with sudden and dangerous softness. "I could say the same about you concerning his sister. Look at you. My son's handsome face disfigured by a Jinn." She walked closer and cradled Python's cheek, caressing the wound with motherly tenderness.

Python turned away from her, but she persisted and he gave in, closing his eyes and swallowing.

Lilith stopped her caresses and tapped his cheek harshly. "You are just what the Book has called you—a fool who will fall victim to his own ambitions. And all because Naamah succeeded in so many ways where you did not."

Python opened his eyes, a truly wounded and angry look tightening his face. "What I do—I do for all demons," he hissed under his breath. "Now what have you done for us lately? Besides throwing your affluent pleasure parties?"

Lilith shook her head and laughed. "Parties that you consistently crash uninvited," she said smoothly. "How dare you use my chambers as part of your little rat maze. How dare you spy on my servants, and on me. Do you think I don't notice you? Do you think I don't feel your eyes on me at every silent moment? Or hear your pleading voice, begging for my affection?"

Python's face became even tighter. He breathed hard as Lilith leaned in closer.

She was tall, strikingly beautiful, and if only for the fact that she was his mother, completely beyond his reach.

"I will win," he said at last, with eyes suggesting he was sure of himself.

"How?" Lilith demanded.

Python didn't smile, but his tone sounded confident. "Do you understand what the Archon's visions meant? She is more powerful than Lucifel. She is one step below the Father. No—perhaps equal to him. And I needed to know what I was dealing with, because I proclaim right now with complete faith in myself that I will watch the Archon destroy Lucifel. I will see Angela Mathers ascend to the Throne of Hell. I will nurture her, and the trust she has in me, and then I will kill her when she's past her pitiful usefulness and rule Hell. *With you, Mother, as my chief slave.*"

Lilith drew back, a disappointed expression washing over her face. "You're insane," she murmured. "Why didn't I kill you when you were a chick? I always knew you were an abomination."

Python closed his eyes, wounded even more than before. But his face was as steely as ever. "Don't count Angela Mathers out just yet. With her, I will show you a new world. Starting NOW."

Sophia couldn't help herself anymore. She had to watch, she could do nothing, and for either her or Angela, it was the end.

Python knew too much.

"ANGELA," she screamed in a piercing voice, her soul shuddering with pain. "ANGELA!" Sophia turned to Python, her soul burning with anger. "STOP IT!"

Python must have had enough. He grabbed Sophia, ripping off the fabric that had tied back her wrists. Clasping Sophia's white sapphire star pendant, he regarded it with a cold smirk. He let it drop back against her chest. "Demands from a prisoner aren't quite so intimidating, my dear. How long has it been," he whispered to her, "since you've seen what Hell is really like? Do you remember your old master? She's been waiting for you. Perhaps it's time for a family visit?"

Lilith stepped back into the shadows with a sigh of ludicrous disgust. Something in her had given up on her son, but it wasn't wicked enough to kill him. She was just leaving him to his fate as she saw it.

Sophia screamed one more terrible time.

Python's triumph was in his words. He dragged Sophia out of the room. "Lucifel awaits."

Thirty-two

*Traveling through that meager portion of Hell,
I realized something sorrowful. With the odds
against them the demons had worked to capture
whatever light was left to them in a world of
endless darkness.* —ANGELA MATHERS

The Kirin continued on until Angela thought her entire life was nothing but dust, hunger, thirst, and pain. Her body ached and throbbed in the saddle, and her leg muscles screamed with stiffness. Yet Kim galloped ahead without any signs of weariness, riding his Kirin like he owned it. Well, his foster father *was* a demon. Kim had probably experienced many things Angela would never know or completely understand. Just like how she didn't know or completely understand Kim himself.

He was risking his life to take Angela to Lucifel and put her on Lucifel's Throne. That demanded some kind of gratefulness on her part.

Even so, she couldn't help worrying about him. Angela had slapped Kim across the face, but in reality she'd been slapping her old self reflected back at her. They were too much alike. He was making the same mistakes she had made in her past, and might even be throwing his life away for a dream she couldn't share.

Under better circumstances, maybe they could have lived happily side by side. But this was a different world, and no matter what Kim believed, peace wouldn't come for either of them just because Angela sat on a Throne she never wanted.

He was too much of a dreamer.

Angela tried to breathe away the tightness in her chest. There was no denying it. The connection between their souls was there. She felt for Kim, and perhaps in some way loved him. So the next thought struck her with horror: what if that connection went wrong and her ascent in any particular direction meant Kim's fall?

Fears she couldn't fight any longer attacked her mind from every direction, and as they did, Angela's soul threatened to bleed away. She tugged on her Kirin's reins in terror, desperately trying to spring ahead while more ghostly riders caught up to them again. The idea of finding Nina among those ghostly riders was like a knife to the heart, but Angela couldn't help glancing at the riders who swerved in closer. At times, she clutched at her pendant so fiercely it cut into her palm. With her awful luck, the pendant would break off and disappear beneath thousands of thundering Kirin paws.

Finally, an enormous stone bridge tipped by spires and lights loomed ahead of them. It spanned in an immense arc reaching from one corner of the city to the other. Angela held her breath and waited for a trap, but their Kirin galloped beneath the bridge without meeting any resistance. No demons walked across it. No guards stood watch. Perhaps the army pursuing her was enough.

Angela swallowed nervously as the bridge's black shadow

passed swiftly over them and dropped back into the distance.

She tried to steal more glances at their surroundings, but they were clearly speeding into the lowest part of the city, and between their pace and the darkness, it was becoming harder to see. Kim continued to navigate without any difficulty, steering his Kirin and Angela's in the direction of a great tunnel marked by enormous pillars, directly at the forefront of Babylon. Now what little signs of civilization there had been dropped off dramatically. The Styx River flowed right through the tunnel's center, but he and Angela were able to gallop along a rocky bank bordering the river on its right.

Angela coughed. Every breath of this awful fog was like inhaling thousands of pins.

They continued, and familiar hieroglyphic writing covered the walls. The symbols grew more arcane and terrible looking with time. Pentagrams glowed everywhere in brilliant, pulsing red.

More pillars flanked Angela and Kim, and the ground sloped down steeply.

They halted beneath an obsidian arch, and Angela grunted as the saddle's pommel dug into her stomach. Kim turned his Kirin around, his pale face looking bloody in the dim light. Angela's Kirin did the same. She parted her lips, already feeling a question on them.

The army was gone.

Noise and cries of frustration echoed from far away near the tunnel's opening. But no ghost or demon appeared willing to cross the barrier between Angela and the beginning of what had to be Lucifel's Altar. Kim dropped from his Kirin and let go of the reins, and the beast snorted and pawed at the ground. Its lean flanks dripped with sweat. Cold blue light flickered along its body and streaks of blood stained the sides of its horn.

Angela's Kirin responded to its mate by stamping the ground impatiently. Angela slid off its back and dropped to the rocks, shouting as her sore feet met the ground.

Her hand burned.

Angela dropped the blue dagger she'd been grasping and it collapsed into a puddle on the stone. Blue liquid trickled through the dirt in rivulets. She cradled her hand, covering the throbbing Grail with the other, wincing at the pain. Her mind flashed to Camdon's relieved face after she struck his ghost with the blade, and a scream threatened to work its way out of her. But it wouldn't bring him back, and there was no point in letting Kim see how awful she felt. Angela leaned against the rocks, trying just to breathe and stand. Her head pounded, her heart ached, her entire body sighed painfully.

Angela's Kirin cantered nervously, pawing at the ground. Suddenly, it gave a fierce cry and raced back toward the army, far away from Lucifel. Its paws thundered against the earth, kicking up dust. Soon, it disappeared with its fearsome mate in a haze of fog.

Angela licked her dry, cracked lips. Her chest felt hollow. She was about to find Sophia—or so she hoped—but too much still stood in her way. For Sophia's sake, she couldn't allow it.

She and Kim stared at each other.

Why did he have to look at Angela like she was so cruel? Kim was the person in the wrong. Not her.

"I won't sit on Lucifel's Throne," Angela said after a long pause. She stumbled, still trying to catch her breath and get used to the ground staying firm beneath her feet again. "I won't, Kim. You can't persuade me or change my mind. So I'll let you choose. Help me rescue Sophia and get out of here. Or . . ."

"Or?" he whispered, his gaze piercing through her.

Angela shook her head. "You know I won't kill you. I can't. I'm not like . . ."

"Me?" he finished for her again. Kim's starkly handsome face actually looked gaunt in the terrible light. He rubbed his forehead, his temples. "Angela," he said, pacing in anguish. "You don't understand. This is your chance to change things."

A deep groan shuddered through the earth. Pebbles dribbled from the ceiling.

Kim stopped and they looked at each other again. "There isn't much time," he said. "A month or two—maybe less. If you kill Lucifel and open Sophia, we can start here. Change things from below, and work up. Python promised me he would help you, Angela. He is on our side. He doesn't believe in Lucifel's role as a god anymore either. I once did—when I was young and foolish. But I can't be led like a child anymore. Things need to change."

"A new revolution?" Angela said. "That sounds too much like a repeat of Lucifel's destiny. I don't see how it will change anything. Besides—I don't know how to open Sophia."

"Lucifel does," Kim whispered. "Why else do you think she wants you down here?"

"You don't know that for sure," Angela shot back. Pain cut through her soul like a rusty saw.

What *would* it mean for Sophia to be opened? Angela never considered that enough.

"That poem I left for you," Kim said. "It's the truth,

Angela. You will be the Ruin. The Ruin of one universe and the beginning of another. It's only humanity's fault that it can't understand the necessity of change."

"Raziel chose a human as the Archon for precisely that reason," Angela shouted. "Because we look at things differently than angels or demons! Sophia is not a 'thing,' Kim. She has feelings. She should have a say in her own fate." Angela caught her breath. Words should have been helping her, but they only made everything feel more hopeless. "In that poem, the Archon is also known by the word 'Covenant.' Isn't a covenant a promise between friends? Well, Raziel made a promise to the Jinn, to everyone. He died for that promise. *I intend to keep it.* And I intend to keep my promise to Sophia. It's the bonds between people that change everything. Not war and bloodshed. Not petty rivalries where a throne passes from one damaged soul to the next."

Kim shook his head. He wasn't quite putting faith in her words, obviously struggling with the validity of her argument.

"I won't let you free Lucifel, Kim," Angela said with finality. "Let her stay caged. That's the punishment she deserves, after all."

"For what?" he shouted back at her now. "For believing in a different world?"

"No," Angela said. "For turning her back on it. But I'm not like her. I'm not running away anymore, or chasing after dreams. Angels or no angels. Raziel told me once that I was living for someone else. I have to believe him."

Kim paused. He looked at Angela with surprise.

"You love her, don't you?" he whispered with real pain in his voice. His eyes widened.

"Who?" Angela shouted.

"Sophia."

Lightning could have struck Angela. Pain, and fire, and a clear light passed through her all at once. She paused, her heart galloping faster than a Kirin. "There are all different kinds of love," she said after a while. "You can't equate my friendship with Sophia to what we—"

"If you say so," he said, smiling sadly. He ran his fingers through his long black bangs.

Angela breathed hard, grasping for her necklace. The tiny pendant rested against her skin like a cold star. Her loyalty to Sophia wasn't at all like the feelings she had for Kim or Israfel. It was something completely different, even if she couldn't quite explain how. There was also no use in trying.

"It's beyond the point," Angela said at last. She hung her head. The temptation to sleep and block out the world forever was clawing at her, and she couldn't let it win. "I can't let you get farther than this, Kim. Not if you won't change your mind, and I know you won't."

"It doesn't matter," Kim said sadly. He turned aside. "You don't really have a choice."

"Why not?"

Python's face appeared parallel with Angela's. He gripped her firmly from behind, his warm hands locked tightly around her wrists. The demon's voice was keen as a knife. "Because"—Python whispered in her ear—"great minds think alike."

Thirty-three

*I resolved on returning Heaven to its former
glory. Certainly, the memories that lived within
me were also my mission.* —ISRAFEL

Israfel could feel the blood drain out of his body slowly. Life
escaped from him second by second. It would be a long while
until he actually died, but these humans had time on their
side. He gasped for air, trying to ignore the burning cuts of
their knives on his wings. By now they probably resembled
Raziel's when the angel fell to his death.

Israfel wanted to tell Raziel they would be together soon,
but there were no words left inside of him.

Besides, Raziel was protecting the Archon. How could he
possibly hear?

Instead, Israfel dreamed. His mind flashed to those moments of his life when he had gazed at the Father, seeing his
Creator for the first time. Why had there always seemed to
be a secret behind those burning eyes? Why had the Father
always looked at Israfel with that terrible longing mixed with
fear? Israfel had time enough back then to try and figure it
out. With Raziel dead and Lucifel gone, the Father had caged

his remaining child Israfel in Ialdaboth and done what he had pleased to Israfel so often, all sense of freedom had vanished.

The testament to that horror lingered within him.

Israfel wrapped his arms around his stomach, trying to protect the last treasure left to salvage everything. He had thought Angela had been crying out for him. Perhaps he had been wrong all along and the voice Israfel heard had been his own. Something in Angela's mysterious soul had merely been reflecting back part of his.

What tied them together? Why was it so hard for him to give up?

You are special, Israfel, Raziel's gentle voice said from his memories. The Supernal angel reappeared before Israfel's mind, still dressed in his beautiful blue coat studded with gems. Raziel's handsome face overflowed with compassion. *Lucifel may not understand you. But I do. There is always more to people, Israfel. So there is more to you—even if all of Heaven believes that they know you inside and out. Don't be afraid to live as that part of yourself. Don't be afraid of who you were meant to be.*

But Israfel *was* afraid. He'd wanted to be normal and whole like Raziel and Lucifel from the start. Instead, he was something in between. Neither truly male or female, he'd been cruelly destined to live in a world defined by others' perceptions and his own desires. "He" and "she'" had become words both defining and imprisoning him, and when Israfel referred to himself as one term, the opposite half of his identity suffered. That suffering eventually taught him to live like a chameleon, favoring the identity most helpful in any circumstance. Finally, and most sadly of all, it ended with becoming what he hoped Raziel loved most.

You are wonderful, Raziel's voice said, echoing gently

within Israfel. *Lucifel and I cannot match you. Only in you is the reflection of the Father seen most clearly.*

If that was true, why did Israfel think of himself with horror? All the jewels, makeup, clothing, and fawning angels in the world hadn't been enough to make up for the reality of how he saw himself. The mirror had always been his greatest enemy. The smiles and desires of others had been his greatest pain. There had been so few exceptions to that rule—but there were still some. Israfel thought of his guardian Thrones Rakir and Nunkir, and their fanatically loyal love. He thought of Tress Cassel's compassion in the face of danger. He thought of Angela Mathers, who had given her heart to Israfel with so much trust.

Had he betrayed that trust?

He would certainly betray it by dying. The Archon's purpose lay with him, and he was about to leave her alone again.

Never before had such weakness swept through him. Not even when Lucifel knelt above him, cried out triumphantly, and infected Israfel with her own shadow.

You can't always be so selfish, Israfel, Raziel said, laughing. They were playing together in his memories as chicks. Israfel had flipped their game angrily when it became clear he was losing. It felt much better simply not to play. But Raziel put the pieces back, offering for Israfel to start their game again. He smiled gently. *Sometimes, you need to lose a little before you can learn how to win.*

How much Israfel would give for those innocent days again.

No—he would see that those innocent days returned. But if he let go of everything here—

Israfel thought all his strength had vanished. He was wrong. Determination scorched through him in a blazing rush. He pushed with his hands and unfurled his wounded wings. They snapped open, thrusting aside some of the humans who had fallen on him. The priests tumbled back in surprise, some of them screaming in terror.

Lizbeth turned and looked at Israfel with horror in her eyes.

Raziel was right. Israfel could be selfish. But there was a time and place for everything, and right now he needed to remember his own pride as a warrior. Israfel had no astral energy left, but now that he'd been losing for so long he knew exactly how to win. Some of the humans advanced on him, shouting exorcisms in the Tongue of Souls.

The pain of the prayers slammed into him like a boulder. Israfel staggered but spread his bleeding wings wide.

He caught the first human by the collar and threw him into the wall. The man cracked into the stone and slumped to the floor, unconscious.

Another human ran at Israfel, swinging wildly at him with a knife.

Israfel grabbed him by the arm, twisted it, and turned the knife on him.

The priest screamed, clutching at his arm. He struggled, but Israfel held him firmly with the knife at his throat.

"*Stop*," he said, in the tone he'd used often as Archangel of Heaven.

No one expected the commanding tone in his voice. Everyone obeyed, staring in terror at Israfel as he held his prisoner close. They knew what he was threatening and were terribly sure he would follow through on it. Perhaps they'd planned for casualties, but they could no longer go through with their cruelty. Father Schrader took the opportunity to break free of his own captors and rush in front of Israfel. He made it clear by his stance that everyone would have to tear him apart before touching Israfel again.

"There is no need to sacrifice yourself, priest," Israfel said to him.

"You're too weak," Father Schrader said, shivering with fear anyway. "It's a miracle you can even stand."

Israfel wobbled but held his ground. "In my world, weakness usually means death," he gasped. "This isn't anything I haven't dealt with before."

But it was. Israfel had never nearly given into despair.

He thought of Angela Mathers's attempts at suicide, and his heart warmed and ached. He knew how she felt, but both of them had to be stronger. Perhaps Mikel's efforts to force Israfel into feeling compassion had been misguided. He'd always felt compassion. He merely refused to let others know. As the Father's prisoner, abused night and day, he had learned not to show a single emotion besides sorrow. But the Father was now dead. Israfel had destroyed him, and with Raziel already dead and the bond of the Supernal angels weakened, the universe was falling apart.

Israfel alone could stop the tragedy. Raziel and Lucifel's children had been special—the offspring of two Supernals. But the chick within Israfel mixed his blood with the Father's, and thus went above and beyond any other creature. Once it was born, with Angela's help unsealing the power within Raziel's Book, the dying universe could be resurrected and a new angelic trinity could rule. The most horrific period of Israfel's life had also given the universe its only hope for a brighter future. Nothing could destroy that hope. He wouldn't allow it.

"Father Schrader," Lizbeth shouted. Fearful tears wet her face. "Step aside! You know we don't have a choice—"

"*There is always a choice,*" the old priest thundered.

Everyone fell silent.

The old priest stared his companions down, shame and disgust all over his face. "You fools. Look at what you've become. This city is a horror. It is falling apart and yet you attack one of the few creatures left to save it. Angel blood?" He glared at a shamefaced Lizbeth and nearly spat at her. "Foolishness! It will only forestall the inevitable. You would rush around as murderers and thieves, the worst kind of sinners, and all because you're assuming the Archon has decided to let humanity suffer. Why not hope? Why not trust in a brighter dream for Luz and for Earth? Must we all be slaves to that awful prophecy of Ruin?"

Some of the priests dropped their knives. A few knelt in shame and anguish.

"Yes," he continued, "pray. But don't be surprised if we deserve our fate. You have no one to blame but yourselves for this angel's judgment. I should have known that some of you would become infected with despair and infect the others along with you. And you, Lizbeth—" Father Schrader shook his head in disbelief. "You should have been Angela Mathers's friend, not her spy."

Lizbeth cried silently. She shivered, unable to look at Israfel, and shut her eyes. "Please, let him go," she whispered, indicating the priest he held captive.

There was no sign of the angel Mikel behind her eyes.

Israfel let go of the priest. His prisoner scampered across the floor, nearly throwing himself into the arms of the others.

"What will you do now?" Father Schrader said to Israfel.

Lizbeth knelt down and cried. "How ashamed I am," she choked out. "God, forgive me . . . what have I done?"

Israfel stared at her. He looked back to Father Schrader. "I will enter the door."

He turned and headed for it, limping slightly. He held his wings high and proud.

"You—you won't kill us?" Lizbeth said, looking up at him with a pale face.

Israfel paused. "No," he said quietly. His wings shivered. Blood dripped to his toes.

"But—"

Israfel pressed against the door, trying to gather his strength. He felt sicker, and the world less stable. His head pounded, nearly blinding him. Of course they deserved to die. But the more he remembered Raziel's smiling face, the less he felt he could judge as he'd judged before. How could Israfel have forgotten those long-ago words he and Raziel exchanged? Was it always true that it took moments like these to remember more clearly?

Father Schrader stepped closer. He offered his arm to Israfel to steady him, but Israfel waved him away. "No," he said. "I will be fine once I leave Earth. Then I'll quickly regain my strength. You must understand—this is the lowest Realm, and it drains us."

"You're ill, aren't you?" Father Schrader whispered.

Israfel looked at him keenly. For a human, the priest was extremely perceptive. "My sister is a virus," he said in a low tone. "Hopefully, I'll rid this universe and myself of the infection soon enough."

Father Schrader looked confused, but then his eyes widened and he nodded in realization. "Thank you for your mercy," he said, kneeling down in front of Israfel. "Please find the Archon. She is human, but she represents the best and the worst of what we are, and that is not Her fault. And if you decide to punish us, punish me alone. I am the representative for these children."

Israfel looked at the others. "Perhaps it is punishment enough for them to know that they can never be what you are."

Lizbeth bowed her head in shame.

"You are special," Israfel added.

Father Schrader nodded and lowered his head. He stole one more glance at Israfel from his low vantage point and sighed softly in surprise. He stared at Israfel as if mesmerized and was about to say something. But another glance from Israfel kept him quiet, and the secret remained between them. No one else needed to know what the priest had realized—Israfel's beauty reflected ineffable desires.

"Cover your eyes until I shut the door behind me," Israfel said firmly.

Everyone obeyed, and he set his hand on the knob.

The iron snake came to life but twisted in pain beneath Israfel's hand, as if his touch burned it. It hissed and spit maniacally.

Israfel yanked the snake hard, opening the door.

He took the first few steps and strength flowed through his body in waves. Quickly, he shut the door behind him.

The light of Earth disappeared, and the door vanished with a gentle sucking sound. Israfel began to descend the dark stairs carefully. The winding journey to the bottom would be tedious, but every moment that passed, his power would also return stronger and stronger. Soon, he'd be traveling, incredibly fast. He was a Supernal angel after all, and in the loftier Realms, miles were seconds.

Already, he anticipated the terror in Lucifel's eyes.

Thirty-four

*Seeing the demon city made me long for what
my own people had cruelly lost. But I carried
the name of our glorious home from my birth,
and true to my sister's hopes, I vowed I would
live to see that glory again.*   —TROY

Troy was as good as dead.

Flightless and weak, she plummeted from the opening
where she'd exited the labyrinth, flipping end over end. Juno
streaked down from overhead and flew beside her, grasping
desperately for Troy's rags and remaining wing.

It was useless.

Troy smacked the rocks. Pain ricocheted through her
bones. The world hazed over, and the light of the demon city
pulsed with her heartbeat, seeming to laugh at her. Juno's
face appeared and disappeared. Troy reached out blindly.
She spread her single wing more and attempted to glide sideways. Her own blood whipped back into her eyes. The roar
of her descent was deafening. Her fingers scrabbled painfully
against the rocky cliff side. Acidic air burned her lungs.

Finally, Troy's nails caught.

She grunted as she dug into the stone of the cliff, her feet slipping intermittently. Hot pain shot through her fingers and fanned into her palms.

Her arms shivered violently from the strain, but Troy held on, taking the time to catch her breath and gather whatever strength she had left. Dizziness plucked at her brain, and she clung tighter to the world. Surely the moment her eyes shut, she would plummet again into death's jaws.

Through a fog of agony, Troy glanced out into Babylon. She could barely discern the immense pillars flanking the Styx River as it flowed beneath the city to the Abyss. Lucifel's Altar lay beyond those pillars. Sophia would certainly be there along with Angela. But the odds of Troy surviving to reach them were now slim to none.

A large cloud of mist swept over her, hiding the city from view. Even though Troy had fallen so far, she and Juno were still very high up.

Eerie laughter echoed from above.

Python was surely coming. They didn't have much time. Juno soared down to Troy's level and hitched into the cliff side nearby. Pebbles sprayed back as her little black nails slid into the rocks. Juno couldn't stop gaping with horror at the wound marking Troy's severed wing. In return for her pain, Troy had been left with numbness and the wild focus that foreshadowed certain death. "I must climb," she hissed weakly to her niece. It drained her dangerously just to speak.

Crawling to the ground wasn't an option. Babylon's plain sheltered plenty of Hounds, Kirin, and others creatures eager to destroy or devour a flightless Jinn. The smartest course of action left was to climb and hide in the thicker acidic fog near the cavern ceiling. Juno looked up, her eyes widening at the distance they still needed to travel.

She nodded and began to move.

"*No. You must escape*," Troy gasped. "The demon will have his revenge on me and let you go. You must survive to lead the Clans."

Juno said nothing, but from the way she grasped the rocks, it was obvious she refused to leave Troy's side. A haunted expression had erased Juno's usual curiosity and babyish fear. She gripped at the stone, using her wings to propel her higher.

This wasn't good at all. The fog would eventually weaken Juno's wings enough that flight would be impossible.

Juno heaved for breath, her muscles already shaking.

A long hiss quivered through the air around them.

Troy froze and her ears cocked forward. She strained to hear despite the pain threatening to switch off her senses. Python's whispery voice began to weave its way through the mist.

Tell me, High Assassin . . . do you enjoy being flightless?

He laughed sarcastically.

Juno prepared to move again, but Troy clasped her by the ankle.

"*Don't move*," Troy whispered heatedly. "*Not yet.*"

There was always the possibility the demon couldn't see them in the fog. He was searching for them, trying to get a reaction out of Troy or her niece that would give them away.

You know, I have to admire you, Python's cool voice continued. *All of this misery just to kill your half-Jinn cousin. But I'm afraid no matter how much I sympathize, that noble mission of revenge stops here. Didn't you know, Troy? Without him, Lucifel can't escape her ancient cage. That doesn't fit well with my plans, I'm afraid.*

Troy's eyes widened. She bit back her frustrated scream. In a cruel instant, it socked her like a deadly punch to the chest. Was that why Kim had been adopted by a demon father? Troy thought of the bonds keeping Lucifel imprisoned. Adamant would be the most likely metal the demons had used to shackle her. It was an element impervious to astral energy. But that only applied to creatures like angels, demons, and Jinn.

Not someone in between the two.

Your silence suggests you're surprised? Python's words echoed from every direction. *So was I. Unfortunately for your delusional cousin, you've enchanted me into forgetting my promise that you'll perish miserably. Oh no, I have plans for you, Troy.*

Juno lost her grip. Her foot slipped from beneath her, flipping loose rocks into the air. The noise of her scrabbling rang like thunder.

Troy stared at her in horror.

Python's words seemed to hold a deadly smile of victory. *You, High Assassin—and you alone.*

His enormous triangular head broke out of the fog. Fangs snapped at Juno.

She barely dodged, flapping her wings and screeching in pain. Just as Troy feared the mist had crippled Juno's ability to fly.

Juno lost the rest of her grip and fell.

JUNO! Troy forgot everything else like a dream and dropped with her.

Not so fast, you clever winged rat. Python's shadow reared up on Troy, intending to stop her from following. *Are you really so eager to die?* His huge serpentine body had wrapped itself around a rock jutting from the cliff next to them. Troy would never get around him. His jaws loomed before her, his eyes tormenting her like the nightmare of a hundred Hounds at once, promising only a future without Juno and without dignity.

There was so little she could do—and then Troy thought of something.

As she fell, she raked her nails across his eyes.

Her fingers caught for a second and then her grip ripped away.

The snake contorted wildly. A dreadful scream tore through the air. Python hadn't expected Troy to sacrifice her life to save her niece. Now his curses rang out with hideous ferocity over the plain. Juno might die, and Troy would die with her, and whatever torments he'd planned for her could never be.

His shrieks followed Troy like a nightmare, but she ignored them and heard only her niece's fearful cries. Juno had slowed her descent by spreading her wings, but it wasn't enough.

She was too weak. She continued to fall, and Babylon grew larger beneath her and Troy. Lights appeared again. The cloud cover broke for good. The city looked like a valley of spires and black spikes. Pyramids glittering with light beckoned. Finally, Troy caught up to her. Juno stared up at Troy, her little mouth widened into an "O" of amazement.

Troy wanted to shut her eyes. These were her last moments. Instead, she kept them open to make sure that Juno saw nothing else besides her aunt looking back at her. Troy used her single good wing to steer herself in Juno's direction and they collided painfully. Troy dug her nails into the chick, and Juno screamed.

She tried to direct them both toward a mound to their left. Troy connected with it hard. Juno tore out of her arms with a shuddering sound. Something soft met Troy's legs and arms, and she tumbled. There was a brief second of more air before the hard earth and a searing pain hit her.

And then there was nowhere left to fall.

Thirty-five

All my life, I had prepared for this moment.
Now, I knew my mistake. —KIM

Angela didn't have it in her to say a word as Python pushed her closer to Lucifel. The demon sometimes gave a small smile of victory, or at other times lost himself in some kind of trance, as if he conversed with an invisible person in an invisible world. Or maybe he was talking to someone far away. But Angela's helplessness was undeniable as Python clutched her hands and dragged her along.

Her head ached. Her entire body cried for sleep.

Kim also remained silent. He followed with his head down, unable to look at Angela. Every so often, he sighed deeply. He would squeeze his eyes shut often, fighting off inner turmoil.

Gradually, the scenery changed. The tunnel they walked through narrowed, and they entered a passage that struck Angela into horrified silence. Bodies had been melded seamlessly into the stone walls. The arms, legs, and wings of countless demons and angels jutted out at her, though most remained frozen for eternity in curled-up positions. Yet some had unblinking eyes that certainly held souls behind them.

These eyes followed Angela as she passed.

"They are curious about you," Python said softly, breaking from his trance. "It's not every day that Hell might get a new ruler."

"Why are they in the walls?" Angela said in a small voice. She could barely find it in herself to keep walking. She shivered and stumbled over a rock. "Are they alive?"

"They keep the demons of Babylon alive," Python said, staring ahead without a glance for the prisoners to his right and left as he walked. "They are traitors, prisoners of war, or sinners according to our laws. Here, they will spend the rest of their eternity, giving energy to us and providing as needed for our civilians. Although considering the circumstances, perhaps their usefulness is long since past."

Angela glanced at them furtively, a hot rage welling up inside of her that overpowered her fear. Her heart ached with pity and pain. "What an evil thing to do," she said firmly.

"You mean necessary," Python said in an ironic tone.

They came to an enormous Gate set into the rocks. Its thick iron bars gleamed in the dim light. It was becoming more difficult to see, but Angela had certainly seen enough. Two angels flanked either side of the Gate. Their bodies had been set into the walls like the others, but they were not frozen in place. Instead, the wall was more like a nest for them. As Angela, Python, and Kim approached, they began to move.

Angela's throat tightened. Her breathing quickened. These angels looked familiar.

One looked male, with tangled black hair and sparsely feathered wings. The other was a female with silver hair, though her wings were even more degraded by the mist.

That's right. They're just like Israfel's guardian Thrones.

Angela remembered what terrors they had been. She paused, uncertain. Kim's footsteps paused behind her. His breath sounded ragged and fearful. He touched Angela's shoulder, as if to pull her back.

"Don't worry," Python said, continuing ahead. He smiled grimly. "Lucifel's Thrones will not harm you, my dear. Lucifel knows you will be arriving soon after all. It's all part of the plan. Even I know she'd be a fool to murder you just yet . . ." He glanced at the dreadful Thrones without a hint of fear as he passed. "Down, pups," he whispered at them maliciously. "No treats today, I'm afraid."

The twin angels glared at him with wild eyes, but merely rustled back into position.

There was a heavy *clank*.

The Gate's doors swung open. Lucifel's Altar appeared in a haze of red light. Pentagrams glowed from the walls, and a gigantic pentagram marked the middle of the floor. Python paused right at the threshold, pushing Angela into the chamber with a hand to the small of her back.

For a second, she hesitated. Fear coursed through her like fire. The Grail burned her hand, bunching tears of pain at the corners of her eyes. A sickly scent pervaded the room.

Worse, there was an ever-watchful, ever-searching presence.

This was why she'd come here. It was why Angela went through so much torment. She knew this moment would arrive. Yet it was more awful than she could have ever imagined.

"Good luck, Archon," Python whispered in her ear ominously. "*You'll need it.*"

He pushed her deeper into the room. As they entered, the Gate clanged shut behind them.

Angela froze. She could barely think or stand.

High above, Lucifel hung amid a web of chains, her limbs shackled at her wrists and ankles. She looked unbelievably pale in the dim light, almost sickly. Angela had encountered Lucifel's shadow and destroyed it a year ago, and that experience had been dreadful enough. In person, Lucifel was lithe, almost delicate looking. But her commanding presence sent a person's soul reeling and fractured it asunder. She hung in the chains, seemingly asleep. Grayish hair hung in her eyes. She looked much like Israfel, but her hair was shorter, and her entire body was covered in black clothing that had been restitched a thousand times, as if everyone was too afraid to simply touch her and change it.

Kim stepped beside Angela, staring up at the reigning Prince of Hell.

He swallowed, closing his eyes.

"You won't become a coward on me now, will you?" Python whispered to him.

Angela struggled, but Python's grip was firm.

I should have stopped Kim before we even got as far as the Watchers. But what could I do? I couldn't kill him. I can't be that kind of person—like Lucifel.

"You won't change your mind about taking Lucifel's place?" Kim said to Angela, not even looking at her.

She trembled, but her voice was firm. "No."

Angela's voice echoed and she thought Lucifel would awaken. The angel stayed asleep.

"All right." Kim sighed painfully. He turned and grabbed Angela by the arms, pressing their lips together so hard it hurt. "I'm sorry," he said, anguished. Then Kim tore himself away and approached Lucifel step by terrible step.

Angela wanted to pull him back and scream. "Kim—"

A low rustle erupted from the other side of the room.

A person huddled to the right of Lucifel, her wide eyes reflecting back the red light. Her face was terrified, but someone had tied fabric around her mouth, keeping her from talking. Then she moved so that a pendant on her chest caught the light and tossed it back like a star. Her features became more visible and familiar.

SOPHIA!

Sophia shook her head violently, trying to tell Angela something.

Angela stared at her, helpless. She tried to fight her tears. Her throat tightened even more, cutting off her air. Her vision swam. Her mind raced as she glanced around wildly and tried to think of a way to save them both. Suddenly, Python grabbed her by the chin and turned her around to face him. "You've made it," he said in her ear, his fingers pinching her face painfully. "Congratulations. Now for the prize, Archon. It awaits. The Throne of Hell will be yours in a few precious moments. All it takes is the courage to do what you know must be done."

She tried to wrench free, noticing with horror that Kim was fast nearing Lucifel. Kim's pale face became suffused with awe as he gazed up at the Destroyer Supernal.

"Look," Python whispered as he watched, his orange eyes bright with eagerness. "She is about to awaken. Then, all you need to do is open the Book of Raziel, take what belongs to you, and snuff her out like a flickering flame."

Tremors rocked through the earth beneath them. Angela stumbled.

Pebbles dropped from the ceiling.

A shudder rippled through the ground and tossed Sophia to the side. The fabric slipped from her head, and with her mouth free, she sat up and screamed at Angela. "STOP HIM. STOP KIM."

"Hush, darling," Python hissed. He snapped his fingers, and the fabric wrapped itself around Sophia's mouth again. "It looks like the Book doesn't believe in you, Archon. Well, I do—"

Angela turned and kicked him hard near the waist.

Python grunted, clutching at his stomach. He laughed between gritted teeth. "Isn't it terrible when people betray you? When they disappoint your hopes?" he said snidely into Angela's ear. "What is friendship, really? I think you're about to find out."

Kim's hands reached for Lucifel's chains. They touched the silvery metal.

"*Kim!*" Angela screamed, no longer able to keep quiet. Sophia struggled, her gray eyes wide and tormented. A shiver ran through the air.

Python shrieked.

Angela turned in a panic. Blood ran between Python's fingers from a sudden wound on his face. He pulled away his hand. A familiar pattern of cuts had streaked to life across one of his eyes. They almost exactly matched the cuts Troy had set in Python's cheek.

Troy was alive. She had hurt Python—somehow. Had he sent a part of himself to fight Troy while they walked toward Lucifel?

With a loud cry, Angela twisted out of his grip and pivoted on him. She flung him back against the ground.

Python's face contorted with pain. He cursed under his breath and gazed at Angela and her upraised left hand in panic. With a sharp cry of frustration, his eye gushing, he vanished from sight.

The earth rocked. Angela fell, slamming to the ground amid the sound of metal clanging against stone. Her palms caught her fall, but her teeth snapped together hard. Her head echoed with pain.

Sophia screamed even beneath the fabric in her mouth.

Lucifel's eyes had opened.

Thirty-six

No one can hide from me. To my eyes, the darkness is bright as day. To my ears, a whisper is a roar. —LUCIFEL

The universe shuddered. The gray angel's gaze pierced into Angela wordlessly.

Their souls met like two bolts of lightning, twining together. Lucifel broke the spell to look beneath her as the shackles on her arms opened with bursts of light and fell away to the earth, resting with the web of chains that had surrounded her legs. Kim stared up at her in a trance of awe and terror.

With a gesture faster than thought she reached down and grabbed his hair. Kim's face drained of even more color. He looked at Angela with fear and pain, and then his eyes rolled back in his head.

He collapsed to the ground with a heavy *thud,* seemingly dead.

Angela screamed. She ran for Lucifel almost blindly.

Lucifel waved a hand, and an invisible blow threw Angela back against the wall.

The pain was excruciating. Angela screeched, and her

bones threatened to shatter. Coughing, she crawled to her knees. Without another thought, she changed tactics and hobbled toward Sophia.

Another wave of Lucifel's hand, and the ether rippled.

Angela fell and rolled, her head throbbing. Lucifel swept her arm sideways, and a rock seemed to sock Angela in the stomach. She groaned, frozen with agony as Lucifel approached steadily and stopped to stand over her like a shadow. Slowly, Lucifel reached down and grabbed Angela by the throat, wrapping cold fingers around it. A horrible buzzing sound filled the air, like the noise of a million flies. Black specks dotted Angela's vision. She stared back into Lucifel's blood-red irises and found nothing there but icy disregard.

Sophia's cries were heartrending.

Angela tugged at Lucifel's hand around her neck, her legs kicking the air.

"Well done," Lucifel said, her voice scratchy with misuse, but echoing. She opened her hand, and Angela collapsed to the ground in a heap.

Angela coughed in surprise, clutching at her throat. Her body groaned like it had been crushed and remade again. Pain needled her everywhere. "You—you won't kill me?" she gasped. "After all the trouble you took to get me down here?"

Lucifel's face showed little emotion. "Kill you?" She shoved Angela toward Sophia with the edge of her foot. "You are the only one who can open the Book. I would be a fool to kill you just yet."

"No one knows how to open her," Angela said, turning back and glaring at Lucifel. "So in the end, you're not winning anything. You're free. But for what? For the demons who serve you to imprison you again?" Angela almost laughed through her pain. She glanced at Kim and tried to wish away her painful tears. Her soul ached and burned with agony. "So much for your Revolution. Even Raziel didn't—"

"*Quiet,*" Lucifel hissed, snapping her fingers. A flicker of anger crossed her face.

Angela's mouth sealed shut against her will.

Lucifel shoved her toward Sophia again. Angela grunted, trying to catch her breath. "I'm not the one who brought you here, Archon," Lucifel said softly. "So save your spite, and spare me your lectures. That snake called Python thought he could outsmart me. Perhaps he had reason to. He played you and your ragtag friends for idiots, gaining your trust and betraying it by turns, all so that he can put you on my Throne as a puppet, with his slippery fingers pulling your strings. He's typical of his generation: naive and ambitious— and dangerously bored. I hope you enjoyed his labyrinth. I've let him play within Hell for too long. Very soon, it will be time for the snake to lose his den . . . forever. Besides, he was wrong about the most crucial thing of all . . ."

Lucifel leaned down.

" . . . you're not going to win."

Even if Angela's mouth hadn't been forced shut, she would have gone silent.

She *was* a fool.

Troy had been right to mistrust Python, and Angela had actually believed his lies long enough to think he really did want her as his new ruler. Of course, now his actions revealed themselves for the deceptions they were. Python had deliberately separated Angela from Troy, Nina, and Juno. He'd thrust Angela into his mother's dangerous ball to force visions out of her head. And he'd helped her get to Lucifel, only so that when Angela hopefully destroyed the Prince of

Hell, he could fawn at her feet before turning his treacherous fangs on her as well.

Python's mocking laughter sounded in her ears all over again.

"Friends are only friends when they find you useful," Lucifel murmured. "And so Python was your friend as long as you cooperated with his plans. Now where is he? You see, Archon . . . promises can be broken, just as easily as they can be made. Right and wrong depends on the eye of the beholder, and love is a feverish dream." Lucifel paused beside Angela again.

Angela fell at Sophia's knees. Sophia glared at Lucifel with pained, red-rimmed eyes.

"From the very beginning, I've been planning my moves," Lucifel said gently. "Python couldn't know that his game ultimately suited my purposes. You should pity him. He's as much a victim as you are. Without him, perhaps you would have never made it down here to the Book's side. But now I am free, and you have nowhere to go."

Lucifel snapped her fingers again.

Angela touched her lips as they opened. She was free to speak again. She rocked to her knees, gasping. "You . . . you don't know how to open Sophia. So it doesn't matter . . ."

"Oh, but I do," Lucifel said. "And I plan to watch. It's what you both deserve, after all. For believing that something as ludicrous as friendship is worth dying for. In my world, that's a cardinal sin. I call it blindness."

"No wonder," Angela hissed. "Because you don't have any friends, right?"

Lucifel kicked her hard in the side. For the briefest second, inner pain flashed behind her eyes.

Angela fell, blood dripping where she'd bit into her lip.

"You suffered in chains and let millions of angels die all because Israfel . . . wore the crown you wanted." Her breaths almost refused to pass through her aching ribs. She forced herself to breathe deeper. "But I think . . . there's more. I find it hard to believe you'd destroy the whole universe just because you're still feeling jealous. You show the world an icy demeanor—but I'd bet it's all . . . an act. I would love to know who broke your heart so badly . . . the entire universe now has to suffer for it . . ."

Lucifel stooped down and pulled Angela by her necklace. The chain dug like a rope of fire into Angela's neck. She coughed.

They stared into one another's eyes.

"You're perceptive," Lucifel whispered. "But don't think your pathetic glimpse into the past was enough to figure me out. You can't even begin to fathom why I started that Revolution. You don't know a thing—and here's the best proof of your staggering ignorance. I'm not the one about to let the universe fall apart, Archon. You are. At least, that is, if you refuse to open the Book. Then, I suppose Ruin will be upon us as promised long ago. And by now, I certainly welcome it."

Lucifel gestured and Sophia's cloth fell from her mouth.

"Stop it," Sophia immediately said between her tears. "Stop it, Lucifel. It's not worth it—"

"I have no desire to be preached to by a 'thing,'" Lucifel said quietly. "Stop wasting my time, Sophia, and break the spell of this pathetic friendship. Tell Angela Mathers what she must do to open you. Raziel refused to do it a year ago. How much better for you to speak for him."

Sophia swallowed. She tipped back her head and shut her eyes. "No," she said in a small voice.

"How clever my brother was," Lucifel said. She took a

deep breath and shut her eyes as well. "He told me there was much more to Sophia than locks and keys. That she was better than a box to be cracked. And then, much to my surprise, I learned that to open Raziel's treasure, she needed to be broken after all. But the weapon that breaks her . . . the Key." Lucifel shifted her position, behaving eerily patient. "Tell Angela, Sophia. Where is the Key that opens your Lock—the seal on the Book of Raziel? And just where can the precious Lock be found?"

Sophia shook her head violently.

"*Tell her*," Lucifel said, her voice still low yet resounding eerily like thunder.

"What is she talking about, Sophia?" Angela said, fear creeping into her, stealing away her heartbeats. "Breaking a treasure to open it? What does that mean?"

"I—" Sophia stammered. Tears rolled down her cheeks. "Angela, I'm sorry—I told you not to enter the door! I told you not to follow me . . ."

"I had to," Angela whispered. "We're friends."

"Yes. Friends." Sophia squeezed her eyes shut.

"Tell her now," Lucifel said, glaring at Sophia with threatening eyes.

"No," Sophia said again.

"Now."

"NO."

The ground shivered. Sophia's eyes widened. She looked around with abrupt sadness, as if seeing the devastation for the first time. Finally, she hung her head. "It's my body," Sophia said so softly it sounded like a breath.

Angela's heart wanted to stop. Everything froze inside of her. "What?" she said weakly.

"My body is the Lock of the Book of Raziel," Sophia said slowly.

Angela stared at her.

Sophia's misery was all-encompassing. "So to open me . . . the Key is . . ."

"No," Angela said, a dreadful realization dawning on her. "That—that can't be true."

"It is," Sophia cried, shuddering.

"No. *No. You're wrong.*"

Sophia turned aside. Her personal torment was horrible to look at. Anguish misted over her gray eyes. Normally so deep and flashing, now they held a devastating tiredness.

Lucifel loomed over Angela. "It's simple, you see," the angel whispered. "To open Sophia and save this universe, you will have to murder her with the Glaive, Angela. Why else do you think I would let you arrive on my doorstep? Because I suddenly feel nostalgia for our brief encounter last year? Sophia always knew—and Raziel made certain—that the Glaive is the only weapon in the world that can harm her. Irritatingly enough, he also made sure you're the only soul who can use it for its truest purpose. But can you be like me and stain your hands with the innocent blood of millions? To choose not to kill Sophia and open the Book of Raziel. Well . . . that would be a rather cruel fate for the dying universe wouldn't it? From what I remember, you don't share my dream of eternal silence . . ."

Angela pictured the Glaive in all its sharp beauty, cutting down so many souls throughout the centuries as it rested in Lucifel's hands. She'd always wondered why it existed in the first place. Now she knew. It had always been meant for one person only. Now all of the effort Lucifel had put into dragging Angela into Hell made sense.

This was why Sophia spoke of her own death. Why her anguished heart knew separation from Angela was inevitable. The earth groaned again. Angela fell forward, nauseated. The world seemed to twist and warp, turning back in on itself. She could barely think anymore, hardly breathe.

Lucifel never flinched. Her tall body swayed along with the earth. "Not much longer, and everything falls apart. If you choose not to open Sophia, Angela, and use what is within her to save this universe, you will be the Ruin after all, I suppose. Able to help, but unwilling to do so, you would be condemning every creature that lives to an irreversible fate. Including those you so faithfully call friends. How interesting that you'd find Sophia's soul to be the only one worth saving from utter destruction."

Angela's heart twisted beneath Lucifel's words like it had been stabbed. She was sure something inside of her broke and bled.

"I am not the Ruin," Angela said in a weak voice. "*The prophecy said there can be two who can be the Ruin.*"

"That's right," Lucifel said. She smiled condescendingly at Angela. "Because even if you do use the Glaive to open Sophia—and your noble heart wouldn't dare do otherwise— we both know I'll take the power hidden within the Book a moment later and eradicate you. Then I will be free to use that power to end the existence you'll have so predictably wished to save. This universe may be dying—but it can also be resurrected. I alone can give it the silent revolution it truly needs. No more lies and pain. My new regime will be the longest and most peaceful of them all."

"You *are* insane," Angela croaked. She struggled to stay conscious and think. "Why would anyone want to destroy the universe? What can you get out of not existing!"

Lucifel regarded her with cool pity. "We've had that discussion before. We won't have it again."

But it just didn't make any sense!

Then Angela's eyes widened. Time seemed to slow. She thought of her confrontation with Lucifel's shadow one year ago. Lucifel had clasped Angela by the face and said Angela's features strongly resembled someone dearly beloved. But Lucifel had been equally clear that mysterious "someone" wasn't Raziel.

Now Angela's mind jumped again to the immense creature who had murdered Raziel. The being who looked like her. *The Father.*

Is that what this is all really about? Lucifel's love was rejected by her Creator, so now she wants to end her life and everyone else's? This is all just a giant game of spite?

Angela didn't have any real proof yet. But she had her intuition, and now Lucifel's coldness and cruelty appeared as a mask over her pain. *It finally made sense.* The dead, apathetic look behind Lucifel's eyes was the same as Angela's in the darkest moments of her life; it was the same as Janna Hearst's when she tried to commit suicide off one of Westwood Academy's rooftops.

"You're like me?" Angela said, utterly flabbergasted.

Lucifel didn't laugh at the suggestion. "Not quite," she said icily. "It's not me that has an existence-altering decision to make. Now what will it be, Archon? Kill your best friend or watch the world freeze over and disintegrate slowly, one Realm at a time? Isn't Earth already dying? The Underworld comes next. The home of your ragged Jinn friend . . . perhaps most of those mangy feathered rats are already dead."

Angela stared more, unable to tear her gaze from Lucifel's.

"Angela," Sophia said. "Look at me."

Time sped up again. That's right—she had a decision to make. Whatever Lucifel's reasons might be for wanting the universe's eternal death, it didn't matter right now. All that mattered was . . .

Angela slowly looked up at Sophia, her own eyes brimming with tears. She trembled, showing her hands. The Grail throbbed. It bled. "Sophia, I can't—I can't—"

Sophia leaned forward. Their foreheads touched. Their necklaces clinked together. "It's all right. I knew this day would come." She breathed softly. "It's my fault for sharing a dream. I thought we had time. I thought we had chances. The more we spent time together, the more I forgot my punishment, and why my destiny was so cruel. You were my first friend, and you will be my last. You thought of me and risked your life for me, and that's enough. Now I know that we can't escape this. It's what I deserve for bringing so much suffering upon everyone."

"No. Sophia, please," Angela said, touching Sophia's face, her tears. "You can't just give up. There has to be more to this. There's always more—a reason—"

"Sometimes," Sophia whispered, "friends are just friends. And sometimes, those friendships end, even when we don't want them to. We knew this would come to pass at some point, Angela. Now that the moment is here, prolonging the inevitable won't change anything. If it's me or the universe, choose the universe. Choose Troy, and Nina, and Juno. Choose the people who believe in you—and who need you most. I'm only sorry I thought of myself. I forgot everything because of that dream we were sharing, and that wasn't right."

"Lucifel will kill me," Angela whispered, holding Sophia's porcelain cheek. "Then what will it all be for?"

"She won't kill you," Sophia said. A tear rolled down her

face toward Angela's fingers. "You have too many people on your side. They won't allow it—and you can't allow it for their sake. No matter how much darkness, the light always wins. Nothing can stop it. It's like an ocean taking away the sand. Sometimes we just need to find that light first and hold on to it better. It's the finding that eludes us most. I'm sure of that . . ."

Maybe somewhere deep inside of himself, Python knew that too. Why else would he dream that Angela could destroy someone like Lucifel?

He was proud and ambitious and cruel, but even he didn't want his world to die.

"Though I tried to avoid it, though I swore it wouldn't happen, now I will be the Ruin no matter what?" Angela said, a deep sob overtaking her. "And you will be gone? Sophia. I can't live like that—I can't—not after all this—"

"Yes, you can," Sophia said, pressing against her again. "You can because you can change things. Not Ruin," she whispered. "Revolution. There is such a huge difference between the two."

Angela straightened and stared down at the ground. Lucifel watched them emotionlessly.

"All right," Angela said, shaking. "All right."

Sophia smiled. She pulled away from Angela, a serene light behind her usually fathomless eyes. "Now don't think," she said softly. "Just do what you need to do. Do what needs to be done. Be the ruler this universe needs, Angela."

The ruler this universe needs?

Angela ripped the glove off her left hand. The Eye that was the Grail glimmered back at her, weeping its blue blood.

Sophia slumped, her curly hair falling forward and hiding her anguish. Her tears continued silently.

Lucifel's voice was soft and yet hideously painful to listen to. "You speak like your friendship is some kind of sacred covenant. This moment between the two of you would be touching if it weren't for the lie behind the dream. Decide, Archon. I'm not above cutting the Book to ribbons even if she can't die from the pain. If that's what it takes to make you choose—"

"ALL RIGHT," Angela shouted. Her voice echoed. More rocks dropped perilously from the ceiling.

She stood up on wobbly legs.

"The Glaive," Lucifel said softly. "Summon it."

There's more to me than being the Archon. There's always more . . . I'm also somebody's friend.

Angela couldn't understand what Raziel had done. What connection did she and the Grail share that made it impossible for anyone else to use it like this? Angela steadied herself and dug her nails into the Eye, feeling the warm blue liquid run down through her fingers. The Glaive began to form, lengthening, looking sharp and dreadful, like a blue scythe of terror. Angela gripped it tightly and lifted it over Sophia. Sophia stared up at the blade and shut her eyes, whispering to herself.

"A noble choice," Lucifel said, cold triumph on her face. Her eyes gleamed hungrily.

Angela brought down the weapon.

Thirty-seven

Even a snake can dream. —Python

Angela whirled around, smacking Lucifel hard with the curved edge of the blade.

Lucifel fell with a brief look of surprise, landing on her knees. Her hand grasped at her cut arm.

Angela held the blade at Lucifel's neck, pressing it against her. "I said you were insane," Angela said, breathing hard. "And I meant it. No one comes between me and Sophia. NO ONE."

Lucifel raised her eyebrows in respect. "Until today," she whispered.

The angel's reach was long and lightning fast. Lucifel's wings unfurled in a blinding aura of red light. Her pinions thundering, she grabbed one of the chains lying on the floor and with a flick of her wrist wrapped it around the Glaive, tugging Angela in close. The Glaive's crystal scraped against the metal with a terrible sound.

"Letting the world go for a dream?" Lucifel breathed on Angela's face.

Sophia screamed in the background. Rocks tumbled beneath the fury of Lucifel's wing beats.

Angela spat in Lucifel's face. "For hope," she shouted at her. "But that has nothing to do with letting go."

"So much idealism," Lucifel thundered. "*I can't stand it.*" She struggled with Angela, grabbing her by the hair.

Lucifel's fingers found Angela's face, and then one of her eyes, and dug in painfully.

Angela tried to wrench free. Her head could have been splitting down the middle. She clawed at Lucifel's hand, scratching out blood. The Glaive collapsed, its liquid running down Angela's arms.

Something gave way.

At first, Angela couldn't imagine what. It almost didn't bear thinking about. She only knew that she'd never been in such pain, and that warmth gushed down her cheeks. Sophia screamed like her heart had been torn out. Angela dropped to the ground, torture and agony coloring the whole world. One half of that world was now dark. Black as the Abyss. Angela clutched at her face, wanting to thrash all over the floor.

Lucifel shoved her aside cruelly, stepping on Angela's chest. Her bare foot felt like an iron weight.

"We can do this as long as you'd like," Lucifel whispered. "You have another eye. You have bones, and skin, and blood. I have all the time in the world when it comes to pain."

"You're a monster," Angela choked out.

Lucifel's face didn't change. "Too many words, Archon. Please stop wasting my time. It's either now or later. Even if you escape, I'll find you again. Do you really want more friends to die? Why not make it easier on them and cut out the suffering?"

Angela coughed, struggling for breath. Her head felt

numb. "You know my answer. Sacrificing one person for everyone else—it isn't right. I'll never allow it."

"Oh, but you're not on my Throne just yet," Lucifel said. Her foot slid toward Angela's throat.

A ripple went through the air, sending the world into more shivers. Hair rose along Angela's neck and arms.

Lucifel stopped and straightened quickly. She turned aside, listening. Her red eyes narrowed, and her face became even more cold and deadly. "*So he's here,*" Lucifel whispered. She looked down at Angela expressionlessly, but her tone held the slightest tinge of anxiety. "Don't think I won't resume where I left off. But for now, I'm going to stop this nuisance before he does what he knows best and ruins everything. Nothing ever seems to change."

Lucifel stepped off Angela and disappeared to the side.

In seconds she left the chamber, her long strides taking her away with unbelievable speed.

Whoever had arrived, they were worrisome enough to leave opening the Book for later.

Angela groaned, but with her good eye she could see Sophia weeping.

Pushing to her hands and feet, Angela stumbled to Sophia like a drunk and collapsed next to her. Heedless of the pain, she set to work on the cords around Sophia's hands, ignoring Sophia's protests and her attempts to cradle Angela's head and examine her wounded eye.

"Now," Angela said. "Now. Before she comes back."

Reality warped again. The lights flickered. Angela fought her nausea. She stumbled over to Kim's prone body and nearly fell on him. She touched his face.

Certainly Lucifel had killed him. Yet he only seemed to be

sleeping, and Angela almost thought she could make out the slight rise and fall of his chest.

Rocks fell.

"Angela!" Sophia said. "He's dead! We need to leave quickly!" She stormed over, glancing at Kim with real pity. "That sad soul," Sophia said gently. "This way—" Sophia grabbed Angela by the arm and dragged her out of the empty prison and toward the tunnel.

Lucifel was gone. The Gate was open. Angela stumbled out with Sophia, a hand clutched over her injured eye. Pentagrams flickered around her. Kim was dead? It didn't seem real. Why had he done that to himself? He'd freed Lucifel, and Angela was no nearer to any kind of Throne, nor would she ever be if she could help it.

They nearly tripped over the dead bodies of Lucifel's guardian Thrones. The Devil had killed her own bodyguards in her haste.

"*Hurry,*" Sophia said.

"Wait!" Angela forced her to stop. She staggered and displayed the Eye, thinking of the Kirin that had been her mount, of its flashing body and great mane.

You are mine. Come to me now.

"Where will we go?" Sophia said, hysterical.

Angela thought of Kim, feeling his last kiss. For him, they had to survive. "Wherever we need to," she said.

The pain in her head faded to a dull throbbing. With it, something else coursed through Angela. Anger. She set her teeth, thoroughly aware of what needed to be done. She would go after Lucifel. She would rid the universe of the Devil forever. She needed to, even though she didn't want to. Her mind flashed to the image of Raziel tumbling to his death. Once again, she heard Lucifel's cold promise of war. In the midst of all that, thunder approached her. Angela looked up from her memories, seeing the Kirin rear above them before its paws stamped powerfully against the ground.

"Get on," Angela shouted, helping Sophia into the saddle. Angela hoisted herself up in front of her and kicked the beast's sides.

They rode powerfully. The air whipped behind them. Rocks thundered to the ground.

"Watch out!" Sophia said.

Boulders crashed in front of them. The Kirin reared and leaped over the stones, landing with a heavy thud on the other side.

Angela clung to the beast's reins and mane. Sophia gripped Angela's waist with arms of steel. Her breaths erupted hot and ragged in Angela's ear.

An army of demons waited at the end of the tunnel in utter chaos. Lucifel's passing had been marked by dead bodies, Kirin without riders, and a burning haze to the air. At the noise of Angela's approach, some of the demons regarded her with wild terror. The ghost riders sat in the background, staring at her with blank faces.

"We'll never make it through them," Sophia said, shuddering.

Angela examined them quickly. They were without a leader. Their god had just killed some of them mercilessly. Obviously Lucifel was a god rarely seen, more legend than reality to her worshippers. Many of the demons' perfect faces had blanked over with fear. They glanced around in confusion. Others shouted orders, but few listened.

Angela tugged on the Kirin's reins, praying that it would stop. It merely slowed down, enough for her to display the Eye for the army to see. Some of the demons looked up and

shouted in alarm, while others stared in horrified awe. A few
of the braver individuals examined Angela wordlessly, their
severe faces looking her over. Angela was sure she recognized
the male demon who had presented her during Lilith's ball.
His perfect face regarded her coldly and—though it hardly
seemed possible—with a shred of respect.

Angela had escaped Lilith's and Python's clutches. She
had encountered Lucifel and lived. Now, she also held answers to countless burning questions.

"I am your leader now," she shouted. "Your god has left
you."

The more she looked at Lucifel's subjects, the more she
felt convincing and powerful. Angela passed through them,
the Kirin renewing its speed. Lucifel was ahead somewhere,
and Angela knew she couldn't slow down for long.

"If you want to live," Angela screamed, *"follow me."*

The Eye throbbed. Her head ached. Some of the demons
stayed behind, but most couldn't do anything but obey the
Grail's mesmerizing power and they trotted behind Angela.
Soon they began to shout and hurl forward in a mad gallop.

Angela's left hand burned like fire. She charged through
the ghost riders, and they reared up and began to follow her
as well, intent and perfectly obedient. "They're following
you," Sophia shouted in Angela's ear breathlessly. "Angela,
they're following you! I've never seen anything like this—"

Babylon loomed behind. Before them—the outstretched
plain continued deeper and deeper into Hell, endless as the
breadth of the world.

The air shimmered ahead.

A deep and alien groan filled the misty sky. Another
image began to appear amid the murky fog, like a mirage
solidifying bit by bit. It was another city, so close and yet so

far away. It resembled nothing Angela had ever seen; Babylon was like a faded mockery of its glory. There were crystalline spires and pearlescent bridges, towers and balconies, glass and lights that resembled stars. Galaxies wheeled behind the city, and at its pinnacle, a great stairway more like a bridge escaped into the ether. Now Angela recognized this place. It was the great city where Raziel had plummeted to his death. High above, she could see the glittering bridge where he fell.

A terrible desperation filled her.

She kicked the Kirin's side, and it charged faster. Sophia screamed, clinging hard to Angela.

Flashes lit up Hell's sky. Lightning streaked across the air, and the fabric of reality tore open. Light spilled out of a great portal.

Before it two silhouettes knelt to steady their balance, wings spread. Lucifel was certainly one of them. And the other—

Angela could hear nothing but her heartbeat as Israfel's regal gaze met hers.

Thirty-eight

She rode to challenge me. Her fear had turned to determination. But as long as I lived, I would never let Her reign. —LUCIFEL

Israfel stared at the incredible vision of Angela Mathers leading a great army of riders straight for him and Lucifel. He had no time to feel grateful or relieved. All he could focus on was Sophia clinging to Angela's waist, and the horrid injury on Angela's face. Deadly determination had set Angela's features like flint.

He pitched beneath the rocking earth, falling to his knees. His hair whipped behind him from the furious wind of the portal.

Lucifel laughed coldly. "Welcome to my kingdom," she shouted.

With her shadow destroyed, she was weaker than he had ever seen her, but just as icy and hard. Yet because Israfel knew her so well, he could discern the briefest flicker of terror behind Lucifel's eyes now that they stood face-to-face again.

She spoke with forced apathy. "And here I hoped you

would see it under better circumstances." Lucifel's gaze pierced through him as she continued shouting over the portal's fury. "How is the chick inside you, Israfel? Perhaps when I rip it free and show it to the Archon, she'll know you for the monster you are. Someone who is neither male nor female, and who like a sad ghost should have faded away long ago with the rest of his decadent regime. I suppose the Father's blood has been keeping you alive? It's the only good explanation for your survival. But why bother? So you can force the Archon to share your insane hopes for a future you've already destroyed?"

Lucifel turned and looked at Angela with an eager light behind her eyes. "Look at her. She is a worthy opponent for me. Unlike *you*. It can't be coincidence that she shares the Father's features—even his Eye. Raziel was right. You, and he, and I were broken from the same source. Perhaps the Archon was the final piece to make us complete—"

"*Quiet*," Israfel screamed back at her. He was already infuriated with his weakness in being too late to keep Angela from this horror. He couldn't bear comparing the Archon to a God who no longer existed for them. He couldn't stand the thought of merely being a piece of a broken whole. It brought back too much pain. "*You never did learn to hold your tongue in my presence*. If we are equals now, sister," he screamed louder, "we are equals only in this: that we are weak, and broken, and can no longer avoid our punishment for letting Raziel die."

Lucifel stared out at the angel city of Malakhim with even keener hunger. It was the same look on her face as the day she'd watched millions of angels perish for the sake of her twisted ideals. Throughout the War's chaos and bloodshed, Israfel knew she'd been searching for the Father's attention, and hoping for his pain. Lucifel's jealousy and spite seemed to know no boundaries.

Her thoughts right now were transparent as glass. Nostalgia was sweeping over her, and her expression softened as she once again saw the angelic city's glory after countless millennia of gloom and isolation. Perhaps she'd forgotten how beautiful it was.

Israfel had almost lost his chance to return to it. The portal would collapse at any moment.

It groaned, and the city's image wavered ominously.

Lucifel turned back to him despite the growing maelstrom. Their gazes met and once again they were chicks, with Lucifel crying over the kisses her Creator denied her. Instead, they'd been given to Israfel. But she'd never considered how much he'd actually suffered for them. *You fool,* he wanted to shriek at her. *Look at how I paid for that affection. All of your envy and greed was for nothing.*

Her face twisted suddenly with rage and grief.

Israfel couldn't dodge fast enough.

Lucifel tackled him, her hair and wings lifted behind her by the hurricane of light and wind.

Israfel was slammed to the earth, his wings scraping against the rough stone. He twisted beneath Lucifel's knees.

She lifted her hand, ready to plunge it into his stomach and tear out his only hope, just as her children had been torn away. Once again, they were both reliving that crucial moment of the War, when Lucifel had tried to kill Israfel and the chick inside him with her infectious shadow. It was at that exact moment Raziel had fallen, and they watched his descent to death in horror.

The difference now was that Lucifel's shadow had been destroyed since then, and she was weaker than ever.

Israfel turned and looked at Angela. She galloped toward them, advancing with every second, her blood-red hair streaming behind her like a banner. Sophia clung to her tightly, staring down Israfel with a look of approval that only made him more determined to do what he'd planned.

Lucifel couldn't stay here, free as she was to force Angela to open the Book.

But her return to Heaven might be just as disastrous. And if Israfel didn't follow her to Malakhim, the chaos Lucifel would unleash once she arrived in the city and tried to scale the heights to the Father's nest would be insurmountable. Mikel was sure to infiltrate there somehow as well, helping her mother so that Lucifel could so mercifully end Mikel's life. Yet there was no choice left to him. Israfel wrapped his fingers around Lucifel's throat.

He kneed her sharply in the stomach.

She grunted from the pain, but was already recovering, ready to break his hand.

The ether rippled. The rift that had opened to Malakhim shimmered and threatened to close amid the light and wind.

Lucifel stared at Israfel proudly, evil promise written all over her face. She sensed what was coming next.

Israfel kicked her powerfully, forcing her through the rift.

With a last and apologetic glance at Angela, he entered the light and followed his sister back home.

Thirty-nine

*Even if I had to do it all over again, my choices
would be the same.* —ANGELA MATHERS

Angela had been so close. So close. She heard herself screaming.

Israfel took one more moment to gaze at her, his beauty even more striking with his face dirty and his wings injured. The portal to the angelic city wavered as he disappeared inside, his white wings rippling in the tornado of wind.

Light blinded Angela. A tremendous roar echoed throughout Hell. Her Kirin reared in terror as brilliance rushed like a relentless tide toward her and the army of riders.

Sophia screamed for her, and Angela felt herself slide from the saddle. She was falling, falling.

Stephanie and Nina had been right. There was no escape for her now. Angela was trapped in Hell with no way to return to Luz. Maybe she should have listened to everyone and never gone through the dark door.

Yet when she thought of Sophia again, Angela knew she'd made the right choice.

Perhaps Hell wouldn't be Hell by Sophia's side.

Perhaps this time when Angela fell asleep, she'd awaken to a different reality.

Perhaps Kim had been right all along. Everything now would change.

Forty

Gradually, I forgot the world that had existed before
I touched the Throne. —ANGELA MATHERS

Angela awakened to a room steeped in darkness. Her eyelids
cracked open, and tears bunched at their corners. Her eyes
weren't used to bright light anymore.

Above her, a large orange lamp hung like a sun, its gentle
glow brushing at the sheets covering her body. She lay on
a round bed with a thick velvety cushion, the covers raised
to her chin. She shivered, desperate to gather her thoughts.
Pieces of what had happened returned to her in painful bits.
Lucifel shoving her in the stomach. Sophia screaming. It all
felt like one terrible nightmare though it most certainly had
not been. Slowly, Angela sat up and pressed a cold hand
against her head, swallowing a sour taste in her mouth. The
air still smelled of vinegar, while before her a set of embroidered curtains rustled as if someone stood behind them.

To her right, an onyx table held glasses filled with different liquids.

She picked up one of them, sniffed the contents, and then
set it down gingerly, remembering the drinks at Lilith's ball.

Her throat ached so much, acid could have poured down it while she slept.

I'm still in Hell. Maybe for forever . . . Troy, Nina, Juno . . . maybe they're trapped somewhere too.

Angela shivered, suddenly reliving her agony as Lucifel's fingers dug into her face, feeling once more the intense pain and gushing blood that had followed.

My eye . . .

Hesitantly, she touched it.

It was whole, as perfect as if it had never been harmed. Apparently there wouldn't be yet another scar to add to the collection already smothering her from head to toe.

"Thank God," Angela whispered, settling back against the cushion again, letting out a shaky sigh. But fear continued to tug at her. A strange sensation of wrongness wouldn't let her relax. Had her eye been restored because of the Grail? Angela should have been dead by now after using the Glaive so much. Yet the suspicion had been growing inside of her ever since killing the Hound in Luz, that maybe her body was actually becoming used to how the Grail fed off her life force—that it was learning to adjust.

It was the only explanation that made any sense.

Or maybe it just wants me alive.

No. The Grail didn't have a will of its own. She refused to acknowledge *that.*

Angela uncurled her left palm, intent on gazing back at the Eye. She was sure it would at least be weeping blood again, reflecting the turmoil that had ricocheted through Hell with Lucifel's passing from one world to the other. Worse, Angela had been dreaming of Raziel's death again as she slept, though the instant she opened her eyes the memories faded a little. She looked down at her hand.

The Grail was gone.

Angela stared at the unblemished white skin of her palm.
IT WAS GONE.

She jumped from the cushion, nearly screaming aloud as a
door she hadn't noticed cracked open, letting in some flickering light.

Kim stepped inside with a lantern. He shut the door just
as quickly behind him, setting the glass lamp on a table half
hidden in the darkness. The light played with the shadows of
his handsome face, and his eyes seemed to shine more golden
and breathtaking than ever. His dark hair glistened like a
raven's wing. He looked clean and calm, the exact opposite
of when Lucifel had killed him. Like a dream come to life, he
sat on a musty chair nearby, staring at Angela with intense
seriousness.

She stared back at him, probably looking wide-eyed as
an owl.

"Kim—you're alive," she whispered, clutching at her left
hand. "Thank God." Tears rolled down her face. She wanted
to jump up and crush him to death with a hug, but nothing
felt real. So she just sat and gazed at him pathetically. What if
the minute she touched him, Kim vanished, and she learned
that this moment of peace was an illusion?

He left the chair and sat next to her, embracing her tightly,
running his warm fingers through her hair. He seemed about
to kiss her but drew back suddenly. Was he afraid?

Kim knelt down by her side.

"How did you survive?" Angela said to him. "I—I thought
Lucifel killed you."

"No," he said quietly. "She drained my energy, but
stopped short of taking my life. Even I don't understand why
she spared me . . ." His face looked haunted.

"Well," Angela whispered, "I'm happy." She brushed back a tear.

"I'm grateful for that," Kim said, smiling.

"Why force me to confront her, though?" she demanded of him, anyway, unable to stop. "Why free her in the first place? You have no idea . . . what kind of pain she caused me."

"I do," Kim said, his suave voice cracking with emotion. "But I also believed in you, Angela. Now, my belief has been justified." He stared at her, almost pleading. "Even Sophia knew there was no way out of all this."

"*Where is she?*" Angela said quickly. "Is she all right—"

"Sophia will be in shortly," Kim said, smiling jealously as he noticed the overwhelming worry in Angela's tone. "She's fine. She had to go and speak to your caretakers, but she'll be back soon. You're in Hell, Angela. But everything is already changing. With Lucifel gone, Lilith has lost all desire to murder you. She is actually your fiercest protector right now, insisting that you must stay so the civilians of Babylon don't panic and revolt even more than before. Most aren't even aware their Prince has left them. Lilith knows the illusion must continue, and that the odd loyalty you've commanded from some of Lucifel's soldiers must remain. I don't know what you said, but they are looking to you as their leader now. If you refuse Lucifel's Throne, more innocents will die."

There was an awkward and painful pause.

Lilith wanted vengeance for Naamah's death, and it didn't feel possible she'd change her mind so soon. The danger in the air threatened to choke Angela's breath away. Kim's hopefulness was almost tragic. He was grasping at anything. Angela's mind turned back to the Grail she had shown to the army of demons and ghosts. Horrid fear rushed through her like a hot flood. "Kim," she said, showing him her left hand, "it's gone."

"I know," Kim said just as softly, staring at her with an odd expression. He never took his eyes off her face, seeming to focus more on the left side.

Perhaps she was wrong about not having new scars after all.

"What . . . what is it?" Angela said. She reached for the eye Lucifel had injured.

Kim grasped her hand tightly. "Angela, do you feel the same? Does your face hurt at all?"

A sinking feeling overtook her instantly. "No. Why?"

Kim sighed. He paused for a moment, and then he leaned over and plucked a mirror from a table.

"Look at yourself," he said, grim as ever.

Angela took the mirror with shaking hands, her heart racing, and her muscles tightening. She lifted it up to her face as slowly as she could, ignoring how Kim held the lantern closer so that she had the best possible view.

Her face was the same as always, too thin and very white.

Both eyes were whole.

"I don't—"

"Look closer," Kim said gently. He moved the lamp even nearer.

Oh God. Oh no. NO.

The flashback was instantaneous, horrendous. Once again she was inside of Raziel, staring down the terribly beautiful creature that had torn his wings to ribbons. That creature—the thing that was both an angel and every beautiful nightmare combined—half of its terrible face gazed back at her in the mirror clasped between her hands.

The Grail was now Angela's left eye.

It had traveled within her body, leaving her hand to fill the void Lucifel had left in Angela's face.

A thousand horrors and just as many regrets shot through her all at once.

Angela wanted to throw the mirror and scream. She wanted to cry.

There was a long moment when she considered doing just that. Instead, she bit her lip, tipped her head back, and sucked up her pain, squeezing her eyes shut, trying to be strong for the people who now depended on her to live. The room spun without her looking at it. She nearly passed out, but held on as tightly as she could to the waking world. Images and ideas burned into her mind even as it threatened to fog over. What did this mean? Lucifel had said that only Angela could use the Glaive to open Sophia. That had to be because the Glaive was a part of Angela somehow. Everyone commented on the mystery of her soul, and why Raziel had chosen her as the Archon out of millions. Angela knew instinctively it had to do with this terror gazing back at her.

A sudden and deadly weakness swept over her.

"Who am I?" Angela stammered, dropping the mirror and clutching Kim's arm. She swayed, feeling sicker than before. "Who am I . . ."

Kim grabbed her tightly. "You are the Archon," he said, embracing her again and stroking her hair. But his voice trembled with the mystery between them. "And I am by your side, as I promised."

No. There's more to me than that. So much more.

"You might tell me you don't need me," Kim murmured in her ear. "But I can't deny this desire that burns in me so painfully. If I can't be with you, let me be next to you. Give me that. Look at me, let me kneel by your throne, and I will be happy. It's all that I have."

Angela looked at him and touched his face. He held her hand to his cheek and kissed it with trembling lips. Warmth and pain flowed through her all at once. Her cheeks burned with her blushes. "Kim," Angela said weakly. "What about Troy?"

He shook his head, unable to answer.

"Let me forget her for a while," he said. A tear trickled down his face. He shivered. "Just for now."

Angela rested against Kim's shoulder.

The moments passed, and Angela stared out into the shadows, thinking hard. As the haze over her mind lifted, the certainty of what came next burned brightly before her like a flame. She could not stay and rule in Lucifel's place. Whether Angela escaped to Heaven or back to Luz, she needed to leave as soon as the opportunity arose. Hell was too much of a danger, and she hadn't forgotten there was a powerful faction of demons who'd always wanted her dead. If it was possible, Angela also needed to somehow reach Lucifel again and bring her to justice before her despair consumed even more souls.

But most important, she needed to figure out a way to open Sophia without killing her, which was out of the question as long as Angela lived.

Absolutely everything depended on it.

Angela would never give up. She had promised Raziel to save Israfel. She had promised Troy, and Juno, and Nina everything in her power to give to them. Those oaths were too sacred to her to break. How would she escape Hell, though, to keep them?

So much already stood in her way.

"Now, we will be here always," Kim said. "Now, we can start over again. Everything can be what it was meant to be and should be. There is nothing that can come between us anymore."

Angela clutched at her necklace, rubbing her finger against the feather and the star it cradled. As long as Angela remained trapped in Hell, she would at least have to make sure that things changed. Sophia was right. It was not time for ruin. A new order had arrived.

Angela gazed at the mirror where it rested again on the table, unable to tear her gaze away from the familiar reflection staring back at her.

The light has to win this time. There has to be a revolution.

Babylon was almost beautiful from such a high vantage point. Yet not as much as Luz. Angela gazed out of the enormous window, her fingers pressed against the smoky glass. Her mind returned again and again to the snow and ice of Luz, the beauty of the candles in every home, the sweetness of a holiday that had ended so soon. What would happen to all the blood heads in Luz now? She could only imagine, and it tortured her. At some point, Angela would return and make everything right. There wasn't much time—she knew it—and it left her silent and pensive too often.

She barely noticed when Sophia stepped beside her.

Sophia hummed a familiar tune. It was Israfel's song. The same one Angela had used to open the door to Hell after she'd smashed Python's iron snake.

Israfel left to follow Lucifel. But I know—he thought of me. He felt sorry. So do I.

"Do you know where that song comes from?" Sophia said after a while, not taking her eyes off the city.

Sophia continued humming. The earth trembled a little and went still, as it had continued to do for a few days.

Angela watched the regiments on the plain of Babylon filing into orderly ranks. She swallowed nervously at the idea of leading them again. Now she looked the part, with a long coat and slim-fitting boots. Bare feet were for demons and angels, not humans. Angela also refused to wear her hair up, but let it fall loose to her waist. She often wondered how long it would be until she also had to wear Lucifel's shackles. The idea terrified her. "No. Where does it come from?" Angela said, grasping Sophia's hand impulsively.

Sophia put her other hand over Angela's and turned to her.

"It's an ancient song," she said in her soft sweet voice. "Older than time itself."

"That's not possible," Angela said, smiling.

Sophia shook her head, as if to say it certainly was. "The first notes of the song," she continued, "sounded in a Realm so high that the human mind cannot truly conceive of it. The initial verses speak of a Garden of Shadows, and the last speak of a ring that imprisons the soul. The Garden is paradise and the ring is love—or at least, that was what I intended those symbols to mean."

Angela stared into Sophia's stormy eyes. Shock burned through her. "That song—it's yours? *You invented it?*"

Sophia turned to the city again. "Yes," she whispered. "Often it crossed my mind that the poetic images were too vague, too easily twisted into another meaning entirely. How many have interpreted my words the wrong way?"

Angela couldn't answer her.

Sophia held Angela's face and brushed a slim finger near

the Eye. Angela sighed and squeezed Sophia's fingers. It seemed they'd both been thinking of so many things. "I've known my fate," Sophia said, "since the day Raziel opened my eyes in this new body, giving me a chance at redemption. Sophia, he named me. The word means wisdom in the Tongue of Souls. But the name is ironic, I think." She lowered her head. "Angela, do you remember how I told you that I died in childbirth long ago?"

"Yes," Angela whispered. "I was afraid for a while that you had lied to me."

Sophia glanced at her quickly. "Lied?"

Angela shook her head. "It just—didn't seem right." She couldn't look Sophia in the eyes. "You seemed too fragile for something like that. Nothing about it made sense to me."

Sophia sighed. "No. I don't blame you." Her face took on that distant and almost frightening expression. "Angela, when I died, I fell into darkness. I also took the universe with me. My soul, my secrets, my power have been reborn thanks to Raziel. Thus, I am the Book of Raziel. But I am also only a meager fraction of my former self. The idea that I am a Revenant of Lucifel was the lie. I am Raziel's creation, but only using parts of myself that already existed. I died once, and I can die again. Now, I am terrified it will be because of the same sin."

There was more to terrify Angela. The idea that Sophia was someone or something she would never completely understand was perhaps the worst.

"What could you possibly have done?" Angela said, touching her hair. "Sophia, I don't care why you think you are being punished. You won't die again."

"I promised one year ago today to be by your side always," Sophia whispered to Angela. Tears slid down her smooth cheeks. "And I want to be. But I also wanted more for you from the very beginning. For me, it was never about your destiny as you made it. It was always about your happiness . . ."

Angela rubbed away one of Sophia's tears. "You're talking like you've always known me," she said.

But that can't be.

Sophia laughed softly at that. "I sound like a mother, don't I?" she said.

"You're not a mother," Angela said gently. "You're more than that. There's always more."

Kim had accused Angela of loving Sophia. Angela couldn't explain then, but she felt he'd only scratched the surface of something deeper. Love felt like too small a word for certain feelings. Maybe they'd have to make a new one. Lucifel had used the word *covenant*. Perhaps that was truly more appropriate.

"You're right . . ." Sophia said. She gazed back out into the city of Babylon, her face settled and cool. The clouds near the cavern's far-reaching ceiling rained down fine crystals. Angela had sensed the growing cold in the mere few days since she'd arrived. "Merry Christmas," Sophia said abruptly, breaking the spell. "I wanted it to be better for you."

"It can be right now," Angela said, tapping her necklace. They smiled at each other briefly and held hands before the world, defiant of the darkness in front and ahead of them. It didn't feel right to be completely happy, but Angela felt it was okay to at least be grateful for each other. "Sophia, I know it might hurt you, but—tell me about your children one day."

Sophia's face hardened a little. "I won't be telling you much you don't already know," she said slowly.

Her tone suggested an end to the conversation. The mystery within it would have to remain so for a little longer.

Angela looked out into Hell. She thought of Juno's little rock resting safe and sound in her skirt pocket where she'd left it. She thought of Camdon Willis, and where his soul had gone after touching the Grail. Because that was all she could do for the people who meant anything to her right now—think, hope, and pray. Troy never responded to Angela's mental calls—hopefully meaning she was too far away to hear, not dead. "I've been wondering about Troy and Nina and Juno . . . Maybe Python was right when he said that Nina was dead and Troy betrayed me . . ."

"He wasn't," Sophia said firmly.

"How do you know?"

Sophia looked at Angela with a chiding expression. The Grail throbbed, sending ripples of warning fire through Angela's entire being. Somehow, Angela thought she could see a pair of burning orange eyes, staring right back at her, like a flash from the farthest corners of her mind. Fear touched her, her heart ached. Python wasn't dead, nor was his ambitious game perhaps over. The protection of Hell was no real protection at all.

Sophia's voice held only a hint of the approaching storm. "Like I told you from the very beginning," she murmured, "never trust a snake."

Forty-one

Even the Devil played my game to
satisfaction. —PYTHON

A foot jabbed Troy sharply in the ribs. Pain shot through her body.

Her dreamless sleep shattered instantly. She was alive, yet the thought held no relief. Troy awakened gasping for breath, spitting out the bitter dust that had found its way into her mouth. Her muscles felt torn in nine different directions. The spot on her back that marked her missing wing throbbed horrendously. Troy shuddered as a hand grabbed her by her rags and lifted her up. Icy cold metal latched around her neck.

Her energy returned in a hot rush. Troy thrashed.

She hissed and spit in her captor's face. Slowly, the demon's features emerged in the wan light of Babylon.

His pale face was almost half hidden by his mop of violet-streaked, sable hair. The scales above his eyelids glittered under reams of purple eye paint.

Python dropped Troy back to the rocky earth, his snake-like eyes watching her keenly. He shook his head, pushing back the hair in front of his face. Three long cuts layered one of his eyes. Python rubbed at them with a sour twist to his mouth. His other hand firmly grasped the chain that connected to the collar around Troy's neck.

Juno! Where was she?

Troy glanced around frantically, searching for her niece amid the cold light of Babylon. They had landed somewhere near the outskirts of the city. The softness that had somewhat broken their fall revealed itself to be a mound of Kirin carcasses and trash. The stench would have been unbearable to anyone, but with Troy's highly developed sense of smell, it was almost a torture. To her right, the city rose above her jagged and menacing. The lights played with her eyes and made the act of thinking painful.

Juno was gone. Even her scent seemed to have faded, which meant she'd been absent for quite a while.

She could have been eaten or captured. Anything.

"Looking for that ragged little chick?" Python said, yanking hard on Troy's chain.

The collar dug into Troy's neck. She had no choice but to look right at him. Troy snarled coldly and threatened to lunge at his face. "*Where is she, snake?*"

"Irritatingly alive," Python said. "At least, that's my best guess. By the time I medicated my injured eye and arrived to find her corpse, she was long gone. I wanted her to die, but I wasn't about to throw my looks away for a dream." He smiled coldly and tugged even harder on Troy's chain. "So the little mouse left my house. And she left her aunt behind as well. Interesting. I thought you both shared a better relationship than *that*."

Troy didn't bother answering. Juno wouldn't abandon her outright. There would have to have been a good reason.

Despite the overwhelming smell of trash and decay, there was no scent of fresh blood. Juno had to be alive. Fury hadn't returned from rescuing Nina Willis's soul. Troy couldn't help but feel both Fury's and Juno's absences were connected to that fact. But Python didn't need to know how they'd kept him from winning that particular part of his game.

"What do you want with me?" Troy snarled at him. She grabbed at the collar around her neck, trying to break it somehow. There was no use. It wouldn't budge an inch.

"Don't even try," Python said. "That collar is made of adamant. Not even Lucifel herself could break it. No—that would take someone like your half-breed cousin, I'm afraid. But I doubt he'll feel up to the task any time soon. Lucifel's shackles left him a bit . . . drained."

Troy froze. Fire rushed through her veins, and her heart pounded.

"Oh, that's right. I'm so sorry. You couldn't possibly know the news that has the elite of Babylon seething—or at least the part that doesn't know how to stay quiet and obedient." Python seemed to gloat, but his face held no happiness. "Your lovesick cousin succeeded, Troy. His unique hands freed Hell's blackbird from her cage. Lucifel has escaped her regime, and she partly has you to thank for it. If you'd succeeded in your mission as the High Assassin, perhaps we'd be having a much different conversation. But at least take comfort in your cousin Kim's courage. You're more alike than you think. I detested him every other minute, but I'll admit that his blind resolve was enthralling."

Troy felt suffocated, like the world rather than the collar choked her.

All she could cling to now was the idea that if Kim had

gotten so far, maybe Angela had also been alive and present.

If Troy could reach Angela, there was still hope for them all.

"I love it when your clever mind works." Python's face burned with excitement. "It makes your eyes so fierce and bright. To survive such pain and come so far—no wonder your race honors and fears you like they do. Perhaps that's why they named you after the city I helped destroy. Hope always seems to linger where it's least wise to believe in it." He rubbed the links of the chain that made up Troy's leash. "Wondering about the Archon, Troy? She's just fine. Though we'll see how long she lasts with my mother for a protector," he ended ominously.

Troy lunged for him again.

The chain twanged harshly. She crashed back to the earth, scraping her knees.

Python stepped backward, staring at her long nails. "Easy," he hissed under his breath. "I wouldn't want to have to muzzle you."

"Let me go now," Troy said to him, gritting her sharp teeth. Her words erupted dark and certain. She dug her nails into the earth and split a few rocks beneath them for emphasis. "Because I promise if you don't, you'll be sorry for it, snake. Wasn't mutilating your face enough? Next time, I'll make sure it's your heart. I won't eat it, of course. Far too much venom for my taste."

Python's expression chilled. He snapped the chain, almost throwing Troy into the dirt again. "Watch your tongue, my dear," he said. "Temper temper. But keep in mind from now on—you're the flightless bird on the leash."

"I won't fail to keep my promise," Troy said viciously.

Her ears pressed back into her hair. Her entire soul froze over with purpose. "I never do."

"Neither do I," Python said. "That's why we're going to Babylon together."

Troy stilled, her entire being quivering. She couldn't go to Babylon when Juno was alive but missing. Even killing Sariel could wait for that. The broken Jinn Clans needed a Queen, and Troy would never be that Queen as long as Juno lived. There was no doubt in Troy's mind anymore about her niece's suitability for the role.

Python laughed grimly. "The Archon thinks she's gotten out of my labyrinth. But mazes don't necessarily need walls to continue. All they really need are people's hearts and desires. I can't wait to see the look on her noble face when I show her the great High Assassin at my heels like a Hound. Shortly afterward, all of Hell will be there with you. But I'm a much more patient demon than I look, so I'm willing to start one individual at a time." The demon stooped down and gazed directly into Troy's eyes. "The universe is my chessboard, and I still have a few pieces left to play. Even better—I have the best piece at my disposal, the Queen."

He smiled, showing all his perfect teeth.

Python spread his wings in a blinding flash of reddish light. The cold lights of Babylon gleamed across the metal holding them together. The fine fog in the air wafted away from him like smoke. He yanked on Troy's chain, jerking her painfully toward the city in the most humiliating way possible.

She stood anyway, her feet cut by rocks as he continued to tug. Against her will, she followed him.

The city waited for her like a pair of shiny black jaws.

At that moment, Troy made her decision. If she did become Queen of the Jinn, she would destroy Babylon utterly and raze it. And if she couldn't do that, she would help the Archon destroy Heaven, Hell, or whatever else came in the way of a newer heaven and a better earth, one dying Realm at a time.

But Troy didn't need to say anything aloud.

Python glanced back, and his suddenly quiet demeanor told her enough. He had seen the future in the icy terror of her smile.

Omega

Luz waited for the Archon amid a whirlwind of snow and darkness. Blackbirds and crows converged on the city, screeching and crying over its impending ruin.

Earth shivered, and the ocean threw up enormous waves that licked the lower levels of the poorer human dwellings.

All this passed beneath Nina Willis like a dream.

Nina soared with the crows over Westwood Academy, wheeling and turning through the icy winter air. She was now one of them, and yet infinitely superior. But despite Juno's warnings for Nina not to lose herself in exhilaration, her new wings had an agility to them she'd never expected, and she couldn't help testing them time and again. Flying was wonderful enough, but flying through the snow was even better, and Nina tumbled with Fury over and over for the sheer bliss of it, plummeting to the roaring sea only to streak up back into the clouds at the last possible second.

Nina had not died in Python's labyrinth. Thanks to Troy, Juno, and Fury, she'd instead been given new life that could last as long as she wished.

Her soul was in the body of a crow exactly like Fury's, but the difference was that unlike most Jinn creations, Nina could leave that body if she wished. The rest of the Jinn had found Nina's talent inexplicable, but she knew it all had to do with Angela. Nina wanted to help her friend, and that had made something impossible, possible. Her promise had become her reality, perhaps because it had been deserved. Troy would certainly understand.

There had been doubt and confusion in her before each death, yet now Nina unswervingly knew her purpose. The souls waiting to fight on the Archon's side in Heaven needed someone who could intercede between them and Angela.

Nina was the only person in that position to help.

First, though, she needed to return to Luz and gather more allies. She streaked above the Memorial Cemetery graveyard, calling for the hundredth time to anyone below willing to fight. Already she heard answers from those whose spirits had yet to escape Earth's dimension for good. Soon, when the time arrived, she could tell them when they would rise and where they would go. But before that crucial hour, she needed to visit a trustworthy friend and tell him to prepare.

Follow me, she said to Fury in her thoughts.

Fury banked to the left and soared with Nina to a series of high turrets crowning Luz. More crows followed them in a gale of birds. The wind screamed at them, while the city below glowed like a star set in the sea. Darkness had set forever over Luz and Earth, and it would not lift until Angela either saved the universe or let it collapse. Nina was certain, though, that Angela would succeed and bring the sun back to a city that had not seen it since time immemorial. She was sure above everything else that the light would return.

She landed with her new crow's feet on Father Schrader's windowsill. Nina shifted on the ice-slicked stone and tapped with her beak on the panes. All around her, more crows landed side by side, chattering furiously.

In the city streets, people looked up and pointed at the enormous flock of birds commanding the skies above Luz.

The old priest stood within a circle of his peers. Noticing Nina, he waved them away and ran to the window, opening it quickly. He stepped back and she and Fury glided within, landing in a circle of priests and novices who stared at them with wide and fearful eyes reflecting beams of candlelight.

A few rested on their knees, half hidden by the shadows of a never-ending night.

Father Schrader stared at Nina solemnly.

Fire burned through her, and she left the crow's body and stood before him as a vaporous form. She recognized her own hands and feet and body, though they were now transparent. She stood firmly, gazing at every person in turn.

"Nina Willis," Father Schrader said in an awestruck voice. "Did the Archon send you?"

A stronger fire coursed within her, and she sensed her master, Juno, returning.

"No," Nina said. Her voice echoed like a song.

The priests and novices looked at one another, murmuring with apprehension.

Nina raised her hand, gesturing for silence. "She didn't send me. I chose to come on my own. But I want to tell you that the time has come to make your own choice. Will you stand on Angela's side, or will you stand against her? She is in Hell now against her will. But she will return soon and will forever take her place on one throne or another. There is no escaping her destiny, and I know, because I couldn't escape mine. The hour is upon you, everyone. When Angela arrives in Luz again, what will she find? I hope you do the right thing."

"She will choose Ruin," one of the novices cried out in

fear. "So what does it matter if we are on her side or not! She is our destroyer—"

"Ruin doesn't always mean darkness," Nina said quickly. "Sometimes, it takes the ruin of an old order for a new one to rise. Sometimes it means change."

"Revolution," Father Schrader whispered to himself. He nodded slowly and turned to one of the priests to his right. "Gereth, grab me the book on the top shelf to your left side."

The young man obeyed and handed the book to the old priest. Father Schrader flipped through it hurriedly. It fell open to a set of verses hastily scrawled in black ink. Nina listened as he read them aloud.

The darkness grew, and yet his weary face held a hope that was a light.

The sound of thundering wings circled Luz and echoed throughout the air. The candle flames in the room flickered at his words, and then unexpectedly brightened.

> *Swiftly rushes the blood-red tide.*
> *In the city of revolving stars She rides,*
> *Where the Crown awaits,*
> *And angels have flown,*
> *Near the watchful Eye of the great unknown.*
> *Ruin ever present, Ruin ever near.*
> *Behold the death of the hour of fear.*
> *Now, the light of the Eternal Year,*
> *Shines on us singing,*
> *The end is here.*

TO BE CONTINUED

Glossary of Terms, Places, People, and Things

Abyss: the lowest dimension of Hell; Raziel was the first creature to explore the Abyss; shortly after he returned to Heaven, he created Sophia.

Angel: intelligent beings that reside in the upper dimensions of the universe known as Heaven; beautiful and powerful, they are thought of as the pinnacle of creation; angels are known for having striking eyes, feathery hair, and abilities ranging from flight to telekinesis.

Angela Mathers: human girl discovered to be the Archon, she is known for her striking red hair, blue eyes, and preternatural skill at painting; Angela's family abused her from a young age, and her arms and legs bear numerous scars from an attempt to kill herself that backfired, killing her parents instead; from childhood, she has had visions of Lucifel and Israfel that have since revealed themselves as the angel Raziel's memories.

Archangel: formal title for the angel whose authority is below God alone; Israfel was the first Archangel; the current Archangel is Zion, one of Lucifel's children.

Archon: arcane name for the human protected by the deceased angel Raziel's spirit, now known to be Angela Mathers; since the Archon is a messiah figure with the ability to ultimately save or destroy the universe, her power is wanted by various factions of Heaven and Hell for their own purposes; she is the only being who can open Raziel's Book (Sophia).

Azrael: name of the Angel of Death who guarded deceased human souls; he was destroyed by Angela Mathers after she entered the Netherworld for the first time.

Babylon: a dimension of Hell; the city of the demons.

Binding: name for a contract linking a human soul with a Jinn's; this contract ends only with the human's death, usually at the hands of the very same Jinn protecting them.

Blood head: a derogatory name for any human with red hair, which is thought to be one of the Archon's distinguishing features; it refers to a prophecy wherein the Archon will "have blood on Her head, and blood on Her hands."

Book of Raziel: a mythical book created by the angel Raziel that contains all the secrets of the universe and an immense power; it can only be opened by the Archon with a special Key; those who try otherwise are fated to go insane; surprising to most, the Book of Raziel's true form is a doll-like girl named Sophia.

Brendan Mathers: Angela's deceased brother and Stephanie Walsh's informal boyfriend; he became infatuated with Israfel and treated his sister cruelly; he was killed by the demon Naamah in St. Mary's church and now exists as a soul forever in service to Israfel.

Camdon Willis: Nina's half brother; he has a strange interest in Angela and feels guilty for Nina's death.

Celestial Revolution: Lucifel's failed rebellion against Heaven, also known as the War; the end result was that a third of the angels followed her to Hell to start their own regime and imprisoned her; it is commonly believed that Lucifel instigated this war because she wished to be ruler of Heaven instead of Israfel.

Cherubim: an order of angels that guards the highest dimension of Heaven.

Chick: term for a young angel, demon, or Jinn.

Clan: in the realm of the Jinn there are six tribes or clans; the Sixth Clan is the most powerful; Troy, the High Assassin of the Jinn, is a member, as is her sister Hecate, and niece Juno; the Sixth Clan's symbol is a crow's foot.

Covenant: refers to Raziel's ancient promises to the Jinn that he would free them someday from their harsh existence; the Archon has long been expected by the Jinn to fulfill this promise.

Crow: derogatory term for an angel, demon, or Jinn, often used among their kind as an insult; also, many Jinn familiars take the shape of a black crow.

Demon: intelligent beings that reside in the lower dimensions of the universe known as Hell; beautiful and powerful, they are either former angels or direct descendants of those who have fallen; demons share many characteristics with angels though they often wear tattoos signifying their rank, and their wings are in varying states of decay from Hell's acidic mists; most demons worship Lucifel, but there are some who wish the Archon to rule in her place.

Devil: the formal name for Lucifel among most humans; in its plural form it refers to the Jinn.

Dominions: the angelic term for the dimensions that make up the universe.

Emerald House: formerly the cult headed by Stephanie Walsh called the Pentacle Sorority, it has now been renamed by

Angela Mathers; it is named after Lucifel's Grail, which resembles an emerald in color, and its symbol is a green eye.

Ether: the substance that composes much of the universe, it can be manipulated by angels and demons to perform feats of telekinesis; it is believed that angels and demons use etheric currents to fly, even without the use of their wings.

Exorcism: a method that can be used to injure or banish an angel, a demon, or a Jinn to another dimension; very powerful exorcisms can kill creatures like Jinn or their familiars.

Eye: another name for Lucifel's Grail, as it resembles a large emerald eye and sometimes even blinks or weeps.

Fae: former angels who left Heaven to dwell on Earth and live in symbiosis with host plants; most Fae are believed to be extinct; Tileaf, a Fae dwelling in an ancient oak tree, had been abused by Luz's Vatican officials for her powers; she managed to show Angela Mathers part of Raziel's mysterious past before dying; a portal to Hell could be found beneath her tree but it has since been sealed away.

Father: the angelic name for God.

Feathered serpent: intelligent, serpentine dragons with feathered plumes crowning their heads; they live in the high dimensions of Heaven; the most infamous of these creatures sided with Lucifel during the Celestial Revolution and became the demon Leviathan.

Fury: Troy's familiar in the body of a crow; she was once a human girl, but remembers little of her previous life.

Glaive: Lucifel's fabled weapon used in the Celestial Revolution; it is a pole arm made entirely of crystallized blue blood with a sharp blade at its tip.

Grail: see "Lucifel's Grail."

Grand Mansion: the building in Luz where some of Westwood Academy's most formal affairs are celebrated; enormous angel statues line the steps to its entrance.

Half-breed: derogatory name for half-human, half-Jinn offspring; most are killed at birth; Kim (Sariel) is the only one known to exist.

Heaven: the highest dimensions of the universe; home of the angels.

Hecate: the deceased Jinn Queen and Troy's sister; she believed in the Archon and was murdered by rival Jinn, who feared she had become delusional in her hopes to rule; Juno is her only surviving child.

Hell: the lowest dimensions of the universe; home of the Jinn and demons; its uppermost levels are known as the Underworld.

High Assassin: Jinn term for their most illustrious and deadly hunter, second only to their Queen in respect; Troy is the current High Assassin and is a legend throughout Hell for her lethal skills.

Hounds: voracious predators of Hell that share characteristics with sphinxes; they are thought to be fallen Cherubim, and are one of the only creatures Jinn fear.

Ialdaboth: the highest dimension of Heaven, accessible only to the ruling Archangel by a spiraling bridge; Ialdaboth was the first Realm to be inhabited by the angels but has been abandoned for millennia; Israfel was imprisoned here against his will by the Father.

Israfel: the Creator Supernal and Heaven's first ruling Archangel, legendary for his beauty and charisma; his once defining bronze-colored hair and wings have since bleached to a shocking white; he disappeared into Ialdaboth at the end of the Celestial Revolution and had been presumed dead for ages; Angela Mathers was infatuated with Israfel, but found him shockingly changed from the person he used to be; he has been slowly dying since Lucifel infected him with her shadow during the Celestial Revolution.

Jinn: intelligent beings who live in the dimensions of Hell known collectively as the Underworld with a society structured into six ruling Clans; they are descendants of angelic offspring judged to be imperfect and thrown into Hell to fend for themselves or die; beautiful but savage, they are known by humans as devils; out of all the angelic races, they have had the most contact with humans.

Juno: the only surviving heir to the Jinn throne, she is Hecate's daughter and Troy's niece.

Key: the object that can open the Lock sealing Raziel's Book; its identity and whereabouts are a mystery.

Kim: a half-Jinn who pretended to be a novice in Luz to get close to the Archon (Angela Mathers); his Jinn cousin Troy is hunting him out of revenge for killing her uncle, who was also Kim's father; he is also known by the Jinn name Sariel, given to him by his father.

Kirin: creatures of Hell that vaguely resemble horses but have sharp horns, paws, and bioluminescent eyes and markings on their bodies; they are often hunted by the Jinn, and their horns are used in Jinn headdresses.

Lilith: the most powerful female demon in Hell after Lucifel; Python's mother, whom she sired with the feathered serpent Leviathan.

Lock: the seal on the Book of Raziel; it can only be opened by the Archon, though the whereabouts of the Key that will enable her to do this are a mystery.

Lucifel: the Destroyer Supernal responsible for the Celestial Revolution at the dawn of time; Lucifel fled to Hell with the demons but rules her regime as a god imprisoned by her own worshippers; her ultimate goal is to use Raziel's Book to silence the universe, but why she wishes to do so remains a mystery; most believe she has gone insane from her long imprisonment; Lucifel sent her shadow to confront Angela Mathers, but Angela destroyed it, weakening her; Lucifel has the ability to drain a person's energy or kill them with a touch.

Lucifel's Grail: a mysterious eyelike pendant in the possession of the Jinn, first embedded in the hand, and now in the eye of Angela Mathers; it was initially worn by Lucifel and has fearsome powers; most who look into its depths go mad; its origins are a complete mystery; the Grail must bleed for the Glaive to be formed.

Luz: an island city off the American continent, officially under the jurisdiction of the Vatican; Luz's most well-known feature is Westwood Academy, the school that has become a haven for gifted students as well as "blood heads"; it has been besieged by increasingly foul weather for at least one hundred years; technology is outlawed in Luz; Angela Mathers has since learned that Luz is the connecting point between Earth and the other dimensions, and is thus a portal for the supernatural.

Malakhim: a dimension of Heaven; the city of the angels.

Mastema: the most powerful male demon in Hell, and Archdemon under Lucifel; Kim's foster father; he wanted Kim to destroy the Archon when She appeared.

Memorial Cemetery: a large grove near Luz's western coast that was once a park; it was originally famous for the enormous oak tree at its center—Tileaf's tree—but is now a graveyard dedicated to those who died in one of Luz's greatest storms.

Mikel: a female angel who claims to be Lucifel and Raziel's daughter and sister to Archangel Zion, she has been presumed dead for millennia; Mikel has no real body, so she must possess a host in order to communicate; she was responsible for letting the demons know the Archon existed, effectively setting events in motion; Mikel possessed Nina Willis after Angela accidentally summoned her to Earth; Angela then brought her to Tileaf; once Angela's ally, Mikel's true allegiances are now shrouded in suspicion.

Naamah: demon and foster mother of Stephanie Walsh, now deceased; she'd sincerely hoped Stephanie was the Archon; Lilith considered Naamah to be like a daughter and holds great bitterness over her death; Naamah was responsible for killing Angela's brother Brendan.

Netherworld: a dark and forgotten dimension where human souls used to gather after death; it was emptied by Angela Mathers, and the souls within, who claimed allegiance to the Archon, went to a higher dimension to await her rise to power.

Nexus: the highest existing dimension, known to be the dwelling place of God and where all souls, whether human or angelic, must eventually return after death.

Python: one of the most feared demons in Hell; the son of Lilith and Leviathan, he can take on the form of a feathered serpent like his father.

Rakir & Nunkir: Israfel's guardian Thrones, whom he raised since they were infants; Rakir is the black-haired male and Nunkir is the silver-haired female; both were critically injured in the battle against Lucifel's shadow.

Raziel: the Preserver Supernal and creator of the Book of Raziel (Sophia), well-known for his wisdom and gentle disposition; he was thought to have committed suicide after his lover Lucifel failed in her rebellion against Heaven; he is believed to be the Archon's guardian spirit, and his presence near her soul has given her his distinctive red hair and blue eyes.

Ruin: the most common term for the dark messiah known more secretly as the Archon; many prophecies predict the Archon will choose the side of evil and destroy humanity.

Sariel: Kim's Jinn name, given to him by his deceased Jinn father; Troy always refers to him by this name.

Sophia: the human form of the Book of Raziel; though commonly regarded by others as as a "thing," Sophia has a strong personality that belies her delicate appearance; she told Angela Mathers that her body was created by Lucifel as a Revenant, with the ability to be destroyed and resurrected by Lucifel as long as Sophia is in her power; she said she originally died in childbirth, which Angela has come to believe is a lie.

St. Matthias Church: an old church in Luz no longer in use; it is the place where Angela and Israfel first met.

Stephanie Walsh: a blood head witch now imprisoned in Luz's sanatorium; at one time, she was suspected of being the Archon and headed Westwood Academy's infamous Pentacle Sorority; she is the demon Naamah's adopted daughter, and is indirectly responsible for Brendan Mathers's death, as well as the deaths of many other individuals in

Luz; Stephanie went insane after Lucifel possessed her, forcing her to try and open Sophia against her will; she was in love with Kim (Sariel).

Supernals: the highest-ranking angels of all; they are three siblings, Israfel, Raziel, and Lucifel, known collectively as the Angelic Trinity; unlike most angels, the Supernals have six wings, but they rarely reveal them all; they were created directly by the Father and are immortal and with immense power.

Theban: the demonic tongue; in its written form it resembles a scripting of curves and sharp lines.

Thrones: the angelic rank acting as bodyguards for higher-ranking angels; most Thrones have a deformity of one kind or another; they are suspected to be derivatives of the sphinx-like Cherubim.

Tongue of Souls: otherwise known as Latin, it has the power to harm or bind angels, demons, and Jinn.

Troy: the greatest Jinn city in the Underworld, destroyed millennia ago by an alliance between the angels and demons that was Python's work; it is often used among the Jinn as a given name, and is the name of the current High Assassin of the Jinn.

Underworld: name for the dimensions in Hell that are home to the Jinn.

Vapor: the term for a Jinn familiar; they are a human soul within an animal body, usually that of a crow, cat, or dog; Vapors communicate with their masters through telepathy.

Vermilion Order: a growing coalition of blood head students at Westwood Academy who wish to segregate themselves from the remaining student population.

Westwood Academy: an illustrious school that is the only haven for blood heads in the world; maintained and run by Vatican officials, Westwood derived its name from the enormous oak tree (Tileaf's tree) that could be found in Memorial Park, near the western coast of Luz.

Witch: a female human who can conjure angels or demons.

Zion: the currently reigning Archangel of Heaven; one of Lucifel's legendary children, presumed to have been executed long ago.